THE ELEMENT OF FIRE

Widowed by Ireland's Great Famine, Ellen Rua O'Malley flees to Boston. With her are Patrick and Mary, her two surviving children and the 'silent girl', rescued from the hordes of the dispossessed. Boston in the 1850s is the best place for a woman to be and there, awaiting Ellen, are the stability of a new life and Lavelle, the man who loves her. Desperate to shake off the Old World, Ellen is driven by her own demons to put everything at risk – and Boston, on the brink of Civil War, seems to mirror her own conflict and battle for survival.

THE ELEMENT OF FIRE

by

Brendan Graham

Magna Large Print Books
Long Preston, North Yorkshire,
BD23 4ND, England.

British Library Cataloguing in Publication Data.

Graham, Brendan
    The element of fire.

    A catalogue record of this book is
    available from the British Library

    ISBN   0-7505-1893-6

First published in Great Britain by HarperCollins Publishers 2001

Copyright © Brendan Graham 2001

Cover illustration Portrait of girl © Attard
Background view of Boston © Hulton Getty
by arrangement with HarperCollins Publishers

Brendan Graham asserts the moral right to be identified as the author of this work

Published in Large Print 2002 by arrangement with
Harper Collins Publishers Ltd.

Magna Large Print is an imprint of Library Magna Books Ltd.

Printed and bound in Great Britain by
T.J. (International) Ltd., Cornwall, PL28 8RW

Although this work is partly based on real historical events, the main characters portrayed therein are entirely the work of the author's imagination.

Dedicated to the memory of
'The Coot',
Fr. Henry Flanagan O.P., Newbridge College
(1918–1992)

Sculptor, musician, teacher, friend

ACKNOWLEDGEMENTS

A number of people generously assisted me with advice, research material and general sustenance, throughout the writing of this book.

In Boston: Staff at Boston Public Library, in particular Curator of Humanities William M. Grealish; at Thomas P. O'Neill Library, Boston College, Kathleen M. Williams; Ruth-Ann M. Harris, Adjunct Professor of History and Irish Studies, Boston College; Joan McAllister at the Boston *Pilot*; Michael and Colette Quinlin. A special thanks to Dr Eileen Moore Quinn, Anthropology Department, Massachusetts Institute of Technology. In Ireland: Staff at the National Library of Ireland; R.V. Comerford, Professor of Modern History, National University of Ireland, Maynooth; Hugh Duffy; John Hassett; Séamus Duffy; Dr Inge Leipold; The Tyrone Guthrie Centre, where some of the writing was done; Kim Mullahey, who did initial background research. To Nicholas Pedgrift in London and Tom Best in Toronto. To the people at HarperCollins*Publishers*, Ireland, UK, Australia, New Zealand and Canada, a sincere thanks for everything. In particular, special thanks to Adrian Bourne, Managing Director,

Trade Division, UK, and to Editorial Director, Patricia Parkin – for patience beyond virtue, and to Georgina Hawtrey-Woore and Sara Walsh.

Finally, to my wife Mary and my family – for forbearance and endurance – and with a special word to Grainne and Niamh for transforming illegible handscript into intelligible typescript and to Donna for a critical reading of the final draft – *buíochas om' chroí.*

Brendan Graham
February 2001

'The element of fire is quite put out;
The sun is lost, and th' earth...'

'An Anatomy of the World'
JOHN DONNE (1572–1631)

1

1848 – Ireland

It was a grand day for a funeral.

A grand August day, Faherty thought.

The coachman, a thin, normally talkative fellow, with a tic in his left eye, held back now. Cap in hand, he waited, a respectful distance from the graveside.

He had brought them here, deep into the mountains and lakes of this remote Maamtrasna valley. The red-haired woman, her twin daughters, one dead, one alive; the son, and the orphan waif, silent as a prayer, beside him.

The silent one was a mystery to him. A week ago – the first time he had brought the woman back here from the ship at Westport – the girl had appeared out of nowhere and attached herself to them, running near naked alongside his carriage for miles. Not a word out of her mouth, not even begging.

He wouldn't have stopped if it hadn't been for the woman. She had taken pity on the girl, saved her from almost certain death. Since then, all through the last few days, she had been like a shadow to the woman, quiet as a nun. God knows, he decided, seeing the woman kneeling over the grave – settling into it the tiny white flowers of the potato plant – someone would

11

want to watch over her. It was surely a strange thing to do – potato flowers on a grave. The way she ran down from the hillock here. Ran, barefooted to the bare-acred field, on past the tumbled cabins and, like that, snatched up a fistful of the flowers from the derelict potato beds. Before that the child's shawl – 'Annie's shawl', she called it – must be another one she lost – twined it round the hands of the little dead one, like rosary beads.

Now her fine, emerald-green American dress was ruined with kneeling in the clay, but she didn't seem to notice. Just kept repeating the child's name over and over: 'Katie! Katie! Oh, Katie *a stór!*' Faherty wondered what she had been doing beyond in America, with her three children here? Not knowing whether they were dead or alive. He watched the shape of her stretch backwards. She was hardly the thirty years out – a fine woman. He turned his head slightly, so as not to be watching her that way.

Out of the corner of his good right eye, he glanced back along the curl of the valley, with its lake of green glistening islands. There wasn't much here for her – a few patches of hungry grass. Not a beast in a field. Hard to get a morsel of food out of a place like this – even before the potato rot. Nothing but rocks and stones and water everywhere, as Faherty saw it.

The sun was bothering him, causing his left eye to jump even more.

Hard on her though, sailing all this way to find them, and then one of them up and dying, just when she thought she had them safe. Hard on the little one left too – she must be only the nine or ten years, same as the other little one they were burying. A split pair they were – one taken, one left behind, the two of them the spit of the mother, hair like it was spun out of hers.

The boy was a *biteen* older, maybe two or three years. Distant from the mother – for leaving them, Faherty supposed. Didn't look like her either, dark, must have taken after the father. But then, what else could the woman have done? Her husband already put into this spot and their cabin thrown down. What had she left here, only the *gossoors* and no way of supporting them? The boy would understand in time – give him a few years, and a few knocks in life. He'd understand all right. Still, it must have been hard.

The woman was straightening, dusting down her dress, wiping the earth from her feet, readying to go. She was tall, for a woman. His eye, practised for horse flesh, put her at seventeen hands, maybe even the seventeen and a half. A hand or two above his own five feet four inches. A fine *ainnir* of a woman. She wouldn't wait a widow long, Faherty thought. He crossed himself, slid on his cap again, fell in behind the silent girl as they descended the burial place, the same as they'd come up, in single file, the boy leading. Next, the living twin, followed by the mother, then the girl and himself.

It was a strange thing the way, when they had set out on the journey here ... the way she had carried the child, not letting on at first that she was dead at all, just bad with the fever. He supposed the woman had her reasons. In case

13

they'd take the girl from her, throw her into the lime pit, maybe. Faherty didn't know what in God's name she wanted to be hauling all the way out here for, to this wild place, making a thing of it. Sure, weren't people dying like flies on every side, on account of the Famine, half of them getting no right burial at all. Faherry was well used to death by now. When you were dead, you were dead. She could have buried the child back in Westport, in the Rocky, and saved them all this trouble. The Rocky, if it was a quarry, was consecrated to take the fevered dead. Sure, wasn't half the countryside already flung into it!

He picked his way down the Crucán, the sweep of the Maamtrasna valley unnoticed before him.

Nell had strayed from where he'd left her, snaffling the sweet grass of the long acre which bordered the mountain pass road. The horse was tired from all the travelling. He patted her neck, relieved she hadn't wandered too far. Back here, in the valleys, a wandering horse wouldn't last long.

'I'm sorry, Nell...' he whispered into the animal's ear, so the woman wouldn't hear him, '...dragging you all the way out here where they'd eat you, quick as look at you.'

As they rounded the bend, skirting the edge of the lake, Ellen held the three of them into her: Patrick crooked in her right arm, Mary in the near reach of her left, half-lying across her, half-smothered in the lap of her dress. The girl then beyond Mary, but within the circle of what remained of the family. Ellen watched the back of

Faherty's head, rolling from side to side as it did when he spoke. Now, he was saying nothing, unless talking to himself.

She looked out at the Mask, probably seeing the lake for the last time, not caring if she never saw it again. Nor the valley, hanging there around it, so green, so empty, so full of death, the sun spilling over it as if nothing in the world was wrong. As if it were the Plains of Heaven.

Faherty's head stopped lolling for a moment. She watched it half-turn towards her.

'It was a grand day...'

She hardly heard him, her attention drawn to his jumping eyelid. It must be a nervous thing. He was probably nervous as a child, she thought.

'...a grand day for a funeral, ma'am!' he said, meaning it.

2

For the rest of the journey around the lake she never spoke. Faherty too was silent.

He never heard her even weep. It was all too much for her, he thought. Sorrow and guilt – a bad mixture. If she *keened* it out of herself, got shut of the grief, it would be better for her. But after this, it would be easier. Beyond in America with only the two to care for – and the silent one, if she took her with them? At least they had a chance, somewhere to go to, out of this God-forsaken place. Not like the poor devils here,

15

wandering the roads scouring for scraps, arms and legs stuck out of them like scarecrows. Eyes burned into the sockets with fever. No sound. Only the bit of a breeze rattling through bared ribs. Wherever they were headed it didn't matter, they'd get nothing, neither food nor sympathy. It was the same all over – a land full of nothing. The only hope a quick leaving of this life and Paradise in the next, if they were lucky.

Faherty wondered about Paradise, the Garden of Eden. Was it like the big houses once were? Hanging gardens; carpets of flowers; servants at every turn; fruit on every tree. And long rows of lazy beds, the fat lumper potatoes tumbling out of them, begging to be eaten. He wanted to ask her was America like that.

Mairteen Tom Anthony, a big *bodalach* of a fellow from the foot of the Reek, once told him how the buildings were so tall in New York, that when he first went out there the roof of his mouth got sunburnt from standing all of *a gám* looking up at them. Faherty wasn't sure if Mairteen was tricking him or not. America turned people into tricksters – even an *amadán* like Mairteen Tom.

Leave her be, he decided.

It was still light when Nell edged them past the conical-shaped reek of Croagh Patrick, so she made Faherty bring them straight to Westport Quay. As they passed the workhouse gates hundreds clamoured, seeking admittance. Hundreds more, near naked and starving, sought to clamber over the top of these, calling for 'relief

16

tickets' that would grant them soup; sole sustenance for one more day.

'There must be three thousand inside, if there's a soul,' Faherty opined, 'and as many more outside wanting in.'

They sloped down Boffin Street, past the boatmen's houses and the gaunt Custom House still, in the reign of Victoria, designated the 'King's Stores'. Here, fuelled by hunger, six hundred in rags milled in desperate hope, battened back by militiamen. Nearby, cart-followers, employed to protect the grain when being transported to the town's merchants, waited, slinking on the margins of the famished until called to their cold duty.

Another angry crowd sent up cries of dismay as a ship from Marseille discharged its cargo of wheat, beans and chestnuts, while behind a clipper of Constantinople lay by, bursting with corn from New Orleans, and flanked by Her Majesty's revenue cruisers. Behind the ships were the island drumlins of Clew Bay – giant hump-backed whales, silhouetted against the purple and crimson of the dying day. Ellen leapt from Faherty's carriage. One of the ships must be Atlantic-bound.

Westport Quay throbbed with all the mixed ingredients of quay life. Pampered gentry and a starving commonality jostled equally with tide-waiters and landwaiters, while elbow to shoulder with the herring- and oystermen of Clew Bay, shipping agents of indifferent character plied their raucous trade.

'Passage to Amerikay!' they called, thrusting

17

beckoning circulars into the hands of all who would snatch them from the surrounding chaos. She took one.

At WESTPORT
For PHILADELPHIA
To sail about 10th October
The splendid first-class
Copper-fastened, British-built ship
GREAT BRITAIN.

She pushed it back against the agent's hand. 'Today ... these ships ... America?' she shouted above the din. The agent, a puffy little fellow in an important hat, gave her the once-over.

'Yes ma'am, to the exotic city of New Orleans,' – as if he'd ever been there – face creasing into a red-veined smile. A well-heeled mark, this one – a bit soiled about the hem, but had the where-withal for passage, he'd wager, unlike most of them here.

'No... Boston, I want Boston!' she impressed on him, impatient that he didn't already know.

'Boston, New Orleans, Philadelphia – it's all America!' he expounded – what did the woman care? 'Four to a berth, splendid provisions and a quart o' water a day. Is it just yourself, ma'am?'

She left the sound of him puffing away behind her, and through the pandemonium eventually made her way to the offices of John Reid, Jun. & Co., Ship Agents.

Mr John Reid, Jun., an affable-looking man in his fifties, had 'no intelligence, in the coming weeks, of any ship Boston-bound. But we are sometimes surprised by what the tide brings in,' he informed her, helpfully. Her only course of action, he advised, was to keep daily watch at the quay and enquire of him regularly. He could promise her 'a ship fitted with every attention to the comfort of passengers for Québec, before three weeks was out', adding, 'Québec being but a tolerable land journey from Boston'.

She was dismayed. Here she was, her two remaining children secure, and no way out of Ireland. She wondered about Québec, about taking a chance, but feared for the ship Mr Reid had described as 'fitted with every attention to the comfort of passengers'. She had seen these 'comfort of passengers' ships before. 'Coffin ships' and rightly named so. Then to land on Québec's quarantine island – Grosse Île, with its seeping fever sheds. She could not subject them to that, she told him, so declining his suggestion.

3

'Ne'er mind, ma'am, something will crop up,' Faherty tried to console her with, when she found them again. 'I'll take you to The Inn on the North Mall,' he offered. 'You can rest up there a while.' He imagined a lady like her wouldn't be shy the tally for the innkeeper, his second cousin. 'It's for ever full with agents and customs men. I'll put word with the owner, a dacent man,' he said, without naming him, 'to keep an ear out on their talk.'

Again Nell carted them, this time up against the slope of Boffin Street, through the town's Octagon and past the Market House, a fine, ashlar-built, two-storey, with pediment roof and louvred bell cote.

It reminded her of Faneuil Hall, in Boston's Quincy Market. But Boston was a city much advanced on Westport. In turn the Octagon, with its imposing Doric column at variance with the inched-out life of those below it.

She felt the children dig in closer to her as they passed the stench of the Shambles where the butchers of James Street rendered carcasses. Faherty yanked Nell to the right, away from the gated entrance to Westport House, home to Lord Sligo, and took them instead along the North Mall.

On this tree-lined boulevard, with its leafy riverside, the poor huddled, congregating outside the place to which Nell delivered them. Faherty nudged the horse forward, shouting at those who blocked their progress, 'Get back there! Let the lady through! She's had a sore loss this day!'

Ellen, aware of the pitiful, near-death state in which most of his listeners were, and embarrassed by Faherty's words, bowed her head. It didn't seem to bother Faherty, who skipped down from his perch, tied Nell to the hitching-post and then helped her and the children alight.

The near-dead gaped at them, shuffling out a space through which they could pass. Some made the sign of the cross as she approached, respectful of her loss.

Faherty gentled her in under the limestone porch, solicitous for her well-being, and bade her wait while he sought the keeper.

Inside was a sprinkling of red-faced jobbers, stout sticks in their paw-like hands, the stain of dung on their boots. Beef-men in this 'town of the beeves' – *Cathair na Mart* – as she knew it by name. She wondered who it was bought their beef, in these straitened times? Merchants with money, she supposed. Some of the beeves would end up in the Shambles they had just passed. Some would go out on the hoof, heifered over in ships to help drive those who drove the hungry machines of England's great industrial towns. Not a morsel would find its way to the empty mouths of those outside.

The tug at her arm recalled her from England's mill towns. It was Mary. 'Patrick's not here!'

Ellen spun around. The boy was nowhere to be seen. She bade Mary and the silent girl wait and rushed for the crowds outside, impervious to everything except that she must not lose him now. Down the Mall she saw him some twenty paces away, on his knees in company with a ragged boy, scarce older than himself. She ran to him, ever fearful of ... something – she didn't know what.

She reached him, relieved to see he was not harmed. 'Patrick, what...?'

'I was only helping him,' Patrick said, defensively.

The other boy, a tattered urchin with vacant stare, backed away, afraid of what this frantic and well-dressed lady might do to him. *'Tá brón orm,*

21

ma'am' – 'I'm sorry, ma'am' – he said, fearfully, in a mixture of Irish and his only other word of English apart from 'sir'.

She spoke to him in Irish. This seemed to help him be less cowed. Nevertheless, he kept his eyes thrown down as he told his story.

They lived five miles out on the Louisburgh road. His parents stricken with Famine fever, had hunted him and his two younger brothers, eight and six years, 'to Westport for the soup-tickets'. So the three had set off, he in charge. At the workhouse, he was too small to make headway against the clamouring crowds. Instead, he had followed the flayed carcass of an ass, bound for human consumption, and stolen some off-cuts, which he and his brothers had eaten. After sleeping in one of the town's side alleys, he had awoken, planning to come here to The Inn, the headquarters of the Relief Works' engineer, 'looking for work, to get the soup that way, ma'am', he explained.

Unable to arouse his two younger brothers, he thought they still slept, 'sickened by the ass-meat', eventually realizing they lay dead beside him. Then he had stolen a sack, put their bodies inside and carried it over his shoulder 'to get them buried with prayers'. At the Catholic church on the opposite South Mall, he had sneaked in the doors on the tail of a funeral: 'for a respectable woman like yourself, ma'am – she was in a coffin'. But, while the church-bell tolled the passing of the 'respectable woman', he had been ejected on to the streets with his uncoffined brothers. Again, he had carried his sack back to The Inn, hoping against hope to get food. Food that would give him enough strength to find a burial place for his dead siblings, 'till I fell in a heap with the hunger!'

That was what Patrick had seen – the boy collapsing, the sack flung open on the road, from within it the two small bodies revealed. Not that he hadn't seen plenty dead from want before. It had to do with Katie, Ellen knew.

She made to approach the boy. He, still afraid that he had caused some bother to her, backed away. She halted, hunkered down, then called to him. Slowly, he approached, head down, arms crossed in front, a hang-dog look on him as if waiting to be beaten. She reached out and enfolded him.

'You're a brave little *maneen*,' she said, feeling his skin and bone, his frightened heart, within her arms. 'We'll get them buried. And we'll get some soup for you,' she comforted, wondering as she spoke, what in Heaven's name she would do with him then.

After a few moments, she released him and went to Patrick. 'You did right, Patrick, to go and help him,' she said, and held her son against her. 'I was so afraid I'd lost you again.'

Patrick made no reply, neither accepting nor denying her embrace. She was a long way yet from his forgiveness.

Grabbing the sack, she twisted the neck of it closed, not bearing to look inside. The weight of the corpses within resisted her, each tumbling for its own space, not wanting to be carcassed together in death. She didn't know how the boy had managed to carry it for so long.

Then Faherty was beside her. 'Ma'am, are you all right?' he panted, all of a flap, seeing her struggle with the sack.

'We need your services again, Mr Faherty,' she said grimly.

Puzzled, he looked at her, looked from Patrick to the boy, then to the sack, finally back to her, his eye jumping furiously all the time. She saw the realization dawn on his face, the ferret-like look he darted her way.

'You'll be paid, of course!' she answered his unspoken question.

'Right, ma'am, I'll fetch Nell.' He made to go, all concern for her well-being now abated. Money was to be made. He turned. 'And what about him, ma'am?' He nodded towards the boy beside her: 'You can't save all of 'em.'

'I know, Mr Faherty. I know!' she said resignedly. Of course she couldn't take the boy with her. She would have to release him again on to the streets, to take his slim chances. How long it would be before he, too, joined his brothers, either coffined or uncoffined, she didn't know.

Later, in the bathroom down the hall, she filled the big glazed tub with buckets of steaming water. She dipped her elbow in. Maybe it was too hot. She waited until it was barely tolerable then went for Patrick, scuttling him along the corridor in case some dung-stained jobber got in ahead of them. She undressed him and bustled him into the tub, all the while Patrick protesting strongly at this forced intimacy between them and her all too obvious intentions.

'I'm clean enough! I don't need you to wash me!' elicited no sympathy. She was taking no chances after the episode with the boy and his dead brothers – who knew what they carried? She rolled up her sleeves and scrubbed him to within an inch of his life, until his skin was red-raw. He thrashed about in the water trying to get away from her but to no avail. She did not relent until she was satisfied he was 'clean', until she had found every nook and cranny of his body. Then, lugging him by each earlobe in turn, she stuck long sudsy fingers into his ears, to 'rinse' them. When she had finished he was like a skinned tomato. Sullen, jiggling his shoulders so as not to allow her to dry him with the towelling cloth. She gave up, threw her coat over his shoulders and led him back to the room. 'Dry yourself, then,' she ordered him.

The two girls she put together into the tub. She was not so worried about them. But even from Katie they might have taken something; and much as she didn't want to think of it, she had to be careful about that too. Disease passed from person to person, even from the dead to the living. Ellen thought the girl would be shy about letting her touch her. This proved not to be the case. Mary, though, seemed to recoil from the girl, not wanting their arms and legs to touch, get entangled. Maybe it was a mistake putting them in the bath together, so soon after Katie. She was as gentle as she could be with Mary, kept talking to her.

'Katie is with the angels in Heaven, with the baby Jesus ... with–' She paused, thinking of Michael, the steam of the tub in her eyes. 'I was too late ... too late *a stór* ... but they're looking down on us now ... it was hard, Mary, I know ... and on Patrick ... and Katie too, with your poor father laid down on the Crucán and me fled to Australia. What must have been going through your little minds?' Maybe it would have been better if she had taken Annie and with the three of them, crawled into some ditch till the hunger took them instead of her splitting from them. But how could she have watched them waste away beside her, picked at by ravens, their little minds going strange with the want of a few boiled nettles, or the flesh of a dog. She thought of the boy and his brothers – or any poor manged beast that would stray their way. She had had to go, it was no choice in the end – leave them and they had some chance of living, stay and they all would surely die.

Mary, head bent, said nothing, her hair streaming down into the water, red, lifeless ribbons. What *could* she say to the child? She pulled back Mary's hair, wrung it out, plaited it behind her head.

'God must have smiled ... when He took Katie. He must have wanted her awful badly...'

Mary turned her face. 'Then why did He leave me?' she asked limply, boiling it all down to the crucial question.

'I don't know, Mary,' she answered. 'There were times when I prayed He'd take all of us. He must have some great plan for you in this life,' she added, without any great conviction.

How could the child understand, when she couldn't understand it herself – the cruelty of it – snatching Katie from them at the last moment. She fumbled in her pocket, drew out the rosary beads.

'The only thing is to pray, Mary; when nothing makes sense the only thing is to pray, Mary,' she repeated.

Already on her knees, arms resting on the bath, Ellen blessed herself.

"The First Joyful Mystery, the ... the Annunciation,' she began.

They had to have hope in their hearts. The sorrow would never leave, she knew, and maybe there would never be full joy in this life. But they had to have hope, keep the Christ-child in their hearts.

She and Mary passed the Mysteries back and forth between themselves, each leading the first part of the Our Father, the Hail Marys and the Glory be to the Father as it was their turn. Once, before the famine, there were five of them – a Mystery each.

The silent girl gave no hint that she had ever previously partaken of such family devotion, merely exhibiting a curious respectfulness as the prayers went between Ellen and Mary through the veil of bath-vapour – the mists of Heaven. Ellen's clothes were sodden, her face bathed in steam, the small hard beads perspiring in her hands. The great thing about prayer was that you didn't have to talk to a person while you prayed with them. Yet souls were joined talking to each other, while they talked to God. She beaded the last of the fifty Hail Marys. There was only so much time for prayers and she whooshed the two out of the tub before they could get cold.

Afterwards, she boiled all of the clothes they had worn, along with her own, before at last climbing into the tub herself. It was a blessed relief. When she had finished rinsing out her hair she lay there, head back on the rim of the tub, her eyes closed. Everyone and everything done for. A little snatch of time to be on her own. Just her and Katie.

The memories flooded back to her. How when she'd send Katie and Mary to the side of the hill for water, they would become distracted, forget. Instead, would lie face-down on the cooling slab of the spring well, watching each other's reflections in the clear water. Then, when she called them they would scamper down the hill to her, pulling the bucket this way and that until half its contents was left behind them. The times when she did the Lessons, teaching them at her knee what she had learned at her father's knee, passing it on. While Mary would reflect on what she had learned, Katie just couldn't. Always bursting with questions, one tumbling out after the other, mad to know only about Grace O'Malley, the pirate queen of Clew Bay, or Cromwell and his slaughtering Roundheads. God, how Katie had tried her patience at times! The evenings, when as a family they would kneel to say the rosary, Katie's elbowing of Mary every time the name of the Mother of God was mentioned, which was often! At *Samhain* once when the spirits of the dead came back to the valley, Katie had thrown one of the bonfire's burning embers into the sky. No amount of argument could shake her belief but that she had hit an 'evil spirit' with it.

That was Katie, a firebrand herself, filled to the brim with life. But she had the other side too; like the time she had dashed to the steep edge of the mountain as they crossed down to Finny for Mass. It had put the heart crossways in Ellen. But Katie had returned safely and clutching a fistful of purple and yellow wildflowers, a gift for her mother.

Her fondest memory of Katie was of the time when Annie was born. Katie had crept to her side, to be the first one to see 'my new little sister'. Like an angel touching starlight, one tentative finger had stretched out to touch Annie's cheek. How Ellen herself had cried at the beauty of the moment, then laughed at her own foolishness. Katie, as always, asking the ever-pertinent question. *'A Mhamaí*, why are you crying when you're laughing?' And she couldn't answer her. They had lain there together, she and Katie and Annie, into the gathering dawn; touching, whispering, rapt in wonder until the others came. Both of them now snatched from her, Annie in far-off Australia, Katie on her own doorstep.

'You in there!' The loud rap at the door startled Ellen. 'You've been there all night, we have others waiting!' The gruff voice of Faherty's cousin was matched by further rapping.

'I'm sorry,' she called back, clambering out of

29

the tub, 'I'm coming.'

She was relieved when she opened the door to find he had gone downstairs. Briskly she padded along the corridor, marking it with her wet footprints, the only sound ringing in her ears, not that of the gruff innkeeper but a child's question.

'Can we make wonder last, *a Mhamaí?*'

And her answer, those two and a half years ago. 'Yes, Katie, we can.'

Back in the room, Patrick, Mary and the girl were already asleep. She dried herself freely, nevertheless, keeping at a discreet distance from the window in The Inn's west wing. The window looked out across the Carrowbeg river. Directly opposite she could see St Mary's Church, with its imposing parapet. The thought of the boy with the sack being evicted from the House of God because of his wretched condition angered her. Why had she felt responsible for the boy – as she had for the silent girl? Why for some and not for others, when thousands were dying? Faherty had told her thirty-nine poor souls had received the last sacraments in that day alone.

'And it's the same every day, ma'am. Monday to Sunday. They say there's thirty thousand of the destitute getting outdoor relief around here – and they'll be joining with them soon enough.'

She could well believe it. Thirty thousand in one small area. She wondered if there was any hope for the country at all. But why didn't she feel as bad about these, about the nameless hordes, as she did about the boy? She had never asked his name. That way, he was just a boy, any boy. But she was ridden with guilt when after giving him some food and a few coins with which to send him off, he had thanked her saying, 'I'll pray for you, ma'am.' Faherty was right, she couldn't save them all. But what would the child do, where would he go? For how long would he survive?

The limestone façade of St Mary's looked back white-faced at her from the South Mall. Nothing much had changed since she had left Ireland. If you had money you lived proper and you died proper, as Faherty might have put it. You had the Church behind you. Otherwise it was a pauper's life and a pauper's grave.

This thought reminded her she needed to be careful with the money. She had depleted what she had carefully squirrelled away over many months in Boston, by coming to Ireland. Now, with The Inn, and who knew for how long, and the extra cost to Faherty for the two coffins, she had eaten further into her reserves. The silent girl could only come with them because Katie wasn't. If they had long to wait in Westport, Ellen might not even be able to afford that passage. She would be forced to leave the girl behind. At one stage, she had almost decided to disentangle herself from the girl and give her to the nuns, if they'd take her.

The waif, who watched and shadowed her everywhere, seemed to be a manifestation of the past dogging her, a spectre of loss, separation, Famine. It unnerved her the way the girl never asked anything of her, just was there like a conscience. But, given a little time, she might make a companion for Mary. Not that anybody could replace Katie; it wasn't that. But maybe Mary might find some echo of her own unvoiced loss in the silence of the mute girl, some small consolation in her companionship on the long journey across the Atlantic.

Now, Ellen prayed across the waters of the Carrowbeg to the House of God that she would not have to change that decision. She closed her mind from even having to think about it. Instead, she tried to recall what it was Faherty had said about the church opposite. About the inscription from the Bible that its foundation stone carried?

'This is an awful place. The House of God.'

Faherty knew all these things.

4

The days dragged by. Each day she trudged with the children to the quayside and scanned out along Clew Bay for the tell-tale line against the sky. Each day they returned dispirited, almost as much by what they had witnessed on the way, as by the lack of a ship. Was there to be no let up in the calamity? The scenes of despair and deprivation seemed to her to have worsened. Drooplimbed skeletons of men – and women – hauled turf on their backs through the streets, once work only for beasts of burden. When she mentioned this at The Inn, they laughed at her naïveté.

'There's not an ass left in Westport that hasn't

been first flayed for the eightpence its pelt will bring, then its hindquarters eaten,' a well-cushioned jobber jibed. 'Now the peasants who sold them have to make asses of themselves!'

She was shocked at the indifference of the commercial classes to the plight of 'the peasants'.

Nervous of everything, she kept the children close by and was cross with them if they wandered, terrified that she'd lose them. That they'd be swallowed in the hordes of the famished who filled the streets with the smell of death and the excrement of bodies forced to feed inward upon themselves.

Once she traipsed them with her to Croagh Patrick. They climbed to where they could look across the dotted archipelago of the bay, out past the Clare Island lighthouse. She could see no tall ships, only boats far out, maybe tobacco smugglers, or those ferrying the contraband Geneva, an alcoholic liquor flavoured with juniper and available from under the counter – if asked for – at The Inn.

They climbed higher for better vantage, Ellen straining her eyes against the gold and green of sun and sea. Here, on this age-old mountain, St Patrick had fasted for forty days and forty nights. 'Those who worship the Sun shall go in misery ... but we who worship Christ, the true Sun, will never perish.' In the writing of his *Confession* the saint had denounced the sun and its worshippers. Now she prayed to the sun to bring them a ship. Sun-up or sun-down, it didn't matter, as long as it came. To the west her eye caught a rib of white stone rising heavenwards against the bulk of the mountain. A 'Famine wall' going nowhere, built on the Relief Works to exact moral recompense from the starving stone-carriers. They in turn given 'relief'; a few pence in pay, a handful of soup-tickets.

She remembered how on the last Sunday of summer, Reek Sunday, as it was widely known, the *Clogdubh* – the Black Bell of St Patrick – was brought there for weary pilgrims to kiss, for a penny. Black from the holy man pelting it at devils, they said. She had never kissed it. For tuppence, those afflicted with rheumatism might pass it three times around the body, for relief. Another superstition of the shackling kind that bred paupers to pay priests. Like the legends about the reek itself. Legends, she guessed, grown to feed misery and repentance, to keep the people out of the sun.

She thought of ascending the whole way – making the old pilgrimage, beseeching the high place where the tip of the mountain disappeared into the lower heavens, to send a ship. But what was it, anyway? Only a heap of piled-up rocks, only a mountain. And what could a mountain do? Still, she called the children and followed the path to the First Station. Seven times they shambled around the cairn of stones intoning seven Our Fathers, seven Hail Marys and one Creed. She wondered why *once* of everything wasn't enough, why it had to be seven times.

Then she turned her back on St Patrick's mountain, angry, yet disquieted by her rejection of it, and dragged them down the miles with her to Westport. Westport, relic of the anglicization of

34

Ireland. A Plantation town of well-mannered malls, the canalized Carrowbeg outpouring the grief and suffering of its hapless inhabitants.

St Patrick and the Protestant Planters could have it between them.

5

Whether her anger had moved the sullen mountain, or whether it was merely favourable winds, the next morning produced a miracle. A ship out of Londonderry – the *Jeanie Goodnight* – had rounded Achill Island under cover of darkness and now sat at the quay: and she was Boston-bound. Word of the ship's arrival had spread like wildfire, igniting all of Westport into frenzied quay-life once again. The Inn emptied.

Ellen left the children behind her in the room, admonishing them not to leave it. Wild with excitement, she threw off her shoes and ran barestockinged all the way to the office of Mr John Reid, Jun., the dress hiked up behind her like a billowing sail and with every stride storming Heaven that she wasn't too late.

The quay was teeming with people. Would-be travellers clutched carpetbags to their breasts – food and their entire earthly possessions within. Many were young, single women, who vied for ground with barking agents and anxious excise men. While late-arriving jobbers had their own solution, jabbing at obstructive buttocks with their knob-handled cattle-sticks.

Already the ship agent's door was mobbed, cries of 'Amerikay!' ascending at every turn. Call the damned at the Gates of Hell. Like it was their last hope.

It *was* her last hope. If they didn't embark on this ship, who knew when another would come. She and her children would be fated to stay in Ireland. Her money would run out, and in time they would sink lower and lower, until they, too, ended up on scraps of pity and charity and the off-cuts of ass-meat. She lunged into the crowd, all thought of her gender put aside. Nor did the opposite gender give ground to her, unless she took it. Pushing and elbowing, she scrimmaged her way forward until she reached the front.

'Mr Reid! Mr Reid!' she shouted, money in her fist, shaking it above her head. 'Passage for four to Boston!' she beseeched.

At last he beckoned her forward, she banged down the money onto his desk.

Fifteen minutes later she left, four sailing tickets to Boston clenched like a prayer between her two hands.

Their passage was secured.

The children were overjoyed, Mary more restrained than the others, at the thought of leaving Katie behind. Ellen wondered if the silent girl really understood what all the excitement was about. Sometimes, you just didn't know with her. But the girl clapped her hands, looking from one to the other of them, her hazel-brown eyes shining, her pert little nose twitching with delight.

Thrice daily, morning, noon, and at eventide, Ellen went to check on the *Jeanie Goodnight* lest the ship slip out again unexpectedly, just as she had ghosted into the western seaboard town.

Three days later they were headed out into the bay, Westport behind them in the mist, like a shaken shroud. She hated the place. Its workhouse which had taken Michael; the hordes of its hungry, clawing to get aboard the ship ahead of her, the lucky ones, their passage paid by land-clearing landlords.

Once aboard, she had changed her clothes, shaking the stench of Ireland out of them, then boiled them. As the *Jeanie Goodnight* threaded its way through the drumlin-humped islands, she was aware of the Reek to her left, the cursed mountain always looking down on them, which-ever way you went, by land or by sea; watching, judging. She wouldn't look at it directly. It was part of the Ireland of the past drawing away behind them. An Ireland of Famine; of vacant faces and outstretched hands – an island of beggars, no place for her and her children.

There they had been, she, Michael, all of them, back there in the mountains, waiting, year in year out, for the potatoes to grow. Beating their way down the road to the priest to give thanks, prostrating themselves, when they did grow; beating their breasts in contrition for imagined sins when they didn't. Then, trudging over and back to Pakenham's place to pay the rent, hoping he wouldn't raise it on them when they had it, grovelling for clemency, citing 'the better times to come' when they hadn't.

Always on their knees, giving thanks or pleading. They were to be pitied, the whole hopeless lot of them. It wasn't the mountains of Maamtrasna that imprisoned them, or the watery arms of the Mask that landlocked them. It wasn't even, she knew, the landlords and the priests. It was themselves. Going round in circles, beholden to the present and beholden to the past, with its old *seafóideach* customs, handed down from generation to generation. Tradition, woven around their lives from before they were born, like some giant web. She wanted to strip it all away from her now, never return. If it wasn't for Michael and Katie back there on its bare-acred mountain, in its useless soil.

'*A Mhamaí...*' The tug at her sleeve startled her.

It was Mary. The child's eyes, though dry, were blotched from rubbing. Mary would try to hide it from her that she still cried over Katie. That was her way. In the days they had waited for the ship, Ellen had talked to her and Patrick about the need to be strong; the child now beside her looked anything but. Though her first instinct was to take Mary in her arms, Ellen instead led her to the bow of the ship.

'See, Mary! See out there beyond the horizon – the place where the sea meets the sky?'

Mary nodded.

'Well, out there is America–'

'Is it like Ireland?' Mary interrupted.

'No, Mary, it isn't. America is a big and rich country not like Ireland at all.'

Mary fell silent. Ellen, sensing the child's disappointment, pressed on. 'It will be better than

38

Ireland, Mary, I promise you it will be better. But we are going to have to be Americans. We must forget we are Irish. Leave all ... all that behind us.'

Mary turned from looking out ahead, trying to see this land where they would be different people. 'But, *a Mhamaí*–'

Ellen stopped her, gently. 'Mary... you mustn't call me that – "*a Mhamaí*" – any more. We are going to be Americans now. People don't say that in America. From now on you must call me "Mother"!'

The child said nothing – only looked at her.

'It's all right,' Ellen said, taking her by the shoulders. 'Nothing's changed. We're still the same between us in English as in Irish,' she smiled. 'Do you understand?'

Mary once more looked out between the deepening sky and the widening ocean, trying to see beyond where they met. Out to this place, this America.

'Yes ... Mother,' she answered, giving voice to the strange-sounding word – the wind from America holding it back in her throat, so that Ellen could scarcely catch it.

Out they tacked, past the Glare Island lighthouse, tall and solid-walled. Its white-painted watchtower, lofted heavenwards two hundred feet, would see them safely past Achill Sound. 'A graveyard for ships,' Lavelle had told her before she had left Boston. It was his place, Achill. This island, cut off from Ireland's most westerly shore. 'Achill – wanting to be in America,' he always joked.

She hadn't yet broached the subject of Lavelle with the children, except in a general fashion, like she had mentioned Peabody; both as people in Boston with whom she conducted business dealings. She would have to tell them more about Lavelle – that they were partners, but in business matters only. Albeit that she was fully conscious of his affection for her, and in turn regarded him highly, it was her intention never to remarry. She would be true to Michael to the grave. If, thereby, she was denying herself the tender comforts of marriage life, and a father's guiding hand for her children, then so be it. That was the price to be paid of her troth to Michael.

An eddy of breeze swirling up from Achill Sound made her shiver slightly. She loosened then re-knotted the blue-green scarf Lavelle had given her at Christmas. She had four long weeks at sea in which to reaffirm her intentions.

The *Jeanie Goodnight*, a triple-masted emigrant barque, with burthen eight hundred tons, and a master and crew of nineteen, was constructed of the best oak and pine Canadian woods could yield. On her arrival at Westport she had disgorged four hundred tons of Indian corn, twelve hundred bags of the dreaded yellow meal; flour, Canadian timber and East Coast American potatoes. There had been a riot, the poor seeking to seize what supplies arrived with the ship. It was the only way they would get food, by taking it.

When Patrick raised the question of inferior food being shipped into the country crossing with superior food being shipped out, all she could say was, 'It doesn't make any more sense to me, Patrick, than it does to you. I don't understand these things.' It really didn't matter what food there was, good or bad. The famished had scarcely a penny between them with which to buy it anyway.

Soon they had sailed beyond the reach of Achill Sound, leaving behind her last view of Ireland – disused lazy beds climbing towards the sky over Clew Bay.

The voyage was a good one, the elements favouring them so that the copper-fastened *Jeanie Goodnight* sat steady and proud in Atlantic waters. Ellen kept themselves to themselves. Their fellow passengers were a mixed lot. Above deck were the commercial Catholic classes – shopkeepers, grocers, middlemen – and those called 'strong farmers', taking what possessions they had, fleeing the sinking ship that was Ireland. There was too a good sprinkling of voyagers from Londonderry and the northern counties.

It surprised her to hear talk in their brittle way of 'the calamity biting deep in Ulster'. She found it hard to reconcile the notion that those who called on the Hand of Providence to strike down the 'lazy Irish Catholics', should also be stricken by the same levelling Hand.

'Planters', or 'Scots Irish', as Lavelle called them; Irish, but not Irish. And they *were* different. More sober in dress and demeanour than the boisterous middlemen from the southern counties. Two hundred years previously, they had

41

been brought in from the Scottish lowlands, and given Catholic land. In return, they were to 'reform' Ireland and the Irish. This zeal had never left them. She had seen them in Boston. Hard work and privilege had kept them where they were – looking down on the 'other' Irish, every bit as much as the 'other' Irish – her Irish – despised them.

These Scots Irish on board the *Jeanie Goodnight* already spoke of Boston as if it were theirs, naming out to each other the congregations where they would gather to worship; giving no sense that they were leaving anywhere, only of arriving somewhere else.

Below deck, sober demeanour counted for nothing. Nightly the scratch of fiddles and the thud of *reel-sets* staccatoed the timbers, as the peasant Irish *ceilidhed* their way to 'Amerikay'.

The 'cleared', passage-paid by landlords happy to see the back of them, at first rejoiced openly at their leaving. Then, inhabitors of neither shore, they floundered in a mid-ocean of conflicting emotions, fuelled by dangerous grog and more dangerous fiddle music.

Along with the 'cleared' a large body of those below deck were single women from sixteen to thirty years, those Ellen had noticed at the quayside. 'Erin's daughters', fleeing Famine and repression. Most would find their way into the homes of affluent Boston as domestic servants to become 'Bridgets'. Others would sit behind the wheels of the new-fangled sewing machines in the flourishing clothing and cordwaining shops of the Bay Colony. Others still would become

42

'mill girls', in the Massachusetts mill towns of Lawrence and Lowell. There, their fresh young bodies would make the machines sing and the bosses happy, their spirits thirst for the fields of home and a cooling valley breeze.

In Boston, the agents of those same factory bosses would be waiting on the piers, to corral the fittest and strongest of these young women, to put shoes on the feet of America, clothes on American backs. She had seen it so many times on the Long Wharf when the ships came in.

And she had seen the jaded 'Bridgets' traipse down to Boston Common with their silver-spoon charges, glad of an outing and a few mouthfuls of fresh air. And the threadbare needlewomen, bodies like 'S' hooks from fifteen hours a day, every day, shaped over their machines.

America indeed promised much. But it took much in return.

Each evening those below were allowed on deck for an hour to cook what little they had on the open stove before being driven below again. Once uncaged, they tore at their carpetbags like ravenous dogs, until the meagre contents contained within, spilled over the timbers. A few praties, a bag of the hard yellow meal – 'Peel's Brimstone', after the British Prime Minister who sought to feed the starving Irish with it, until it sat like marbles, pyramided in their bellies. Sometimes she saw a side of pig or the hindquarter of an ass, smoked or salted for preservation. Finally, the carpetbags carried a drop of castor oil for the bowels – to clear out Peel's yellow marbles.

Once, horrified, she watched as a young lad, no older than Patrick, was flung from the carpetbag mêlée by a much older man, his father. The boy careered against the tripod supporting the cooking cauldron. But his screams, as his arms and upper body were scalded, served to distract none but his mother from the frenzy taking place. Ellen ran to summon the ship's doctor but the boy's frailty was unable to sustain his sufferings and he expired before relief could be administered.

She noticed, the following evening, that the tragedy stayed no hand from the continuing brawls for carpetbag rations.

Again, Ellen kept the children close to her, having found the silent girl one evening to have disappeared and crept amongst the carpetbaggers, peering into their faces, searching out a spark of recognition between any and herself. Ellen could still get nothing from her, nor did the girl speak to either Mary or Patrick.

At first the strangeness of being on the ship had seemed to frighten the girl – as it did Ellen's own two children. Then, she became fascinated by it. Looking out on every side, running quickly from windward to leeward, watching the land slide away behind them. Or, facing mizzenward, almost, it seemed to Ellen, *listening* to the flap of the wind in the masts. Other times she would find the girl staring for hours into the deep, ever-changing waters, finding some kinship there, amidst the white spume, the dark silent depths. What was ever to become of her, Ellen wondered. She would have to give her a name. She

44

couldn't be just the 'silent girl', for ever.

The thirty days at sea, whilst giving Ellen time to regain herself, had done nothing to restore her with regard to Patrick.

He still resented her for deserting them and didn't seek much to conceal it either. Ellen had decided to let things take their own course between them, not to rush him. But Boston wasn't far away – and Lavelle. If Patrick didn't show some sign in the next week or so of coming around, then she would have to sit him down anyway and tell him about Lavelle. Already, when she had returned to Ireland to retrieve the children, her changed appearance and failure to return sooner had caused Patrick to accuse her of having a 'fancy man' in America.

6

Three days out of Boston, she spoke to them of Lavelle. 'I want to tell you about Boston...' she began. 'There are a lot of houses. Big, big houses and a lot of streets. Not like our little street in the village, but long, long streets and every one of them crowded with people,' she explained.

'Like Westport?' Mary ventured.

'Like twenty Westports all pulled together,' she answered, 'and the sea on one side of Boston and the rest of America on its other side.'

Mary's eyes opened wide at the idea. Patrick

45

stayed silent.

'And Boston Common, itself as big as all Maamtrasna. Where people walk and children play in the Frog Pond and skate in the snow. And,' she drew in close to them, 'a giant tree where they used to hang witches! And,' she moved on, seeing the frightened look on Mary's face, 'horses that pull tram carts – you'll love going in them.'

'When we get there you'll be going to school to learn all about Boston and America, and lots of other things besides,' she went on, wondering what she would do for the silent girl in this regard.

'Will you not be doing the Lessons with us any more, *a*–' Mary started to ask and corrected herself, 'Mother?'

'Well, Mary, I think you and Patrick are too grown up for me to be still teaching you at home. The best schools in the whole, wide world are in Boston. It will be very exciting for you both with American children ... English and German children ... children from everywhere,' she told them.

'Will they be like us?' Patrick spoke for the first time.

Ellen, not sure of what he meant, replied, 'Yes, of course they will. They'll all be of an age with yourselves, bright and eager to get on,' she said, thinking she had answered him.

'No, but like us – Irish?' he countered.

She had to think for a minute. 'Yes, yes, of course there will be children like you, who have come from Ireland. Did I not say that?'

Patrick pressed his point. 'And what about those?' he pointed to the deckfloor, 'those below there?'

'Well I'm sure they'll all be wanting education,' she half-answered. The way Patrick looked at her told her he knew she had tried to skirt his question. She decided to plunge straight on, into the deeper end of things. 'Now, as well as the schools, you'll meet some people in Boston ... who – who have helped me...' She slowed, picking out the words. 'A Mr Peabody, a merchant who owns shops...'

Patrick watched her intently, searching out any flicker or falter that would betray her.

'Mr Peabody helped me to get started in business and a Mr Lavelle, a friend...' she could feel Patrick's eyes burning into her, '...who saved my life and helped me escape Australia to get back to you. Mr Lavelle works with me in the business.'

There, she had gotten it all out and in one blurt. It was so silly of her to be nervous of telling them, her own children.

Neither of them had any questions, Mary's face lighting up at the news that Mr Lavelle had saved her mother's life.

'Oh, he must be a good man, this Mr Lavelle, to do that ... a good man like Daddy was!' she added.

'He is,' Ellen said, more shaken by the innocence of Mary's statement than by any hard question Patrick might have asked. It was what she had wanted to avoid at all costs – any notion that Lavelle was stepping into their father's

47

shoes. He wasn't. God knows, he wasn't.

Soon they were within sight of America, evidenced by increased activity in every quarter of the *Jeanie Goodnight*. Ellen still had not resolved the problem of naming the silent girl. Calling her by no name seemed to be so soulless. How well she had come on since Ellen had first found her. Or rather since the girl had first found them, on the road towards Louisburgh. Now, if only she'd speak – tell them what her name was. Ellen determined to try again with her.

To her horror she found the girl part way up the rigging, seeking a better view of America. Petrified that she'd fall, Ellen anxiously beckoned for her to come down.

The girl jumped on to the deck, smiling at Ellen. Tall and dark-haired, her frame now filled out the skimpy dress that, a month past, had hung so shapelessly on her. Still looked scrawny but at least she was on the way.

'What's your name, child, and where did you come from?' Ellen asked. The girl, eyes still alight with the rigging fun, just looked back at her – happy, forlorn, smiling, such a mixture, Ellen thought. She must have her own pinings and no one to share them with.

The one and only time the girl had spoken, at Katie's burial, it had been in Irish. She probably had no English. Ellen tried again asking her name, this time in Irish. English or Irish, the silent girl made no response. Ellen was sure the girl heard her, understood her even, but, for whatever reason, could not, or would not, reply.

'We have to get you a name, child,' she said, touching the girl's face. 'A name to go with those hazel-brown eyes and that pert little nose of yours. A name for America.'

The deck was now getting crowded with sea-weary travellers, jubilant at the sight of land before them. Before she could progress things further with the girl, Mary ran at her all of a tizzy.

'Is that it, is that Boston?' she burst out, more like Katie than anything, unable to hold back the excitement the sight before them evoked. Patrick too arrived, his forehead dark and intense with interest, but not wanting them to see it.

Ellen felt her own spirits quicken. Momentarily forgetting her quest for a name, she began pointing out places to them. 'Look at all the ships! Remember, I told you. And all the islands, let's see if I still have names for them?'

Mary laughed at the strange-sounding names as Ellen tried to get them right.

'Noodles Island, Spectacles Island, Apple Island and Pudding Point!' she rattled off, pleased with herself.

'No shortage of food here in America then,' Patrick cut in, trying to deny them the moment.

Ellen ignored him. 'And that's Deer Island! We'll have to stop there for ... for the people below, for quarantine ... that they have no diseases,' she hurried to explain.

And their eyes were agape at the size and splendour of America, with its tall spires distantly spiking the heavens.

'There's the harbour way ahead,' she pointed out, trying to distinguish the Long Wharf, 'where we'll dock. Beyond that is the State House and Quincy Market.' They heard the quiver of recognition in her voice as she tumbled out the names, all foreign, all strange to them. 'Further up is Boston Common – I'll take you there.' She hugged the three of them, this time leaving out the witches. 'On the higher ground at the back – you can't see it clearly from this far – is Beacon Hill, where once were lit the warning lights for the city if it was going to be attacked.' She gabbled on, childlike, dispensing all she knew to them. 'And there's a place up there called Louisburgh Square – like Louisburgh back home – where we found–' She stopped, looking at the silent girl in front of her. 'Louisburgh – that's it! That's it!' She laughed excitedly. 'We'll call her after the place where she was found, and the place she is coming to! Louisburgh – we'll call her "Louisa".'

Ellen looked from one to the other of them. Mary smiled, nodding her head up and down. Patrick signalled neither assent nor dissent. '"Louisa" – it's a good name, a grand name,' Ellen went on. How easy it had been in the end – naming the girl. 'It'll suit her well! Oh, everything is working out fine! I knew it would once we came to America!'

The silent girl, who had drifted a few paces off from them, sensing the commotion turned from looking at her new home, the place she was now being named for.

'Louisa!' Ellen took the girl by the arms, dancing them up and down with delight – like a girl herself. 'Louisa – welcome to America!'

The girl just looked at her, before turning her attention back to the sight of her adopted home, indifferent in the extreme to her new appellation.

'It's not even an Irish name,' Patrick mumbled, more to himself than anybody.

Ellen, nevertheless, heard him. 'You're right, Patrick... it's not,' she said sharply, fed up with his surliness.

'It's American!'

7

Lavelle was waiting on the Long Wharf for them. As they disembarked he waved, a big smile creasing his weathered face. It was easy to pick him out on the thronged jetty, his well-built frame setting him apart as much as the casual colours he favoured – a russet-coloured jacket; a wheaten homespun shirt – colours of the season. But he wouldn't have thought of that, she knew, watching the bob of his head – like summer corn in the autumn sun. He never looked Irish, the way Michael did – 'Black Irish' with the Spanish blood. Lavelle always looked Australian, reminding her of the bushland, the baked earth, the wide-open spaces. She was pleased to see him, but nervous, none the less, about how the children might regard him. Of her own reaction to him she was clear. He was her business partner, her good companion. She would reinstate that particular relationship from today and that relationship only.

He was restrained when he moved to greet them through the milling crowds, but shook her hand warmly.

'Ellen, it's good to see you again! You're welcome back! And who are these fine young ladies and gentleman?' he went on, unsure of how to deal with her return.

She saw him stop for a moment as he took in Mary, looked for the missing Katie, then at Louisa, it not making sense to him.

'This is Patrick,' she intervened. 'Patrick, this is Mr Lavelle of whom I spoke ... and this is Mary,' Ellen introduced the nine-year-old image of herself. 'And this is...' she paused as Lavelle's gaze transferred to the silent girl, '...this is Louisa, who has come with us to Boston.' She saw the question still remain in his eyes. 'We had to leave Katie behind ... with Michael.'

He caught her arm, understanding at once. 'Oh, I'm sorry, Ellen. So sorry – you've had so much of trouble ... after everything else to...' he faltered, unable to find the words.

'Well, we're here,' she said simply. 'At last, we're here.'

'And how is it in Ireland?' Lavelle moved on the conversation.

They would talk later of Katie and this girl Louisa who, when he made to greet her, seemed not to notice him. She was deficient of hearing, or speech, or both, he thought.

'Ireland is poorly,' Ellen answered him, 'Ireland is lost entirely.'

'And what of the Insurrection – the Young

52

Irelanders – we read something of it in the *Pilot?*' he said, referring to the Archdiocese of Boston's weekly newspaper.

'The Insurrection failed – I brought you some newspapers, *The Nation*,' she answered. 'There was much talk of it in Ireland and aboard ship. I have little interest in it. Now we are here and Ireland is...' she turned her head seawards, '...there.'

He heard the weariness in her voice. God only knows what she had gone through to redeem her two remaining children.

'Mr Peabody enquires after you frequently,' he said, in an effort to brighten her up, knowing how much she enjoyed her dealings with the Jewish merchant.

'Oh! And is he well himself, and the business – how is it?' she asked.

'Both Mr Peabody and the business continue to thrive,' he told her with a certain amount of satisfaction, she noticed. Things must have gone better between him and Peabody, in her absence, than she had hoped for.

The children were agog at Boston's Long Wharf, stretching, as Mary put it, 'from the middle of the sea, to the middle of the town'.

'City,' corrected Patrick, showing he was a man of the world, not like his sister who knew nothing. 'It's a city!'

If Westport Quay swirled with all the varied elements of quayside life, then here, in Boston, it was as if the mixed ingredients of the whole world had collided together. Tea-ships, ice-ships, spice-ships. Syphilitic sailors, back from the South Seas, poxed and partially blind, bringing home with them 'the ladies' fever' and the stale stench of flensed whales. In their midst stood sinless and sober-suited Bostonians cut from the finest old Puritan stock; anxious for merchandise, disgusted by this new influx of paupers and the sanitary evils accompanying them.

The hiring agents of the mill bosses sized up this fresh supply of factory fodder. 'Labour!' they hollered, to the sea of 'green hands'. 'Labour!' they called, winking and smiling at the wide-eyed Irish girls. Seeking to seduce with smiles, as much as with dollars, those they considered 'sober of habit, sound of limb and with good strong backs' – as they had been instructed. One man's 'sanitary evil', it seemed in America, was another's 'strong back'.

The children's heads turned at every step, gawking at this and that, each new sight and sound of Boston a greater wonder to them than the one before. Like the gaudily bedecked sailors of various hue, reeking of spices and perfumes from the far reaches of the Orient, chattering in unintelligible tongues. Or a few freed slaves from the South silently bullocking the heavy cargo. She had to prevent them from staring.

'But that man ... he's all black, what happened to him?' Mary couldn't contain herself.

'He's a Negro – from Africa,' Ellen hushed her.

'But will it rub off?' Mary persisted.

'Only if you shake hands with him, Mary,' Lavelle cut in solemnly.

Mary's eyes opened even wider, craning her

neck to see this man who would change colour at a touch.

'Mr Lavelle should have more sense, Mary, ignore him!' Ellen rejoined. 'Some people have a different skin to ours, that's all – and it doesn't rub off!' she stated emphatically, more to Lavelle than to Mary. Nothing she had told them about America had ever prepared them for this, for Boston's Long Wharf.

And the Irish. Everywhere the Irish; shouting, laughing, crying, mobbed by relatives who had crossed the Atlantic before them. Others, solitary young girls clinging to their carpetbags – no one to meet them in this throbbing kaleidoscope, this frightening place. Like motherless calf-whales they were, these daughters of Erin floundering unprotected in the great ocean of America. Easy prey to the welcoming smile, the outstretched hand, the familiar lilt; to their own, the Irish crimpers and 'harpies', who would flense them of everything.

'I can see that Boston is as busy and bustling as ever,' she said to Lavelle, full of being back in the place.

'And bursting at the seams – thousands have arrived these past months – mostly Irish,' he replied. 'The bosses are happy; "green hands" from Ireland mean cheap labour,' he continued, 'but the City Fathers are not, thinking pauperism and Popery both will sink Boston!'

She didn't care much about either bosses or Brahmins. Boston, bursting or not, was such a far cry from what she had left; the tumbled villages, a famished land; silence – no hope. Here there was hope. To her, the city with its crowded chaos, its cacophonous quay-life, rang out with the very music of hope.

'Stop, Lavelle! Stop here!' she called out of a sudden, almost forgetting. 'I want them to see it!'

Lavelle 'whoaupped' the big bay mare he had hired for the day and had scarcely pulled them to a halt, when gathering up her skirts she leapt from the trap-cart.

'Come on, come on!' she beckoned to the children, shepherding them across the mouth of the busy wharf.

Lavelle stayed where he was. She was as impetuous as ever, he thought, watching the long straight back of her weave through the crowds. He smiled to himself – the factory bosses would be glad of a back like that! Three months since she had left and he had thought about her every day, wondering what awaited her in Ireland. Wondering when, if ever, she would return. Then, these past few weeks, scouring the pages of the *Pilot* for shipping intelligence and hoping for a fair wind to bring her back.

She looked a bit racked, he thought. Her face, the way she didn't smile as big as he remembered. The furrow above her lips – the one he could never help watching, fascinated at how its fine fold rose and fell with the cadence of her speech. It didn't fall and rise so much now, as if she was holding it back, keeping it in check. Still, it was a wonder at all that she looked as well as she did. She must have been too late to save them both, whatever had happened. That must have near killed her, would eat away at her for ever, he knew. This one, Mary, with the *dos* of wild red hair on her – how like Ellen she looked. Going to be tall like her too. He could see it now, as together they rounded the corner of the building away from him. The girl was quieter, less impetuous, more of a thinker. But maybe that was down to the foreignness of the place and him being present. And all that had happened.

The boy had made strange with him. With his unruly black head and sallow skin, he looked more like he'd come off a ship from the Spanish Americas, than Ireland. He was unlike her in every feature. Lavelle wondered about the boy's father, her husband. It was her strong attachment to his memory that was holding back her affections. He had been hoping that when she stepped down from the ship, she would be wearing the scarf he had given her. But she wasn't. He wondered, what she had told the children? Or, if she'd thought much on him at all these past three months?

And the girl – the one who said nothing, only taking you in with those big brown eyes. Where had she appeared from? Maybe she was a neighbour's child, orphaned by famine. Nearly more orphanages than groggeries in Boston too, so fast were they springing up. She'd probably put the girl into one of those – run by the Sisters. He 'gee'd' the horse, threading it gingerly after them, glad that he'd painted the sign. It would be a surprise for her. She was standing in front of it, her finger outstretched, reading aloud the strange-sounding words to the children. She turned, hearing the clip-clop of the horse.

57

'Mr Lavelle's been busy painting, I can see,' she said to them. But it was meant for him, he knew. '"The New England Wine Company",' she read out the larger letters again, then the smaller ones underneath, '"Importers of fine wines, ports and liqueurs". That's us!' she said to them with a little laugh. Even Patrick seemed impressed, looking at her, then at the sign over the warehouse, then back at Lavelle, trying to piece it all together.

'You're a merchant, Mother!' Mary said, flushed with pride in her, yet seeming not in the least bit surprised.

'I ... I suppose I am,' Ellen replied, never having thought of herself in that way.

They went inside, Louisa remaining close by her, Mary and Patrick going from rack to rack examining the cradled bottles and the labels with the unusual writing wrapped round them.

'Fron-teen-nyac, pair ay fees' – Frontignac, Père et Fils – she tried to explain, 'the people we get the wine from in Canada. Frontignac, Father and Son,' she went on, watching them watch her as if she was some stranger. And in truth she was. Their memories of her were as far removed from the woman now before them, explaining French wines, as Massachusetts was from the Maamtrasna valley. An ocean in the heart's geography. It would take time.

'Bore-dough,' she pointed to a ruby rich red, 'the place the wine comes from in France.'

It was a strange thing, Patrick thought, for her to know about, her and the 'fancy man' that kept watching him and kept smiling at his mother.

Ellen was well pleased at what she saw. Lavelle

had kept the warehouse solidly stocked against the coming season and the winter closing of the St Lawrence river. Furthermore, he had secured her new accommodation.

'In Washington Street between Milk and Water Streets, near the Old Corner Bookstore,' he told her. 'I know you like to be at the centre of things, and it's bigger, more suitable now with the children.' She had surrendered her old lodgings, not knowing how long she would be away. Her belongings Lavelle had stored in the warehouse, and more recently moved to the new address, paying the rent to secure it against her return. He himself continued to live where he previously had, in the North End, though it was 'now being over-run with the poorest of our own'.

The Long Wharf led them into State Street, New England's financial heart, its temples of commerce close to the city's importing and exporting lifeline – the wharves. Lavelle took them left at the Old State House, down along Washington Street, its patchwork of buildings, filled with apothecaries, engravers, instrument-makers and 'Newspaper Row'. Signs and hoardings jutted everywhere, higgledy-piggledy, while canvas awnings over the footwalks, provided shelter from the rain, shade from the sun, for those with dollars to spend.

Four flights of stairs they climbed of the high-shouldered building, which itself stretched upwards above the world of commerce below. The effort was repaid in full when arriving in their rooms she saw, across from them on the corner of Milk Street, the nestled campaniles of the Old South Meeting House; how they ascended like a pinnacled prayer to the steepled sky.

She knew she would love it here 'on top of the world', as she said to Lavelle. They had three rooms. One large, with two windows, for living in, and above that, two smaller rooms, each lighted by dormers, for sleeping. The larger one for herself and the girls, the smaller for Patrick. She had considered giving the three children the larger one, her taking the lesser room. But Patrick was of an age now.

It was close to everywhere. The Wharf and their warehouse, the Common, shops, churches, schools. The Old Corner Bookstore – which she had commenced frequenting before she left – now only a hen's footstep away. Beneath their roost, on the next floor down, were commercial offices. Below that again, suppliers of mathematical instruments, while a sewing shop for ladies' garments and a dye house occupied the street level of the premises.

She was grateful to Lavelle. He had gone to some trouble to find this place, knowing how much she preferred the rattle and hum of city life above the quiet of some numbing suburb. The frantic commercial life of 'Hub City', as Bostonians liked to call it, was rapidly devouring all available space here at its centre. She wondered how long it would be before trade and commerce would drive further out the dwindling number of inhabitants, like themselves. Where they now stood would soon enough fall into use as an instrument-maker's den, or a sewing sweatshop.

But while ever they could remain here, she knew she would be happy.

When she had thanked him again, Lavelle left and she began to settle them into their new home, high above the world of clarion calls and the street noise of Boston, far from the hushed valleys they had known.

8

Jacob Peabody made an exaggerated fuss of her when, the following week, she came to visit him at his premises on South Market Street across from Faneuil Hall. On top of the Hall's domed cupola, its weathervane – a copper grasshopper – spun from side to side, busily welcoming her back.

Now Peabody, white-domed and wrinkle-faced, grass-hopped from behind his counter to welcome her, rubbing his hands on the white apron he kept on a peg, but which she had never seen him wear. 'Ellen! Ellen Rua!' he exclaimed, both arms outstretched, a bleak shaft of October sun diagonally lighting one eye and a flop of his white hair, vesting him with a kind of manic enthusiasm. He clasped her to him. He not being quite the match of her in height, her head ended up over the shoulder of his well-seasoned cardigan. In its wool the smell of salted hams, spices from the East, tobacco from the Deep South, all indiscriminately buried there.

'Jacob, I'm going to reek of pork and spices just

like you,' she laughed. 'Let go of me! Anyway, I thought it forbidden by your beliefs to sell certain things,' she added, unable to resist poking fun at him. He laughed with her, held her back from him, the snow-white eyebrows arched, the canny eyes taking her in.

'Ah, Ellen, you are as beautiful as ever. Weary from your travels, I can tell...?' He paused. 'And beyond that a certain sorrow...' He had never changed, could tell everything and then never hesitated in its saying. 'But underneath,' he went on, 'your spirit has not changed. Look at you, the first minute you are here flinging the beliefs of an old man in his face. It's good to have you back – back home in Boston,' he beamed. And he clasped her to him again in his pork and spice way.

It felt good to her to be back. And Boston was home. The sounds, the smells, the bustle of Quincy Market, the air spiced with possibility instead of the pall of oppression which hung over Ireland. And good old reliable but mischievous Jacob. He had been a tower of strength before she had left on her journey to Ireland.

He made her tea, Indian, from the Assam Valley, closed his door against the world and bade her sit. 'I want to hear *every* word, Ellen,' he emphasized. 'I've missed the music of your voice – the Boston drawl has little music to it – as flat and as cold as the Quincy marble that built the place!'

Whatever about missing her, Jacob still didn't miss any chance to snipe at his adopted city. Some day she'd ask him about that and Papa Peabody, as he called his father, and the change of name from something Jewish to Peabody. Whatever his origins, Jacob had built up a commodious store on South Market Street. It was frequented alike by well-heeled clientele from Beacon Hill, the literati of Louisburgh Square and Boston's rising middle class. Always well stocked with the exotic and the oriental and anything in between, pickled gherkins to spiced Virginia hams, 'Peabody's' did a thriving business.

When she and Lavelle had first arrived in Boston, they had decided that rather than she go to the factory gates and Lavelle to 'build railroads to build America', they would invest in some business. The wine had been her idea, after Australia – being all that she knew apart from potato picking in Ireland. She had written to Father McGauran, the chaplain she had befriended in Grosse Île, with the idea that she could import French wine from French Canada. Through the old *Seigneurie* connections of the Catholic Church in Québec's province, Father McGauran had found them Frontignac, Père et Fils, Wine Merchants, importers of *vin supérieur de France.*

Soon the deliveries came. Crates of full-bodied reds and clean-on-the-palate whites, from the châteaux of Bordeaux and Burgundy. Sparkling *mousselet* from the chilly hills and chalk caverns of Champagne. Darker-liqueured aromas too, matured in oaken barriques; coveted by angels in the deep cellars of Cognac. All signed with the flourished quill of Jean Baptiste Frontignac, their quality guaranteed with the red waxen seal of the French cockerel. At first, she had approached the Old English-style merchants of Boston – the

Pendletons and Endecotts. Politely but firmly they had turned her away, astounded at her nerve, she only 'jumped-up Irish and selling French wines!'

Finally, she had happened upon Peabody's place. Although at the time uncertain of his motives – the way he had taken her hand, lingered over it – Jacob had taken a chance on her, when no one else would.

She too had taken a chance on Peabody, devising an 'at cost' agreement with the merchant. The terms by which it operated guaranteed that she and Lavelle would deliver him the finest of wines and brandies, at cost, taking no profit. Peabody, when he had sold their wines, would then split the profits with them. Further, she had convinced Peabody to give their wines a separate display from the rest, near the entrance, on shelves specially constructed by Lavelle. It had been a risk but it had worked and Jacob had opened a second such store.

As the story of her journey to Ireland unfolded, Jacob Peabody again held on to her hands, rubbing them underneath in the fleshy part, but not in the suggestive, wicked way that was normally his wont, but of which she took little notice. Now, he comforted her, his sharp eyes on her face watching, understanding.

It surprised her how much she opened herself up to Jacob. Not nearly so much had she to Lavelle. To this Jewman, who had changed his name to survive in Nativist Boston – a city as zealous in attitude to Jews as it was towards 'papist Celts' – but had closed his shop to listen to her story. When she had finished, it was as though a great weight had lifted from her.

Peabody waited before speaking. She had suffered much, more than most who had found their way here to the Bay Colony. But she had an indomitable spirit. Time and America would heal her loss, if she let them. She was angry now at the 'Old Country' and all it had inflicted on her. But that would pass. He hoped that, on its passing, it would not be replaced by the misbegotten love for their native land, so often the fruitful cause of insanity among the Irish here.

At last he spoke. 'Ireland is behind you now, Ellen,' he said tenderly, still stroking her hand, like a father. 'A new life in the New World beckons. Try, not to forget, but to remember less. It works, Ellen, believe me, it works.'

'Thank you, Jacob ... for listening ... for everything.' She leaned over and kissed his cheek. How wise he was. What he had told her was like something her father – the *Máistir* – would have said. 'Try, not to forget, but to remember less.' It was good advice.

She could never forget; that would be a betrayal. But she could remember less, without letting Ireland and its Famine gnaw at her insides, eat up her capacity for life.

They sat for a while, exiles both. Trade had been good for Jacob and things had gone well between him and Lavelle – 'her young helper', as Peabody insisted on calling him. She didn't correct him this time, just thanked him again, with the promise she would be back within the week to talk about 'clarets for Christmas and champagnes for the New Year'.

As she walked back from Peabody's, Boston, with its busy streets, its banks and fine tall buildings, seemed indeed to be the hub of the universe. The buildings that, when first she came there with Lavelle, crowded in on top of her, taking patches out of the sky, now signified something else – progress, getting ahead. Looking upwards instead of downwards.

She wanted to be part of all that now, instead of on her hands and knees clawing at lazy beds for the odd lumper missed by the harvesters, up to her eyes in muck. What good were grand mountains and sparkling lakes, when you had to crawl, belly to the ground, in order to fill it? An empty craw sees no beauty.

Faneuil Hall, the spiralling Old South Meeting House, the Grecian pilasters of the State Street buildings, Beacon Hill – these would be her new mountains. The harbour with its wharves and docks, its busy commerce – her new lakes. It was all here. Everything Ireland wasn't, this place was.

'Try, not to forget, but to remember less,' she repeated to herself.

9

In her efforts to 'remember less', Ellen in the following weeks threw herself with abandon into her new life in Boston. Lavelle had indeed done well while she was away. He had kept Jacob's two stores fully stocked and the merchant reasonably happy, despite Peabody's frequent mutterings about it not being the same 'since Mrs O'Malley deserted me and sailed for Ireland'.

Lavelle had also secured a new outlet for the New England Wine Company, in the developing suburb of West Roxbury, far enough away not to damage Peabody's business.

'What he doesn't know won't bother him!' was Lavelle's dictum. Ellen wasn't so sure.

'It's a bit underhand – Jacob's been a good friend to us and our business,' she said to Lavelle, resolving to tell Peabody herself at the right moment.

The children seemed to take up so much of her time, but she was happy 'doing for them', busying herself more with domestic matters than business. In this she was forced to rely, to a greater degree than she thought fair, on Lavelle. If during the daylight hours she did not manage to get to the warehouse, then at evening Lavelle would call on her to discuss matters of business, bringing various documentation of invoices and receipts. Because of the nature of their arrangement with Peabody, resources had to be prudently managed – something to which she had always applied herself vigorously. She looked forward to these evening visits, finding some time for titivating herself in advance of them – between household chores and the children. This total reliance on Lavelle would, she knew, be but a temporary measure, until she had settled them into suitable schools.

Situated in the 'Little Britain of Boston' – the non-Irish end, of the North End – the Eliot School was one of Boston's better public schools for boys. Nominally non-denominational, pupils nevertheless sang from the same hymn sheet – the Protestant one. Too, the official school bible was the King James version. However, Eliot School had the best spoken English in Boston, fashioned no doubt from that bible of the city's non-chattering classes, *Peter Piper's Practical Principles of Plain and Perfect Pronunciation.*

Ellen wasn't unduly worried about the Protestant ethos prevalent in Boston's public schools – the 'little red school houses' as the Boston Irish called them. Patrick would receive a more liberal education at Eliot than in the narrow Catholic schools, the 'little green school houses'. She, herself, would see to his spiritual needs outside of school. At first Patrick resisted her choice of schooling for him, but finding Eliot School populated with a good sprinkling of other Irish Catholic boys, his resistance diminished.

Mary's future, Ellen decided, would be best served by placing her with the nuns. She saw no contradiction in this, relative to her plans for Patrick. Boston, in terms of schooling for girls, particularly young Irish and Catholic girls, far surpassed that available to its young men, mainly due to the influence of the 'Sisters of Service'. Mostly Irish or the American-born daughters of the Irish, the nuns were a group of free-spirited and independent-minded young women who had eschewed marriage in favour of the economic, social and intellectual independence the Sister-

68

hood offered. What Ellen liked about them was that having liberated themselves, they had a more liberal view of other women's roles in society. Orders like the Sisters of Notre Dame de Namur, where she would send Mary, sought not to prepare young immigrant women solely for marriage, but to lead lives of independence and dignity. This would provide the pathway to spirituality, rather than that followed by most young Irish women – the bridal path.

The nuns would be good for Mary.

With regard to Louisa, Ellen had much with which to occupy her mind. She had grown a great fondness for the girl but still wondered about her – where had she come from? Her family, if any?

The *Pilot* ran regular columns of the 'lost' and 'missing' Irish – those who had become separated *en route* to the New World, or who had moved deeper into the American heartland before family had arrived from Ireland to join them.

Each week Ellen read the 'lost' notices, relaxing only when nowhere among them could she find a description to match that of Louisa. She agonized for weeks as to whether she herself should put in a notice, seeking any family of the girl who might be in America. Reluctantly, she came to the conclusion that it was 'the right and proper thing to do', as she explained to Patrick and Mary, 'and pray that we don't find anybody!' she added.

For a month she had inserted the notice, hoping it would go unanswered.

Female child – of about twelve or thirteen years, unspoken. Tall, with dark brown hair and hazelwood eyes – found among the famished near Louisburgh Co. Mayo 20th day of August 1848. Now living in Boston. Seeking to be reunited with any members of family who may have escaped the Calamity to the United States.

To her despair, she had been flooded with respondents. With each one her heart sank lower, fearing that this would be the one to claim Louisa, lifting again with relief when it was not. In turn, she was filled with guilt at her own selfishness, then sorrow at the disappointment carved out on the faces of those who came with so much hope but left again, empty-handed. Faintheartedly they would apologize with a 'Sorry for troubling you, ma'am!' or 'I was hoping 'twould be her,' some would say, awkward for having come in the wrong.

One young woman from near Louisburgh arrived brimful of hope. She had, she said, been told that her young sister 'had been taken pity on by a red-haired woman, rescued from the famished and brought over to Amerikay'. She had searched high and low, doggedly traipsing each mill town. At nights waiting outside until, disgorged in their thousands, the mill girls poured out into the streets. Ever afraid her sister had been among them and that she had missed her in the crowds.

'Was it to Boston she came?' Ellen enquired, wondering if the young woman's task was fruitless from the start.

'To Amerikay, anyway!' she replied, as if 'Amerikay' were no vaster than the townland of her home village. 'She has to be here somewhere, if it's true what they say!' she added, defiant with faith. The girl had no idea where her sister was, would spend a lifetime looking for her in 'Amerikay'. Probably never to find her – in this life at least, Ellen knew.

'You have to keep looking,' was all she could limply offer the girl.

'I do – them that's still alive back home are always asking for news of her – she was the youngest ... but I'll find her yet, I will!'

Ellen's heart had gone out to the young woman, her hopes dashed once again, yet still full of faith, still resolved to finding her sister.

'Thanks, ma'am – this one is very like her,' she said of Louisa, 'but it's not her. She's a fine child, God bless her, I hope you find her people.'

She spoke to Lavelle about it. 'There are thousands upon thousands of them still searching for their lost ones, still hoping to find some trace. It's heartbreaking.'

'They've done a right good job, the Westminster government,' he replied, scathingly, 'scattering the Celts to the four corners of the globe. Keeping us on the move, wandering, like a divided army trying to find itself. One day that army will regroup–'

'Oh, Lavelle!' she had chided him. 'I'm not talking about armies or the British Empire. You should've seen the look on that poor girl's face – she will search all of America, search till the day she dies. Louisburgh, and all that's in it, will have long since disappeared before she finds her sister.'

As the months passed the number of enquiries about Louisa, originally from Boston and the greater Massachusetts area, reduced. Then a trickle from the further-flung regions of New York, Montana, Wisconsin and even Louisiana, found their way to her door clutching old issues of the *Pilot*, clinging on to even older hopes. Eventually the stream of people calling dried up completely. Only then did Ellen allow herself to be fully at ease, previously having measured out to herself only small, fragile rations of relief as each month had slipped by.

Louisa herself bore all of this with apparent equanimity, Ellen having assured her in advance that this course of action was not an attempt to get rid of her. Again reassuring her, each time someone called, of how much both she and the others loved her. Some callers took just one look at her, knowing immediately she wasn't the girl they sought. Others inspected her more intently, peering into her face, asking questions: 'Does she ever utter a sound at all?' or 'What name has she?'

Always, Ellen had the feeling that Louisa understood. Once or twice she had faced her, asking, 'Louisa, can you hear me – tell me if you can hear me?'

The girl had just looked at her lips as she spoke, so that Ellen didn't know whether she was avoiding looking directly at her, or merely trying to understand in that manner. Either way she got no response, only the killing smile.

Although Louisa did not converse with anybody she was yet such a part of their lives; always there, soaking up everything. If not, indeed, through her ears, then through her eyes, and, in some strange way Ellen couldn't define, just through her presence. She resolved to take Louisa to a doctor.

'I can find no physical defect in the child, Mrs O'Malley,' Doctor Hazlett confided in her after examining Louisa. 'It may be that the abject circumstances in which you found her have locked a portion of her mind, a portion in which she still remains,' he offered, referring to their pre-examination discussion.

'What am I to do, Doctor?' she asked.

'The answer lies not with me,' he replied, 'but the answer, if anywhere to be found, will be found in Boston – the cradle of the sciences. I propose sending you to Professor Hitchborn for further consultation.'

'What kind of professor?' Ellen worried.

'Professor Hitchborn is a doctor of medicine – a graduate of the Harvard School, but shall we say he deals more with what the eye cannot see and the ear cannot hear, rather than with what they can.' With this conundrum still ringing in her ears, he bade her 'Good-day!'

Professor Hitchborn failed to elicit any utterance from Louisa after four visits. Ellen hated going back to 'the old stiff-neck', as she called him, but continued to do so for Louisa's sake. Always, Ellen seemed to leave these visits with the feeling

73

that she herself was somehow to blame. That her own motives in first saving, then adopting Louisa, were not morally pure, thus causing Louisa's condition. It troubled her. If Louisa felt that she was a burden on them, they had only held on to her out of guilt and a sense of duty and not out of love, then maybe Louisa's silence was fear. Fear that if she was found to be able to hear and speak, to be not so dependent on them, she would be packed off again, to an orphanage, or worse, to the streets.

Finally, it was Mary who decided for Ellen what to do regarding Louisa. 'Send Louisa to school with me, I'll look after her!' she appealed to her mother. Ellen had at first been doubtful of this solution and considered keeping Louisa at home, giving of her own time to the girl's education. It would be difficult, but somehow she would manage. Mary's entreaties of 'Please let her come – I can help her!' won the day. After consultation with the Mother Superior, it was agreed the two would be put side by side in the classroom at the Notre Dame de Namur School for Girls.

Ellen delivered them on Louisa's first day, both girls bursting with a mixture of excitement and nervousness. Ellen herself was every bit on edge as they were, the day being for her not without its tinge of sadness, too.

'The last leaving the nest,' she said to Lavelle when he called to see her that evening.

He perked her up, telling of his escapades as a young scholar, and asking about her own schooldays.

74

'They were spent in timeless wonder with my teacher – my father,' she told him, falling into 'remembering' for once.

Mostly though, she was 'forgetting'. She read with an appetite Lavelle found hard to understand. Newspapers, periodicals, handbills, anything from which she could glean more information for herself and her children about Boston and 'America-life'.

Though he could still raise a smile, even a laugh from her, Lavelle thought she had gone into herself a bit since returning to Boston. It was to be expected, he supposed, added to by the preoccupation with getting the children settled into their new environs.

At times, she teased him about Boston's belles, and while there were many among them who flashed their eyes at the handsome Mr Lavelle, none caught his in return, as he expected she knew.

Lavelle, since she had left, had been busy in more ways than one. His geniality and easy manner had led him to form acquaintances with some of Boston's more go-ahead Irish community. He prevailed upon her to visit the gathering places with him, thinking she had 'rarefied herself from all things Irish'. This she had agreed to on occasion but only for his company. She couldn't say she enjoyed hearing the endless stories of 'Old Ireland' – and in the old language. Steadfastly she refused to sing the times when song and dancing broke out, even when Lavelle himself, armed with his fiddle, hurtled the bow across its strings. At the first of such gatherings, he had introduced her as 'Ellen Rua'. Afterwards, she had corrected him.

'It's just "Ellen", Lavelle, plain "Ellen"!'

'Why?' he challenged.

'It just is. "Ellen Rua" is in the past,' she answered.

'I understand your wish to forget the past,' he said, 'but this is something more than that.'

'What is it then, Lavelle?'

'It's a denial of who you are,' he stated matter-of-factly. 'You've been known since a child as "Ellen Rua", your parents ... Michael ... your neighbours...'

'Well, they are all of them gone now and so is "Ellen Rua",' she insisted. But he would not be put off.

'You're also denying your Irishness, the language, everything... Since the moment you set foot back here, you don't want any part of it.' he accused.

'Would you blame me?' she retorted. 'And you, Lavelle, what do you want?' she challenged in return. 'Only your notion of a red-haired Irish *colleen* – a *Kathleen Ní Houlihan* – who you can hold on to as your dream of Ireland?'

'An Ireland that's dead and gone...' she continued, the blue-green eyes firing up. He watched, saw the furrow between her lips and nostrils rise and fall like he remembered. Deepening its well, swelling its narrow ridges. '...and in the Famine grave. An Ireland that all of you are trying to hang on to, filled with mist and grog and dewy-eyed *comeallyes*. Living for the day when you'll all rise up and send an army home to

76

rout "the auld enemy"!'

'And why shouldn't we?' he answered calmly, taking no small delight at seeing her in such an impassioned state. 'Isn't it the English that have us the way we are?' he added, giving as good as he got.

10

With the children now settled in their respective schools, she had, as she had hoped for, more time to devote to the business of the New England Wine Company, so taking some of the load from Lavelle's shoulders.

Coming up to Christmas was their busiest time; Peabody was demanding and irritable, wanting stocks early, pressing for replacement stock immediately, arguing that with the large volumes he was now taking for two stores, rather than one, she should be 'beating down the French with their high prices'. Lavelle made extra shelving to try and appease him. He looked after all activities related to shipping, warehousing and deliveries. She saw to the ordering, the banking and the documentation, being, as Lavelle put it, 'better able to hurl the pen' than he was.

Twice weekly she called on Peabody at Quincy Market, soothing his irascibility, he wanting to hold her hand at every turn, still referring to Lavelle as 'that young helper of yours, not much between the ears'. Mockingly he asked her to 'make an old man happy this Christmas and marry me, Ellen!'

She, in turn, telling him, 'Don't be exciting yourself, Jacob, with all that talk or you'll get a heart attack and never see the Christmas. I'll be neither an old man's sweetheart, nor a young man's slave.'

Jacob feigned hurt, 'rejected again' ... then laughter... 'Ah Ellen, what would I do without you to brighten the day?'

What was it about men, she wondered, that they were distracted so easily? If they had a few children to bear and rear, it would soon soften their coughs. Always thinking about their 'scythe-stones'! She'd heard the valley women, when they huddled to talk, often laugh that – 'It's the last thing to die in a man – the scythe-stone – if it was ever any good for anything but sharpening a blade in the first place!'

She loved the way that in the Gaelic you could talk 'round' a thing, with everybody still knowing what you meant. Say it without saying it. The Americans never talked in the 'roundabout talk' – she missed that, much and all as she tried to distance herself from her previous life.

Despite everything, getting the children settled, easing once again into the business, she hadn't really fitted back into Boston life as she would have hoped. She didn't know what it was. She still grieved for Katie, guilt always suffusing the grief. Once started her thoughts would then run to Annie and Michael, until she would have to go and hide in the dark of Holy Cross Cathedral, or slip away to sit in the cold of the Common under the Great Elm. No matter how busy she was, how she was furthering their lives, there was always the void, the big aching void, always waiting to claim her.

Lavelle had been her one constant, steadfast in everything. He laughed and poked fun at how she worried over things, her single-mindedness. Kept at her, forcing her not to take herself too seriously. At first this irritated her, but he didn't stand for that either, and she found it hard to sustain any measure of annoyance with him, such was his enthusiasm for 'life to be lived'. And the children liked him. Even Patrick, though he'd never say it, had softened towards Lavelle.

They had all gone on 5 November – 'Pope's Night' – to see the Orange Parades, with their Kick-the-Pope bands. Patrick was agog at the display of anti-Catholic paraphernalia and the aggressive clatter-thump of the lambeg drums, the manic drummers facing each other 'hoop to hoop', malacca canes banging out deafening military tattoos.

'But ... they're Irish too!' Patrick protested, as Lavelle tried to explain the sashes, hard hats and anti-Irish slogans.

'They are and they aren't, Patrick!' Lavelle responded. 'Their feet are on the same island as us at home,' and he laughed, 'they've even stolen some of our jigs and reels and fifed them into marches, though they'll never admit to that. But their hearts are for ever in England.'

That was the moment, Ellen knew, when Patrick had begun to change towards her 'fancy

79

man', as he once called Lavelle. The boy identified with Lavelle's antipathy towards the Orangemen and their bitter, threatening music. To his credit, Lavelle did not encourage Patrick, make a thing of it, as he could have done. And she noticed it had gone on like that, in little fits and starts that bonded them, without any great scheme being behind it.

Without any great scheme, either – certainly on her part – things had settled into a comfortable pattern between herself and Lavelle. He was as much a part of the neighbourhood of her new life as the Old South Meeting House, spiking the sky across from where she lived, or the Long Wharf, spiking the sea. Like these boundaries of heaven and ocean, always there, securing this exciting New World of hers, so too was Lavelle. Not that she was unaware of his physical attractiveness, the way he sometimes collided with her, would catch her arm, steady her up, and give that grin of his, causing her a momentary embarrassment. Once or twice he held her longer than necessary, startled her by his nearness, said something like 'Boston life hasn't softened you yet, you're still a fine woman,' then laughed and let go of her just as suddenly again.

At Christmas, after he had dined with them, tramped in the snow, laden with presents for the children and her, she wasn't totally unprepared when he asked her.

She had gone down the flights of stairs ahead of him, held the door, looking out into the abandoned stillness of Washington Street. No hawkers' cries, no noise of commerce, the Old

South Meeting House cribbed in white. No sound at the Hub of the Universe, only his voice, clear and as impudent as you please, passing her, going out into the dampening snows.

'You know, Ellen, we should get married after Lent!'

She never answered him at first. Giddy in the moment, she drew back, waited until he was outside, half-turned for home.

'You know, Lavelle,' she said, mocking his impudence and laughing, 'I had the same notion myself!' And, despite all of her previous resolve, it was out before she knew it.

She watched after him, his boots crunching the snow, the flakes haloed on his head, whistling his way down Washington Street – some old jig-time tune she half-remembered.

In the New Year, little doubts had begun to raise themselves about whether or not she was doing the right thing. She hadn't remained steadfast for long. Getting married again was against everything she once held; against 'being true to the grave'. But that was just it – that was part of the old ways. Here in Boston, it was different. After a suitable period of mourning a man and, to a lesser degree, a woman might marry again. Still, it was only three years.

Not that she ever forgot Michael. Not for one single day, nor would she, ever. But she had great ease with Lavelle. He had no fixed notions like some of the other men about where women fitted – mostly in front of a baking oven. Maybe it was his time in Australia, where women tamed the

81

harsh bush as much as the men did. Whatever, there was ease and comfort between them, and she liked his off-the-cuff manner. He granted her respect, but not too much. Even the way he had asked her – going out the door – as if not caring if she had said 'yes' or 'no'. Herself and Lavelle would be a good match.

She had told the children on the following day, St Stephen's, when she herself was more composed. Mary, she thought, took it well. Patrick less so, but without the level of opposition from him, which she had expected. The excitement somehow catching her, Louisa too joined in, running to kiss her as Mary had done.

By early Lent, she had cast her doubts aside. She had made her bed, now she must lie in it. At times, even, the thought of lying in Lavelle's bed caused her a shiver of expectation.

Spring saw her preparing for the rites of marriage as precepted by the ever-expanding Archdiocese of Boston. Purity in thought and action,

The Inviolata to the Blessed Virgin...
Inviolata, integra et casta es, Maria...
Stainless, inviolate, and chaste art thou, O
  Mary.
Nostra ut pura pectora sint et corpora...
That pure our minds and hearts may be...

Nobody 'forbade the banns' – read out on three consecutive Sundays at Holy Cross. Each week she sat through their reading, mortified lest somebody would shout out objecting to her intended marriage. Worse still that without her knowing it, some prudish biddy would slink around to the sacristy after Mass and coat the ear of the priest with poisoned whisperings about her. Then she would be quietly summoned, the reading of the banns suspended, she and her children shamed.

When the day finally came, the wedding was grander than anything she could have had back home. Much grander – and in a hotel too. While she was against wasting too much money on frippery, there was a sense of statement, as Lavelle had put it, 'That we're not paupers any more. That we're no longer the Famine Irish!'

So she had relented, rigging the children in new outfits, had cut for herself a dress from a *foulard* of silk, thin and soft and cream in colour. Lavelle too, hatted, cravated, looked every inch the fine Boston gentleman. The day itself was a great success and seemed to spin out for ever. As indeed it did – into the next morning. 'It's in danger of turning into a wake...' she whispered to Lavelle, in a private moment, '...if it goes on any longer!'

And she had sung, especially for him, *'Úna Bhán'* – 'Fair-haired Úna', one of the great love songs, not as she should have, she felt. She hadn't spoken a syllable of Irish for eight months. Now the words felt clumsy in her mouth so she trimmed the song from its forty-odd verses down to a dozen or so.

Peabody, whom they'd invited but didn't think would attend, to her delight, if not wholly to Lavelle's, presented himself for the after-wedding festivities.

'I might as well close up shop completely if I was observed entering a Roman church,' he confided to her jokingly. 'It reminds me, Ellen – it reminds me...' He started to tell her something after she'd sung, then changed course. 'That song – what does it say?' he instead asked.

'It's a song from Connemara, two hundred years old,' she explained, 'composed for the woman Úna, whose father would not let her marry beneath herself. Being kept from her beloved, she died. He seeing her laid out, remembers her beauty – like the music of the harp always on the road before him. His love for her so great it she had come between him and God. There, that's all forty verses of it in Irish, in one in English!' she laughed.

Peabody, after he had thought for a moment, remarked, 'Isn't it a strange song to sing on your wedding-day, Ellen – a song about death?'

'Oh no, Jacob! That's the beauty of the song – it's not of death, it's of great love. He would lose God for her,' she answered, impassioned.

Peabody looked away from her into the revelry beyond. 'I suppose a life without great love is like that – a losing of God,' he said. He was speaking of his own life; she waited, silent. 'The tenacity of true passion is terrible; it will stand against the hosts of Heaven, rather than surrender its aim, and must be crushed, sent to the lowest pit, before it will ever succumb – something I heard once,' he mumbled, by way of explanation.

'Jacob – were you ever...?' she started, wanting to ask him.

'It's something I have observed, Ellen,' he inter-

84

rupted, deflecting her, 'about the Irish. How at once happiness and sadness can co-exist. Your wakes are laced with merriment, your weddings with lament. It is a peculiar twist of character. Little wonder the English find you a disconcerting race to govern.' Peabody laughed a little.

'We're no different from any other peoples,' she said gently, thinking of him, rather than the Irish or the English.

'Oh, but you are, Ellen!' he said, rising to the argument. 'There's a blackness within your race, a perversity. Nothing is allowed to be as it is. Love must be death. Death must be love. Everything turned on itself.'

'Jacob, come along. This is most unlike you to be so dark, on such a day.'

He apologized, and she was drawn back into the merriment, sorry she had started it all by explaining the song to him.

She had some difficulty pulling the children away from all the excitement and settling them down across the hall from where she and Lavelle would spend their wedding-night. Later, as she undressed, thinking about the day, waiting for Lavelle, the song came back to her. 'Úna, wasn't it you that went between me and God?' What a thing for a person to live with! It was unimaginable to her – throwing over God for love.

She hiked up her nightdress, knelt by the bedside. She'd shorten the prayers a bit tonight, didn't want to be still out of bed when Lavelle came up.

Besides, Boston in springtime had yet quite a nip to it.

11

The very next day they moved into the new quarters Lavelle had found for them in Pleasant Street. They had decided they should rent, until they were better fitted to buy a place of their own. The fear always being with them both, that if overstretched with borrowings, things took a turn, the banks would then tumble them out of the house, evict them. She and the children already carried that scar. It was something she'd never put them through again. With the rent it was less of a risk. They'd still have a bit aside to tide them over, if a reversal of fortune came about.

She had hated leaving Washington Street, in the end it was marriage, not commerce snapping up every parcel of space which had forced them out.

The Pleasant Street house was in a neat terrace, with its own hall-door and a shiny letterbox low down – while Washington Street was never her own hall-door. A slab of granite stone stepped up to this one, which Mary thought 'very grand'. Louisa meanwhile was fascinated by the brass lettering, running her finger around the welcoming curvature of the number that would be her new home, 29.

Inside there was a short hallway, a kitchen, a parlour and a 'good room', as Ellen regarded it. Upstairs three bedrooms, two commodious, one less so. 'That one's for you, Patrick,' Mary couldn't resist teasing. Out back was a small yard and a cabbage patch. It was all perfectly adequate. She could do a lot with it, and at least they wouldn't be crowded in on top of each other.

They were hardly in the door, solid and black apart from the two light-giving panels of frosted glass, when it resounded to a vigorous knocking. On the step outside, Mrs Harriet Brophy fixed the tilt of her snug hat, pushed back an unbiddable wisp of hair and waited to present herself to her new neighbours. A trim dart of a woman from the Donegal–Derry border, she had already espied them.

'Newlyweds,' she had heard, 'with three grown-up children,' she had exclaimed to 'himself', hand to her mouth. 'What's the Christian world coming to at all, Hector?' 'Himself' wasn't much interested. 'Bringing down the neighbourhood, that's what. What have we got to leave our children, if not a decent neighbourhood?'

'I'd just like to welcome you all.' Harriet Brophy beamed as Ellen opened the door. 'I'm your neighbour – a few doors up.' Ellen bade in the woman, who sparrow-hopped over the threshold. She had a paper with her, something wrapped inside. 'For luck,' she said, 'for the house.' Ellen opened it. 'A piece of anthracite to keep winters warm,' the woman said. 'A handful of salt, to keep the table laden.' And in a small bluish bottle, 'A sup of holy water to sanctify the home.'

Ellen thanked her, moved by the woman's thoughtfulness, but Harriet Brophy wouldn't hear of it.

'Och, for nothing at all – I think the custom came from Scotland first, except it was a sod of turf then, instead of the anthracite, and probably whiskey instead of the water!'

She had thin bony hands, Ellen noticed, which she fluttered like wings when she spoke, and a waist like a wasp. The smallest *bitteen* of a woman, Ellen thought, that she had ever seen. But she insisted they come with her to her house for tea.

'Himself is out and won't bother us!'

Ellen looked at Lavelle.

'You and the children go, I'll take care of things here,' he smiled.

At tea, Mrs Brophy, as Ellen knew she would, filled her in on Pleasant Street life. 'Nice neighbourhood, Americans and the likes of you and me,' she confided, 'hardworking people, none of the other Irish, you know what I mean ... from the ships.' Then, stretching her thin *scrogall* of a neck and leaning forward. 'And no blacks, Mrs Lavelle.' Harriet Brophy pursed her lips, narrowed her eyes and gave a knowing nod to Ellen. 'You'll be all right here, Mrs Lavelle, nice neighbours to look out for you here!'

And so it was, with Ellen settling into an ordered continuum of life with her new husband, two children and 'the fosterling', as Mrs Brophy referred to Louisa.

By the summer of 1849, the number of Irish in

88

Boston had swollen to a quarter of the population, the weight by which they were arriving almost suffocating the city. Each one bringing his or her own story of the distressful state of Ireland.

Half of all the city's paupers were Irish. Many having left the workhouses of Connacht, found only in Massachusetts the State Lunatic Asylum – alcohol and the tug of home combining to make sanity elusive. Half of the male Irish who did manage to find work were labourers. Of the females, two-thirds of all cooks, housekeepers and laundresses in Boston were Irish. Ellen marvelled at the resoluteness of her people. There was no going back and the Irish would work at anything. Boston bosses welcomed the increasing supply of green-hand drudge horses, who would work for next to nothing, $1.25 a day or less. How they kept body and soul together for this – labouring a twelve- or thirteen-hour day – she didn't know, except it was an everyday miracle.

The *Pilot* carried regular letters detailing the trials and tribulations of the new arrivals:

For the promise of $2.00 a day, I was carted halfway across America. When we got there, they said it was a mistake, the most they could give was a dollar a day, with cents a day gone for the first month for the cost of getting us here.

A couple of Tipperary lads and me started complaining about what they had promised first when the ganger from Clare says, 'Well Paddy, start walking!', and he pointed his finger to the east. 'You should get there by Christmas!'

It was only June then, so we stayed.

She used it with the children. 'Life in America is not all honey and gold. Keep to your books, it's the only way for us Irish to "up" ourselves!'

She herself didn't come much into contact with the masses of Irish who polluted the neighbourhoods of the North End and Fort Hill, though it was hard to avoid them, the way they spilled over like treacle into the areas around the docks. New vessels, holds bursting with more Irish peasantry, arrived with worrying regularity.

'The city is swamped with them!' she said to Lavelle. 'We'll all be over-run by the Famine, as much here as at home,' was his comment. 'It would never have been let happen in Devon or Cornwall, only in John Bull's Irish province,' he added caustically.

She was still careful of the children, and kept them in as much as possible lest they came into contact with the other Irish from the ships, be diseased by these new arrivals. Things had gone well for them and she wanted nothing to go wrong now.

The French wines and brandies supplied to them by Frontignac, Père et Fils, Montréal, found their way steadily off the shelves of Peabody's two stores – and likewise from the shelves of their newest customer, Higgins of West Roxbury – and on to the finer tables of Boston. There to be frequently served by the swelling number of 'Bridgets', who arrived almost daily to inhabit the plush parlours of Roxbury and Beacon Hill.

Once, when visiting Peabody, the merchant had introduced her to one such of his customers. This gentleman, having disposed of the normal courtesies, confided in her: 'We have one of your countrywomen amongst us – "Bridget" – excellent girl, clean and no trouble; the children adore her.' Ellen was pleased for him. The gentleman sallied on. 'She's the very best "Bridget" in all of Chestnut Street, my wife assures me!' he said, smiling at her.

'Really?' she smiled back.

He, mistaking this for interest, continued. 'Every home in Boston should have a "Bridget". They require some training, but are so genial by nature. We hear so much of the turbulence of the Irish character. Perhaps geniality is more particular to Irish womanhood?' he said, thinking he complimented her.

'So, they have become nameless?' she replied brusquely.

He looked at her, surprised at her obvious lack of geniality.

'If they are all to be called "Bridget", then they are all without identity,' she stated, with little patience.

'Oh, not all, madam!' the gentleman from Chestnut Street assured her. 'Our "Bridget" is a Mary, and next door's is an Ellen; they are all named with their own names, eh, before becoming "Bridgets",' he explained, wondering at her slowness, and why on earth Peabody had ever introduced them in the first place.

Whatever about the turmoils Boston was experiencing with Bridgets or otherwise, she and Lavelle settled into a happy and tranquil state. 'A pool of contentment', was how Mrs Brophy ('Wasp-waist' to Lavelle) described it. Harriet Brophy had an opinion on most things in life – and most people. Furthermore she was not one bit backward about coming forward with these opinions – in whatever company she might find herself.

'He, Mr Lavelle, is such a dashing man, always good-humoured. It was made in Heaven … made in Heaven, Mrs Lavelle, as my own and...' she added quickly, '...all good marriages most surely are,' she informed Ellen.

Ellen, was careful not to reveal too much of anything to Harriet Brophy, for by the following Sunday after Mass the whole parish would have it. But 'Wasp-waist' was right about her and Lavelle. They were 'a pool of contentment'. Lavelle was everything the woman described him as and more, being as well an industrious worker and a good father to her children and 'the foster-ling'. Ellen knew he would have liked a child of his own and she was full in her desire to grant him that wish. But so far they had not been blessed.

Lavelle never asked, but every month or so he would look at her. When she said nothing, she would see the hope dashed from his eyes. But it never lasted with him, nor did he ever attach any blame to her, saying only she was the 'plenty of all happiness' in his life.

Once she had told him that for the six years before Annie was born, she had been barren.

'She must have been born hard,' was all he said,

'taken a lot out of you.'

Sometimes of an evening he spoke of Australia, its vast bushland, its sounds, its redness. She neither naysayed nor encouraged him in this. Australia had been a dark experience for both of them. But it had, after all, been where she had first met him.

'You miss it,' she stated, during one such reminiscing.

'I suppose I do, Ellen,' he told her. 'I grew up on an island, wild as winter. Australia always reminded me of that wildness, though it was hot and red instead of wet and green. I miss the wide-open spaces, the smell of the gum trees – the silence. This Boston's a noisy place.'

'It is that,' she replied.

'Would you ever return?' he asked, turning the question on her.

'No...' she said, '...to neither. Australia is a far country and Ireland even farther in my mind. I'll do with being buried in America.'

12

Whatever about dying in America, living in America was an excitement that barely disguised itself. There was always something happening, some new discovery. She followed the newspaper reports of how life was progressing in her adopted homeland as assiduously as ever.

'See, Lavelle, all we need is a chance! A chance

to prove ourselves. We can be as good as the rest!' she said, reading of how the electric telegraph, developed by two County Monaghan brothers, had carried a message from President Polk throughout the United States. 'They have five thousand Irish employed and are as well building a railroad across Panama to join the Pacific and the Atlantic oceans!'

Lavelle was not so impressed. 'And why wouldn't they, at a dollar a day on the broken backs of their countrymen?'

'Lavelle, why do you always down your own, those who have advanced in America?' She was annoyed with him.

'Because if we don't say how America was built – at what cost – then it will all soon be forgotten,' he answered. 'Forgotten that Paddy's shovel filled the coffers of this Commonwealth, the same way that Paddy's green fields filled the granaries of the British Commonwealth. Everything has a price.'

'At least the Paddies here have a chance, a chance to be part of *this* Commonwealth,' she answered him.

'Commonwealth me arse!' he said, forgetting himself.

She ignored his outburst. 'You're still caught up in the wrongs of Ireland, and all of that ... all of what we've left behind us,' she said, calmly.

'But have we left it behind us, Ellen?'

'Well, I have,' she said, more firmly.

Her assiduousness in gleaning every scrap of new information from the periodicals and magazines led her to a most unexpected bounty – Mr Horace Mann, an educator of high standing.

She read how Mann, following travels in Europe, had published a report on a new departure in the education of deaf-mutes, a sort of 'silent talking', advocating it be introduced to the schools in America, Her hopes were raised for Louisa and she pursued this new avenue whereby in Germany 'the deaf can now read on the lips, the words of those who address them, and in turn use vocal speech'.

When, all of an excitement with this news, she sat them down and through Mary tried to explain it to Louisa, she was met with total indifference. Not the hazelnut eyes sparkling with hope as Ellen had expected. Not the joy such news must surely bring. Louisa, it seemed, did not want to be liberated from her affliction. Almost as if she wanted to remain locked away in her own silent world, Mary to be the sole key-holder.

It perplexed Ellen. She tackled Mary on the matter.

'I think she's afraid of something,' Mary told her.

'But what, Mary? It can only be to her benefit.'

'I don't know, Mother. She wouldn't tell. Maybe she likes being the way she is ... not part of everything.'

That night, she tucked Louisa into bed, prayed with her as always, whispering the prayers up close to the girl's face, so that Louisa could at least see the shape of their sounds, feel them, if nothing else. The child, hands angelically clasped, lay there, eyes fixed on her adoptive mother's lips, until the final breath of blessing. Then Ellen folded Louisa's arms across her bosom in the shape of a diagonal cross, pulled the bedclothes up about her neck, and pressed her lips to Louisa's forehead. She sat with her longer than usual, caressing the girl's brow, soothing her to sleep, with touch and talk.

'It's all right, Louisa dear, you won't have to do it any more. Sleep now, and don't be fretting yourself. I only wanted what I thought was best, but maybe I was wrong. Maybe, after all, I was wrong.' She put her face next to Louisa's, fingered the hair back from her far temple. 'My little fosterling.'

She remained until Louisa had fallen away from the world and its noise.

Despite the huge influx of paupers, these years were Boston's golden years and the city continued to grow and prosper in every direction. At the Massachusetts General Hospital, an ether anaesthetic had been used on the operating table for the first time. It was the start of a new era in surgical medicine. Where previously brandy and even opium had been used, now ether – the 'Death of Pain', as Bostonians proudly proclaimed, had arrived.

The ether of the Irish – alcohol – continued to provide the 'death of pain' of deprivation, disease and displacement, suffered by the city's immigrant population. This, despite the fact that Ireland's Temperance priest, Father Mathew, had visited the city to admonish the frequenters of

Boston's twelve hundred taverns about 'the evils of the bewitching glass'. But nothing, it seemed, not even the ethered Irish, could hold back the city's progress.

Added to its horse-drawn streetcars, on which one could travel for a nickel, Boston now had eight railroads, bringing twenty thousand people daily into the city. She vowed that one day she would travel every single one of its new iron roads.

The Cochituate Water System had already opened to meet the increasing demands of a swelling population and much to the delight of Boston's children, the Frog Pond on the Common was now regularly filled with water from Lake Cochituate. She had taken the children there when first it opened and Mayor Josiah Quincy had ordered a column of water to rise eighty feet above the Pond – immortalizing himself in water with a sky-high statement that Boston's citizens would never again be short of it.

There was nothing, it seemed, Boston and its citizenry could not achieve. The city filled her with a breathlessness as much for herself as for what it opened up for her children. Regularly, she brought them to the Frog Pond, to skate and tumble and laugh on its winter ice, to wade in its cooling waters in the summer, often taking one of the horse-drawn trams to make it a special treat. The Long Path, which diagonally traversed Boston Common, was her favourite stroll, a walk long favoured by those in love. She explained its tradition to them.

'A young man, too timid, perhaps, to directly

propose to his Boston beauty, would ask, "Would you take the Long Path with me?" If she said "Yes" it meant she would marry him. They would never part. But,' Ellen paused, 'if she stopped to rest – here perhaps, under this gingko tree, it meant she didn't love him.'

'Oh...' said Mary, looking around for the ghosts of lost love, 'that's so sad – but at least she'd not said "No!".'

'That was it!' Ellen explained. 'The young man was spared that embarrassment. So ladies, if any young beau asks to walk the Long Path with you, consider carefully if you should rest along the way,' adding, 'I'm sure no young lady of Patrick's choice would ever rest!'

Patrick, however, was not impressed and though he regularly accompanied them to the Common, at fourteen was less interested in marriage-making than in watching the hay-making, a custom that still persisted. Unless, of course, she recounted stories of Paul Revere and the Sons of Liberty, and the military history of the Common, long a mustering-ground for armies of every flag and allegiance.

The Great Elm commanded attention from every element of the family, even boys. The giant tree, whose protective branches offered one hundred feet of shade, stretched heavenwards for seventy or eighty feet. But if Heaven was its aspiration, Hell was its application, for the Great Elm was once a place of executions. Witches, martyrs, adulterers alike, all swung from its gallowed limbs. United in fascination, all three would close in around her, fearing its embrace, wanting none the less to hear its dark history retold yet again. Tales of 'the Puritans', or of 'the Reverend Cotton Mather', who stalked the condemned, seeking to save their souls from a fate worse than death – eternal damnation!

'Tell us Mary Dyer!' Mary asked, though by now, they knew the story well.

The Quaker girl had left the early colony, protesting the banishment of another young woman dissenter. On her return she was imprisoned and saved only from the tree by her son. Instead of her life she was banished for ever from the Bay Colony.

'Mary came back again,' Ellen told them in hushed tones, 'to fight for her freedom. But the death sentence previously given had not been lifted. Mary still refused to repent, because she had done no wrong.' Ellen paused, looked into the branches above them, before delivering the final verdict. 'So the Great Elm took Mary Dyer.'

'And her ashes were scattered on the ground here,' the young Mary O'Malley put forward, fearfully.

'Yes, we should be careful where we tread,' Ellen told them, herself almost frightened by the notion of it.

The Great Elm where the dead and the living came together had a sobering impact on all of them. Yet, time and again, Ellen was drawn back to it. Sometimes, she would sit alone there, waiting for them while they played. It reminded her of the Reek – strange, silent, overshadowing. More than its trunk and limbs was the Great Elm, just as the Reek was more than its rocks and steep crags. Tree and mountain, both seemed to her to be warnings posted on the path of life. Grim, penitential listening places, for the strayed and the wayward. While the Long Path had its whisperings of love, the Great Elm had other darker intimations. Of love betrayed. Murmurings too of the terrible consequences its infamous gibbet had wreaked on the necks of those betrayers. She had yet not told them those stories, lest, in innocence, they should have sympathy for adulterers.

13

It took her into the following spring 'to put a shape' on No. 29. But she was not foolhardy, hunting down bargains – crockery ware on Washington Street, 'sensible' curtains from the Old Feather Store, a thick-in-the-hand, good-wearing Turkish counterpane for the floor of the good room; sturdy chairs, slightly shop-soiled, a chip or two gone from them but still perfectly good for sitting upon.

Lavelle did the heavy work – painted and decorated and put a *snas* on the backyard. Then Patrick wanted to 'get at' the gone-to-seed cabbages, but at her request left it. She decked the front and back borders of the cabbage patch with small yellow flowers – a Latin name, ending in *'ium'* – she couldn't remember when Mary had asked her. Peabody had told her when he'd given her the seeds, but she'd forgotten. The other two sides she left open, so she could 'pluck the new cabbages, when they grew', she hoped.

Eventually, the house was the way she wanted it; for the moment, at least. She had one other idea for the good room, but that could wait a while.

Lavelle, who had always maintained close links with those Boston Irish interested in the 'Irish Cause', had recently begun to attend meetings for the repeal of the Union of Ireland with England. She would have preferred he didn't, that he'd leave 'the past to the past'. Lavelle's view was that 'the past never goes away – the past is a road – always coming from somewhere and leading somewhere else'. She couldn't win with him, so she gave up trying. She did once remark that with his increasingly frequent absences on 'matters of Ireland', 'Now that the house is settled here, I have a mind to move back to Washington Street – and you could pay court to me every evening, as before!'

He knew she wasn't serious, grabbed her and kissed her, laughing as he exited the door.

She read, instead, sitting at the rosewood bureau he had restored, her book on the baize-covered writing surface, vanishing her away from the world.

Her visits to the Old Corner Bookstore had been less frequent since they moved here, yet more precious. So that when she did go there she lingered over its store of treasures, lovingly fingering the gold-lettered spines, imprinting into memory the works and the lives within. The

101

English poets: Wordsworth's *Lyrical Ballads*, Blake's *Songs of Innocence* and *Songs of Experience* – the two contrary states of the human soul – Byron and Donne. These were her favourites, opening her eyes to an England, pastoral, passionate, spiritually provocative, different from the 'perfidious Albion', she had known, an England of Cromwell and Queen Victoria, 'The Famine Queen'.

At Christmas, Lavelle had presented her with *Legends of New England, in Verse and Prose*, by the Massachusetts-born John Greenleaf Whittier – 'to wean you away from old England'. And she was much interested in New England writing. Emerson with his spiritual vision, his belief that all souls shared in the higher, Over-Soul, that nature is spirit, rang with a resonance close to her own, one which the organized pulpitry of the Catholic Church could never achieve for her. The women writers of New England, she also sought out, as much for their 'Bloomerist' agenda as for anything. However, the Old Corner Bookstore, Lavelle's 'Repeal' meetings, and even the aggrandizement of No. 29 were only the trimmings of life in Boston. The education of her children, the steady growth of the business, and the unerring stability of life in general was what mattered, what she had always craved. What now was within her keeping.

The children all were flourishing. Patrick at the Eliot School, Mary, and even Louisa, with a little additional schooling from Mary, at Notre Dame de Namur. Peabody had now opened yet a further store, his third, in the affluent suburb of

West Roxbury. And she had settled more easily than she had expected into the marriage life, seldom a cross word between them, Lavelle, unlike many, remaining sober in manner. Mrs Brophy's 'pool of contentment' continued to surround them, if not indeed deepen.

She thought that maybe the time was now right to try again some of Boston's better establishments which had once refused her, given that they themselves were better consolidated now. But upsetting the arrangement with Peabody worried her.

'We are too much in his hands already,' was Lavelle's view. 'I wouldn't put it past Peabody to go directly to Frontignac himself. What's stopping him – except you?' he added, teasingly.

She swiped at him with her apron. 'You might be right, Lavelle,' she teased back, 'but underneath everything, Jacob is all business,' adding more seriously, 'he is at no risk financially. That is what's stopping him. He doesn't pay until he sells. Nobody else affords him that arrangement.' She paused. 'But if we are to give the same terms to enter business with others, then what little reserves we have will be strained. We will need to approach the banks – or R.G. Dun, the credit agents!'

'Well we didn't give it to Higgins...' Lavelle started, referring to the customer he had secured while she was in Ireland; a steady, but not startling account. 'I mean, I wouldn't...' he corrected himself, so as not to appear critical of her arrangement with Peabody. 'The city is bursting at the seams. It cannot develop quickly enough.

There is such wealth here that we can scarce go wrong by expansion, and without having to extend excessive credit,' was Lavelle's final word.

She told Peabody of their plan, reassuring him that they would not supply anybody within a certain radius of his own stores.

'I wondered how long it would take you. Of course, you must expand – God forbid anything should happen to me!' was all he said. 'Come, sit now a while and we will discuss life, instead of business – all only business with you Irish,' he mocked.

She was relieved at his generous response. There were times when Jacob seemed more interested in philosophy than profit, and she did love these discussions with him. He seemed to know so much, quoted freely from poem and psalm alike and had such seeming wisdom. How like her father he was in that respect. Yet, unlike the Máistir, Jacob never revealed much about himself; his defence to veer off into being flirtatious with her, if she probed too deeply. Not that he needed much excuse for that either.

'Jacob, how did you come to know so much ... of everything?' She had decided to try some probing of her own. 'Was it from your father or through schooling?'

'Neither,' he quipped, 'but from gazing into the eyes of beauty. Much wisdom is to be found there.' Then he turned it around, asking questions of her. 'That song at your wedding – I was reminded of it again recently,' he began. 'The "Úna" in your song intrigues me. Love beyond

104

death? Death in love? Which is it?'

She laughed; he always did this. 'It is both ... it depends,' she answered vaguely.

'On what?'

'On the love, the lovers – you know that, Jacob!'

'And is this love a common thing, do you think, or only in songs?' he pressed.

'It is uncommon. If it were common, it would not be written about.' She tried to bring the discussion back within the framework of the song but Peabody was having none of it.

'So, there is love and there is love. One, the common kind for the many and the other – great, tragic love – for the few. Is that it?'

She knew where this would lead. He could be wicked, Peabody, the way he forced her to uncompromise her thinking.

'Yes ... I suppose so, Jacob,' she parried.

'What begets the difference, Ellen Rua?'

It was the first time he had called her that since she had spoken of it to him on her return to Boston – about how she had shortened her name, dropped the 'Rua'.

'I don't know, Jacob, and don't call me by that name.' She stamped out the words at him.

'Do you know the Four Elements of the Ancient World, Ellen ... Rua?' he repeated provocatively.

'Of course I do!' she said, angry that he still persisted with her old name. 'Earth, wind, water, fire,' she reeled them off.

He held up his hand. 'Fire – that is it, the Element of Fire. That is what begets the difference, Ellen Rua.'

Sometimes he was hard to follow, the way his mind twisted and darted.

'The Element of Fire? What on earth are you talking about, Jacob?' she asked. 'And I told you – it's Ellen!'

He ignored her reprimand. 'That is the difference between love for the many and love for the few – the Element of Fire,' he answered, as if it were all self-evident. Then, seeing the look on her face, he continued, 'Fire smoulders, it burns, it rages, it purges and purifies, it engenders great passion ... and it destroys.' He paused, took her hand as if passing some irredeemable sentence on her.

'You were named for fire, Ellen ... *Rua.*'

The talk with Peabody had unsettled her. What was he at with such a statement? That she was named for fire, the element that destroys! Jacob was trying to bait her, to stir something in her. Maybe some tilt at Lavelle and herself? But why? While Peabody was dismissive about Lavelle, he was hardly suggesting that she didn't love him, that it was merely a marriage of convenience? You never knew with Jacob. Sometimes she felt that if she were to encourage him, he would be quite willing to draw down the shutters, pull her into the storeroom, and fling her on to the nearest flour sack, or chest of tea from the Assam Valley.

He was capable too. More than once when he embraced her, he had pushed in close to her, so that even through her underskirt she could feel his 'scythe-stone'. Whatever about Jacob's 'scythe-stone', his mind was sharp and dangerous, always trying to cut through her thoughts, to lay them bare.

She didn't speak to Lavelle about her discussion with Peabody except to say, 'My fears were unfounded, Jacob was most generous at the news.'

'I don't trust him, Ellen; and neither should you,' was Lavelle's response.

'He has always been upright in his dealings, give him some credit,' she defended Jacob with.

'It's not in their nature, the Jews.' Lavelle would give no ground to her argument. 'While there's money to be made, they're trustworthy. When more is to be made elsewhere, then see how far their trustworthiness stretches,' he challenged.

'Lavelle, you can't say that. They're not all the same, no more than all the Irish are fighters and drunkards,' she retorted.

But Lavelle was not for turning. 'History teaches us – didn't they betray the Saviour for thirty pieces of silver?'

'That was just one, Judas,' she responded.

'Yes ... His friend,' Lavelle retorted. 'Kissed Him and betrayed Him, and the rest – all Jews – stood by while it happened. How well the like of Peabody got started here. The wandering Jew will get in anywhere.'

'Jacob was *our* saviour when–' she started to protest, but he cut her short.

'I know you and Peabody have talks, and I know, too, that at the start, he was our saviour, but he is too familiar in his talk with you, and,' he added, 'how he looks at you!'

So that was it. How could Lavelle possibly

think that Jacob was a rival for his affections? Nevertheless, this side to him pleased her somewhat, and brought a small flush to her neck. She went to him, embraced him.

'Oh! Lavelle, please stop it!' she chided. 'You know he looks at every woman under fifty years of age like that, it's just his way. Jacob has never made any indecent approaches to me – yet,' she teased.

He laughed with her, kissing her fiercely. 'All I say is, beware the Judas kiss,' was his final word.

Later, on her own, she raked over what had passed between them. She hated it when Lavelle got like this about Jacob and the Jews, as if he never saw the parallels with the wandering Irish, or the Irish who betrayed their own for the Queen's shilling. She did remember her father telling her about the Jews, condemned to wander the world for ever because they had crucified the Son of God. How they were buried standing up, not like other people, laid out flat. Whatever was the reason for that? She had never doubted the *Máistir*'s teachings before. All those years growing up, all those years after his death, his voice had come to her, guided her like a beacon in times of trouble. Strange how here, under the shadow of Beacon Hill, he hardly ever spoke to her now. Had he deserted her?

Or, she wondered, had she deserted him?

She encountered the same problem as before with the Pendletons, Endecotts and the others – 'the wine Whigs of Boston, old world Sassenachs', as she described the merchants to Lavelle.

Polite but definite 'no thank yous'. They still wouldn't deal with her because she was Irish; by definition, a Catholic. It must change, she thought. Some day, surely it must change. But it didn't help her now in their hunt for new customers. She continued to search, now looking among their own – the coming Irish. Those who had 'upped themselves' out of the North End and into the South End, in the process forcing the second-generation Yankees to move onwards.

The palates of these burgeoning Irish middle-class now sought a little more refinement than Boston's one thousand groggeries once supplied them with and still did to their less elevated countrymen. So, on a train journey to Dorchester, she found 'Cornelius Ryan's Emporium', boasting 'wines, whiskies and refined liquors'.

Ryan, a sly but affable Tipperary man – or 'Tipp'rary', as he pronounced it, had come to America before the exodus caused by the Great Famine. Like many he had started his first enterprise in the corner of a tenement basement. Things had obviously gone well for him.

He rolled his 'r's like the Scots and gave her an order for 'half a crate of the "Bordelaux"', putting back into that region the syllable previously denied to Tipp'rary. She thought it a peculiar twist of his speaking but didn't correct him. 'Till I see how it goes ... and half of the white too – you can put them all in the one box,' he added.

Riding back to the city to the sound of steel on

steel, she wondered why she wasn't more excited about finding this new outlet. When she and Lavelle had first started she would have been beside herself to have found a new customer, *any* customer. Now it didn't seem to matter an awful lot to her. But it should have. She let her thoughts wander far from Tipp'rary and Cornelius Ryan.

What she loved on such journeys was the way you could lose yourself in the sway of the train. Fix your gaze on everything, your mind on nothing; let the world swirl by. It was a wondrous thing, the way the trains were going everywhere, pushing out further and further, finding out America. Far from trains she grew up – many's the day barefooted, going over the bent mountainy roads and back again – twice or three times the length of these train journeys in and out of Boston – it not even bothering her.

Everything was so easy here, once you got a foot on the ladder. Neither she, nor the children, wanted for a thing. No mountain roads, no bare feet. Theirs was a secure and comfortable existence and showed every sign of remaining so. Strange how everything had worked out well in the end, if she could call it that – without Michael and Katie and Annie – but it had. It surely had.

She was no longer one of the potato Irish; nor would her children be singled out as such. What harm if in Boston's public schools her son had to recite the Protestant Ten Commandments and the Protestant Our Father? Or read the King James Bible that he was made to bring home for the 'edification of your family', as the Headmaster of Eliot School had so delicately put it. It was all much of a muchness to her. 'Bishop John', as the Catholic prelate of Boston was familiarly called, could rant and rail against Anti-Popery all he liked. In the end it didn't make one 'Amen' of difference. She had always maintained it was 'how you came into the world and how you went out of it' that mattered. Even to be born hard and bred hard, if, in the end, you died easy – in the grace of God – wasn't that it? And it was the same, she thought, for black, as for white, for heathen, as for Christian, for Sassenach, as for Jew. The main thing was to see that her children got a good education, Catholic or Protestant. To ready them for this life – and the next.

One evening while reading, waiting for Lavelle to come in from one of his Repeal meetings, she heard a noise outside. Thinking it was him, she looked up. There, darkly framed in the window, were the head and shoulders of a woman. Gaunt, sunken-eyed, a rag of a headscarf about her, the woman scratched at the windowpane, her withered finger bent against the glass. The sight of her startled Ellen. But when she opened the door the old woman was gone.

The woman was so frail of limb, that she reminded Ellen of those poor souls ravaged by Famine that she had once seen along the Doolough Pass Road between Westport and Delphi. That day the wind had whipped up along the Pass, swirling the wafer-thin phantoms to a watery grave in the Black Lake. The memory sent

111

a shiver over her and she crossed herself. 'No use thinking of all that now, is there?' she said to herself, before closing the door and running upstairs to the children. Probably just some poor old beggarwoman looking for a crust of bread. Then, maybe got frightened and took off.

'Too much reading, agitating the mind,' Lavelle had brushed it off with when he had come in later.

14

Whatever about frightened beggarwomen or imaginary phantoms from the past, she knew him the minute she opened the door.

He didn't recognize her as instantly. Then the surprise in her face, her intake of breath, alerted him. He looked at her hair. The long-maned tumble of it, that he would have known, was long gone. Instead, much shorter tangle of curls was rather severely nested to the back of her head and securely pinned above the high-necked collar of the dress she wore.

'Ellen...! Ellen Rua...! Can it...?'

The man, whom she had only known as the 'Shanafaraghaun man' in Ireland all those years ago, couldn't seem to finish the question. Not that he had ever been much for words, if she remembered him correctly. She nodded, as dumbstruck by his appearance here in Boston as he was by hers.

'Mrs O'Malley? Lavelle...?' He looked utterly perplexed. 'You are Lavelle's wife?' he tried.

'Yes,' she said simply, without still yet showing any hospitality towards him, trying to come to terms with his appearance.

'You remarried?' He seemed unable to take in what she had just confirmed. 'But ... I ... thought you were in Australia?' he fumbled, trying to make sense of it all.

'I was,' she said, not making it any easier for him.

How many more questions had he, this man who had led Michael to his death? This man without a name, but the threat of whose name she had once used to guarantee her children's safety. She should offer him in. He was obviously acquainted with Lavelle. She hesitated.

'I have recently arrived in Boston, and I call merely to pay respects to your husband – to Lavelle,' he explained, as if reading her mind.

Her instinct was to ask him more. Why was he in Boston? What was his connection with her husband? Instead, she eased the door towards him. She could never forgive him for Michael's death – him and his 'causes'.

'Thank you for calling, Mr...'

'Joyce,' he filled in. '*I'm* sorry, I forgot you didn't know.'

'*I'm* sorry, but my husband is not at home,' she said.

He donned his tall hat, gave her a pleasant smile and left.

Once the door was closed, she leaned against the inside of it. He was the harbinger of death,

113

this man, and she feared his appearance here might be as fateful for Lavelle as it had once been for Michael. This Mr ... Joyce, if that were his name, he who, Michael once told her, had proclaimed, 'The sword is a sacred weapon.' She had remarked on it then, had never forgotten the words. It was such a frightening image. Making it all right, holy even, to take life, putting the name of God on a killing blade.

Later, when Lavelle came home, she told him, 'You had a visitor today.'

'Who?'

'The Shanafaraghaun man – as I know him. It seems my past follows me to Boston.'

'Your past – the Shanafaraghaun man?' Lavelle paused, perplexed.

'Mr Joyce, he calls himself now!' she said, helping him.

'Joyce – he is already here?' Lavelle seemed surprised. But it also seemed to her that he was expecting the man.

'Who is he?' she asked.

'He comes to Boston via Van Diemen's Land. He had some part in the failed insurrection of 1848,' Lavelle answered.

'The Young Irelanders?'

'Yes, the Young Irelanders. But how did you know him?' he asked.

'I knew him from before ... that he was a Repealer. Don't you remember?'

Now Lavelle did. 'He is the same man?' he asked, rhetorically, 'who led the attack ... with Michael. What a strange coincidence,' he said, his mind recapitulating how when Michael had died,

114

she had used this man's name as a threat against her landlord to keep her children safe.

'It is too strange, and not to my liking that he is here in Boston,' she replied. 'So-called revolutionaries,' she continued. 'Imagine it, seizing a poor widow-woman's house to start a revolution – were they all mad?' she asked, wanting to dismiss Mr Joyce and his co-insurrectionists. 'Fighting the Crown from a cabbage patch!'

'Ballingarry was ill-timed,' Lavelle responded. 'The people wanted potatoes instead of pikes, and the priests were against it. But it wasn't a failure!'

'Of course it was a failure,' she contradicted him.

'No, Ellen, the English made the usual mistakes, this time sending the leaders to Van Diemen's Land, letting them live. But all the Crown got were live martyrs instead of dead ones!'

She didn't want to hear this kind of talk. 'What does he want here in Boston, with us?' she demanded.

'The same as every true Irishman ever wanted – repeal of the Union with England,' Lavelle answered.

'Pshaw the Union!' she returned. 'Isn't it more important for us to repeal the laws of Massachusetts so that we have equal rights for our children, like other white people, and not be kept down like the blacks? We had enough of that back home.'

Lavelle seemed taken aback by her attack. 'You've changed, Ellen, changed so much, lost the fire for freedom you once had.'

She looked at him. 'There are different freedoms, some worth fighting for, some not. Some you never get anyway.'

'Ellen,' he countered, his composure regained, 'you well know that in Ireland, the land still belongs to the few. The many live from hand to mouth in circumstances far worse than the slaves of the South. Thousands upon thousands still crowd in here, forced to flee from their own country. That is the most basic freedom – to be in your own country, to live off your own land. *That* is worth fighting for,' he said strenuously, in one of the longest speeches she had heard from him. It was the company he was keeping of late.

'Lavelle, I don't want us to argue now,' she answered. 'I've done enough, lost enough for the "Ould Counthry". What I have left I want to hold – you, the children. Don't, please, drag us back into all of that. I'm worried by him being here.'

He could see that the man's visit had troubled her greatly. 'It'll not affect us, Ellen – the family,' he said, trying to reassure her, 'but it is only if the ones who have succeeded abroad, like us, agitate, that change will ever come at home.'

She was afraid for him, angry that he and the Joyce man would use America as a mustering ground for Irish dissent. Distressed that everything she had struggled for would be put at risk by time-worn ideals and would-be revolutionaries, recently reduced to hiding in cabbage patches.

15

If Ireland was Lavelle's cause then her own hands soon were full with another, one much closer to home than Ireland's: Patrick.

At the Eliot School the boy, now fifteen and 'starting to have a notion of himself', had protested against reciting the 'Protestant version' of the Ten Commandments. When the teacher insisted, Patrick had resolutely stood his ground, stating that he would recite the Ten Commandments, 'but only the right version'. Things had come to a head and Patrick was caned with a rattan until his hands bled. He had refused to cry and left the classroom. A number of the other Catholic boys had walked out in protest, some of whom brought him home to her.

She nearly died when she saw him, ashen-faced and the blood splattered all over his hands. She bathed and bandaged them but could not stop the bleeding, while Mrs Brophy, who had come to see 'what all the commotion was about', scurried off for a doctor. He subsequently rushed Patrick to hospital, declaring, 'The boy is so savagely cut, he may lose a finger or two.' She went with him, frantic with worry. To her great relief, Patrick did not suffer the predicted loss. However, his hands were so sore and so heavily bandaged that she was obliged to spoon-feed him for the following week, undressing him at night for bed, dressing him again in the mornings. Mary and Louisa were equally solicitous of Patrick's well-being, waiting on him, comforting – as much as he let them. Lavelle wanted to deal with the schoolmaster who had flayed the skin from Patrick's hands, but Ellen restrained him, until she had decided what to do about Patrick.

Even under such harsh circumstances for Patrick, she was glad to have him at home. Just the two of them, for a change. Putting the food into his mouth, her fingers touching his lips, or dabbing his chin with a napkin, where clumsily she had spilled some broth, was at first awkward for them both, bringing back to her the memory of a previous intimacy. When, at ten years of age and dying of hunger, she had force-fed him from her breast, with Annie's milk. She could tell by him now, easing some bread into his mouth, that it was his remembrance too.

After the first day or so, things relaxed between them. He never complained. He was so like Michael in character, as well as in countenance, she thought as she washed his face. She held back the black-curled hair to dampen his forehead, her face next to his. 'You're so like him, Patrick, so like him, in every way,' she whispered. Then, it all flooding back on her, she was forced to leave the room, Patrick wondering if he would ever make any sense of understanding his mother.

So outraged at Patrick's treatment were the other Catholic parents whose sons attended Eliot School that the next she knew, Bishop John was on her doorstep, in his wake the ever-attendant Mrs Brophy.

Tall and well-built, 'a fine stock of a man', as Lavelle described him, Boston's newest Bishop, John Fitzpatrick, was as cultivated as he was popular. Bostonian by birth, he moved equally within both communities of his diocese. As frequently dining with the Brahmins of Beacon Hill or discoursing with the Scots-Irish in the Thursday Evening Club, as he was to be seen rambling about on foot, visiting with the ordinary, mainly Irish, folk of his flock.

Although she had never met him, Ellen attended his Masses in the cathedral on Franklin Street, taking Holy Communion from his hands regularly. A powerful preacher, Bishop John spelt it out to his congregation in no uncertain terms that they should forget the old squabbles of Ireland and concentrate instead on getting on with life in Boston.

Now, all flummoxed at his sudden appearance, she was rising from kissing the ring on the proffered hand. 'My advice, Mrs Lavelle, is that you engage legal opinion and execute charges against the schoolmaster for this violent assault on your son.'

'Your Lordship, I am removing Patrick from Eliot School to another. It was my mistake to send him there in the first place,' she said, anxious for no continuance of the upset.

'You must not do that!' Bishop John counselled. '*That* would be a grievous mistake. If you do not press charges, this unhappy occurrence may manifest itself again. Other Catholic boys

119

will suffer as Patrick has.'

She could see the sense in that.

The Bishop continued, 'Secondly, if you or the other Catholic parents remove your children, then the bigots will have won. You must immediately send Patrick back to Eliot School, as soon as he is recovered,' he advised, telling her that, 'The Catholics of America are protected as equally by the Constitution as are those of the Protestant faith. We must use those constitutional rights to effect change.'

She could not argue against what he was saying, only she didn't want any trouble – she'd seen enough of that. She said nothing, left him to carry on.

'Education for the success of our children is of crucial importance, Mrs Lavelle. *Crucial,*' he emphasized, 'and of course, school laws must be observed. But – and only by non-violent means – our children must resist all prayers and ceremonies foreign to their religion, within the public school system, and we, as parents and priests, must support them.'

Nervously she intervened, as one would a sermon. 'Your Lordship, but they are only children. How can they resist the authority of the school?' she asked, afraid of the consequences of what he was suggesting.

'You are thinking of Patrick now and the suffering he endures. But our children are more than children; they are soldiers, soldiers of Christ, as Patrick has so ably demonstrated. If there are enough soldiers then they become an army, and an army is not so easy to resist – even by the public school system!'

'Begging your Lordship's pardon,' she found herself still disagreeing, 'but one army begets another.'

'You leave it to me, Mrs Lavelle,' Bishop John assured her. 'Neither you nor Patrick will be left to stand alone on this matter.' He touched Patrick's dark head. 'Well done, young man, and you're a handsome fellow too – the black Irish!' He proffered his hand again to her and she knelt to it.

Bishop John was as good as his word. He wrote forcibly to the Boston School Committee about Patrick's treatment, citing the wider theological issues involved, as well as the unconstitutionality of imposing one set of values and beliefs on pupils of clearly different backgrounds and religion.

Patrick went back to the Eliot School, and while there was no formal acknowledgement of wrongdoing by the school, things did change. Shortly thereafter, pupils as a whole were not required to publicly recite the Lord's Prayer.

Lavelle was mightily pleased by all this, proud as Punch of Patrick. She, on the other hand, was glad when it was all over, and felt it was only bringing attention to themselves.

It did. Patrick himself became something of a hero, if not to his teachers then at least to his Catholic classmates and even, somewhat grudgingly, to the other non-Catholic pupils. Ellen, too, achieved some element of reflected glory from her son's stance. 'He didn't lick it off the ground, Mrs Lavelle,' Mrs Brophy complimented. 'You have him well-tutored – well-tutored indeed – and the Bishop himself was here, lovely man. It shows you what's what ... the Bishop coming and all!'

And when she called back to Cornelius Ryan's Emporium, she was met with, 'I heard about that boy of yours – a good lad.' Cornelius Ryan leaned over the counter towards her. 'They have them Orange bibles in all the schools about here,' he confided, keeping an eye on the door. 'Grand people, grand people. Some of them come in here; the teachers too,' he continued. 'But they're not the same as us, Mrs Lavelle, nah, but grand people all the same. Grand people,' he repeated, as if wanting to offend no one.

She wondered if Cornelius Ryan would be as quick to refuse an 'Orange' dollar, planked on the counter of his Emporium, as he was to praise Patrick's refusal to read the 'Orange' bible. Cornelius Ryan, thereafter, ordered only full crates of the 'Bordelaux, from that grand Mrs Lavelle woman – the mother of the O'Malley boy!'

16

Fall, she loved fall.

On the Common, the red and gold leaves, fiery-embered emblems of a dying summer, fell winterwards in one last glorious sunburst. Soon the cooling Atlantic chill would roll inwards from the coast, preparing the Common for the blustery snowstorms in its wake. Snow that would quickly weave its winter-white mantle over everything. But fall – the in-between season, after the excitement of summer – always seemed, to her, to settle things down.

The summer madness that had touched Peabody had lightly passed over him and, for the most part, it was business as normal. And business was good. Bordeaux instead of Byron, port instead of poetry; everything in its place. And, as if to herald the new fall, Boston of 1851 was finally linked with Montréal via the Grand Junction Railroad, thus breaching another frontier. In line with Boston's usual penchant for announcing its advancement, three days of celebration followed. Canada and the North were now opened up for commerce with the Hub City.

For Ellen and Lavelle it meant that the railroad could now carry their fine wines from Montréal all year round. Now the New England Wine Company, previously dependent on ships that plied the St Lawrence, need not hold so much stock against a transportation route frozen solid four to five months of each year. She resolved, in time, to travel the new railroad, make her own maiden voyage to Frontignac Père et Fils.

She resolved, too, this fall, to improve herself further, her original plan when she had first come to Boston, perhaps join one of the evening clubs for ladies which Mrs Brophy kept harping on about. They sounded interesting and educational – if all the ladies weren't too alike her breezy neighbour with the buzzing tongue. And

123

they couldn't be, Ellen thought.

Boston ladies had, like the trains, continued to breach new frontiers for themselves, unlike any other society in America. In the mill towns of Lowell, Lynn and Lawrence, the women of Massachusetts had already raised their voices, through the Women's Trade Union League and reforming organizations like the Nine to Five Association. And more importantly, their voices had been heard, their vision of a better working world for women gilding the way for the Massachusetts model to spread nationwide.

These mill girls from the farms of New England, later joined by the tenement Irish, bonded together to form a Sisterhood of Toil, and refusing to let the spirit of freedom imbued in them be crushed by the daily grind of the five-storey textile mills. Life was more than 'sun-up to sun-down', six days a week, in the company of clattering looms, rotating spindles and flying shuttles – 'all enough to dizzy a girl'.

'Mill life,' Ellen explained to Mary, 'was the tyranny of employment replacing the tyranny of unemployment.' Mary, thirteen now, had recently engaged her mother in a number of debates on these matters arising out of a visit to Notre Dame de Namur by Bishop John. The Bishop had spoken to them about their new home in America. That while they could never forget their old home, it was best not to be looking over one's shoulder. A tramcar might be ahead of you! Bishop John had then 'preached', Mary said, 'as if he were in the pulpit', about the role of young ladies, and older ladies, too, in the New World.

'He thinks a woman's place is in the home!' Mary stated Bishop John's case, making it clear that it was not a view she necessarily shared.

Ellen could not resist a smile, hearing her child speak so.

Mary continued. 'He said that Boston was leading the way, with women in the marriage life leaving the home and going out to work. That it was becoming a fashion ... and not a good one!'

Ellen broke her silence. 'Well, it's a fashion that's here to stay – whether Bishop John likes it or not!' she said, trying not to speak too disparagingly of Boston's most senior prelate. 'Work is plenty for the men. But there are so many "green hands" here, it has driven the wages down. Women have no choice but to work.'

'They have, according to Bishop John,' Mary replied. 'They have the choice to stay at home while the men fight for higher wages, and the Bishop would back the men. He believes that "God's creatures must work to live, not just live to work".'

'What if it wasn't just for the wages?' Ellen put to her. 'What would Bishop John say then?'

'If women just wanted to work?' Mary paused. 'I think he's still against it,' she answered. 'Bishop John says the most rewarding job in the eyes of Holy Mother Church is marriage life and being a mother. That the mother educates the man.' Mary was nothing if not well briefed.

'Bishop John has a lot to say on it – for a man, Mary!' Ellen laughed.

Mary nodded, asking, 'But what do you say on it?'

Ellen considered her answer. 'I suppose if a woman has a parcel of children she'd be hard put to work sun-up to sun-down six days a week, outside the home, as well as inside it.'

Mary nodded again, but had yet another question. 'Is that why the Irish girls who come to America stay single and don't go into marriage life?'

Ellen thought before answering. 'I was too young, Mary, when I married your father. Just turned seventeen when I saw him at the Pattern Day Fair in Leenane.' She started remembering, but pulled herself up. 'But then, they were different times in a different place.'

'Imagine – you were only four years older than I am...' Mary said, wonderment in her voice, '...but you fell in love with him?'

Ellen looked at her child, imagining how she would look in four years' time, seeing in Mary's face how she, herself, must have looked back then. She had been a mere child. Then she had gone from child to mother in the space of a year when Patrick was born. That was the way it was. She had nursed him and reared him while still seventeen, as if she had been born to it. And she supposed she was; women were.

'Ah ... love him ... indeed I did, Mary, but I hardly knew the meaning of the word.' She held Mary to her. 'Don't worry about it, *asthore*. There's always time for love afterwards. Here, in America, you can "be somebody"; be anybody. There, in Ireland, you could be nobody. Just keep working the same hard acre, year in year out. Marriage was a way out, an excitement. This is why I brought you all here to Boston – to give you a different way out, so you could all "be somebody".'

'Does "being somebody" mean I might never get married and have my own little babies?' Mary got right to the point.

'Mary, whssht child! Do you hear yourself talking? Sure you're only a *gossoor* yourself. But no, it doesn't mean that at all!' Ellen hoped she hadn't overstated her case. 'To "be somebody" means to "be somebody" for yourself, whether you have a marriage life or not.'

Mary nodded – but she had one last question. 'Then...' she paused, trying to find the right words, 'did you not love our Daddy, our first Daddy ... and if you were in America, does what you said mean that you wouldn't have married him?'

Mary always saved the hard questions until last.

'I did love him, Mary, very much, from the first day I set eyes on him. I think no matter where I was in the world, it would still be the same.'

'Even if you were seventeen?'

'Yes, Mary, even if I was seventeen.'

That seemed to satisfy her, at last. God, the child had such an exasperating way of turning everything back on you. Still, it was to be encouraged in a girl who was going to 'be somebody'.

She resolved to rummage out for Mary an essay she had read in *The Lowell Offering* titled 'A Society for the promotion of Industry, Virtue and Knowledge'. She found the article and the following evening, Mary read it aloud.

'Resolved: That the wages of females shall be equal to the wages of males that they may be enabled to maintain proper independence of character...'

'I like Betsy Chamberlain,' Mary declared after she had completed reading all of the author's resolutions.

'So do I,' her mother concurred.

At the other end of the scale from the mill girls were the 'gorgeous pedants'. Ellen delighted in reading of Margaret Fuller, she who first had introduced 'Conversations' into the parlours of Boston for the gorgeous pedants. These ladies of 'incomparable intellect', as regarded by themselves, in wintertime engaged in 'high parlour conversation' while dressed in every finery that money could buy. But they shared, if not their finery, at least one thing in common with the mill girls of Lowell – the opinion that there was 'more to life than a dress, a pudding and a beau'.

In one sense Ellen admired the gorgeous pedants, almost as much as she did the mill girls. It was unthinkable that this would have happened for women in Ireland. The male-ridden Catholic Church would have stomped it out. 'Rosary beads and rearing children was as far as a woman could go there,' she said to Mary, another evening when pursuing their own 'conversations'. 'Beading and breeding!'

Louisa sat with them, listening almost, Ellen thought, moving her head, first towards her when she spoke, next towards Mary, watching their mouths. Then the girl chalked something on her slate board and passed it to Ellen.

'Bloomerism?'

Ellen looked from her to Mary. 'Bloomerism? What do you know about Bloomerism?'

Louisa pointed at Ellen's mouth, then put her hand to her own, moving her fingers as if drawing sound from it, wanting Ellen to talk.

'Bloomerism? What kind of a pair am I raising?' she laughed. She began, speaking slowly for Louisa's benefit. 'Even here in Boston, the Church denounces Bloomerism – pegging it "the end of family life as we know it". But I don't think the women here, either the mill girls or the high-society ladies, will be shaken from their views by the threat of a Bishop's crozier!' Maybe some of the newly-arrived Irish might, she supposed. 'Bloomerism is here to stay and I think we should be a part of it,' she told them. 'Cooking, dressing and loving we can still – do as the Church commands, but we can do more, much more.'

Mary agreed wholeheartedly, while Louisa cleaned her board and scribbled a new word. 'Yes!'

Ellen determined somehow to be part of 'the new movement for the advancement of women in society'. While she empathized with the militant mill girls, she didn't see how she could be a part of their movement. Neither had she the intellect, and more importantly, the entrée to be a gorgeous pedant. She would have to settle for some in-between grouping, probably a mixture of mid-parlour Bloomerists, some 'reformers and abolitionists' and a sprinkling of the likes of Mrs

Brophy, interested in 'a bit of gossip-talk and getting out of the house'.

So she threw in her lot with the 'Daughters of the Commonwealth'. She was put forward for membership by Mrs Brophy as 'a woman of faith and fortitude who, having snatched her children from the jaws of famine in the Old World, has instilled in them those same virtues, so desirous, in the New'.

There were twelve Daughters of the Commonwealth. No more, no fewer. That was the rule. And any such organization worth its title had rules, and a constitution by which its members lived. A new 'Daughter' could join only when there had been a defection, or ejection, of a sitting 'Daughter'. The latter unhappy circumstance had never afflicted the 'DOCS' – Lavelle's abbreviation – as yet. But there had been a defection which had allowed Ellen to go forward.

'Like the twelve apostles we are,' she told Lavelle.

'And who is to play Judas?' he jibed.

'You have Judas on the brain!' she mocked, pleased that she had at last made this further move towards improving herself.

The twelve Daughters of the Commonwealth met weekly, on Monday evenings, in a room at Faneuil Hall, also the venue for Trade Union and Anti-Slavery campaigns. A motley assemblage, as Ellen had imagined, of mid-class Bostonians, 'upped' Irish, and one or two who professed 'no affiliation save that of gender'. Life would be lively among the Daughters, Ellen imagined.

130

Topics for discussion could be anything under the sun and were proposed, seconded, and voted on, a week in advance.

'To allow time for reflection and reading,' Mrs Brophy had explained to her.

Men could not attend except in the capacity of 'invited speaker'. Allowing men to be present was 'the death of many such a grouping', Mrs Brophy also opined as they travelled home together after the first meeting, '...they being a distracting influence and inhibiting the different way in which we think'.

Ellen revelled in the discussions, the arguments, the broadening of the mind. But no matter how great her own interest was in the DOCS, it palled by comparison with Mary's, who with Louisa in rapt attendance peppered her with questions before and after each meeting. So much so that Ellen began to worry if she had encouraged them too much in their Bloomerism.

'The discussions,' she reported to Mary and Louisa, 'are as diverse as Boston itself. Freedoms in general are high on every agenda. The "freedom of black Americans"; the "freedom of workers from industrial slavery"; the "freedom of women from domestic slavery"; "freedom of expression"; every "freedom" imaginable.'

There had even been a discussion on 'To Bring Back or Not Bring Back The "Third Row"', which she avoided telling them about. The infamous 'third row', traditionally the row in theatres where Boston's ladies of the night arrayed themselves, often attracted more attention from male theatregoers than the stage itself.

However, the bedizened third row never sat easily with the strongly puritanical streak of Boston's ruling class and Mayor Quincy had banned the tradition, effectively dismantling the third row.

Ellen had thus found herself in the midst of a lively debate. Some supported the 'removal of vice from our midst' stance. Others excoriated 'male laws which would seek to enchain female bodies', while Mrs Brophy was firmly of the view that 'if a man got good cooking at home', as she put it, 'then he would not sup outside of it!'

The Daughters of the Commonwealth would keep the third row, if only by a narrow majority. Little wonder then, Ellen thought, that Bloomerists were charged by Church leaders with being the 'free-thinking cesspool out of which moral dangers crawl into society'.

Eventually, as she knew it would be, it was Ireland's turn. The 'Great Calamity on Erin's far shore' caused some outpourings of concern in Boston, supported, indeed, by some generous outpourings from Boston's well-laden coffers. Strangely, the city's ruling elite did not consider the tens of thousands fleeing the 'Calamity' to be worthy of the same concerns, once landed on Boston's near shore. These new immigrants were a scourge, a pestilence. Those fleeing one 'Calamity' became the Calamity themselves, in Boston. Ellen wondered how the Daughters of the Commonwealth would view the issue with the problem now on their very own doorsteps.

'Renaissance or Revolution, the Future for Ireland?' was the declared topic, and there would be a guest speaker.

17

The women applauded when he had finished speaking. All, that is, except Ellen. Not that he hadn't spoken well, with clarity and passion. He had. She knew he would come to her. He had noticed her silence, her sign of disapproval.

He had done this before – spoken to groups, maybe even crowds. The way he had posed a question then paused, giving them all a chance to consider the answer. Before he supplied it. *His* answer, as if he replied for all of them. He was quite arrogant, she thought, with his slightly gaunt, black-eyed poet's face, and his talk of revolution.

'Ellen Rua!' He insisted on putting the old badge on her.

'It's plain "Ellen" here!' she said to him, surprised that he was still in Boston, unsettling things, as she saw it.

'You did not agree with my sentiments?' he asked, ignoring the frostiness of her reply.

'Ireland and its revolutionaries have well failed us, Mr Joyce ... then and now,' she answered.

If he was stung by this, as she intended, he concealed it well. 'Perhaps it is we who have failed Ireland, Mrs O'Malley?'

'Lavelle,' she corrected him for the second time. 'It's Mrs Lavelle, Mrs *Ellen* Lavelle. We have not failed, Mr Joyce, we have survived. Our duty is not to Ireland, it is to our children. You and men like you come here to distract us from that cause!' she accused.

'I know what you have suffered,' he said, not arguing with her. 'It is through the suffering of its people that a country is reborn.'

'Reborn is it?' she retorted. 'Men are full of words. High ideas... What do you know about birth or death, except what is in your books?'

He flinched, but didn't rise to her. 'The idea must first be born, before its realization,' he replied, watching her.

'And what "idea", Mr Joyce, do you have for us – the "Daughters of Old Ireland" – here in America?' she said, mockingly. 'Will you have us drilling on Boston Common, then sail back over the ocean and lay siege to London? Will we be America's first "Petticoat Armada"?'

She was aware of having raised her voice; Mrs Brophy and the others who circled nearby had fallen silent. She didn't care, she was sick of it all; him, Lavelle, the Repealers. The revolution was not back in Ireland against the English Queen; it was right here in Boston. Better working conditions, a fairer chance at life, equality in the schools, something to be done about the tens of thousands of Irish living in squalor. He kept looking at her, he too oblivious to all but this 'Daughter of Erin' who railed against his philosophies, railed against Erin itself.

'I am glad my talk stimulated you so, Ellen Lavelle,' he smiled. 'As your talk has me!'

On the way home Mrs Brophy reproved her, in her usual round-the-houses kind of way.

'Oh, my, Mrs Lavelle, what an exciting evening – that nice gentleman Mr Joyce seemed to take a great interest in your point of view.'

Ellen agreed. It was easier than enduring the usual non-stop babble from the woman. But Mrs Brophy wasn't for shaking.

'Did you notice the love-spot under his left eye?' Mrs Brophy beaked on, referring to the small dark spot on the man's skin.

'I did, Mrs Brophy; a *ball seirce* we used to call it–'

'Wasn't it very fetching, very fetching indeed, dark and brooding, like himself?' she insisted.

'I found him to be both arrogant and opinionated, Mrs Brophy.'

'Well, he met his match in you,' Harriet Brophy said, sparrow-hopping about her. Ellen thought the woman intended it as a compliment.

Now she'd get nothing but Mr Joyce and love-spots for the next week, unless some other diversion popped up to distract Mrs Brophy. And one usually did – on a daily basis. She offered up a silent prayer that the days of this week would be no different.

Maybe it was a mistake – perhaps she wasn't cut out to be part of such a gathering, to be too mannered. She should instead just concentrate on the fundamentals of life, the children, Lavelle, the business. Not be trying to rise above her station, forgetting who she was, where she came from, getting notions. 'Going before herself' as they would put it, back in the valley villages.

Lavelle was at home waiting for her. She didn't give him a chance to greet her, still in her hubris

135

over Mr Joyce. 'Why is it, Lavelle, when we are prospering in the plenty of a new country, that some want us to be still shackled to the rag and bones of the old country?'

He never answered her. 'Who was the speaker?' he asked.

'Your comrade-in-arms, the Shanafaraghaun man, Mr Joyce, or whoever he is – he doesn't much speak like the people of Shanafaraghaun that I know,' she levelled at him.

'We have a duty to the old–' Lavelle began.

'We have no duty,' she interrupted him. 'It's guilt, Lavelle, that's all. Guilt that we escaped. Guilt that we left misery behind us. Guilt is strangling us.'

18

Despite having done business with the Frontignacs for the past number of years, she had never met with them. All her correspondence had been by letter, since Father McGauran had first put her in touch with them. Now with the opening up of the Grand Junction Railroad to Montréal, it was timely to meet with Frontignac, discuss new supplies from France, and terms of business in general. Peabody had always maintained that she should be enjoying a more favourable set of prices from the Frontignacs because of the growing volume of business from Boston.

It was perfectly natural for her to go rather than

Lavelle. She was the one who conducted all such dealings – 'hurling the pen' as Lavelle put it. He himself was more comfortable with 'hurling the hammer', keeping the warehouse in order, doing repairs, building new racking, and everything to do with freighting the wine both inwards and outwards. 'I am the hands and feet of the business; you, Ellen, are its face and mind,' he often remarked. Besides, the journey would be good for her, Lavelle knew. She had become increasingly fraught of late, seeing faces at the window, arguing vehemently with him over Ireland's cause. Obviously, too, had vented her spleen on Mr Joyce. And he had no fears for her safety, although a woman travelling alone might invite some small surprise. She too was glad of the opportunity. She would have time to herself, time to see more of this vast land; time to think.

The journey necessitated her having to forgo the next meeting of the Daughters of the Commonwealth. She knew that her absence would afford them the occasion of discussing her recent behaviour. Let them do what they wanted, censure her, let her be the first to be ejected. She had had to say what she had said.

Maybe she had been a bit hard on Mr Joyce. It was over Michael. Now this man was back like a ghost to haunt them, bringing the past with him. She feared for Lavelle, afraid that he was involved in some conspiracy with the man. Was she now to lose him too? She loved Lavelle dearly. No matter his politics, he was everything to her; steadfast, loyal – would move the world for her. It didn't

137

bear thinking about, that like Michael he too could be taken from her.

The train rattled onwards, leaving Boston behind, losing her to the past receding outside her breath-misted window.

Then it ground to a halt – some commotion ahead – 'bears on the tracks'. They had been warned not to leave their carriages in such an event. Her face continued to press the window, looking out into the soul of nowhere. She was unaware, of the man who had entered the carriage as it was stopped, and now stood behind her.

'Am I again the fitful cause of such trouble on your face?'

She turned, some sense of what she had been thinking about telling her it was him.

'Oh, Mr Joyce... !' she fumbled for the words.

'I am journeying to Canada to speak,' he said by way of explanation. 'This time, I hope, to a less hostile reception than Boston afforded me. I trust, Mrs Lavelle, that your reason for travelling is therefore not the same as mine!'

It was the first time she had seen him laugh. She was embarrassed. How long had he been watching her?

'I can assure you it's not, Mr Joyce,' she replied, unable to resist a smile.

He sat down across from her, explaining how, through the crowds, he thought he had seen her board at Boston, but was himself late and had taken the nearest carriage. He had decided then to come looking for her, taking a chance with the bears.

'You are *not* coming to Montréal to hear me speak?' he asked in mock disappointment. 'Perhaps this time to heckle me?'

'It matters not to me where you speak. Canada is, I am sure, as America is, a land of free speech,' she said, a little more coolly than before. He waited before replying, then leaned towards her.

'I am sorry about your husband ... Michael...' he said seriously, his granite-dark eyes locking with hers. She could not help noticing the tiny macula, Mrs Brophy's 'love-spot', high on the rim of his left cheekbone, near his eye. 'He did what he did for you, Ellen, not for me, you must know that. But I am sorry none the less. The assault on Pakenham's house was under my command – Michael was my responsibility.'

She remembered. She knew that this man, with his non-Shanafaraghaun speech, spoke the truth. Michael, his mind altered by hunger had wanted to 'do something' against the way Pakenham had been grinding them down. Feeling he had failed her and the children, his 'doing something' was Michael's way of being restored in her eyes. She was as much to blame for his death as this man was.

His voice broke in on her thoughts. 'Some must die for what they believe in,' he said gently. 'Most of us are denied the opportunity.'

She believed him, this strange man. He would embrace that opportunity if it arose. Death to him would be a victory. If your oppressor killed you while resisting him, you were not defeated, he was. She studied him. He had an intensity with which his face seemed constantly alight, the

139

tiny dark macula set in brooding contrast. Tall, and slender of build – like a girl, but not soft – he was, indeed, a man of the sword. She saw it in him. To use it or die by it.

'I should thank you for being guarantor of my children's safety. You must think it ungrateful for me not to have done so already.'

He nodded, neither agreeing nor disagreeing with her. At times he said so little – until something fired him up – only looking into her all the time. Part of her wished he would leave, go away to wherever on the train he had come from, but she had yet things to say to him.

'I don't want you to encourage Lavelle in your ways.' There, she had said what she had been thinking.

'Lavelle is...' He stopped, changing his mind. '...his own man...'

But she knew it was not what he had started out to say. However, Lavelle being his 'own man' had the effect of preventing her speaking further to him on Lavelle's behalf. He smiled, awaiting her next question.

She wondered if he was married. She thought not. What kind of marriage life would it be for his wife? A man who spent half his time living in the shadows, traipsing the world, fomenting trouble, the other half in prisons. In the window she caught the side view of his face, landscaped with her own, imprinted on America. A man consumed with only one passion – Ireland.

'Do *you* ever think of Ireland?' He surprised her.

'I am American now,' she answered.

'Is that why you've shorn your hair – and your name – to cut away the old life?'

She wasn't ready for this directness, but didn't falter. 'Yes! To tell the truth, that is it.'

'And is the truth only to be told in the English language?' He was trying to snare her now, like Peabody.

'There isn't much use for the old tongue here. It's hard talking the price of pigs to Germans and Jews,' she gave a little laugh, 'in Irish!'

He didn't share her sarcasm. Probably didn't see much humour in life anyway, she thought.

'Do you ever sing any more?' He was actually worse than Peabody with his questions, diverting from subject to subject.

'No,' she answered, then remembering, 'once only – on my wedding-day ... for my husband,' she said pointedly.

'Never since?'

'No.'

'To sing is good – it releases the soul. What was your song?'

She told him.

'Would you sing it for me now?'

She looked at him askance. Was his mind altogether gone? His head, at some stage glanced by a bullet? He stared at her, like a boy would, awaiting a favour.

'I ... couldn't, not here ... on the train,' she found herself saying, when she should have just refused him outright.

'Sing it for me, Ellen Rua – I'm sorry, Ellen ... sing it for me!' He leaned forward, physically willing her.

'No, I don't know you ... I don't sing any more!' she eventually got out, his nearness unnerving her.

'You don't sing any more?' he said, drawing back as if she had told him she'd lost her faith, deserted her God. 'I remember you, Ellen, hair to your waist, the beating heart of the Maamtrasna valley, fiery steel to your dear husband's resolve.' He pushed his face closer to hers again. 'Don't you know what you were?'

She looked at him, disconcerted by this new turn in the conversation. All because she no longer sang!

'You were hope,' he said passionately. 'Hope for a people long dashed with hopelessness. Your courage, the sacrifices you made, it gave those people hope. To them, Ellen, you were the symbol of a new Ireland, rising out of the ashes of Famine–'

'Stop it!' He was mad, this man sitting across from her, mad with the extreme madness of zealots. 'I was none of that, Mr Joyce,' she said, controlling her voice. 'I was a wife like many, destitute and with a dead husband. I was a mother – once with four children,' she paused and he saw the line cross her face, '...who lost two – like many.'

'You did, Ellen, you did,' and he took her hand in his. 'You are the living story of Ireland.'

She withdrew her hand, shaken by his fervour. 'I am not. Whatever it is you want me to be, I am not.'

It was Peabody all over again, trying to fashion her into some imaginary 'element', make her something she wasn't – a symbol. Something *they* wanted her to be.

'You have grown comfortable in Boston,' he said, unruffled by her rebuttal. 'Prosperity has embraced you. It is the great danger – we are at our finest in adversity.'

There he was again, explaining her to herself.

'What danger?' she demanded. 'Isn't it what everyone who has come here with nothing wants, to make something of themselves?'

He continued, plausible, passionate in his beliefs. 'What we are now facing in America, is that we, the Irish, will become what we once despised in others. *We* are becoming the next generation of colonizers – the new Imperialists.'

'Riddles and *ráiméis*, Mr Joyce. We only want a better life for our children than the cabin-life *we* had. That's all. We want nothing more.'

He was troubled, this man, twisted of vision, locked in some fatal embrace with a mythical Ireland. And he saw her as some kind of *speirbhean* – 'woman from Heaven' – who in the vision poems appears as lover to the sleeping poet. He the poet, she Ireland.

'I am not Ireland!' she said aloud. 'I am no *speirbhean*. I am flesh and blood. Look! Feel!' and she grabbed his hands and clasped them to her face, held them there so he could feel her skin, her cheekbones flushed with anger. When she tried to push them away again, he resisted, momentarily.

'To Ireland in the coming times, Ellen Rua. In the coming times,' he whispered, drawing his fingers down from her cheeks.

He left as the bears were cleared and the train

143

groaned into life again, swinging down from the door like some long black wraith of a highwayman. She turned, pressed her face to the window, its welcoming coldness dissipating her anger. Then with her finger she traced the outlines of her face on the glass. All it revealed was herself, everything as before, no noticeable difference. She trailed back a wandering wisp of hair from between her forehead and the glass, weaving it around her finger. It had held its lustre well these last years.

'Ellen... Ellen Rua,' she whispered. Was she always to be Ellen Rua?

Everything had been falling so well into place for her in Boston. Life, as she had hoped, was falling into a predictable and well-ordered sequence, and nothing and nobody was going to turn her from that course. Outside, the tall trees of Canada deep-dimmed the woods. Then for the most fleeting of moments the reflection in the glass was not hers. She drew back, frightened; it reminding her of something she couldn't place. She looked to see if anyone stood behind her. When she looked back at the window again, it was only her own face she saw. But of course it was. She was out of sorts a trifle, upset at all his talk, and that nonsense of symbols and 'women from Heaven'. She snuggled into the corner of the carriage and closed her eyes, a comfortable warmth coming over her as she settled her thoughts on Lavelle and her children.

To her annoyance, Mr Joyce appeared again, this time to assist her alight from the train at Montréal. Courteous to a fault, he proferred a helping hand. She, careless in the moment, miscued the landward step and stumbled awkwardly against him, her face striking his shoulder. He steadied her.

'Flesh and blood,' he smiled, repeating what she had earlier said to him and heightening her embarrassment. He insisted on accompanying her to the hotel. Some connection between the 'thinner numbing climate of Canada' and the 'onset of dizziness'.

Montréal was teeming with life and bustle, colour and smells. She loved it immediately, its glittering turrets and steeples, the mountain behind it, the 'flowing road' of the St Lawrence river before it – two miles wide but choked with *bateaux*, sloops and raftsmen poling their timber platforms over its scudding currents. Île de Montréal, with its timber kings and river barons, its scarlet-costumed Iroquois, plumed and proud. Blue homespunned girls breezily clogged along in their *sabots* – the shoe boot – hollowed from wood. English, Irish, Americans, Jewish, French-Canadians – all were here. Not even in Boston was there such an assortment of accents. Scots Presbyterians were here too, who with traditional Calvinistic determination had first arrived, millstones in their travelling bags, ready to grind and conquer.

'The Scots are the new *Seigneurs* here,' Stephen Joyce explained. 'They are the captains of commerce. You will see their mansions on Mount Prospect and Dorchester Boulevard, town houses, what would elsewhere be considerable

145

country retreats. They ride to hounds when not in their counting houses and generally take their cue from London.

'*Les Anglais*,' he continued, 'those who are English, and that includes us Irish – the Anglophones – have little love for the Francophones, who reciprocate the feeling in full measure.'

She didn't care about the divisions between Anglophones and Francophones. She wanted to explore the leafy culs-de-sac, linger over the market stalls brimming with iron pots, mirrors and the pelts of beaver, mink and otter. Side by side with them the smell of syrup of maple, and assorted brandies vying for bundled stall space with vermilion dyes, ground from cinnabar into a brilliant red-wormed pigment.

A red-coated regimental band crossed them, stamping out its brass-thumping tune, trying, as it were, to do down the other sounds and colours of the city. By comparison, Boston seemed dull and conservative.

'You like it here, I can see,' he said.

'Oh!' she replied, 'do I reveal myself so easily?'

'Not very often,' he answered, being kind.

'Your own disposition seems much lighter?' She arched her eyebrows in a questioning manner. He had relaxed considerably since their encounter on the train.

'It is the company!' he complimented her.

'Oh ... thank you, Mr Joyce.'

'Please call me Stephen – and if in return I might call you Ellen?'

'As, on the rare occasion, you have already ... Mr *Joyce*,' she emphasized. Then she laughed,

146

seeing his serious look at her imagined reprimand. '...Stephen!' she added, still laughing.

Her laughter was compounded by the sight of a pig who had run amok among the marching band, either attracted to, or distracted by, the music. Soon the hapless band was hopelessly out of step, the once-rousing march dismembered into a series of syncopated 'oomps' and 'pahs'. The demented pig had meanwhile begun to snout the breeches of the tuba-player, obviously deciding that the instrument's low-pitched grunting was an invitation to fight or to mate. She thought it perfectly in keeping with the place.

Where she was to stay, the Hôtel Fond du Lac, was also where he would stay. She would have preferred him to be at a distance from her. Things were happening, coincidences, connections with the past. Coincidences she had never trusted. She'd seen her share of them, often to her benefit. But with whatever good there came of apparent coincidences, also came the sense of some design being constructed about her. By the time you understood that design, it was too late. You were by then central to it.

'What a pleasing coincidence, that we share the same accommodation. Fate, to some end of its own, must be flinging us together!' he commented, as if reading her thoughts.

He was most definitely not of the valleys. He had that arrogance, born of station, common to none of the local men she had known. She ignored his remark.

'Please do me the pleasure of dining with me. I would consider it a great honour.' His enthusiasm was flattering.

'Your engagement…?' she protested.

'My engagement waits until tomorrow.'

It was foolish of her. He would not have asked her otherwise. Now she had given him an opening, or would have to refuse him outright.

'Thank you, Stephen, I'm afraid I can't.'

'You have other plans?'

'No … but–'

'Then I insist, Ellen. You cannot dine alone in a foreign city. And Montréal is so foreign – so French!'

She looked at him, expecting that half-mocking smile. She was sure her life would not be at risk if she dined alone.

'French? I am surprised,' she said, playing him at his game. 'Montréal is full of Scots, English and Irish!'

She saw his long brows rise, framing the question. 'Unless … you consider it an impropriety to dine alone with a man who is not your husband?'

'Impropriety had not entered my mind!' she replied, perhaps too hurriedly, rising to his bait.

'Well then, my company has overtaxed your patience. I am sorry.'

He had disarmed her – what was she now to say to him? She laughed, and was pleased at the flash of bewilderment that showed in his face.

'Don't be so serious about everything, Stephen. I'll be happy to dine with you. And you'll know full well when my patience is overtaxed,' she added for measure.

'I hope that day is never,' he said, smiling.

She was surprised at how generous his smile

148

was, once he let slip the hauteur which normally governed his countenance.

'At seven then?'

'At seven,' she replied.

19

She was ten minutes late.

Their earlier badinage had seemed to relax him and he talked, if not openly, then at least more freely about himself.

'Secrecy is an unfortunate necessity,' he offered by way of explanation. 'Spies of the Crown are everywhere and Boston is as much England as is Dublin.'

She could only imagine at what he hinted – wondered if, indeed, some of it was just in his head. He had ordered champagne, imported by Frontignac, Père et Fils.

'The French betrayed us at Paris when we sought support for 1848; they scarce do anything else – but we forgive them everything for their champagne!'

She rarely imbibed alcoholic beverages. Tasted, yes, but she had seen too much of their ill-effects on her countrymen. He raised the slender long-stemmed glass, toasting her.

'Some civilization will remain in North America while Canada remains partly French.'

He held his glass aloft, watching, waiting until she had wet her lips with the drink, the *mousselet*

149

catching the tip of her tongue, fizzing there, melting with the warmth of her mouth.

'Thibaud IV, the Comte de Champagne, it was who first brought the Chardonnay vine to France from the Crusades,' he told her.

She interrupted him. 'And the reverend Doms of the Benedictines continued the godly work, nourishing it in the chalk pits of Champagne, safe-keeping its secrets in the cellars beneath the Abbey of St Niçaise.'

'You know about champagne?' He smiled at her.

'It is my business to know,' she answered him.

'So...' he continued, 'champagne is a holy drink crusaded for by *Comtes*, benedicted by monks. Let us enjoy it!'

She took another sip of the 'holy' drink. He did, after all, have a sense of humour. She put her glass on the table. She had to ask him this question.

'You're not Irish,' she challenged, 'the way you speak ... you're a "Planter".'

'Yes ... a "Planter",' he replied, 'my people were from Scotland, but I am in all other things Irish.'

He grabbed her arm. 'Hear me out!' he said.

'I knew you were different, but this – Scots-Irish, a "Planter" masquerading as a patriot...' She shook her head in disbelief, unable to reconcile the contradictions in him. He was too good to be true, this dark and intense man, who just appeared and disappeared, bringing trouble everywhere with his poet's talk, making himself out to be a man of the people.

'Listen to me, Ellen,' he said forcefully. 'Am I to be for ever damned by history, by the sins of the past? I am as much of Ireland as you are. I was born there and shall probably die there.'

'You can't–' she started.

'Can't? You mean I have to be Catholic and poor to claim Irishness?'

She fully realized that this was exactly what she had meant.

'And if I tell you that further I was educated at Trinity, the "Devil's College" as your prelates would have it, does that make me even blacker than the "black Protestant" you see before you?' he demanded of her.

This was why her children had not been harmed while in Pakenham's care. The man had influence indeed, more than she had counted upon. That of a common faith with the landlord.

'You are a fraud, Mr Joyce, I'm leaving!' As she rose, he again caught her arm, forcing her to sit down. Then he told her his story.

'After the flight of the Earls O'Neill and O'Donnell, to Spain, their lands in Tyrone and Tyrconnell were forfeit to the Crown. We, the McCoists, were small tenant farmers in the Highlands of Scotland. It was the barest of existences. London had, beyond its own purposes, no interest in us. Like thousands of others, we came to Ireland to survive. In return for land, our duty was to "cultivate, colonize" and in particular "civilize" those parts of Ulster to which we had been transplanted. One such "civilizing" process was to alter the name of Derry to Londonderry. To my shame, a McCoist hand was involved.'

She listened, fascinated by his revelation.

'Streets within the same Ulster towns became

known either as the "Scotch quarter" or the "Irish quarter". My forefathers, stout Presbyterians all, moved eastward to County Down, hated alike by Catholics and Anglicans, who classed us as "dissenters". On Sunday, the McCoists would set out from the Down coast to Stranraer in Scotland to receive the Holy Sacrament, forbidden us in Ireland by the English Church. Thus fortified we would return again across the Irish Sea to our new homeland.'

'But your name ... how did you come to live in...?' the questions tumbled out of her.

'Eventually the fugitive Catholic rapparees left behind by the O'Neills and the O'Donnells came down from the Mourne mists attacking the settlements, with their short pikes and swords...' He fell silent, the telling of it paining him.

'Please go on,' she said, wanting to hear it all.

'It was November. Portadown was attacked, the English and Scots rounded up. Men, women and children ... Annie McCoist ... who was in childbirth...' he faltered '...her child half delivered, was in that condition driven from her bed, stripped naked and with her other children herded to the bridge of the Blackwater. Annie, by every account a dignified woman, pleaded, not for her own life, but that she be allowed complete the delivery of her child and her other children be also spared.'

Ellen's heart shuddered, fearing what was next.

'From the midst of the jeering crowd, a young swordsman came – "You are brave for a 'Planter' woman," he shouted. "We should remember you." With his sword he sliced a collop from each of Annie's buttocks and threw them to the clamouring crowd. She, her half-born child and her other children were then prodded with pikes until they leapt from the parapet to the drowning waters. One, a child of eleven years, Elizabeth, who by God's saving grace was swept to shore, was then stunned on the head by a gallant rapparee and pushed again into the life-taking tide.' He paused. 'Such was the fate of the McCoist womenfolk. As for Annie's husband, he, first having had his feet fried was buried alive, his Catholic gravediggers, it is said, taking great pleasure in hearing him cry out to them as they tumbled the earth upon him, until they could hear him no more.'

She saw the tears fill his eyes, then spill over, the grievous scars of two hundred years. She reached to him. 'Stop, you don't have to go on, Stephen!'

'Oh, I do, Ellen, I must, if you can bear it,' he said, drying the black pools of his eyes.

She nodded. She couldn't really bear it, so sickening, so clear it was in her mind's eye. 'Oh my God, Stephen! Oh my God! It's, it's...' The horror of what he was telling put her beyond words. It couldn't be true, it just couldn't be. 'No one would ... Catholics ... we...' She struggled to come to terms with the enormity of it.

'It all happened as I have described, perhaps the telling through time ... exaggerated...' His voice trailed off, mitigating the crime of her creed. '...it is ever in my dreams. It speaks from my bones!'

She kept hold of his hand, her own shaking,

almost recoiling from touching the teller of such atrocities.

'One McCoist out of all survived,' he continued, almost inaudibly. 'He fled south and west – to Joyce country – your land. Stuart McCoist became Stephen Joyce. The people, at first suspicious of the stranger, eventually accepted him. He married a local girl, a Catholic. They lived more or less untroubled and had four children. Two hundred years later ... I am here.'

'*Madame, elle voudrait encore du champagne?*' The waiter, armed with a white cloth, held the bottle at the ready.

She declined; the *cru* of Crusaders, blessed by Benedictine monks, was far from her troubled mind.

Later, in her room, unable to sleep, she lay on the knotted *macramé* bedspread. Above her beams of mighty cedar trees, their barks still preserved, darkened the ceiling.

She had excused herself, but shaken and unsteady as she was, he had escorted her to the room, apologetic for ruining the evening. Now, no matter how she tried, she could not expunge from her mind the image of Annie McCoist, in that most sacred of moments ... and the young man who had cut collops of flesh from her buttocks, desecrating her.

Outside her window, dominating the skyline, the twin towers of Notre Dame stood, their giant bells tolling the passing day. *Le Gros Bourdon*, the largest, dedicated to the Virgin Mary and St Jean-Baptiste, seemed to shake the very timbers above her. The second largest, inscribed to Queen Victoria, boomed in reply. She tried to pray, to be in communion with the Catholics of Montréal, to be rid of Annie McCoist. But the sound of the bells only clogged up her head. She imagined the cedar beam directly above her would crack with the sound, blood spill out of its wound, giving life to the shapes on its crinkled bark. Jean-Baptiste, sword in hand, Salome screaming and the Queens of Heaven and Earth, Virgin and Victoria, dancing to the flutes and drums, on the bridge at Portadown. She would drown in the sound of it all, before the bleeding cedars finally fell, crushing her.

He rapped on the door the following morning. She was still asleep atop the bedspread. He was perturbed at her disarray. Would he summon a doctor, fetch some resuscitation salts from the apothecary? She assured him she would be altogether fine, she would rest, take the air once she had restored herself. The Frontignacs could wait until the following day.

She was touched by his concern for her, agreeing to dine with him again, on his insistence that he be given the 'opportunity for reparation'; that it would be a 'lighter occasion'. She wondered though about his meetings, thinking them more clandestine than the open address he had given in Boston, and at how he was again free to dine with her.

In the afternoon, she walked first to Bon Secours Market with its silvery dome. It reminded her of Quincy Market and Faneuil Hall.

Her spirits lifted, she visited Notre Dame. The Basilica, with its neo-gothic twin towers, was the largest structure in Montréal. It was built, she learned from a cloying sacristan, under the architect James O'Donnell, an Irish Protestant from New York, who converted to Catholicism during the course of its construction. 'He died of a broken heart, unhappy at how his dream was disfigured.' The sacristan pointed to the vulgarly-spotted columns, the interior décor, then led her to the right of the altar. 'The architect lies buried at the foot of this first pillar.' She thought how appropriate and on the way out left a donation, while the sacristan watched her, satisfied.

Protestants building Catholic churches, Stephen part-Scots, part-Irish, part-Planter, part-patriot. Nothing was as clear as she had once imagined it to be, wanted it to be. It was easier when things were clear, had dividing lines.

And the bells pealed while she wandered among the slender forms of the Lombardy poplars to the rear of the Basilica. 'It was a mistake to cast them in England,' the sacristan had confided to her, earlier, in his broken English. '*Le Gros Bourdon* – the Great One – taller than a man, developed a crack. It was a sign. Had to be recast.' He shook his head. 'They should have known.'

She sauntered along, following the curve of the buildings which, in turn, followed the curves of the meandering streets. Tin rooftops, silvered against the sky, bespoke the ice-cold winters when wood in large quantities would be burned to drive back that shivering season. Fires,

Montréalers had learned to their cost, could shoot sparks to roofs made of the same timber which gave them warmth, destroying their town. It was a hard lesson. Now it was tin instead of timber. Other roofs – Victorian mansard – sloped down on every side to meet her. An opening on du Port Street sequestered between large rectangular blocks of dressed limestone, drew her to its ancient iron-studded door. She wondered who or what it was the door wanted to keep out, or perhaps even keep in?

And windows, Victorian, Venetian, and the small circular *oeil-de-boeuf* – an eye to the world. Other windows held iron pins to secure sheet-iron shutters, Montréalers believing 'the night air to be unhealthy'. She had never seen such windows, more still nestling beneath crow-beaked corbel stones, which jutted into the streets, guiding her way, like the hands of the eyes of Montréal.

She must have walked for miles, leaving the windows behind, when she came to Château des Messieurs on the western slopes of Mount Royal. The Château was set in rolling meadowlands with the wooded slant of the mountain forming an idyllic backdrop. It was the jewel of her afternoon. Within the vineyards and orchards of the former mission house of the Gentlemen of St Sulpice, she could see its cassocked inhabitants. Some walked singly, breviary in hand, at prayer. Others in silence, stood black-statued in the secluded corners of the ornamental gardens. Château des Messieurs – the 'priests' farm'. She approached, seeking entrance, more to imbibe the spirit of solace the place offered than the

157

water she asked for.

The *madame* was welcome in the Lord's name. The château was, she discovered, now a retreat house and 'Le Seigneur Jesus had directed her footsteps here to pray – to confess', the monk who admitted her explained. After her experience of the previous evening, she felt she had indeed been led here. In the tiny chapel of Our Lady of the Snows, she confessed to sinning against what Jesus had signified to be the greatest of His Commandments – 'Love thy neighbour as thyself' – she had not shown charity of thought to Stephen Joyce, a troubled man.

She confessed her strange swooning images being unsure for this aberration which of the Commandments she had trespassed against. The Monsieur, in absolving her, reminded her of the dangers of 'bewitching beverages' and 'the occasion of sin the solitary company of unwedded persons of the opposite gender might present'. Having made her penance, 'one decade of the most holy rosary, to petition Our Lady of the Snows for a guiding hand', she remained a while in the silence of the chapel.

She had never before heard of Our Lady of the Snows, but then the mother of God had so many names – 'Our Lady of Good Hope', 'Our Lady of Sorrows', 'Star of the Sea'. Wherever she was needed, she was named for. It was a consoling thought. The White Virgin, she imagined, pure as the snow from which she appeared, brought safe passage to *voyageurs* and *coureurs de bois*, cut off from the world in the far trapping-grounds of Canada.

And she thought of Stephen Joyce. She had been wrong to judge him so harshly and had only begun to relent in her opinion when driven to do so by his terrible story. That was not true charity – when there had to be a reason. She resolved to be more tolerant. Her mind went ahead of her. The rapparees, the Catholics who had committed such atrocities, to which 'Our Lady' did they pray? Everybody – even butchers – prayed to some God, some Our Lady.

She blessed herself, sorry to be leaving this haven, but anxious lest she be late again for him.

20

She arrived as he did. He was fully himself, as of old, she thought – almost. His concern for 'how she had been today' was genuine, lacked that air of peremptory enquiry she had previously detected. Oh, she should stop this ... this tick-tacking at every nuance of speech and manner. Resolved 'that it be a more joyous occasion', he called again for the Comte de Champagne, clinked glasses with her. She smiled.

'What is it?' he asked.

She didn't tell him. But somehow out of the ring of the crystal, the voice of the mild-mannered Monsieur repeated itself. His admonishment concerning the twin perils of alcohol and 'single company' framed in mid-air between them.

'I'm damned, doubly damned,' was all she would say.

He listened with rapt attention as she relived her day, images of the city spilling out of her, ribboned with colour and sound and windows.

'You are in love, Ellen – with Montréal,' he laughed.

And she was, with this swirling, spinning top of a city. But she wanted to hear more of him. His story of the previous night had been stopped short by her own revulsion at it.

'Are you sure?' he asked.

'Yes!' she said, confident of her new state of mind.

So he told her of how, over the generations, his family had become 'more Irish than the Irish themselves'. How he had seen the injustices visited on the people and how, at Trinity College in Dublin, he and others of the 'landed class' had resolved to do something about it. 'Love of one's country is not in the exclusive grasp of the Catholic population,' he reminded her.

Her own view had always been that there were two Irelands, Protestant and Catholic. Rich and poor. That was the divide.

So a band of them, poets, Protestants, and Trinity nationalists, had come together and joined with O'Connell, the Catholic Emancipator. They split with him again when the 'great man' sold out to passivism and nepotism, they the Young Irelanders, prepared to use force if necessary to sunder the Union with England. The French, whom they looked to as allies, had betrayed them. In a last-ditch effort in the

Tipperary foothills, their damp squib of a revolution at the Widow McCormack's house had gone awry and been hastily extinguished.

'The Crown, as ever, was cleverer than we were…' he went on. 'Juries were packed, convictions gained. But rather than hoisting us on a scaffold, the British banished us, knowing that nothing moves the Irish as much as an executed martyr.'

'You were spared because you were "gentlemen",' she said plainly. 'Had you been peasants you would have been hanged.' She had followed reports of the uprising, subsequent trials and deportations, on an almost weekly basis in the *Pilot*. 'And had you been truly of the masses then the revolution might have succeeded. You failed because you were "gentlemen" – a different class and creed. The people would not follow you,' she stated, in as non-accusatory a fashion as she could muster.

'Freedom is not a finite moment in time,' he answered her. 'The moment we seized was but one in a long march of moments, each with its own momentum until, together, they become an unstoppable army. There will be a time for freedom, of that I am sure.'

'But it is not now,' she cut in, 'not here. Why waste your life on such dreams?'

He leaned towards her. 'Without dreams, Ellen, we have nothing – we are nothing!' he said, the light of dreams smouldering in his eyes.

'No, Stephen, you are wrong; dreams are for those who have nothing but dreams,' she countered.

'What is your dream, Ellen Rua?'

She ignored the slip with her name. 'My dream is no dream at all!' she answered. 'It is to live in the world. To do, to see. To make do. To put some order on the everyday things of life.'

'While we do not dream – and love – we are dead,' he said, full with the passion of his belief.

'That's only poet's talk, imaginings, it is not how the people live – or die,' she countered, adding the old saying, 'When hunger comes in the window, love goes out the door – and dreams too!'

He considered this a moment, a quixotic curve on his lips. 'What about dance and song, are we to be dead to them also?'

'They have their place,' she answered, carefully choosing her words, 'but it should be a little place, to the side of living, not at the centre. Like dreams, they too are only shallow conceits – distractions.' She knew her reply would not please him.

'Ellen,' he said, 'it is strange to hear you talk like this, like one of Boston's merchant classes, concerned only with squirrelling away...'

'Squirrelling away, as you call it,' she interrupted, 'providence for the future, is not to be sneezed at. It is a trait many of our own countrymen would do well to foster.'

'So we should trade our slavery to a famined soil for slavery to the Yankee dollar, swap one form of bondage for another?'

'*Fonds d'artichaut, madame?*' the waiter interrupted. She looked at her companion, wondering what the question was.

'Artichoke hearts,' he said, the intensity leaving his voice.

As the waiter retreated, she continued the argument.

'The reality is that it is the women, the "Bridgets", not the dreamers, who have "squirrelled away" and sent home a million Yankee dollars, "biddy-money" to free their families from the slavery of the soil. Yes, the "Bridgets" are slaves, but slaves by choice–'

'But yet slaves,' he interrupted.

'Slaves?' she echoed, her voice rising. 'The "Bridgets" are the real heroes, the revolutionaries. By doing, not dreaming, they are changing the way Ireland at home and Ireland in America will for ever be.'

'Why are you so engaged with this?' he asked. 'Is it because you, Ellen, are neither "Bridget" nor dreamer?'

He was right. She had sought to deny her previous life, her wild imaginings, her delight in the elemental. How she would dance above the ground – the wind and the rain spinning her – the dark waters of the Mask spitting and seething, for her daring to dance on its shores. She had even shut out the whispered mysteries of her father's voice.

She kept her gaze on the stream of bubbled air surfacing from some invisible space at the bottom of her glass. She was the *cuvée* – the blend – of all things past, outwardly the calm surface, inside her, though, like *mousselet* rising.

'I changed my name,' she said, as if that answered anything. He had waited, watching her

163

while she went through it all.

'Nothing changes the way we are, Ellen. Nothing!'

She looked at him, leaning forward towards her, no harshness in what he was saying. Irritated by his perceptiveness, she lifted the glass, laughed and inclined it towards him. 'To the way we were and the way we will be,' she toasted, feeling the liquid dance on her tongue.

When the violinist approached, she didn't understand a word he said, except that it was French. She thought she caught the word *'musique'*. He had flashing eyes and a drooping moustache which undulated up and down as he spoke in his rapid-fire French. Underneath was revealed a near-perfect row of ivory-coloured teeth. All was set off by a colourful patriot's *tuque*, atop black, shoulder-length locks.

Stephen came to her rescue. 'What he is saying is, "Would *madame* like to choose a piece of music to dance – to celebrate the happy occasion?"' He nodded towards the champagne. 'He thinks we are newly married!' Stephen laughed.

Ellen was unsure whether to believe him; he wasn't much given to humour. But before she could say anything, he had spoken to the musician.

'Madame voudrait une valse irlandaise?'

'Non monsieur, non!' The musician shook his head, looking at Ellen, but talking to the *'monsieur'*. *'Une valse, oui! Mais une valse irlandaise – non!'* He now directed both look and speech at her, his arms outstretched, as if she

164

should understand everything. *'Pour vous, madame, ça doit être une valse ou un quadrille québécois – "La Valse du Coeur Glacé".'*

Ellen waited for an explanation from Stephen; the musician obviously seeking some direction from her, arms raised again in mild exasperation.

'He would like to play for *madame* a piece of music from Québec – "The Waltz of the Frozen Heart",' Stephen explained.

She looked from one to the other of the two men. '"The Waltz of the Frozen Heart",' she repeated, 'for me?' She saw the funny side of it and started to laugh. 'Tell him,' she directed her French-speaking companion, 'that *madame* wishes him to play his damn Québécois waltz then.'

Whatever way her wishes were translated, it seemed to please the violinist, who removed his stockinged cap, curtsied in front of her, and extended his bow towards an open area of floor behind him. Before she fully comprehended what was happening the back of her chair was being held with Stephen saying to her, *'Madame ... la valse.'*

'The Waltz of the Frozen Heart' was exquisitely beautiful. She was conscious of the other people who remained in the room watching them, thinking they were honeymooners perhaps. Mostly, she was conscious of the nearness of her dancing partner. Tall and sinuous, his arm a guiding pressure on the small of her back, he moved easily, if with more formality than she was used to. The strict Protestant upbringing, she thought. Going into a turn, he pressed the heel of

165

his hand into her spine, the wheel of the dance inadvertently pulling her closer to him, causing her cheeks to gain colour. She hadn't danced since her wedding-day, but how quickly it all came back, the body needing only the touch of the opening notes to awaken its dormant rhythms. She had known nothing of the music of Québec – its Acadian melodies a *pot-pourri* of mellifluences which wended and wefted intricately, until you were not outside listening, but intertwined within. The waltz, looser in three-four time than its Irish equivalent, was neither as predictable. The melody, travelling one path, would twist off, serpent-like, into some less certain by-way of runs and slides. Clipped beats, missed beats, major to minor – and all the way back again. It took her breath away.

As she turned she glimpsed the fiddler watching them through half-closed eyes, the moustache drooped low, almost touching the strings, locked with them in this *ménage-à-trois*. 'The Frozen Heart', she imagined to be locked in the icelands of the Far North, red, unbeating. Stilled in the white bosom of the deepening snow, awaiting the release spring would bring.

Or was the tune the voice of the human heart? Unloved, unused, frosted over by pain or timidity? A heart suspended, awaiting the release only true love could bring. 'Listen to the music!' she said to herself, she thought. But as if in response, the man pulled her closer, until his sunken cheeks brushed her hair. And the notes wrapped around them like the skin of silk, lightly but surely, binding them into the dance. Then she felt the great wound within the music. It was a heart betrayed, she was sure of it now, for ever frozen. Afraid to be freed, safe where it was within its own wastelands.

'It is the same cry as the cries of the souls in Hell...' she whispered to him. '...for ever denied the love of God.'

It frightened her and she told him she was retiring.

21

She didn't see him the next morning.

Jean-Baptiste Frontignac, he of the flourished pen, and one of the *fils* of Frontignac Père et Fils, expressed great pleasure at seeing her. He conducted her on an extensive tour of their cellars, introducing her to some clarets from the higher terrains of Bordeaux, of which she was hitherto unaware. While expressing himself pleased with the degree of business *'madame* and Boston' had brought to the family concern, the foppishly dressed younger Frontignac wondered, ever so politely, if Boston could provide 'further possibilities'.

By way of reply, she presented him with her latest set of orders, showing a substantial increase. In return, after private consultation with Frontignac Père, Frontignac Fils agreed a modest discount. Further, they would convey goods to her by the railroad from now onwards, ensuring better continuity of supply. Her meeting at Frontignacs, having been successful, she was happy at the prospect of returning home to Boston.

Any separation from her children and Lavelle was not to be desired. Besides, this journey had been unsettling. The coincidence of everything. This man from her past on the train. The hotel ... the dance ... the beautifully wounded music of 'The Waltz of the Frozen Heart'. She still could not fathom her reaction to it all. It was like when, in the past, she had sung particular songs, her soul had seemed to leave her body, be at a removed vantage – hearing and seeing herself. This was something the same. While in one body, she was there in the dance, it was as if also she inhabited the space beside the violinist watching herself and the man perfectly cadenced in rarefied motion. Almost, as if she were the tune itself – it pulsing out through her in quavers and semi-quavers from wherever it lay, in the ice-mountains of the singing Arctic. It was danger-ous to have one's emotions disordered by music. She trembled at the remembrance.

The journey homewards was uneventful, and the tall welcoming spires of Boston seemed another world from the one in which her thoughts had recently dwelled.

They had all been glad to have her back, excitement running high, wanting to hear all the news of her journey.

Later, she had been reassured by Lavelle's lovemaking and her own response to it, and while she told him about the encounter with Stephen Joyce on the train, she did not tell him of the later events. Later, she wondered about this, while Lavelle slept, feeling some guilt at her omission. A guilt undeserved by those same events, she told herself, before finally turning to sleep.

22

She invited Peabody to dine with them at Christmas. Jacob had no family here in Boston that she knew of and she often sensed in him a feeling of loneliness. He himself was partly to blame, inclined as he was towards irascibility and pepperiness. His customers, she imagined, liked this quirkiness of character but only when engaged in purely commercial transactions. Peabody added to the general spice that was Quincy Market. But, on a level of social intercourse, his idiosyncratic character might be the ruination of an otherwise well-toned Boston evening.

Recently Jacob had been full of the fact that 'Boston was getting true religion at last' with the news that 'the city's first synagogue, only the second in all of Massachusetts, will open here by next March'.

'Pray, Ellen, that it will not be on the seventeenth of that month, else we will have to call it St Patrick's!' he had mocked. She knew he was not part of the regular Jewish community; but he

169

had hinted to her on more than one occasion about 'declaring' himself.

Lavelle, she knew, was not all that keen on Peabody joining them. She, on the other hand, liked his querulousness and the way he half-said a thing, letting it hang there. He was such a relief from the ordinariness and orderliness of much of her daily life in Boston nowadays. Jacob, for his part, had seemed mightily pleased by her invitation, touched even.

A week before Christmas, Lavelle asked if 'we have room for another at table?' When she enquired who it might be: 'It is our friend, Mr Joyce.'

'Thank God we have invited Peabody!' she said, recovering herself. 'There will, at least, be somebody for me to converse with on a topic other than the "Great Irish Revolution".'

'He is a friend, Ellen, a compatriot,' Lavelle pointed out. 'Like your Peabody, he is adrift in Boston. It is the least hospitality we can offer.'

She was surprised at how she had responded. It was a presentiment; Peabody and the man from Montreal at the same table. She didn't like the idea.

She loved Christmas, the stillness brought on by the snow; the seasonal excitement; the bells and baubles; new clothes for the children; the sense of anticipation at the coming of the Saviour – all of it. The preparations, which added to the extra work in ensuring the many-layered cellars of Boston were well stocked with 'Christmas cheer', did nothing to daunt her spirits.

Lavelle, however, was agitated. 'They've gone

and elected Seaver as Mayor!' he rushed in to tell her. 'You know what that means?'

She knew, but did not see how it would unduly affect them.

'Benjamin Seaver is a "Know-Nothing", Ellen.' Lavelle stressed the words.

'I know!'

'You know! Eighty thousand Irish Catholics in Boston and we elect an anti-Catholic, anti-Irish Mayor. We'll have convent-burning and "Pope's Nights" all over again,' Lavelle protested.

'If we stick to minding our own business, it won't affect us one bit,' she chided him. 'We're not Irish any more,' she continued, 'we're Americans and we have a Constitution to protect us, Know-Nothing Mayor or not!'

'Sometimes I cannot fathom you at all,' he said. 'Should we not be concerned, if not for ourselves, then at least for the thousands pouring in here from Ireland?' he challenged. 'And for the thousands already here trying to set a foot on the ladder of the American dream, to be shaken off again like rats by the Know-Nothings?'

'The Irish have their own to look after them – the Church,' she said, wishing the conversation to be over.

'Ellen, *we* are their own. We should reach down, pull them up that ladder.'

He walked around the room at his wit's end trying to get her to understand.

'Lavelle!' she said, annoyed at him now, always having these arguments when she was up to her eyes. 'It's fine for you men with your mist-covered dreams, wanting to change the world with your meetings and secret organizations. That's all fine ... but...'

'But what, Ellen?'

'We are not so secure here in America as you might think. The children have still to be schooled. You would risk all that for someone else's quarrel?' she charged him.

'No, Ellen! You know I wouldn't, but it isn't someone else's quarrel. It's ours! We can't live our lives as if we were separate from it all. I'm sorry for rising you but it bothers me.'

She embraced him. 'Forget about it now – for the Christmas.'

Lavelle was so passionate about issues; always was. Like she used to be, she supposed.

At Christmas, when Stephen Joyce arrived he kissed her hand. This time it was 'Mrs Lavelle'. She smiled to herself. In Montréal he had called her 'Mrs O'Malley', before that, 'Ellen Rua'. Now it was 'Mrs Lavelle'. Three names, three different sides to her; like the Holy Trinity.

When Peabody arrived he was in high spirits, announcing that he was 'here to celebrate the company, but not the Feast'. She hoped Jacob wasn't going to be difficult. She was on tenter-hooks enough as it was. Peabody had brought some gaily-wrapped gifts for each of the children, which he refused leave to them to open 'until we have dined'.

However, her other guest, on presenting her with a rather heavy box 'in gratitude for the hospitality of mine hosts', insisted she open it there and then, hoping 'its contents would add to

172

the gaiety of the evening'.

The contents revealed themselves to be champagne – the same they had shared in Montréal. She felt the colour drain from her cheeks, then return again, making her hot and clammy. What was he doing, seeking to unnerve her in her own house? Damn him, she thought.

'I know that bringing champagne to this household is akin to bringing ice to the icefields,' she heard him say, as if trying to lessen his effrontery.

It seemed an age before anyone else said anything and she wondered if Lavelle had noticed her state. Maybe she should have told him. But what then if Stephen had done as he had just now done, how would Lavelle have regarded that? He had taken the risk that she had not told Lavelle. He had known. She was troubled at his presumption that she had something to hide. Later, while the men and Patrick remained in conversation and she, Mary and Louisa prepared the meal, she tried to recall all of the events in Montréal. Everything was clear, their conversation, the setting of the table, the champagne, the violinist. How, from being merely a tune for her pleasure, it had turned into dancing with him. Then, everything had become a swirl of music and movement set against the slow motion of his voice. A voice, like another instrument, between the sounds, saying things to her. Things indefinite that she now couldn't remember. Peabody came up behind her, startling her.

'Don't do that, Jacob!' she said, fraught that he had caught her unawares.

'I just came to help – the Revolutionaries are in full swing!' He nodded towards the dining-room. Annoyed, she wiped her hands and cast aside the cloth she held. 'You are not yourself, Ellen,' Peabody began, when Mary and Louisa had left for a moment. 'Haven't been for a long time – but this evening–'

She had no time for this now and brushed past him for a ladling spoon. 'Mary, can you help me with this?' she called into the other room.

'Your guest ... you knew him before?' Peabody was intent on aggravating her. She never acknowledged his question. 'Interesting fellow – not really one of you though, is he?' he persisted.

She continued to bustle around Peabody ignoring his prattle. God, it didn't take him long. 'Here, Jacob, make yourself useful, carry this in for me!' she ordered, handing the sauce-boat full with thick brown gravy into his flapping hands. 'Be careful, it could scald you!' she said, half-wishing it would.

When she re-entered the room, she noted that the conversation to which Patrick had enthusiastically attached himself broke off.

Ellen was seated between Lavelle and Stephen with Jacob across from her. Then beside Jacob, Patrick, with Mary and Louisa squeezing in at the end corners of the table. She should have gone ahead and purchased a new dining-table rather than sticking to her surprise plan about the pianoforte. Mrs Brophy had such an instrument, and had informed her that 'both your girls show great interest in the pianoforte when they come to visit'. So Ellen had started them with lessons on Tuesdays. When Miss Wigglesworth, their tutor, reported that 'the progress of both would be much accelerated with regular practice', she had decided there and then to start putting by. It would take a while, but then Harriet Brophy had been in Boston long ahead of them and had only in recent years acquired a pianoforte. She had gone once to Miss Wigglesworth's to hear Mary and Louisa play and to be sure both showed great promise. Mary deft and precise, Louisa more awkward of style but more ready to explore her own expression of a piece. She smiled down at them, her two *angelitos*. They could make do with the table for now, be squashed at the end of it for one day. They would have their piano, soon.

'To have Jew, Protestant and Catholic at the same table must be an unusual combination for many, if not all of Boston's homes this Christmas,' Peabody launched out.

'It will, Mr Peabody, be the common way before the century is out,' Stephen Joyce replied, adding, 'and German and black and whatever other combination one can dream up!'

Despite her fears Stephen made no reference directly or indirectly to their meeting in Montréal. Nevertheless, she was acutely aware of his presence so close to her at the table. She was glad when, having eaten, the children had been excused. It provided more space, more distance between her and the man. A few times she felt Peabody's eyes on her. But then, even when she was in his company alone, he was for ever inclined to try and dissect her thoughts.

The conversation ranged far and wide, eventually arriving at the continuing controversy over slavery and the freeing of fugitive slaves by Abolitionist mobs.

'Where will it all lead to?' Peabody posited. 'What with relations between the cotton Whigs of the Northern States and the slave-holders of the Southern States continuing to deteriorate. That's the nub of it – commerce, nothing to do with the rights of man.'

'If the black man in the South is liberated then they will swarm like locusts over cities of the North which espoused their cause, like Boston,' Lavelle answered. 'They will flood the mills and factories and tunnels – working for nothing,' he continued. 'The Irish will suffer. They will be the new slaves chained to unsupportable wages. The Irish will be the new blacks.'

Ellen entered the conversation. 'No, Lavelle,' she countered, 'it is an issue greater than an economic principle. All men and women, black and white, should be free. It is an absolute principle, it speaks to the spiritual not the corporal, the soul as much as the body.'

'Spoken like a true Bloomerist, Ellen!' Peabody applauded.

'I agree with Mrs Lavelle that freedom is an absolute principle. Whether one wants it or not, one should get it!' Stephen added.

'If there were to be war between North and South, to which side would you two gentlemen be disposed?' Peabody inserted, changing the whole generality of the conversation.

'I would declare for freedom, and the North,' Stephen said out clearly, as she knew he would.

'And you, Mr Lavelle?' Peabody asked.

'I would be with the South,' Lavelle answered, 'until our own people have risen out of their poverty. They have suffered far longer than the slaves of Alabama, who enjoy a better existence, are better fed and better housed than the free peasants of Connacht.'

'You see – that is how it will be...' Peabody seemed pleased. 'Friend against friend, father against son, brother against brother. Irishman against Irishman. Houses and countries divided against each other in America's cause. Maybe even Jew against Jew, though we are thin on the ground below the Mason-Dixon line,' he joked. 'And you Ellen, seated as you are between North and South. How do you say?'

'I say it will not come to war – that this is only the talk of foolish men,' she answered.

'Then let us talk of women,' Peabody rejoined, relishing his role as mischief-maker.

'And what would you know of women, Jacob, except foolish women?' She couldn't let the chance pass.

The two other men laughed, and Peabody himself smiled, good-humouredly conceding her remark. 'Indeed, Mrs Lavelle, but leaving personal experience aside, I have heard it often said that it is the women of Boston who are effecting most change on the city, not the men.'

'How so, Mr Peabody?' Lavelle asked.

'Firstly, take the mill girls,' Peabody outlined, 'and the needlewomen – thousands upon thousands of them driving the petticoated engine of Massachusetts industry. Now that they have organized, they hold sway everywhere.'

'That is hardly revolutionary,' Lavelle intervened.

'Perhaps, but if the women were to withdraw labour Massachusetts would crumble,' Peabody argued. 'Secondly, beyond that, the Catholic "Bridgets" clean, feed and,' he stressed, *educate* half the children of Boston's elite. Think of that effect on the minds and disposition of the upcoming generation – tolerance, eradication of religious bigotry. For will the city fathers of tomorrow turn on the hands that nurtured them as children today?'

'You exaggerate the case.' This time it was Stephen.

'No, I do not!' Jacob was quick to his own defence. 'It is the women, the women of Ireland, who are building America, not you Irish patriots! The women build it by stealth, but build it they do, just as surely as do pick and shovel.'

Ellen was enjoying this. Lavelle and Stephen were not, she could see. 'Go on, Jacob,' she encouraged him, 'you're doing well!'

'Is it the women or the men who travel in greater numbers to our shores?' he asked her.

'The women,' she answered.

'So, you are superior in number,' Peabody continued, ignoring the two men. 'And here also you are single, rejecting the chains of matrimony, *choosing* when to marry, if at all. You have shaken off the old taboos, become free.'

Ellen was fascinated. Peabody would have been

as at home in the learning halls of Harvard as he was in the city's market stalls.

'So!' Professor Peabody concluded, putting out a hand to Lavelle and Stephen. 'While Irishmen in general are fractious, given to intoxicating liquor and wandering throughout America, Irishwomen stoke the industrial hearths of America, and the hearts and minds of its young.'

'But it has always been so, Mr Peabody,' it was Stephen, 'and yet the fair gender have so far failed to lead society forward, as men have.'

'Yes, yes, yes – but here in Boston the women talk to each other, that is the difference. Have you not seen the "Bridget Conventions" at the edge of the Common, meeting regularly, with their prams, to discuss all matters? Women are meeting everywhere in Boston. Am I not right in believing that Mrs Lavelle is a member of such a gathering?'

'Yes, Jacob, you know that I am.' She didn't like it when he turned it personal to make a point.

'The Daughters of the Commonwealth?' he asked.

'Yes,' she said, a little curtly.

'And what are your discussions centred upon?' he asked.

She thought for moment, running her mind over the various topics. 'Everything, I suppose – the future,' she answered for simplicity's sake, conscious of Stephen's presence, and their 'differences' at one such discussion.

'There, you see!' Peabody said triumphantly. 'Then each goes home and discusses the Bloomerist view of "the future", if not with hus-

179

band, then with sons and daughters who will shape "the future"!'

'It is a damned petticoat conspiracy, Jacob,' Lavelle said, in mock seriousness. 'Will it ever succeed?' he added.

Ellen was reminded of the 'petticoat whalers', those doughty women who followed their wayward husbands to sea. 'We did it on the whaling ships; better than any priest or parson, reformed those floating palaces of sin,' she said, half-seriously.

'Chastity – that's it, that's what gives women their power,' Peabody put in, 'Mrs Lavelle has cleverly brought the conversation to the central issue!'

'Chastity?' Lavelle and Stephen echoed together.

'Yes, chastity – it is the greatest of all the virtues,' Peabody lectured. Ellen was sorry she had given Jacob the opening. 'For if a woman is chaste,' he went on, 'then she is likewise strong in all other virtues. If, on the other hand, she has a weakness of virtue in this respect then she is blemished in all respects.' She watched him as he spoke, casting about the room like a pulpited preacher – Peabody the grocer, the professor; now Peabody the priest. 'Chastity is woman's greatest power – it entrusts the young and innocent to her. It brings her a moral elevation which allows her to admonish her husband, and it empowers her with the courage and fortitude to be a guiding light for the society in which she finds herself.'

'Well spoken, Mr Peabody. It is a subject dear to you?' Stephen framed a question.

180

'And you will know,' Peabody continued, ignoring him, 'that the daughters of Erin, the daughters of the "Virgin Isle" as it is referred to, are among the most noble of all women in this respect.' He inclined his head towards Ellen.

She did not like this turn in the conversation. She knew Peabody of old. He would try to reduce everything to the particular and the personal. But there was no stopping Jacob now.

'No matter how low their fortunes sink, through circumstance or illness, there is a line below which they themselves will not fall. They are hardly ever, if not never, to be found among the ranks of those bedaubed and bedizened women who until recently inhabited the third row of our theatres.'

This was not the conversation for a Christmas table. She was glad the children had been excluded from the company. She made to get up.

'Mrs Lavelle, I am almost complete,' Peabody pleaded. 'Apologies for my inconsiderateness.' She had no option but to wait until he was finished. 'Why is this?' he continued. 'Is it because they uphold the influences of the "Old Country" regarding the sacred duties of wife and mother, or because the darkness of the confessional is the ultimate deterrent?'

'Really, Peabody, you go—' It was Lavelle.

'No, Lavelle,' she interrupted, knowing what Peabody was at. 'These are questions which obviously tax Mr Peabody's mind. They are quite fundamental to society – fear or duty. If you ask me, Jacob, and I know you do, my answer is that it is neither fear nor duty. It is a sense of self – our

181

bodies are the temples of the soul,' she said, flintily, flashing him a smile.

'A good answer, Mrs Lavelle,' Stephen said. 'But I have one last thought on the subject, then perhaps we should let the matter rest.' She was glad of his intervention, wondering what this last thought would be. 'Is it humanly possible for passion and chastity to co-exist?' the poet-patriot posed to the table.

'Plato, my friend, Plato had the answer...!' Peabody jumped in, eager to keep the conversation going. He was in his element, Ellen thought. Unfortunately so.

'No, Mr Peabody, I think not,' Stephen, in turn, interrupted, in his definite way. She was pleased to see Jacob taken down a peg. 'The question is,' Stephen continued, 'not of the relationship *between* two people, whether platonic or otherwise, it is the more interesting one,' he paused, looking around at them, 'the one of the conflict which the co-existence of passion and chastity might cause *within* the person, and,' he finished with 'which, if either, of these two "virtues" would be the victor?'

She rose, calling for Mary and Louisa to help her clear the table. It was a curious note on which to conclude, she thought, Mr Joyce, surprisingly, having the last word over Jacob.

Later, when they bade their farewells, she was glad to see the back of both of them.

23

The doings of Christmas took her mind away from all other thoughts. But the new year of 1853 was scarcely ushered in when, like January snows, the old feelings of restlessness set in on her again. She didn't know what caused them to rise, only that of late they arose with more frequency. Nor did she have a remedy with which to assuage them. They just came and went of their own accord, filling her with a feeling of helplessness at her failure to control them. The restlessness was temporarily broken only by the arrival, the following month, of the upright pianoforte with three brass pedals. No one she knew of in Ireland had one. The house rang with its music, Mary and Louisa continuously jostling for position on the brocaded stool which accompanied its arrival. It was a joy to her – their animation, their love of the instrument.

The infection of their enthusiasm, the fumbled pieces finally falling into perfection, caught up not just the practising duo but the whole household. Lavelle took a keen interest in their playing, once or twice taking down his dusty fiddle and rosining his bow, trying to cross his jigs and reels with Bach's baroque, until they all threw up their hands in despair and laughed.

Patrick, too, would linger and listen, wondering aloud when his sisters were going to learn 'some

Irish airs'. But after a while Ellen found that even the uplifting charms of Bach or Handel seemed only to occupy her mind for the duration of the piece. Indeed, after a while, far from staying the growing restlessness within her, the music seemed only to encourage it to feed upon itself. The constant practising by Mary and Louisa jangled on her nerves, the melodies resonating throughout the house mocking her own internal dissonance. Then she would flee from the house, so as not to be cross with them, walk up and down the Long Path or sit under the gnarled boughs of the Great Elm, seeking answers. She had no reason, she told herself, to be as she was – no 'why'. She was assiduous at church-going, regular to the confessional. Once, she broached the topic with her confessor.

'It is the soul pining for God, yet turmoiled by the Devil. Attend regularly the sacraments. Fulfil all your wifely duties,' he advised.

And she did – fastidious in all things, delighting in some.

The rosary beads, which from habit she always carried, she now used more frequently, fingering them for solace, silently sliding over the Hail Marys and the Glory Be's. Then at Mass, at that most holy of moments, the Consecration, while all others bowed their heads, she would watch over the edge of her arms as the priest held aloft the chalice. As the sacred mystery of transubstantiation was enacted and the wine became the Blood of Christ, she would join herself with His ultimate sacrifice. 'This is my Blood ... offered up for you.'

'Acceptance, or lack of it, in your case,' Peabody advised, was her problem.

She argued with him. 'But Jacob, how could that be? In every role I carry out all that I should; I am happy here. Boston has been our saviour after what we once suffered–'

'Ah!' he cut in. 'Suffering. We all seek to flee it. Yet, when we leave it behind we wonder what is missing from our lives. We are born to suffer, Ellen, not be free of it,' the merchant philosophized.

'I know that, Jacob, but it is as if a malaise is upon me. Why, I don't know, but the lifting of which I deeply desire.'

Peabody gave one of his wicked little laughs. 'Is it the sallow man at your Christmas table?' he taunted.

'Of course not, Jacob!' she said, annoyed at him. 'What nonsense to come up with when I am seriously seeking your counsel.'

He always did this – some personal effrontery, some searching probe.

'I am sorry,' he quickly apologized, 'I am merely exploring all avenues. We men do not have the nose for such things as the gentler sex does. I am afraid I am of no help to you. You must be your own salvation,' Peabody said, washing his hands of her problem.

And so she determined to be. It had been a mistake to instigate the discussion with Peabody. Between his poets, his philosophers and his insufferable games of entrapment, he was too clever by far. She needed someone to talk to who understood this *mí-ádh* – this malaise – that was on her. Maybe it was a woman's thing. Would it be a topic for discussion by the Daughters of the Commonwealth, she wondered? One topic they had discussed was 'Should Women Learn the Alphabet?', and it had opened up into a lively two hours debate on learning and intellectual thought. Something like that maybe, perhaps 'Should Women Have Feelings?'. Or even more specific, 'The Restless Spirit – a Woman's Malaise?'. But how could she bring it up? What if none of the others had experienced what she was experiencing? She would be exposed, look foolish, selfish in her own preoccupations, have Mrs Brophy confiding in her on the way home that her feelings were 'nothing more than an attack of the vapours'!

She could almost talk to Lavelle about it. He would be concerned, listen to her. But then, by even raising it, would she be betraying a dis-loyalty to him? Perhaps his mind, like Peabody's, would jump to the most unlikely of conclusions? No, she would not risk causing any doubt to rise in him. She loved him too dearly for that.

And even if she did raise it with Lavelle, she still could not tell him about Montréal – the dance. Part honesty was worse than no honesty, for under the guise of revealing a thing it strove to conceal its core. But by not telling him was she acknowledging some untowardness on her own part? Some slight betrayal? Yet, if she did tell him, now, would it not also signal that she had strayed, however briefly, from wifely propriety? That the truth might be disguised by distance of time. She

186

decided she couldn't risk talking to Lavelle, or it would all come out.

In desperation, she tried to summon up the *Máistir*. He would understand, he always had, about the heart's yearnings. He never listened to her with the ear only, but with the ebb and flow of the spirit, until whatever her worry was washed between them, tidal, unspoken. But she could not get a clear image of her father. Even that was failing her now. She sat under the Great Elm, fighting to hold back the tears, turning her head back over her shoulder, so that the 'Bridgets' wheeling their prams would not see her and talk about her, when they gaggled together with news of the 'doings' on the Hill. In a while they would disperse again with their blue-blooded charges, disappearing behind the purple-paned windows of Chestnut Street.

'An oversight,' Peabody had jested, when first she had asked him about those windows, 'resulting from an excess of manganese during their manufacture in the real capital of Beacon Hill – London.' The residents apparently considered them 'distinguishing', leading Peabody to further scorn. 'The kernel of the problem being not so much an excess of manganese as an excess of vulgarity!'

Ellen herself liked the purple glass. The way the springtime light glanced against the world less ordinary hidden behind the purple divide, then bounced back again, multi-spectrumed, to light up the more ordinary outside world. She had to find her own purple divide, one where her inside world did not interfere with her outside world –

the children, Lavelle, her day-to-day functioning. She should have no need of trying to draw up old comforts like the *Máistir*, then worrying why they would not come when bidden. Life had to be lived – to be inhabited. It wasn't too long a time since she had spared out potatoes, rationing them like indulgences, an extra one for Michael, one fewer for herself. Then, cutting out the purpling, rotting pieces, swaddling them in straw, mollycoddling them like new-born babes, because all that was between themselves and the grave were those miserly few lumpers. She had much to be thankful for now. So much.

'Lord, remember the dead,' she prayed. 'And thank God for the living!'

She stirred herself, headed homewards. That would be an end to it now. She would talk about it no more, to Lavelle, confessor, Peabody, nobody. This peering into herself would have to stop. In the run-up to Easter, Lent had to be faced. A solid forty days and forty nights to eliminate these panderings into which she had allowed herself to slip.

On Ash Wednesday as she shrouded over the piano with Mary and Louisa, Ellen was in good spirits. The piano would remain covered until Easter Sunday. Then, like Christ from the tomb, it would be resurrected, unshrouded, sing again its song while the sun danced. Now, it was right to silence it. Like a monk in a monastery the piano stood, robed with the brown covering cloth she had stitched together, its arched legs already covered with sackcloth, in turn tied with string ribbonlets. This had been at Mrs Brophy's insistence, and was a custom of Victorian England imported into Boston, 'lest the lewd curvature of the supports give rise to scandal', her neighbour had told her.

Ellen was unsure who it was Mrs Brophy thought the shape of the legs would scandalize. But, nevertheless, she agreed, wondering, at the same time to Mrs Brophy, why they 'were so shaped by the wood-carvers in the first instance?'.

'Lutherans!' Goodwife Brophy whispered back through the little aperture between her lips, tucking her chin chicken-like into her neck. There would be no more about it, or the satanic motivations which drove 'Lutheran' wood-carvers.

Lent, as Ellen had hoped, provided some relief from the lack of ease with herself. It was a time of 'spiritual mortifications', Bishop John had preached, 'a time of fasting, abstinence, and penance – a time for the recollected life'.

When, on Ash Wednesday, she had knelt and the priest thumbed the sign of the cross on her forehead with ashes – 'Dust thou art and to dust thou shalt return', a sprinkling of ash had fallen on her nose. She had reached to brush it away, then withdrawn her hand. If she accepted, truly accepted what her Bishop was saying, a speck of ash on her nose didn't matter. Wouldn't her nose, her face, all of her one day, be dust? And maybe soon enough too? That moment had seemed to her to be a turning point, a symbol of her determination to succeed.

Daily, with rising hope, she travelled the Way of

the Cross, shuffling around in silence, bending her knee at each Station. At the Twelfth, 'Jesus dies on the Cross', she would kneel, united in grief with Mary the Mother of God, and Mary Magdalen. The latter, a sinner of low virtue, had washed the feet of Jesus, dried them with her long hair and then stood watch with His mother. The adulteress had wept as those same feet were nailed into the wood of crucifixion. Ellen was much drawn to Mary Magdalen and how the fallen woman had ultimately uprisen herself on the road to redemption.

Each day around her, other shawled and bonneted figures rose and fell in genuflection, redeeming themselves with words, 'O, my Jesus, forgive us our sins ... save us from the fires of Hell ... lead all souls to Heaven...'

Each of them, like herself, had held a hand to the hammer, hammer to the nail. Every day she knelt, imagining her own sin, whatever it was – ingratitude, idleness of mind – a thorn, flying from her soul to pierce the forehead of the dying Saviour.

Weekly, she attended confession, rooting out imperfections one by one; uncharitable thoughts about her neighbour, Mrs Brophy, impatience with her children, her little vanities in hair and dress, her wilfulness, being vexatious to her husband, on every occasion running through the Ten Commandments like a cargo listing from Frontignac. Ticking them off one by one, bottle by bottle, in case she missed any, or had broken any more.

It satisfied her, but only until the following

190

week. Every sin she could find she confessed, and the more she confessed the more she found. Yet every week the sin she wanted to confess above all others seemed to elude her. If she could only name it, label it like the other sins. Maybe it was greater than all the others? Sometimes she became distracted, so she would again run through the Commandments, searching for what she'd missed, wanting to pin down this final flaw.

'First, I am the Lord Thy God, thou shalt not have false Gods before me... Third, keep holy the Sabbath day... Fifth ... thou shalt not kill... Sixth ... thou shalt not commit adultery.'

Peabody, who never missed an opportunity, had once told her of an early 'Irish' bible, whose Sixth Commandment instructed, 'Thou *shalt* commit adultery' – the missing 'not' a printer's error. The bible was withdrawn, 'Otherwise,' he had laughed and taken her hand, 'the world as we know it, Ellen, would come to a standstill!' She concentrated her mind again – Peabody could be such a distraction. Ninth... not covet thy neighbour's wife... Tenth...

Sometimes during Lent Mary and Louisa would accompany her. Some days it was Mary alone; other days, Louisa. Now, here in the church, she stole a look at Louisa, praying beside her. After school, on days Mary would remain behind to help the Sisters, the girl would run to Ellen with a squeeze-the-life-out-of-you embrace. Then she and Louisa would clasp hands, arms swinging between them with happiness, two schoolgirls at walk.

The girl now was intent on the figure bowed down with the weight of the cross, face etched on the towel held by one of the women of Jerusalem.

The Sixth Station was Louisa's favourite, the one where they lingered longest. The girl would gaze on this small act of compassion, by the woman, Veronica, as if for Louisa this, and not the crucifixion itself, was the central moment. Ellen could only surmise that it related to Louisa's own experience, when years previously she herself had stopped along the road to Louisburgh and taken pity on the famished waif the girl then was. When they had completed the Stations, as always they sat together in silence.

Louisa was fifteen now, maybe sixteen, and had shot from a gangling twig into a well-sprung sapling with the nourishment the New World had brought her. Not yet quite as tall as Ellen herself, she would be before long. 'I bend while you grow,' Ellen would say to her. Louisa carried herself well – no sense of *snawvauning* about her. What would she do out in the world in another few years or so, Ellen wondered? There wasn't much of any consequence if you couldn't speak, much less for a *woman* who couldn't speak. Louisa liked learning and music but then what? Still, with God's help, it would all work out.

Mary, who would be fourteen this year, was already clear that she herself wanted further study, 'if it was not a great burden on the family'. Whatever the burden, Mary would have it, Ellen had decided. 'To be somebody', you had to have education. After that, Mary could decide to marry well. Though Ellen doubted, given their conversations about 'settling for a beau, a dress, and a pudding bowl!', that Mary's horizons would rise only to the marriage life, and no further.

Ellen loved seeing the two of them together. Mary, with her shock of red hair, a wildness to it like her own once had, Louisa's straight to the shoulder, dark as a nut, and as shiny. Arm in arm around each other like real sisters, sparkling together in the flower of youth.

Lavelle had been wonderful about the children, not only with regard to Patrick and Mary, but Louisa, too, and reared them as his own. She was particularly pleased that with Patrick, Lavelle had struck up a close friendship. More so as the boy grew older and became more radical in his thinking in relation to Ireland. It was something she had hoped Patrick would grow out of here in America, but to her dismay he had not. It was the one element of their family life that disconcerted her. Especially as he was now of an age, 'a man', as he kept telling them, that he could attend Lavelle's various meetings. Still it was good that the boy had this bond with Lavelle and she would do nought to sever it.

The men in America, she noted, lived more separate lives than the small communities back home allowed them to do. Here, among the Irish, there was 'men's business' and there was 'women's business'. 'Men's' was out of doors, 'women's business' very definitely confined to the inside of the hall door. The threshold between was seldom crossed. She was an exception, combining both male and female lives. Lavelle, for his part, accepted that, while Bishop John, for all his liberal views, did not. Women should make the home, not the money was the Church's view. No matter how much self-denial she engaged in, she doubted if it could extend that far. She was indeed fortunate that with her temperament and Lavelle's understanding, she had the freedom to move between both worlds.

Peabody she had avoided as much as possible since undertaking her Lenten 'renewal'. Without arousing suspicions in Lavelle, she had managed to substitute him for herself on a few occasions in visiting the merchant. Everything was tidy, in its place. Her confidence in her own ability to deal with her malaise grew with each passing day, each Stations of the Cross, each little lessening of self.

St Patrick's Day, in the middle of Lent, was like an oasis in the barren desert of penance and abstinence leading up to Easter. It was a wonderful day, with High Mass at the cathedral, followed by the parade. The whole of Boston, it seemed, was greened and festooned and obligations of fasting and self-denial were lifted for the festivities surrounding Ireland's national saint. However, she resolved privately to hold to her daily routine to further advance her self-discipline. So it was wholly against her better judgement that she agreed to later accompany Lavelle to a 'special meeting at which ladies who support the Irish cause will also gather for a discussion on the un-American Principles of Education in Boston'. This was part of the diocese's ongoing assault against the anti-Catholic bias of Boston's public schools, for which Patrick's case provided so much momentum. The ladies had requested her presence, would have a private room. She, on the other hand, desired no such public involvement, and even less so, the raucous St Patrick's celebrations which would follow the meeting.

'Lavelle, I see no necessity in my going. It's over. Changes have been made,' she argued.

'Have you not heard Bishop John from the pulpit say that while outwardly there is change, there is little change of heart?' Lavelle contended.

'You can't change people's hearts if they themselves don't want to,' she responded.

Despite Lavelle's entreaties, she resisted his arguments to accompany him. It was not until Patrick intervened, saying, 'And what will my friends think if they find out you refused to go?' that she at last relented.

24

The crowd parted silently as she supported Lavelle out of the Windjammer. Panic-stricken she wanted to be well gone before the Night Watch arrived. If only she'd followed her instinct, not gone near the cursed place. Even at the last moment, as soon as she heard the din of untuned fiddle music and the rum-filled raucousness of its inhabitants, she should have turned on her heel, gone home. Why the ladies, or the men for that matter, had to hold meetings in such a den was beyond her.

Now her husband hung on her shoulder, bloodied by a knife-wound. And behind them on the tobacco-spewed floor of the Windjammer, a man lay dead. Never mind that Lavelle was not seriously wounded, or mind that the man behind had died accidentally, fallen awkwardly on a splintered bottle, or that her husband had not initiated the aggression. She could have saved it all for them, if only she had been firm in her resolve. Then the remark about her person would not have been made, Lavelle would not have remonstrated with the man; one thing leading to the other until the knife was produced, Lavelle assaulted, forced to defend his life.

They made it home, no one taking too much notice of two more drunken Irish staggering homewards on St Patrick's night.

Once there, she bandaged his wound, put him to bed then burned his clothes and her stained dress. The last thing they wanted was trouble with the law. Lavelle would be imprisoned; it would be the end of everything. She was still shaking after the incident. The mannered life she now lived in Boston had long removed her from the brutality of her previous life. She clambered into bed trying to still her quailing, trying not to waken him, wondering when the knock would come to the door. He was still awake and turned towards her, grimacing with pain.

'Oh God, Ellen, I killed a man, killed him with my own two hands,' he said, distraught.

'It was an accident – he would have killed you,' she said simply.

He dug his head into her shoulder, racked with remorse. Tenderly, she pulled him to her. She had to help him, get him to forget about it for tonight, sleep and get his strength back. Tomorrow would be a new dawn. He would be more able to cope.

'You're such a good man, Lavelle,' she said, dabbing the *soologues* of perspiration from his forehead.

'Oh Ellen, if anything ever happened to you,' he answered, 'it would be the end of me.'

'Nothing ever will, while I have you to protect me,' she whispered, 'and to love me.'

'I couldn't do much for you now,' he replied, straining a smile.

'Oh yes you could,' she laughed deep down in her throat, the tension still high in her.

She tried to move him into position alongside her. It was awkward, he being unbalanced, unable to put weight on his injured arm. Somehow she managed, Lavelle scolding her for being 'wanton', with him 'almost drained of life', talking the words into her mouth in little gasps. In a while she felt the spasms of his pain become one with hers, the bandaged arm beneath his chest, crushing her, taking the breath out of her each time he rose and fell. Violently she responded, needing her own easement.

'Oh, Christ, Ellen! Oh, good Christ!' he cried at the highest point.

She barely felt him sink his teeth into her

shoulder, the soft part near her neck, didn't know about it until afterwards. Nor did she realize until she had helped him off her that his wound had opened, seeped through the protective bandages, little globules daubing her breasts and ribs. Now, as he slept beside her, she sat up, watching the blood, mesmerized, at how it splayed out over her belly, held for a moment in the dark pool of her navel, before deep-reddening the hair below. As if she herself had been severed from thorax to bowel. She shivered, thinking of the knife that had reefed him, imagining what it must be like, before rising to wash herself.

Then she sat there an hour or two, watching over him, reminding herself that she would have to admit in the confessional to her lack of abstinence on this terrible Lenten night.

Wondering if the night itself would change everything.

In the days following the Windjammer 'incident', she was rushed off her feet between tending to Lavelle and the children and the task of single-handedly running the business. She hired a man to help her with the heavier work. A surly enough fellow, Sullivan from Knocknagoshel, who didn't like taking orders from a woman, and whom she could scarcely understand with his high-hilled Kerry accent. Still, he did the work – after the first tongue-lashing she gave him.

It was better being busy; it kept her mind occupied. Too much wondering about things, like too much religion, was a bad thing. She had cauterized Lavelle's wound herself, coagulating the severed tissue to stop the bleeding, not a doctor for fear word would get out and he be arrested. Miraculously, no knock came to the door. Yet, she imagined, someone must break silence. Not the 'tars' from the whalers. No, they would want no truck with the law, only to hurry back aboard their floating gin-palaces, set sail again for the whaling grounds and the accommodating wahines of the South Seas.

Lavelle's Repealers would also hold fast – not give the Nativist Night Watch any whisper that would have them on his trail. Any 'Paddy' falling into the clutches of the Night Watch would receive short shrift. The Irish would hold together, not be informers.

She cautioned the children against speaking about the 'incident', and told them as little as possible, although Patrick was hard to restrain from wanting to know more about it. She found the boy visiting with Lavelle more than she would have liked. Now they were both heroes, bonded in blood. Both her men. She fought back within her what she considered an inappropriate surge of pride.

Neither did she have time to spend dallying with Peabody, which was a blessing in disguise. While she enjoyed their 'philosophical discussions', on previous occasions he had consciously provoked her in a very personal way, with his talk of 'love and death'. And what was it he said she possessed – or more rightly it possessed her – 'the Element of Fire'? She could do without all that now. The first time she did visit him, he asked about Lavelle. When she told him that Lavelle was 'not well', Peabody was all concerned.

'No danger to life or limb, I trust?'

'No, Jacob, my husband is but mildly indisposed,' she lied, wondering if he knew anything.

'And ... the boy, your son – Eliot School – how fares he?' Peabody enquired.

'Oh, he's fitting in quite well now, Jacob – thank you for asking,' she answered politely.

'Courageous – a bit of steel to his backbone. Well, I wouldn't expect less,' he complimented her. 'It is amazing,' he continued, 'more than circumstance, I suspect...'

'What is, Jacob?'

'Like moths to a flame, Ellen, that's you. You attract ... shall we say ... attraction. The harder you try to avoid it, the more it seeks you out.' She hoped he wasn't going to start his meanderings, had yet to finalize his order. '"Maidens like moths, are ever caught by glare,"' he quoted. 'Byron, Ellen. You should study Byron. He is the poet of passion and fire.'

'Jacob, never mind Byron. The Bordeaux...?'

'Never mind Byron?' he interrupted, throwing out his hands in mock despair. 'Ellen, my dear, you display your origins. Byron *is* the Bordeaux, the *Grand Cru!*'

You couldn't win with him, she thought. '"The best of life is but intoxication,"' he continued, off again on one of his whirls. 'Bordeaux, beauty, Byron, love... "In her first passion woman loves her lover, In all the others all she loves is love."'

'Jacob, stop it!' She had enough of him. 'To hell with you – try selling bottles of Byron to your customers! I'm leaving!' As she fired out the door to the marketplace, she heard him call after her.

'If not Byron then perhaps closer to home – Whittier? "Love has never known a law, Beyond its own sweet will."'

She heard his mad laughing following her until the sun glancing off the gold-domed cupola of Faneuil Hall seemed to drown him out.

The week before Holy Week, the knock at the door she had feared finally came.

She was distraught when they took Lavelle, pummelling the arresting officer's chest, shouting at him. 'It was self-defence ... the man wronged me!' She didn't know what she was saying. It didn't make any difference, they still took him, roughly handling him so that she saw the tell-tale stain creep through his shirt.

'He's wounded, can't you see? Let go of him!' she continued to berate them.

They restrained her, but she followed them through the streets, running to keep pace with the prison cart, damning them with her shouts, until it drew away from her, and she was left there standing, like some tricked harpy. She hadn't managed to see him, not even a glimpse to know that he was all right. Dejected, she made her way homewards. She had thought that with the lapse of time he would be safe, that the incident would be forgotten.

If only she had followed her instinct, not gone with him to that place; kept to what she had planned – away from the Irish. Then, none of this would have happened.

Thinking of him, flung there in a Boston prison

cell, she recalled to her mind the Westport work-house. 'Once in, the only way out was a shroud,' they used to say.

She was sick to her stomach. It had been her fault then too.

The children and Mrs Brophy were awaiting her when she arrived home. She knew by their stricken faces that they had already heard the story of Lavelle's arrest. She embraced them, one by one, whispering some empty solace.

'He'll be all right, Mrs Lavelle. He's innocent of any wrongdoing. He'll be all right. Please God!' Mrs Brophy comforted, making some black tea for her, fussing about the place, grating on her nerves. 'It's a terrible thing, a terrible thing, and Mr Lavelle such a fine upstanding man – I won't delay now, Mrs Lavelle, but if there's anything ... anything at all?' Mrs Brophy offered, backing towards the door; Ellen thanking her, trying to get around her to open it as quickly as possible.

When the woman had gone the children closed in around her.

'We should get Bishop John – he'll help us,' Mary put forward.

'Mr Joyce,' Patrick butted in, 'Mr Joyce, he could do more, he knows about the courts ... things like that. He'll stand by us.'

Louisa came and stood in front of Ellen, her two hands joined, mouthing shapes, telling her something.

'Pray!' Ellen said, that's what the girl was saying. 'That's what we should do first, pray for his safekeeping. Louisa is right.'

So, like when they were children, they fell on their knees around the kitchen table and prayed the Five Sorrowful Mysteries – being as it was the Time of the Cross.

Lavelle's incarceration distracted her from the previous preoccupation with herself. She went to see Bishop John, who received her well, expressing his concern. He would do what he could do, he said, qualifying this with, 'Even today, Mrs Lavelle, it is not freely permitted for the Catholic clergy to visit their flock in any of the State institutions.' This didn't encourage her. 'However,' he added, 'I will make my concerns for your husband's situation sufficiently known to the authorities.'

She thanked him, and left. Whatever little the Bishop could do, it would be a help.

She didn't know where to begin to search out Mr Joyce. He could be anywhere in America or Canada, even back in Ireland. Patrick, too, had offered to make enquiries, but she didn't want to be dragging him into it. In any event she was of two minds whether to try to contact the man or not. They had been drawn too closely together in Montréal. Sometimes, even at her Stations, she found her mind distracted from prayer to that time.

Louisa and Mary now came more frequently with her to do the daily round of vigil, during the lead-up to Easter. One day, early in Holy Week, Louisa alone had accompanied her, Mary remaining to help the nuns with some preparations for the feast-day. After they had completed the Stations, she and Louisa had sat in silence at the back of the cathedral, a flickering candle-wick their sole illumination. The church had temporarily emptied of other pilgrims of the cross. She loved it when there was just themselves.

'I am still in Thy presence, O Lord,' she said, inwardly. 'Speak to me ... in Thy wisdom deliver me.'

What if after Lent, after Easter, everything was the same with her? If the Lord had not delivered her of her malaise? This past week or so, since Lavelle's arrest, it had seemed to recede. But it had not gone away, of that she was sure. At the same time she was riven with guilt that she should still be so preoccupied with herself, instead of with Lavelle. Even though she knew he must be proven innocent. She turned to find Louisa staring at her. Could the girl know? It was said that those deprived of sight had improved use of hearing. Could the opposite be true? That those who had no sound had increased sight – inner sight? She took Louisa's hand, keeping her voice down.

'You understand, don't you?' she asked, their faces close together. 'I don't mean the words – maybe that too – but you have understood, I think, for some time. I am tormented with myself, Louisa,' she continued, in the voice normally reserved for the confessional, 'as much by lack of understanding, as by the thing itself. Till my knees are bruised with genuflecting, till I have worn the varnish off the wood in these pews.'

She paused. It wasn't fair, she knew, to unburden herself like this to Louisa, who couldn't ask her to stop, whose saviour she had once been and to whom now she looked for solace.

'I shouldn't be...' Louisa lifted her hand, holding out her index finger, rotating it slowly. She wanted her to go on. Ellen grabbed the girl's hand, stopping its motion.

'Oh, my child, my dear child – you *do* understand.'

25

Good Friday morning was as sombre as the day itself. Black clouds gathered over the bay, sheeting down grey penitential rain on Boston, as if its hapless inhabitants alone were responsible for the death on Calvary.

It was a bad day to be setting out to visit Lavelle. As she prepared, umbrellaed against the day, she hoped he would soon be out; that it was all some mistake, and she thanked God that Patrick hadn't been with them on the night.

She would be back in time to take them to Holy Cross for the Stations, three o'clock being held as the time Christ finally died. Oddly, the thought struck her as she stepped out into the downpour, was it the 'three o'clock' in Ireland, or in America, that was the correct 'three o'clock'? She supposed it didn't matter.

She hated the thought now of the place she was to visit. Peopled mainly by the Irish – the dregs of

Boston life. However, all thoughts of low-living compatriots were banished when she saw the tall figure of Stephen Joyce rise to greet her in the waiting area. She hadn't seen him since Christmastime and now she was jolted, discomfited by his presence here.

'Ellen.' He smiled, came towards her and took her arm. 'I am sorry we meet again under such circumstances – word came to me.'

She was aware of the firmness of his grip, something in his face at seeing her again. 'Stephen ... I ... I'm glad you're here. Lavelle will be ... thank you,' she got out.

'I have arranged legal representation and will personally post bail. We will have him home to you without delay,' he told her.

He continued to hold her arm until she withdrew it from him. Immediately she thought her action unnecessarily impulsive, ungracious. He was here to help her and had already done more than she would have asked.

'Thank you ... thank you, Stephen,' she said again.

'You have been drenched with the rain,' he replied. 'It is a dangerous time of year.'

'Yes, quite – I'm sure I'll be...' She wasn't sure what she was *sure* of.

'My lodgings are close by. When you have visited with your husband, I will take you there; I have a dry cape.'

She had agreed before realizing it. 'I have to be home before three, to take the children to church,' she put up defensively. Did he – the Presbyterians – commemorate Christ's Passion

206

in the same way?

He smiled, the dark eyes intently taking in her words, her concern. 'Of course. I haven't had you late yet.'

She flushed, remembering her own tardiness in Montréal.

She left him, straightening herself before being shown in to Lavelle, who was in a small cell with two other men. Before she could speak, one of these came to the bars jabbing a finger at her.

'Is this the missus ... patriot?' he said to Lavelle, turning to guffaw at his cohort, who answered, '*Anamandhoul*, Festy ... wouldn't like to layve her too long on her own on the outside!'

The jailer who accompanied her, a stout, able man from the West of Ireland, rapped his night-stick across the bars. 'Get downside you two,' he threatened, in his best Connemara English, 'or I'll overhaul the both o' ye wharf-rats,' he added, 'bilkin' them what's arriving from the old country with nothing.' He left no doubt in Ellen's mind as to in what condition 'overhauling' would leave the two.

Lavelle was overjoyed to see her, reaching out to her through the bars. She grabbed his arms.

'I'm sorry, ma'am, you can't do that – regillations. I'm sorry,' Connemara said gruffly, embarrassed by their show of intimacy.

'It's all right, officer,' Lavelle said.

He looked well, she thought, slightly strained, the lick of hair normally swept back off his face now dangling in the middle of his forehead, giving him an even more boyish look than usual.

'Did you meet Stephen outside?' he asked her.

'Yes,' she said, wondering why it seemed such a hard question.

'He'll explain everything. It's hard to talk here with these two; they'd sell their souls, and mine, for a dollar,' he whispered, his face close to the bars, close to hers.

'Will you be out soon?' she asked, seeking confirmation of what Stephen had told her.

'Soon, very soon, I hope, Ellen...' He paused, as if about to say something else to her. 'How are they all at home?'

'They're worried for you – praying for you – but they're well,' she reassured him. 'You're not to be worrying yourself, do you hear? Everything will be fine,' she added.

'I promise I won't. Listen, Ellen, you should go. I don't want you in here with the likes of these two, they're a disgrace to the name of Ireland. Connemara here, he's all right,' he said, nodding towards the guard, 'a different class of a man.'

She wanted to talk more to him – just to stay there, despite Festy and his fellow wharf-rat, Losty. She needed time. It was all too quick, too sudden. Lavelle behind bars, the visit, the man outside waiting for her. It all made her jittery inside, like she was before Lent began.

'Lavelle...' she began.

'Ellen – go now!' he said.

She wanted to tell him that she loved him, that she'd be back tomorrow, bring the children on Easter Sunday, wanted to talk about all the safe reinforcing things in their lives.

Stephen Joyce took her by the arm, holding the

umbrella over her with his free hand. He never spoke a word except 'this corner ... cross here! ... careful!' Neither did she speak. It was as if the rain beating down on them, drumming them into silence, said it all for them. Like when they had danced, she couldn't think straight, focus on what this was all about: Lavelle's lick of hair, the gruff guard from Connemara beating the bars, the two others, watching her like caged animals. The Stations at three o'clock, the cape, the dance... What had they all to do with one another? With her malaise? She had felt it there in the prison, back worse than ever it was, like a wave sweeping over her. Good Friday, the end of Lent, and she was no further on.

'We're here!'

He let her in. She heard him shake out the umbrella behind her. She turned, fumbling for the top button of her coat. He took her hands away, undid it. Then, one by one, the rest. She stood foolishly watching the top of his head descend as he bent to reach the lower buttons.

Her own hair lay smathered against her forehead, little rivulets of rain running from it, down along her nose, down her cheeks – droplets falling on to his black and already soaking head. Those that did not fall on him found the space between the high-necked paisley print she wore and her neck, cooling her shoulders and her breasts, so that she never moved when he rose in front of her, unlaced her black bonnet and let it fall away. Down her hair fell, down over her face like a wet veil, dividing him from her. When he unshouldered her thick coat she thought the absence of its sodden weight would lighten the pressure she felt. Instead, her only relief was a shiver as the last of the Good Friday rain evaporated into the warm place halfway down her back. When the shivering had taken over her whole body, she didn't allow him even to undress her.

Baggaged up on the bed, her hair blinding her, she pulled at him, sucking in mouthfuls of hair, wondering if she would suffocate before she had done or in the doing itself. She scarcely felt him, as if her body had dislocated itself, disengaged from him, was a thing unto itself, beating about in the air. Her hands found the brass headrail and she clung to it for dear life, imagining it must snap, crash down on his head. He looked up; her thoughts, wild and scattered as they were, somehow transmitted to him.

'Your eyes,' he said, straining a hand to them, 'you're weeping!'

Only then, in the wiping away of them, was she aware of her tears. Above her hands, somewhere on the wall, where part of her was, a church-bell tolled the praying hour.

'Oh, sweet crucified... Oh Jesus!' she cried, as she sacrificed everything.

Calling out with the ecstasy of the damned for her lost Saviour, Lavelle, and the children who waited at home for her.

26

They *were* waiting for her, worried. She was never late.

'I was delayed, but your father's all right,' she blurted out. 'I had better fix myself. We'll get some of it, the Adoration of the Cross at least!'

She dashed upstairs, tidied her hair, threw on a fresh coat and hat and was ready, when she noticed the purplish bruise on her lower lip. She panicked, thinking it worse than it was. Her eyes unclear, still filmed over, she daubed some powder above the lip-line, half-concealing the bruise. 'Bit it while running... Bit it! Bit it!' she panted, convincing herself, her heart racing. She closed her eyes and sighed ... remembering ... part euphoria, part hysterical with remorse and fear. Her heart still palpitating, she herded them out the door ahead of her.

'Come on now, let's hurry!' she ordered, relieved at the mantle of bustling their lateness provided.

When they got there the cathedral was already crowded. She ushered them in, urging quietness. The altar was entirely stripped; no altar cloths, candelabra, or cross. Bishop John was shrouded from shoulder to foot in the long white alb of purity. Around his waist, securing the alb, the girdle, symbol of chastity; about his neck and

211

shoulders, the white-lined amice, signifying restraint. The stole, black for Good Friday, symbol of immortality and innocence regained, was looped around his shoulders, crossed at the breast, like a garment a woman might wear.

So crushed were the pews, they were unable to sit together, Mary and Patrick finding seats further up on either side of the nave. She held back to the rear – couldn't have borne the closeness of them squashed up against her. Louisa squeezed into the pew in front of her. It was the Sixth Station. Thank God, she was behind Louisa, wouldn't have to face the girl when the congregation turned to genuflect towards each Station. She hadn't thought of any of this beforehand. Now it all seemed so important.

'The Sixth Station – Veronica wipes the face of Jesus,' Bishop John pronounced. To her dismay, Louisa turned around, gave her a little smile. She did her best to return it. 'My most beloved Jesus...' Bishop John began the prayers. '...Thy face was beautiful before ... now wounds and blood have disfigured it. Alas, my soul also was once beautiful. But I have disfigured it since by my sins.'

She couldn't focus on the prayers, would only get so far in the response, 'Oh my Jesus, forgive us our sins...' and then be lost to it.

Again, the drowning, her whole body slipping into a kind of post-delirium state, she trying to resist until it oozed over her again, a mixture of sweat and rain, and the saliva seed of her sin. Even the *sream* that had filmed her eyes like a second skin still remained. Like a chrysalis imprisoning her sight. She blinked, trying to unblur her vision, trying to see the faces of the women of Jerusalem; Veronica, full with pity and compassion, Mary Magdalen, the adulteress, now at the foot of the cross, her sins shriven. Snatches of the drone of the prayer floated in and out of her sea of drowning. '...As Christ died for us so too must we be dead to sin.'

And so it went, Station by Station.

'Let us pray' – the Bishop. 'Genuflect' – the Deacon. 'Rise up' – the Subdeacon. The constant genuflecting helped, was like rising up out of her sea to the surface, a chance to breathe. At times, she had to grip the elbow-rest to break her unsteadiness. Would it never end – the 'let us prays', the 'genuflects', the 'rise ups'? Would Christ ever be buried – the stone rolled over against His tomb?

She felt a hand on her glove. It was Louisa. The Stations were over. Now the row in front of her was emptying into the nave, a long shuffling line, to approach the altar for the Adoration of the Cross.

'Behold the wood of the cross ... on which hung the Saviour of the world.'

She had dreaded this moment. What was she to do? Unlike Communion, which required no stain of mortal sin on the soul, every sinner in the place would now file out of the pews, and up to the altar, where the large crucifix held by the Bishop would be kissed. How could she march up, bold as brass, at one with the rest of the congregation after what she had done? She considered sitting it out, hunched there, head in

213

hands. She would be the only one, but she could have had a momentary weakness, a dizzy spell. Who was to know?

Those beside her started to rise. She hesitated, unable to move, caught between Heaven and Hell. Her mind was made up for her when Louisa stood back, waiting for her, at the far end of Ellen's pew. Now she had to move, fall in with Louisa, not give rise to scandal.

The procession inched up the centre aisle. She moved within its impetus, eyes down, not wanting to see anybody. A hand touched her arm. Startled, she looked up. It was Mary, who having adored the cross, now sought readmission to her pew. Ellen stood back, head lowered, feeling the flush of betrayal rise in her. She, Mary's mother, was worse than any Mary Magdalen, who had fallen but then was redeemed. She herself was fully unredeemed, in such a state that she wasn't even sure she sought redemption. In front of her, Louisa's hair, braided beneath a prim little box hat, swung from left to right with every step in a tiny precise motion. Like a hypnotic pendulum, the braid of Louisa's hair drew Ellen forward until she was the next to kneel before the cross.

She averted her eyes from Bishop John, fixing them instead on the alabaster white body of Christ, head hung on His chest. Somehow, she got to her knees trembling over His near-naked body. Bent to deliver her Judas kiss.

'Behold the wood of the cross.' Bishop John proffered her Saviour to her.

She wished it could have been a plain wooden cross instead of a crucifix. It was almost beyond her to kiss any part of His body with her stained mouth. She brushed her lips against the furthest extremity – the blood-dripped toes. The moment seemed to last for ever, the fever in her lips against the cold plaster incongruous. Still bent, she was gripped by an over-riding fear that the crucified Saviour would open His eyes ... speak ... denounce her. That fixed by His denunciation she would be unable to rise. Then she was rising, Bishop John wiping away from the feet of Christ the smudge of powder she had left there.

Later, when they returned to the house, she told them about her visit to Lavelle. They wanting to know more, she wanting to tell less. Finally, she reached the sanctuary of her room, douched herself thoroughly, and was filled with panic, wondering again what she would have done if Lavelle had not been in jail. If he had been there – waiting for her.

On Holy Saturday her whole body ached. Her legs and arms, her neck and back, every joint and sinew, it seemed, ached in a hollow of longing. No matter how busy she forced herself to be, this ache was not assuaged.

She went to church on her own for confession, dreading it, needing it. Otherwise, in a state of mortal sin, she could not receive Communion on the following day. With her husband in prison, that omission might cause some tongues, notably Mrs Brophy's, to wag. In the confessional she went through all her litany of other sins, putting off until the end her reason for being there in the first place.

'Is that all, my child?' enquired the priest, knowing from years of listening that it was not.

'I have sinned against the Sixth Commandment, Father!' She heard the silence fall. A pause and then: 'Are you married or unmarried?'

'Married ... Father!'

'Married,' he stated. In the dark beyond the screen which separated them, she sensed the shoulders ease, his misunderstanding granting her a momentary respite. 'With your husband' – he paused – 'or on your own?'

She did not know how to answer this.

'Well, child, with your husband – did you waste the seed?' He laboured the question, already beleaguered by a long stream of penitents.

'No ... Father.'

'On your own then – the solitary sin?'

The tone was quite impatient now. He pushed his head closer to the grille. She bit into her lip before saying it.

'It was with ... another man.'

'Adultery! Adultery!' he said, as if not believing what he was hearing. 'You committed the sin of adultery?' He turned his face full on to her.

She wanted to tell him to speak lower – if by any chance the children had followed her, and were outside.

'Yes,' she whispered, withdrawing her face from that of her accuser.

'Speak up, woman!'

'Yes, Father – adultery.' In the darkness, she could feel the wrath rise in him.

'You committed the sin of Mary Magdalen – the *mortal* sin of adultery with another man.'

Each word was a nail in her heart. She could only nod.

'And is *he* married, this ... man?'

'No, Father.'

'Thank God.' She heard the expulsion of breath; something saved, she thought, grasping at straws, knowing worse was yet to come. It came with his next question. 'Does this man attend the sacraments?'

She paused, steeling herself. 'No, Father, he's ... not of our faith ... a ... Protestant.'

She wished he'd turn his face away. They weren't supposed to look at you, know who you were; maybe for adultery it was different. She pulled her head further back into the penitential gloom.

'An English Protestant!' he emphasized, scarce believing what he was hearing, damning her with each syllable.

'No, Father.' Her voice was shaking. 'He's Irish!'

'Irish? Irish? He's Irish, this man?' her confessor thundered, until she thought all outside must hear her sin.

'Yes, Father,' she said, stricken into further submission.

'And pray tell me, what is a good...' he paused, reviewing her status, '...an Irish Catholic woman like you doing keeping company with a Protestant in the first instance, whether he be English or Irish?'

She didn't want to say he was a friend of her husband's, incur a further outburst, even louder questions. She fumbled for the answer.

217

'He ... ah ... helped ... helped my family in the past ... in the bad times.' She managed to get it out, trying to make it sound as heroic as she could, as if she had some excuse.

But he was having none of it. 'And now he exacts his reward – is that it?'

'Oh, no, Father! No, it wasn't like...' She leaped to the defence of Stephen – this black Protestant, the occasion of her downfall in the priest's eyes. 'I ... it ... it was my sin ... I–' She stopped herself.

'This man is evil,' he warned, accepting no exculpation from her on the Protestant's behalf. She held her breath, waiting. 'There are those of the opposite faith who are seducers of our womanhood, who prey on the weaknesses of your sex. You must not see him again. Do you understand?'

She wanted to argue with him. It was she who was evil, had given in to herself, to the weakness of her sex, as he had put it. Instead, she found herself agreeing.

'Yes, Father.' She wanted to be rid of him, to be out of there, now that the worst was over and she had confessed. But she wasn't to go that easily.

'Are relations ... normal with your husband?' he asked, more restrained now that she had resolved not to see the man again.

'Yes, Father.'

'Then why did you find cause to go outside your marriage?'

'I ... I don't know, Father. I was weak ... I succumbed to temptation,' she answered, knowing it to be untrue. She hadn't been tempted. It had happened, just happened. She thought of the

Sulpician monk in the chapel of Our Lady of the Snows. The warning he had given her about the 'occasions of sin', a warning she had not heeded. She wished this one would stop asking her all these questions. She had thought he was on the point of doling out her penance, giving her absolution and letting her go. There must be a score of people outside, waiting, wondering – as she often had.

'Do you have children?'

'Yes, the two, Father.'

'Hmm ... a small family,' he reflected, asking, 'you are still of child-bearing age?'

'Yes, Father.'

'Then, to save yourself from further sin, you must pray to God for the blessing of more children – with your husband,' he added quickly. 'And you must never see this man, this Protestant man again. Never – is that clear?' She said it was. 'For your penance – the Stations of the Cross – twice,' he said curtly. 'Now, make an Act of Perfect Contrition and ask the crucified Saviour for forgiveness.'

She closed her eyes, praying with all her resolve, damping down the intruding signals from where her body still remembered him, the words of contrition pushing back the small twinges of delight, crucifying them into the high dark corners of the confessional.

'Oh my God ... I am heartily sorry ... detest my sin ... firmly resolve ... never more to offend thee. Amen.'

He gave her absolution at last, mercifully, the back of his white hand held up in blessing, slicing away her sin in the darkness. She had to control herself from pushing out the door of the cubicle before he had swept across the purple curtain over the latticed screen which divided them.

As she came out into the light, her eyes adjusting to it, those gathered in the confessional pews, studiously kept their heads lowered, resisting as best they could the temptation to look up, take in this scarlet woman who had kept the priest for so long. The woman who had caused him to raise his voice, making them even more fearful of the wrath of God.

If they had looked up, the way they did when people came out who had only small sins and short confessions, it wouldn't have been so bad. This way was worse. Now it was as if they all knew, as if the livid mark of mortal sin was stamped on her forehead, not even other sinners wanting to witness it.

She fled the church. Unable to do her penance now, slinking from Station to Station, whispering and genuflecting, everyone there knowing it was her; sneaking their sly little looks at her as she stood at the end of their pew. She would come back later.

But how? She had to visit Lavelle – if only she hadn't told him she'd come back today; let it wait till tomorrow. But how could she have known? She must visit him. She had confessed, resolved never to sin again, been given God's grace. It was a mortal mistake, but it was behind her now. She had come through adversity before, much worse than this, than her own weakness.

Neither could she go home now and come back

later to the church. The children would wonder, want to come with her. For a moment she considered that if they did, she could pass it off; extra prayers for the not-yet-risen Christ, or for Lavelle's safe return. But then, the second round of the Stations. How could she explain that? But she *must* do her penance, otherwise her sin was not absolved. She knelt at the back of the church, agitated, putting it over and back in her mind – one or two seats up and in a bit, so that those leaving would not pass too closely by.

In just twenty-four hours, everything had become so complicated, so topsyturvy. Whatever way she turned she was trapped by the everyday normalities of her life. She had stepped out of the ordinary and now the ordinary was closing in on her. Her given life, as it should be, defining the boundaries of who she was, of what she could and could not do.

She just sat there, not praying, her thoughts in a maze. Finally, she resolved that she would first go home, then visit Lavelle, returning home once again. She would then bring the children with her back to the church. By that time the queues of penitents would be cleared. She would make one round of the Stations with the children, the other some other time. She worried about attending Communion the following morning if she hadn't completed her penance. And when, if not today, would she make the other round anyway? People didn't make the Stations of the Cross after Easter Saturday – there was no need. Christ was risen then. She would stick out like a sore thumb if she were to do the Stations on

Monday, or Tuesday, be considered to have taken leave of her senses. There was nothing for it except to do her penance now – both rounds. It would avoid complications afterwards, telling more lies to the children.

She got up and walked the length of the cathedral to the first Station. Why couldn't he just have given her them once?

27

'You don't look yourself, Ellen,' Lavelle whispered through the bars to her.

'Oh....!' she said, putting her hand to her face.

'You're not to be worrying about me. Did you get a wetting yesterday?' he asked, continuing to look at her strangely.

'No, I'm fine, nothing's wrong. You're the one in prison.' She laughed nervously.

'Did Stephen explain everything to you?' His face was close to hers.

Connemara watched them, and from back in the cell, Festy and Losty, forewarned to behave themselves for the lady visitor, watched the jailer.

'He did, yes. You shouldn't be long in here,' she said brightly, trying to make the connections clearly in her mind.

'No. He's a good man, Stephen, to have on our side,' Lavelle said, each word having a potency for her beyond what he intended. 'The education always stands to a person – you always said that yourself, Ellen.'

She smiled, making a little noise with her mouth. 'Yes, I know it's hard to talk with the two behind here.' Lavelle nodded backwards, mis-understanding her reticence. 'Maybe they'll be moved by tomorrow. You'll bring the children? Connemara here says it's all right.'

She hoped that Festy and Losty, repulsive as they were, would not be moved. They were a distraction, something for Lavelle to focus on other than on her alone.

'Yes, they're looking forward to seeing you,' she answered positively, glad to be truthful about something.

'And you, you yourself, you're sure you're fine? You look tired,' he asked again, casting his eyes over her face.

She prayed that he wouldn't notice the guilt she felt was written all over it, or the fading powd-ered bruise. If he did either, he didn't say, he let his concern rest.

'Yes ... yes, of course I'm fine – don't worry,' she answered.

It further grieved her that he was concerned over her. His own situation was bad enough. If only she'd told him yesterday what she had intended to say – that she loved him. Maybe it was as well she hadn't. Then it would have been a worse betrayal.

Outside, she half-expected Stephen to be waiting. Half-glad when he wasn't, but half-disappointed too. Stupidly disappointed. She wondered where he was, what he was doing, what did it all mean to him? She must follow the priest's advice – not see him again. She had thought his solution almost childishly simple, but simplicity was what was called for, no ifs and buts. And if by force of circumstance, until Lavelle was freed, she must see Stephen in that respect, then she could meet with him only in that context.

Holy Saturday was kinder of climate than the previous day, lifting her spirits, as if fore-weathering the glory of Easter. She slowed her pace slightly once out of the jailhouse – out of the maelstrom of that hunted feeling, of having to think faster and faster, think ahead of herself. But it would not be wise to over-dwell on the events of yesterday. The why of it, her complete readiness, it seemed, for it to happen, and without a word spoken between them. How did they both know, like two rivers confluencing, coursing into one? Then her abject abandonment of all decorum, all that was virtuous in the marriage act. She turned her mind from the thought. She was certain it was connected with her malaise of spirit; as if her person, aware of how far she was fated to fall, had slowly drawn the veil of melancholy upon her. Now that she had fallen – gone to the pit – she would be free.

Easter morning was glorious. She rose early and watched for the sun rising out of the depths of the Atlantic. Like a saved soul it was, *Lumen Christi* – the light of Christ. It was one of the few concessions to her previous life that she had retained. In those times, she would leave the cabin early and from the high-rocked place near the *Crucán*, would wait for the sun to appear over the fields beyond, in that area on the far side of the Mask known as 'Little America'. She smiled at the tongue-in-cheek nature of the name, now that she had seen 'Big America'.

There, the sun, which came to them from the east, from England, where it never danced, her father had told her, splayed down from Dublin across the plains of Leinster and into the far stoned outposts of Connacht. She remembered how it sparkled and danced, greening the fields out of their darkness; sprinkling down into the Mask, then like a fiery serpent secking out of the darker waters of Lough Nafooey. She always knew, as she watched the sun, couldn't but know that the Saviour had indeed risen.

Here, in Boston, she had no *Crucán*, no high place. But the Easter sunrise was still a source of wonder for her. How the first gap of its light opened on the eastward walls of the tall buildings, expanding upwards until each windowpane in turn became a dazzling crystal, throwing back to the streets below its redeeming brilliance.

'Glory to the Risen God,' she prayed, lifted up by wonder, raised out of her fallen humanity.

She dressed, more eager to meet the day than she could have hoped for, furling the hair back from her temples, pinning it quite severely. Then she plaited it across, but above the nape of her neck, finally interlacing both sides of it into a fusion of red crochet. Her fingers felt its symmetry, knowing that her new bonnet, as yet untried, would perch perfectly on top of it all. When she had walked to Boston's most fashionable hat shop, tucked away between Washington and Tremont, she had already decided not to keep with her favourite green. Delargy, the milliner, had demurred, advising that 'nothing suits better an existing glory than to crown it with a contrasting one'. She was not for moving, instead going for navy; but a blue navy, not a dark dreary navy.

Now, as she secured it with a neat little bow beneath her chin, she was pleased with her navy-blue bonnet. Pleased, too, to note the bruise on her lip had all but disappeared. There was something about a new, blue bonnet.

Mass was a riot of celebration, the statues and crucifixes undraped from their Good Friday mourning, the radiant white, 'first-class' Easter vestments in stark contrast to the penitential purple of Lent. The bells carolled out the good news of Resurrection – *alleluia, alleluia, alleluia.* Children scrubbed shiny as apples, boys in new breeches, girls in fresh frilly dresses, jittery with excitement, accompanied starched fathers upright with new canes, mothers newly bonneted. 'Jesu, Joy of Man's Desiring' never sounded as sparsely beautiful and that morning, He truly was Ellen's desiring. The circular, yet ever-ascending melody of Bach's cantata rose like an invisible ladder, the higher notes seeking Heaven, the *basso* – the footfalls of God – redeeming the earth.

She stole a look to either side. Mary, to her left, was radiant with happiness. Music had become so much part of Mary's life, as much as it once had been of her own. On the far side of Mary was Louisa. She, sensing the movement, turned towards Ellen. The girl's face was in rapture. *They* were angels, the both of them, pure and beautiful angels in the sight of God. Her angels, and Patrick, to her right, her dark archangel. They were her treasures, all that mattered. Almost of an age now to make their own way without her. But not to be divided from her because of her actions – that would be unbearable. She glanced at them again. Louisa, still watching, smiled, as if knowing her thoughts, reassuring her – the child, mother to the woman.

Outside, after the Mass, it was the same; *Exultate* – rejoice, rejoice – and 'Happy Easters', flying through the air like angels. Many sympathized with her about Lavelle. But when the priest sought her out, the same one who had heard her confession, she was truly mortified. She said as little to his enquiry as politeness permitted. If he did recognize her voice, there was no acknowledgement of this in his manner or speech. She spotted Mrs Brophy, bedecked in some gaudy bird-yellow creation, making for them. Ellen was glad of the intervention, despite the woman's opening proclamation: 'She hasn't been herself at all, Father, not since they took in poor Mr Lavelle. Such a fine man – hasn't been herself– have you, Mrs Lavelle?'

Later, before she took the children to visit Lavelle, she warned them of the 'two noxious characters named Festy and Losty who, when not in prison, normally reside in the tenements of Half-Moon Place, and whose language is as foul as the place they inhabit'.

'Are they Irish?' Mary asked.

She replied that they were.

'We were Irish once – like them,' Mary stated simply.

'No, Mary,' she answered her daughter, 'we were Irish and poor, but we were never like them. We never lost our dignity.'

'We *were* Irish!' Patrick picked her up. 'We still are – even if *you'd* like us to lose it!'

She was annoyed at him, always correcting her. 'Patrick, you know that's not true,' she began. 'We'll always be Irish, but you all will, in time and by geography alone, become more American than Irish. You must be prepared for that, not be looking backward to what is dead and buried...' she regretted her choice of words, '...to the past, I mean.'

'I'll never be American,' Patrick protested.

'If one day you get married, your children will be. Then what will you say?' Mary challenged him, in her own quiet way. This halted him momentarily.

'I could be back home in Ireland by that day. Things will have changed there and maybe I'll have helped change them,' he answered back defiantly. 'At least there we were something,' he added.

'What do you mean, Patrick – "something"?' Ellen took up the issue, resenting the implication of what he had said.

'Well, we're nothing here. The real Americans despise us, and you,' he directed the word at Ellen, 'you despise the real Irish – getting fancy things and pianos, trying to be like the Yankees and covering up the feet of them, in case anybody would think we're still "Micks" underneath it all.'

'Well, Patrick...' she started, but he kept going. 'You never mix with any of our own. Never speak a word of our language or sing the old songs – only up with that Mrs Brophy and your Daughters of the Commonwealth, talking *ráimeis* about notions and the place of women in society and –'

'And what's wrong with that, Patrick?' she said angrily, flabbergasted at his attack. The way he had begun to back-talk her of late, she felt like slapping his face, something she'd never done, to any of them.

Before she could continue, Mary interjected. 'We women do have a place in society and a right to our own minds, not just to be traipsing after you men!' she said firmly.

'See!' He jabbed his finger at Mary. 'You wouldn't be talking like that back home,' he accused. 'This place has changed ye to be even talking like that. That was the plot of the English all along – to drive us out of Ireland to another England. Only here it's not called England, it's called America.'

'Drive us out to do what, Patrick? Sure we have a much better life here?' Ellen had had enough of him.

'But that's the price. We end up being like them, so we'll never rise up against them. So we'll forget.'

Ellen couldn't believe her ears – was this some

229

of the nonsense that went on at Lavelle's meetings?

'But,' Patrick continued, still defiant of her, 'there's some of us will never forget – like me and Lavelle and Stephen Joyce!'

She wasn't going to hear any more of this. 'Patrick, Mary, shsst now the two of you! This is not the day nor the time for that kind of talk. Get the feet under the pair of you!' she ordered them.

Lavelle was in good spirits and to her great relief was much distracted by the presence of the children. Mary and Louisa huddled up close to him, unsure of what being in prison could do to a person, nervously delighted at how normal his condition seemed.

'Is it awful in here?' Mary asked, in a hushed voice.

'Well, if it wasn't for these two behind me – it's not such a bad place and the cooking is almost as good as home,' he laughed, catching first her hand, and then Louisa's, mockingly examining their fingers – as if he'd know. 'You're both not practising as much as you should be; I can tell,' he said, adding, less whimsically, 'I miss the music in here.'

'We said a prayer for you in school,' Mary said. 'Didn't we, Louisa?'

Louisa reached through the bars and put her hand up to his face, drawing it slowly downward over his skin. Ellen watched, a turmoil of emotions battling within her. How they loved him, and he them, and she...

'And you, Patrick, how are you? Keeping the

side up?' he asked of Patrick, who hung back a little.

'He don't look a bit like you.' Festy shuffled around the back of the cell.

'Not a one of them do, Festy,' chirruped in Losty and the two of them broke out, guffawing and grunting, and poking each other in the chest with the fun of it all. She saw Patrick's face flush, his fist clench. He would be embarrassed in front of her that they were like this – and Irish.

'Don't mind them, son,' Lavelle said, pointedly. 'They're only gadabouts, parasites living off their own.'

Patrick squared up to the bars. 'I wouldn't take any lip from the likes of those two–'

'Take it easy now, lad.' Connemara stepped forward. 'They'll get their own comeuppance one of these days.'

Patrick was mollified somewhat by Lavelle telling him, 'You're the man of the house now – look after your mother and sisters.'

Then Lavelle told Ellen he had been earlier visited by Stephen Joyce to say that he had secured the legal representation sought. The man, a Mr Erastus Jellico, would wish to speak with her. Stephen would call to make the necessary arrangements.

This set her in a panic. She did not want him calling on her. What would she have to say to him; could what had happened between them happen again? It couldn't, it could never happen again. But what was she to do? To demur would raise questions and, after all, if it helped expedite matters, secure Lavelle's release, then it was all to the good. He would be home more quickly. Then everything would return to ... as it had been before – normal.

She could keep one of the girls at home, so that she would not be alone when Stephen called. But on what day would he present himself? Anyway, what reason could she use to keep either of them with her? As in everything to do with this ... this awful business, every twist, every turn, every connivance, led only to further twists and turns, to further convoluted connivances. There was nothing for it but to resort to her own resolve and the grace of God. It was as simple as that, involved drawing no other person into her schemes.

Simple was best.

28

Monday he did not call.

Tuesday morning she had a visit to make to Peabody. She left a note, in as steady a hand as she could muster, and tied it to the door handle in case he should call and she missed him.

Peabody, who had obviously heard the news from some quarter, was all concern about Lavelle, enquiring after his health and worrying about 'the deleterious effect of even a short stay in such a low place'.

'And your own spirit, Ellen – how is that bearing up?' he asked, scrutinizing her features. She assured him it was fine, but he kept badgering her, when all she wanted was for him to just settle his account – he would have done well with the cognacs running up to Easter. 'Do I detect a certain, let me see … lustre in you, not present in recent weeks?' he enquired, stringing out the words in a way that alarmed her.

She looked at him. '"Lustre", Jacob? With all that's…'

'Yes,' he interrupted, ignoring the surprise in her voice.

'I suppose it *is* the high point of your Christian year,' he went on, trying to fox her. 'The scriptures have been fulfilled, Christ is risen. You have done your forty days of sackcloth and ashes, so you are all redeemed?'

'Jacob, I haven't the time, nor the inclination for your "philosophizations", or whatever you call them. I have to be back for–' She caught herself.

'For what, Ellen? Ah, I can tell … a secret?' He moved to stand beside her, eyes wide with mocking. She had never noticed before the patch of pink skin starting to show through the fine white strands of his hair.

'Jacob, your hair is thinning admirably,' she said, hoping it would deflect him.

He laughed, loving it when she bit back at him. 'You are in a hurry, Ellen, I can see. No time to talk to old "balding" Jacob today.'

She made to move. 'Yes, Jacob, I'm sorry. Some other day.'

'You have an assignation,' he trumpeted, not asking, stating. 'I can tell by your heartbeat,' boldly placing his hand above her bosom. 'Yes,

233

yes, I'm right!' he said, like a crowing cock, the white-crested comb of his head tilted up at her.

She didn't flinch, was used to him by now. 'Yes, Jacob, you are absolutely right,' she said, as straightfaced as she could. 'I have an assignation with a lawyer, and when he has finished securing my husband's release, I shall direct him to turn his attentions towards you for committing a felony on my person!'

He drew back, laughing. 'You are a wicked woman, Ellen Rua, as wicked as I am! What a match we would make in wickedness.' He continued to laugh, rubbing his hands in relish. 'Tell your lawyer to leave Lavelle where he is. I have flours and grains and hams and spices here, but not a *bar-mitzvah* in sight. While you – you are still a young woman and could bear me a brace of sons, a couple of fiery-haired Irish Jews, Paddy and Shamus Peabody. In no time they'd have the running of the whole market!' He was beside himself with mirth at the notion.

'God forbid the thought, Jacob,' she fired back at him. 'And forgive you for thinking it. Pay me now so I can go,' she demanded.

He paid her, watched her thread her way through the crowds. 'Ah! Paddy and Shamus Peabody,' he laughed more quietly to himself.

As her head bobbed out of view, Jacob Peabody still wasn't convinced. She was too cocky by half today, had over-engaged him. And he was right – she had a lustre to her, something indefinable he hadn't seen in her before. 'The Element of Fire,' the proprietor of Peabody's – no heir to his prized hams and grains and spices – mused. But

234

not pleased by his musings.

Pleased with how *she* had handled herself with Peabody, Ellen hurried homewards. It was important to her that she had given him no suspicion that anything was amiss. He would pry that suspicion open, unlocking it further and further until it became a book of evidence. Unlike with his other games, were he to discover her flaw, this one she could not win. Sometimes Jacob displayed a possessiveness towards her which his banter hid, as if he imagined that together they inhabited some special world, which she supposed they did. However slight this trait now was, who was to tell how it would manifest itself, if he were able to find the chink of her guilt?

Jacob was best kept at a long arm's length.

29

He was standing at her doorway, waiting, note in hand.

'I did not know which way to read it. Whether you were hurrying back and I should wait, or whether you were not at home to me?' He smiled, waving the note at her.

She hurried him inside, did not want anybody seeing him waiting for her with her husband in prison. Straight away he came to her putting his hands to her face.

'Ellen, it has been an agony –'

'Stop, don't say it!' She tried to push him away. 'We ... it must not re-occur, Stephen,' she remonstrated.

'Ellen, *it* was not as you seem to refer to it – an unseemly urge. Since first I saw you all those years ... I...'

'No! It's impossible ... no!' She broke back from him. 'It is madness. I have confessed our sin ... *my* sin.' She had repented. 'You have to leave, Stephen. Give me your message and leave – my children will be home!'

He raised his hands. 'Tell me that I am mistaken, Ellen; that you have not harboured such thoughts – for I have ever felt them in your company.'

How could he have? She didn't even know herself until ... it happened.

'No! You're wrong!' she denied. 'It was a different thing – a malaise, some malingering malaise in the face of all my happiness and good fortune since coming to America.' She tried to explain it away, that it had nothing to do with him. That it wasn't he who had altered her feelings, distorted her life.

She saw him withdraw, stung by her words, felt the hollow longing rise within her. The seeping realization that perhaps Good Friday was after all not the purging of her malaise, not the razing of it, gripped her. What if its consummation, the carnal celebration of it, was only the beginning? The terrible truth dawning on her, she moved to him, took his face in her hands, stretched out her fingers over the bone and hollow of his cheeks, and kissed him deliberately for all the years he

236

had loved her.

She met him again on Wednesday at his quarters, this time allowing herself to be naked beside his long body, surprised at how un-squeamish she was.

'We are both damned, you know,' she whispered, Eve-like, into his ear. 'Damned to high Heaven – Stephen Joyce, or McCoist, or whoever you are. It was a rue day you crossed my cabin's door.'

He didn't laugh with her. 'Damned to Hell, Ellen,' he corrected.

'You're too serious,' she said. 'To Hell with seriousness and to Hell with damnation – there's enough of both in this life,' and she bounded up in his bed as if to make her point.

'You, on the other hand,' he smiled, reaching to uncoil her back down beside him again, 'are more unrestrained than I had ever imagined.'

On Thursday, he escorted her to the offices of Erastus Jellico. Throughout, though they were never alone, every fibre of her body seemed to be set in contrasting extremes with itself.

Once in the street again, she turned to him. 'He unnerved me. Do you think he suspects any-thing?'

'Mr Jellico? I am sure he does not.' But she wasn't as convinced as she would have wished.

He took her arm, hurried her along through the streets, the breath clutching at her throat so that she could not even ask him where it was he was taking her.

Soon she had forgotten about Mr Jellico,

forgotten about everything. In the suspended moments of the after-stillness, he asked her, 'Do you remember Montréal – the waltz?'

He reached over, running a finger along the stretched silk of her side.

'And the frozen heart,' she responded. 'I wonder if it is yet loosed?'

He made no answer, encircled her with his arms, danced in the gossamer time with her, until she saw it pinned to the sky outside his window, its white beating lighting the heavens and the earth.

30

The rest of her life had now become nothing more than the time in between the occasions when she could see him. Outside of those meetings, whatever else she had to see to she dealt with in a frantic state. Even when she didn't need to, as if to claw back the time spent away from him. And if life before had been vacuous, and she in a state of suspended animation, now it was a flurry and a frazzle. As if her over-industry was a store of pardon she was building up – plenary indulgences for her sins. Besides, she could not bear to be idle, to dwell on their last intimacy, to let every pore of her body rage for the next. When the children looked at her askance, she offered 'your father's upcoming trial' as an excuse, knowing she was fraying their nerves as well as her own. In the rare moments when logical thought afflicted her, it all made no sense.

She prayed to God that Lavelle would be acquitted, be home to her and everything back to normal. His release became a beacon for her own salvation. She took food only in snatches, yet her blood raced, her body prospered. She was indestructible, surging with energy enough for two people. For the two lives she was now leading.

Everybody complimented her on how well she looked. Inquisitive Mrs Brophy – Ellen checked herself. She must learn not to keep thinking of her neighbour in such a manner. Mrs Brophy was blameless compared with her own actions.

'Why, Ellen, I think it suits you to have your man in prison,' the woman twittered from behind her hand. 'Gives you a rest, I dare say! I wish mine would take such a spell.'

She made a note, mentally, to tell Stephen of the encounter when they were next together. All the little banalities of life took on a new importance for her, if connected to their liaison in even the remotest way. As if they had become the building bricks of the secret life between them.

At night she would lie awake imagining him: his dark intense eyes, the macula, the peculiar twist of his lip – a 'Protestant twist' she called it, 'from Trinity ... handed out with gown and cap'. How in retaliation he would turn her, slap her rump, imprinting her with his long, articulate fingers. Unable to sleep with her imaginings, her body would become turbulent, until she quelled it, damping down its fire within the cup of her hands.

The night Lavelle was acquitted her joy was unbounded. She received him with all the gratitude and love at her disposal and all the fury and passion his absence demanded. She watched over him as he slept the sleep of the innocent, and prayed to all that was good and holy to release her from her affliction. Thankful she was too, that in their first intimacy since she had betrayed him, she had displayed no uncharacteristic act to disquiet him. Again she besought her God to remove this predicament of the flesh from her.

She had told Stephen that 'when my husband is released, I cannot see you again', deliberately naming him as her 'husband' and not 'Lavelle'.

He had agreed, knowing she was right. Adding that, because of his own connection with Lavelle, 'My own honour is greatly tarnished and I should take myself away from this place and from you. How I do not know, Ellen, but I must.'

She did not want never to see him again. 'We could be as friends, as before – nothing more.' The words sounded hollow and unconvincing, even to herself.

He had disagreed. 'We are a danger to each other, Ellen, like fire and ice. One will extinguish the other, or each both,' he had warned.

'You are right, Stephen. God knows, I know you are right.' She hated the admission of it.

'I should visit once with you and Lavelle,' he had answered, as if contradicting his previous

240

thought. 'Else it will seem at odds, that I was in your company in his absence, and on his return, I am absent. After that I must travel again to Canada, then perhaps to Ireland...'

'Montréal?' she interrupted.

'Yes. How I will bear it on my own I do not quite know.'

Nor could she bear to imagine him there without her. 'I will go too.' She had said it before she could stop herself. 'It will be our last time together, the dance will end where it began.'

It was as if another voice had spoken. Not the voice of her reason – she had gone through the arguments a hundredfold in her head. Not the voice of repentance which she had daily promised herself. But it *was* her own voice. She had quaked at this reversal in her, quaked the more that he might refuse her.

He had begun to. 'Ellen ... you ... we cannot or it is lost to us for ever,' he said as if damned by the thought.

'No ... Stephen!' It would be their last time, their very last. 'It will be complete then, consigned properly to its history. I have always wanted to walk openly with you, stand on a hill, watch the stars come down. Let that which is everybody's be ours...' She paused at the enormity of what she was suggesting, the way she was seeking to construct a grand finale to their deceit, dress it in the heroic, like some great Greek tragedy. '...to celebrate the ordinary of life would be a fitting goodbye.'

It had to be finished between them. But equally it could not be left unfinished – furtive, between the gaps. She wanted to spend a whole day with him, two, even three – to put their grand passion to the test, but also to anchor it in the detritus of daily living.

'Montréal will be a step too far, Ellen – it will be a bridge of sighs – but I cannot refuse you ... or myself,' he had answered.

They had decided to wait a respectable length of time after Lavelle returned home. Now she was in a state of constant but sublimated elation, fearing at every moment that her turmoil was as visible externally as it was present to her internally. Somehow, she kept her conscience at bay, rationalizing that this last act was the clearing out of her errantness, that Montréal would be the final purging of her malaise. That by sinning more, her sin itself would be rooted out.

Whilst in prison, Lavelle's wound had received some medical attention and had healed well so that now he was able to engage in some light work. Nevertheless, they kept on for a period the youth who had assisted her during Lavelle's incarceration, as the bullocking of freight was heavy work.

She felt that they needed additional help on an ongoing footing, that there still was more capacity for expansion in burgeoning Boston. Lavelle still was of the view that they were too much dependent on Peabody and latterly she had come round to his way of thinking. Jacob, with his three stores, gobbled up most of their time and effort, and stocks. She had become increasingly aware of his foibles, concerned by his preoccupation with her. They were very much at Peabody's mercy should anything go wrong.

To balance out Peabody's influence on the business required them to expand. This in turn required further expenditure, further capital, further risk. They discussed the options open to them. She, more conservative, was against borrowing from the banks or the credit agency of R.G. Dun. They resolved that in limiting their exposure to Peabody, they should also confine the risk of overstretching their borrowings. This could be achieved by approaching the Frontignacs, suggesting they take a stakeholding in the company, thereby binding them in as partners. In return for their investment the Frontignacs would have an already established entrée into New England. This all presented her with an appropriate reason for travelling to the Northern city. In any event it was fast approaching a year since she had previously visited the Frontignacs – too long an interval.

Stephen had called to visit Lavelle, on the first occasion when she was not there – a Monday evening. By design, she knew; it was her evening for the increasingly irritating discussions of the Daughters of the Commonwealth. On the second occasion she was present.

It had not been as difficult as she had imagined. She left them to talk on their own, joining them for only small periods of time. The sight of them, locked in earnest conversation, seemed to echo the common bond she shared with them. She loved them both. Now, as she breezed into them she saw no contradiction in the idea that they in turn, but individually, would similarly regard her.

Louisa and Mary both had played their Bach cantatas for the visitor in the good room. He had complimented them on their own beauty and their 'beauty on the instrument'. Nor was Patrick ignored, brought into the conversations on politics and the growing 'abolition of slavery' movement, 'conversations befitting a coming young man', as Stephen had called him; much to Patrick's delight, she observed.

Apart from this, she hadn't seen Stephen at all. She had left it a decent time, she thought, since this last visit, three weeks, before furtively depositing the envelope at his lodgings. Inside, the details of their final assignation in Montréal – the date on which she would fly to him on the singing rails of the Grand Junction Railroad.

Full of exhilaration, she hoisted herself on to the train, yet feverish with trepidation that something would go wrong. That he had been away, not received her note, as a result would not be there. She would then be denied drawing it all to a close, in a kind of Montréal Paradiso. Thus, unresolved, it would be a never-ending claw to her gut, giving her no ease until the grave.

As the train jolted her away, she was filled with panic. She had not been steadfast before. What if Montréal was not the *grand dénouement* she had imagined? What if, instead, it served only to advance her addiction? And it *was* an addiction, this craving within her. This ... she hesitated to give it its rightful name ... this lust, one of the Seven Deadly Sins, because it was so obsessive, with no end to it. She shuddered with repugnance at the idea of the creature she had become.

It could not be such a base element as lust. She loved him. With great passion, it was true, but she loved him. With him she lived outside herself, in the air, disconnected – the old Ellen disintegrated, the new one, a phoenix rising, lifting its wings. When she arrived in Montréal, she flung out the carriage door and stood on the platform, searching for him over the heads of the hustle and bustle.

But he *was* there. Waiting, at a discreet distance, raising his hat in welcome, making her heart dance.

31

Montréal was everything she had desired; it was indeed her Montréal Paradiso, all two days and three nights of it.

Strolling together with him, she linked his arm, like a lady and her beau should, with little fear of recognition to constrain her. That evening they dined at the Hôtel Fond du Lac. She wanted to dance, but to her disappointment there was no music.

'The dance is over,' she said wistfully, 'the frozen heart caged once more.'

He read less into it than she did. 'It is only the

musician's night off – perhaps he is meeting his lover!' he teased, making her laugh at the irony of this.

For hours they lingered in conversation, talking of the great and the little wonders of the universe: life, pre-destiny, the nature of love; the transcendence of love over sin; the conspiracy of boundaries – those small rituals which hem and fence and define a life.

'This could never have happened in Ireland,' she mused, thinking of her life before.

'No,' he said, mistaking her, 'we are creeds apart. The union of Protestant and Catholic flesh would be an abomination. Here, we are the symbol of a New Ireland, not merely disunited from Britain, but united within ourselves. When we lie together we consummate the past,' he said with a little laugh, adding, more wickedly, 'the sword of the Boyne is blunted in the bower of *Kathleen Ní Houlihan*. It is the way it should be!'

'It is the way with men,' she sighed, but thinking how less serious he had become since she had first known him.

'What is?' he asked.

'Men seek to change what they love, to exalt it, to make the loved one different from what she truly is, while a woman–'

'While a woman loves not the object of her love but only love itself!' he interrupted.

'No – not at all!' she countered, 'a woman will love a man as he is, his blemishes and failings, not imagining him changed by her love–'

'But scheming for it!' he interrupted again.

'Yes, Stephen,' she laughed with him, 'but that

246

is a different thing – a female prerogative.'

Later, while she lay waiting for him, she wondered if perhaps he was right, if the desire for
love itself was the malaise which had brought her
to this. Peabody and his poets would have held it
so. But she loved Lavelle, was sure of it, and in
return was loved by him.

He smiled, seeing her lying there, like the *peau-
de-soie*, the fiery diadem of her hair splayed out;
below the darker, downy pubescence; she a pale
and vivid offering, of fire and ice.

She knew what he was thinking and smiled
back, the dream-like substance – the *sream* –
again over her eyes. As he arched over her, she
could not think of him as anything but the
ultimate object of all her feelings.

Every sensuality filled, her body ebbed and
flowed to his slightest touchings. And if no great
waves crashed down as before, flinging her
breathless and broken on the shore, then she was
caught in swirling eddies of pleasure. They, like
the ever-constant ripples of calmer seas, swept
endlessly over her.

Afterwards, he read to her: Donne, 'To His
Mistress Going to Bed', from the *Love Elegies*.

'License my roving hands, and let them go,
Before, behind, between, above, below.
O my America! my new-found-land...'

She let the words float over her, before, behind,
between, above, below, sensuously following the
course his hands had taken, re-awakening her

parts. Was she his 'America', his 'new-found-land'? Poets were always describing women as lands. He continued reading.

'...Full nakedness! All joys are due to thee,
As souls unbodied, bodies unclothed must be,
To taste whole joys...'

Words, powerful, easy words of seduction, as if he had any need of them for her, she thought. She would have another poem – a shorter one – before she set the book aside from his hands.

'Twice or thrice had I loved thee,
Before I knew thy face or name;
So in a voice, so in a shapeless flame,
Angels affect us oft...'

It was their story. Written two hundred years before them – between 'Air and Angels', as Donne called his poem – the space she now inhabited.

It was no mystery to her why Stephen had chosen this poem, the loved one undefined, except as a 'shapeless flame'. Unclothed by form or human characteristics.

'It makes love, or the idea of love, the greater, the loved one, the lesser,' she whispered aloud, unravelling it for herself. 'But it is the opposite of love – to create an illusion, a deception for one's self...' She turned her head to him. 'That way, I suppose, one is never disappointed?'

'I am never disappointed in you, Ellen,' he said.

'Perhaps you in me?' She reached out, touching

his love-spot with her fingertip, like a child unsure of what the touching would release.

'In you I taste only whole joys,' she said, paraphrasing a line he had read to her. She put the book aside from him. 'I have had enough of words for now.'

Wordlessly then, from the far dark corners of her mouth, she created her own love poem for him. In tongues, as eloquent an elegy as any fashioned by the seventeenth-century Dean of St Paul's.

Time spun out before them like a silken thread, unhemmed, unbounden, unchimed. One hour was like the next, and no hour called them to be somewhere else. Maybe, after all, in this timelessness these were the selves they were meant to inhabit from time immemorial. Or maybe it was the French thing he had told her; *'l'absence ni le temps ne sont rein quand on aime'* – 'to those who love absence and time are as nothing' – up here in the suspended time-oceans of Canada. Alberta, Alaska, Arctica. First named of the alphabet, ancient, primal. As different from New England as Ireland was from Old England.

Her only indebtedness to the world of New England, and one she must repay while she was here, was to call on Frontignac Père et Fils. To impress upon them the opportunities she and Lavelle could present for them in Boston and beyond. With their financial backing and the superior variety of wines the Frontignacs could supply, she and Lavelle could employ salesmen to travel the ever-increasing network of railroads,

249

taking their wines well beyond the confines of Greater Boston.

So, she sauntered along Dorchester, Montréal's most graceful boulevard, with its fashionable Italianate mansions thick with vineries, and horse-chestnuts alive with humming birds. She was confident of convincing the Frontignacs as to the merits of her plan, invincible in her conviction that it was a good one. A lover's weakness, she imagined. But she must be careful to listen, take cognizance of their reservations, embrace their ideas too; not just parade out her own and Lavelle's.

She had not breathed a word to Peabody. Her plan should not have any effect on their dealings with the merchant of Quincy, but you never knew with him what way he would react. Having concluded her business at Manoir Frontignac she would hurry back to Stephen. A surfeit of happiness suffused her at the thought.

They had enquired about the musician and for tomorrow night, their last in Montréal – their last ever, she reminded herself – had been assured he would be in attendance. It was more fitting he be there as they made their good-byes.

As she mounted the impressive granite steps to Manoir Frontignac, palisaded on either side with hardwood and still thinking of Stephen, she felt the flush of expectancy rise in her again, the roof of her mouth go dry. 'Tasting only whole joys' – the poets had words, even for the unmentionable.

32

That evening she leaned over the table to him, fork in hand.

'I believe it is their intention to themselves set up in Boston, their firm intention!' she stated.

'Merely because they did not approve your plan at this juncture does not mean that, Ellen,' he pointed out quite logically.

'No – but it's not logical, Stephen. It was the words in between the words. I sensed it. They are so polite, the Francophones, but something is at the back of it.' She'd had the feeling the moment the large French oak-panelled door had swung open to admit her to Manoir Frontignac.

'Were you not introduced to the Frontignacs by a mutual friend, the priest in Québec?' he asked. 'They will hardly betray *his* friendship.'

For all his education, he could, at times, be frustratingly pedantic. She put down the fork, aware that she had started to shake it at him. Nothing could be proven; it was her *sense* of what had occurred, an intuition.

'*We* should talk of betrayal!' she answered. 'It would be a fine irony indeed if it were the Catholic merchants of Québec Province who closed me out of business and not the Ulster Scots of Boston!' she said stingingly.

He refused to be drawn by her. 'You still have Peabody – is he not the largest retailer of fine

251

wines in Boston?'

'Peabody?' she exclaimed. 'If the Frontignacs set up in Massachusetts they will seek to deal directly with Peabody. Jacob will hold out against them for a while – because he is made that way – but in the end he will have to go with them.'

'If you believe this to be true, the only answer for you is to find another supplier while you are in Montréal,' he pointed out.

'No!' she answered him, defiantly. 'This is to be our last occasion together. I will not spend it tramping the streets of Montréal, searching out bottles of claret. Maybe you are right, maybe it is not as I see it after all,' she rationalized. 'I can come here again – at another time – if needs be.'

'Later may be too late. It is for only you to decide, Ellen,' he said, knowing she already had.

For her part she didn't want to talk about it any further.

However, the business with the Frontignacs weighed heavily on her for the next day. She was as angry with them for its intrusion into her sacred time with Stephen as she was for any imagined threat to the New England Wine Company. An emotion, she decided, which would make no earthly sense to anybody but herself.

Determined though she was to put all thought of the episode at Manoir Frontignac behind her, the impending sorrow of their parting now rose up before her. As the day wore on, she and Stephen spoke less and less to each other, sharing the unbroken intimacy of the growing silences, as if in preparation for the longer silence awaiting them. She clung to him like a soul adrift, seeking comfort in the physical; consoling herself that she would for ever enshrine these moments in some hallowed place in her memory. Hold them there frozen for all eternity, at times to unthaw them, let them breathe, put flesh on them, momentarily melt them into her own life.

She wondered if her skin would remember. Never before regarded her skin as separate from her other parts until she had been with him. Now it seemed to have its own memory. When he touched her, roved her with his hands, each place on her skin seemed to have its own distinct response. It was not the same as memory of the mind. It was to each part local, this memory of skin.

'All other things to their destruction draw, Only our love hath no decay.' She mouthed the words to herself; Donne – 'The Anniversary'. She would decay, she knew, without him, wither into middle age, forgoing pity, substituting duty, but decaying nevertheless. Would this memory of skin he had awakened in her, would that too dry up with time?

'The element of fire is quite put out, The sun is lost and th' earth.' She said the lines knowing that was how it would be. It was as if the priest-poet, Donne, had seen into her life. She remembered Peabody using the lines, playing with her, prophesying her life. 'You were named for fire ... Ellen Rua.' Now the words rang with a fatalistic aptness. It was all so far removed from what she had known. Where love was simple, often a 'match' made by others, it came with a 'cow or a sow', a bargain made for the cost of keeping a woman. Not many fine rhymes then. Too much living, surviving the next winter.

Yet here in America, Stephen and Peabody, these two men having such influence on her life, spoke to her – about her – in rhymes and images – lines composed by Englishmen. Neither Michael nor Lavelle ever spoke to her through other people's words, and she had never felt the lesser that they hadn't.

Yet, it was she herself who had reached out from that world to the world of poetry and music – and ideas. She wanted it for her children, she had thought, now realizing she had not thought much on them in the last few days. She imagined them safe and well but in that other world. They could not co-exist with her here, be in her mind, a party to her sin. She had stepped outside their world in an attempt to define her own. What chasm between them had now developed resulting from that step?

After tomorrow, when she would attempt to step back inside it again, it would not be the same world, its boundaries would be irreparably broken. A growing part of her now wanted tomorrow to be over, this Montréal madness put behind her. She would redouble her efforts towards Lavelle, the children, the business. The slate would be wiped clean – confession, reconciliation with God and man.

She was filled with excitement as she dressed. Tonight, everything would be right, all misfortune

254

banished from her mind. There would be time enough for that – and the sorrowing dullness – on the long train journey home. And in the days and months thereafter. She wondered what Stephen was thinking of. Was it likewise with him – parallel thought?

The realization hit her then that she was guilty of the same sin towards him as she had accused him of towards her. If she was his *Kathleen Ní Houlihan*, his vision of Ireland, then she too had made him into some kind of mythic deliverer, some romantic poet-warrior, whom she had dredged up out of the past. She had invented a self for him as different from his person as she was from the 'Heaven-Woman' which he had sought to turn her into.

'Ellen!'

She quickened at his voice, set the last lock of hair in its place, ran to him and kissed him fiercely.

'Fionn!' she said, her face alight, naming him for the legendary leader of the Fianna. 'Slayer of monsters, magician, poet,' she laughed.

He looked at her, bemused. What was it that had now intoxicated her mind?

'You're "Fionn"!' she said, laughing now at the look on his face. She shook him to emphasize it. 'Fionn MacCumhail!'

The evening was everything she had hoped it would be. She remarked how resplendent the Hôtel Fond du Lac looked, far raised above the wilderness place – the 'Base of the Lake', from where a century earlier a duo of 'Nor'westers'

255

who had made good, had brought home the name. It had been much improved since the days when it rang with the old songs of the *voyageurs*, and the entrance hall stank with the smell of stacked pelts. Now, the large hall, papered with imitation white-veined marble, boasted female figurines in sequestered niches. A slab of real black marble lay mantelpieced between a yawning fireplace and a large gilt-framed mirror, in which she fleetingly caught sight of themselves. The dancing area, a polished parquet floor of native wood, hosted a large rosewood table. To either side of it dark-leathered mahogany tallbacks sat regimentally arranged, while to each end even larger spindle-backed carvers remained regally empty.

This table had never been occupied. It lay in readiness for the souls of those wandering voyageurs, who would one day return.

The *maître* led them to a discreet window table. Beside them hung long chintz curtains which glazed and spattered with variegated silvers and golds.

'It is like a palace of old, Stephen – was this what you were used to in Dublin?' she asked.

'No,' he laughed, 'the peasantry would never take up their pikes if it were known that revolutionaries frequented such places.'

'Indeed they wouldn't, and shouldn't,' she sparked back at him, unable to decide whether or not she liked the place, if it was only the occasion dulling her senses.

And it was as if the chef had excelled himself for them. Oysters in aspic were followed by a roast of wild game. Then, the *pièce de résistance*, a meringue pyramided with assorted fruits, its foundation a glacé bed of strawberry and citron ices. It really was sinful, but then it was only for tonight – a 'Last Supper', she said blasphemously.

Afterwards, when the moustached *maître de musique* waved his magician's wand over them, she sparkled and spun, dancing away tomorrow's darkness. Stephen held her close, folding her around him when they twirled. As if by accident insinuating his long dancer's legs between hers when he curled her backwards; impaling her against the climax of the ascending *arpeggio*. Held her then, suspended between one pulse and the next, until the descending music caused him to release her again. Bending, yielding, swaying, in perfectly motioned *fléchissement*.

Then, the *joueur de violon* played the 'Valse du Coeur Glacé' without her asking. When she later asked for it again, he flicked back his shoulder-length hair, raised the drooping moustache into a smile and knowingly obliged.

And they danced, floating between the white air and the angels in a place which had no centre.

When they retired, she brimming from the evening, Stephen bade her wait a moment then disappeared.

When he returned he made her close her eyes, holding her hands in front of her, like a child.

'A parting gift,' he said, dropping the neatly wrapped parcel into them.

'A book!' she guessed, before opening her eyes

again, fingers fumbling to loosen the silken string with which it was bound.

It *was* a book. Donne's poetry, including the *Love Elegies*, which he had somewhere found for her in Montréal. She clasped her arms around his neck.

'Thank you, thank you,' she said, 'for this ... a treasure trove of memories.' She fanned through the pages, glimpsing familiar lines. 'Is it the same as yours?' she asked.

'Yes, it corresponds exactly,' he replied. 'Why?'

'If I could, I would have *your* copy – that from which you read to me?'

They exchanged the books like vows, sealing their love in the eternity of verse.

He undressed her then slowly, delicately, as if unfolding a flower of paradise, lest in haste he damage it. She put her hand to his face – a gesture of thanks. Their lovemaking would be the lovemaking of grieving.

Afterwards, they lay separate from each other, in silence. Expressed, yet the inexpressible weighing upon them. Elated, yet the long hunger of the soul, as ever, unfulfilled. *'La petite mort'* – 'the little death' – Donne had written of the depression that descends on the soul after the body has climbed to the ecstatic state, as theirs had.

Her religion had taught her that only at *'la grande mort'* – 'the great death' – would the soul at last be fulfilled, united with the one true object of its desire, God. At that moment she feared she would ever be denied that ultimate unity. She had sacrificed the *'grande'* for the *'petite'*.

'Ellen!' Stephen called into the space above them, 'sing to me.'

Since the time on the train when she had brushed him off he had not asked her. She said nothing, raised herself from the bed, crossed to the window. Outside the *québécois* moon was occluded, brooding behind some dark cloud. Out there too, beyond the city, lay the fertile plains of Montréal, nurtured by the St Lawrence, the river which had first brought her to this country. Beyond the St Lawrence to the north were the great Canadian wastelands, to the east the great wastelands of the Atlantic Ocean. South was Boston – and Lavelle.

Stephen watched while she put her fingers to the windowpane, connecting with the outside, saw the white flesh of her back expand as she breathed in to begin. 'O my fair-haired boy...' She sang, turned away from him, the notes curving along her spine, down her bare legs into the wood, singing themselves through the floorboards to where he lay.

'All joy is gone that we once knew,
All sorrow newly found...'

His eyes followed the rise and fall of her shoulder-blades, the melody seeping out of her body.

'Let no sad tears now stain your cheek,
As we kiss our last good-bye.
Think not upon when we might meet,
My love, my fair-haired boy.'

She paused before the final verse, the moon emerging from behind the cloud to bathe her in its light, fixing her breath like a white rose on the windowpane. She half-turned to him, the moonlight edging her contours, sifting her colours.

She had not sung since her wedding-day, for Lavelle. But it was not this song then, that Michael, her dear dead Michael, so much loved her to sing. She had always thought of it as his song only. But it wasn't. It was hers. Now she sang it for herself, as much as for Michael, or Lavelle, or ... Stephen, who had summoned it from her.

'And there will grow two hawthorn trees,
Above my love and me.
And they will reach up to the sky,
Intertwined be...'

He watched, rather than listened, as she poured forth her elegy for lost love.

'And the hawthorn flower will bloom where lie
My fair-haired boy and me.'

She stood motionless. More than the act of love, the act of singing had transported her into another space and time somewhere beyond the great wastelands. Now, she needed time – a moment of earthly time – to come back, be present to him. To restore the absence of centre, lost to her in song.

She it was who spoke first. '*Ó mo dhúchas* – from my tradition,' she said quietly, as if that explained everything. It was the first of the old tongue he had heard her speak in the New World.

Neither of them slept until they parted into the ordinary Montréal morning it had become.

33

Sweating and steaming, drumming out its own monotonic tradition, the Grand Junction Railroad train drew her ever homewards. Its rhythm at first dimmed her sorrow. Now, each rolling mile was a steel rod, pile-driven into her heart.

How could she face them? What would she say to them? That she missed them, when instead she had striven to drive all thought of them from her mind? When they asked of Montreal – how could she describe it without investing it with the myth of a lover's eyes? And Lavelle – when they were alone and he reached for her? How could she give him her Judas kiss, her Mary Magdalen love? Her body would betray her, as it had already betrayed him.

She prayed, trying to make an Act of Perfect Contrition, discontinuing it when the cadence of the words fell in with the rhythm of the tracks, mocking her.

'O My God,' clacketyclack, 'I am heartily sorry,' clacketyclackclacketyclack, 'for having offended thee,' the clacketyclack, clacketyclack, echoing her hypocrisy ahead of her down the line to Boston. She flicked open the pages of Stephen's book but found no respite there, the once tactile words devoid of all flesh and blood, arid. Her eyes rested on 'Good Friday, 1613. Riding Westward', one of the *Divine Poems*, Donne's later works. 'O think me worth Thine anger, punish me, Burn off my rusts, and my deformity.' She had deformed her soul for love, or its phantasm, contorted her mind into thinking that it was some higher calling; perverted virtue. But she could not deny her emotions; they were as real as sin. She would not let the guilt of what she had done transform itself into yet further guilt – the guilt of denial. Good Friday 1613, or 1853, it was all the same, Donne, like herself oppressed by sin ... now obsessed with death, yearning for his God.

She stared out of the window. The moon hung lifeless in the sky, suspended between the earth and the heavens. Salvation ... damnation? She too had no answer, as the iron horse plunged her between them.

Boston station was a mêlée of welcome, of calls and answers, doffed hats, outstretched arms, hand-clasps. Lavelle, a wide smile on him when he spotted her, ran to her, swept her up, twirling her in his embrace.

'You're welcome back, Ellen.'

She was glad to be home, relieved to see him, to be swept back into their used-to-be world. He peppered her with a mixture of questions and news, and she gabbled back at him with her own mix of answers and questions. He thought she '...looked strained by the journey, but as fine as ever.'

Later, the excitement continued as Patrick, Mary and Louisa, each of them, plied her with more welcomes. Even Patrick, not normally given to such demonstrations, was patently pleased to greet her. Her homecoming was less of a trauma than she had anticipated, the exuberance of the occasion sailing her through it. Still, the knot of dread in her stomach never left, wrenching her more and more as the evening wore on.

Later, she went ahead of Lavelle and dressed quickly for bed, skipping her prayers, not wanting him to see her full naked, to replicate what had gone before. As if in her nakedness she would be exposed, the handprints of adulterous love on her breasts, between her thighs, signposting each act – 'Before, behind, between, above, below'. Unbidden the words flew into her thoughts, her body, despite herself, remembering. She tried to banish them, changing her mind about the prayers, kneeling to make an *Ave*. 'Hail Mary, full of grace ... Holy Mary, Mother of God, pray for us sinners now and at the hour of our death...'

At the 'Amen', she was already clambering into bed.

Half-dozing, facing away from him, she felt his tug at her nightdress. It had twisted behind her. Now, instinctively, she moved to free it.

'Oh Ellen...!' She heard the quivering in his voice, the surge within him quickening her to wakefulness. She turned to face him.

'Oh, Lavelle, I love you ... I truly love you!'

263

She meant it. She wanted to love him even more, to the exclusion of everything, everyone ... herself. For a moment she panicked that the state of liquefaction in which her body was, its additional fluency, would give her away. Bizarrely, she wondered if their two seeds would mix within her, intercoursing, become one?

Lavelle's wanting to kiss her shook her out of these aberrations. She resisted his kiss, afraid of this intimacy – somehow more intrusive, more revealing, than the most intimate act she now consummated with him.

While he slept she thanked God. He had not turned His forgiving face from her. By not revealing her to Lavelle, He had given her a second chance. Feverishly, she sent up Acts of Contrition and Thanksgiving, mouthing them under her breath so as not to awaken Lavelle. Now there was hope, the hope of a new life for them both. She did not mind, now, how the Almighty might punish her transgressions.

34

In the days and months that followed she appeared to have shaken off her old lassitudes, her 'malaise' as she called it. Her spirits were uplifted – even the children remarked on it – and she found a renewed zest for living, and for love.

'Like fresh-scrubbed apples, the pair of you' was Harriet Brophy's observation. 'All rosy and shiny, and ready to be eaten!' her neighbour had whispered.

It had taken her a while to work up sufficient courage to risk confession. Only then did she go, avoiding the cathedral in Franklin Street, to St Mary's Church in the North End. It was almost her undoing, her new confessor every bit as inquisitorial as her previous one. He asked about that confession and if she understood 'the true nature of repentance'. Finally, he made it clear that if she presented herself before him again 'and had continued in that most grievous sin against Holy Matrimony', he would refuse her absolution. Furthermore, at whatever other confessional she might attend, she was to inform her confessor there of this admonition. This did not trouble her greatly, her fervency of resolve convincing her that such a banishment would not be called upon.

Peabody, too, noticed the change in her, and although she was now more readily prepared to enter into verbal combat with him, he seemed less inclined towards pugnacity than before. This newfound conciliatory manner in him almost tempted her to unveil her thoughts about what plans she suspected the Frontignacs had in mind. But she didn't.

Glad she was that she hadn't raised the hare with him when, throughout the following months, she experienced no problems of either credit or supply from the Montréal merchants. It must have been her 'heightened state' while in Montréal that had led her to such unfounded 'imaginings'. Business too, with Peabody and

265

their other customers, continued to grow, but at a pace posing no threat to their own stability.

Stephen, true to his word, did not 'darken her acquaintance' and though she knew Lavelle met with him on occasion to discuss 'Ireland', she expressed only a passing interest in those affairs. Their paths did not cross the remainder of that year, and she forced herself to think about him less and less, following Peabody's dictum – 'Not to forget, but to remember less'.

Boston itself continued to prosper, the harbour with its two hundred docks, handling half a million cargo tons each year. Some work, too, she noted, as 1854 glided outwards, was being done to assist the pauperized Irish, often reported as displaying a 'listless indifference to their fate'. Societies like the Charitable Irish Society and the Irish Emigrant Society, which helped place emigrants out West, as well as locate lost relatives, grew in numbers and strength. The St Vincent Female Orphan Society in the South End, established by the Sisters of Charity, and, she had to admit, generously supported by Yankee Protestants, now housed up to three hundred young orphaned girls, many Irish. For homeless boys the House of the Angel Guardian in the North End, newly founded in 1851, provided a 'moral restaurant' for short-term inhabitants.

She contributed whatever she could afford to these societies. She had been appalled at the poverty and deprivation she had witnessed in the North End, when she had gone to confession at St Mary's, thinking the situation of the Irish there to be by now somewhat relieved. But she

266

had been wrong. They still flooded the city tenements, poverty-ridden, diseased, often more dead than alive.

There were, too, other growing tensions within the city. Abolitionist mobs had begun to set free runaway slaves from the Southern States, spiriting them out of the country to Canada. Slaves arrested by federal troops now patrolling Boston's streets were returned south to bondage, amidst widespread outcry. During one such occurrence an Abolitionist mob murdered a US Marshal, bringing violence associated with the slavery question to a new level in Boston. But while the liberation of black slaves in the South greatly occupied the minds of liberal Bostonians, in stark contrast the ever underlying venom against the Irish was once more whipped into action.

In 1854, another Know-Nothing Mayor, J.V.C. Smith, was elected. The new Mayor actively encouraged feelings of hate against a large proportion of the citizens he represented – Catholics. The Irish, their Catholic leaders suggested, because of the scale of intimidation, 'should keep low, avoid the polling booth – be like guests in someone else's home'.

Lavelle was furious. 'Those shoneens are trying to turn us into lily-livered lackeys. We tugged the forelock long enough in our own country.'

She pleaded with Lavelle not to get involved in the disturbances, also taking Patrick to one side and cautioning him, fearing that his earlier stance at the Eliot School might make him a target for Nativist groups, such as 'The Sons of Sires', founded 'to protect our country from the insidious wiles of foreigners'. 'Insidious wiles', she knew full well, meant the Catholic Church and all its teachings.

One evening Patrick arrived home excitedly waving a handbill. 'These are being given out on every corner!'

She took it from him, an unexplained terror gripping her as she read it... that the sentiments expressed were going to embroil them all in some great calamity.

Americans to the Rescue!
Americans! Sons of the Revolution!!
A body of seventy-five Irishmen, known as the 'Columbian Artillery', have volunteered their services to shoot down the citizens of Boston and are now under arms to defend Virginia in kidnapping a citizen of Massachusetts!
Americans! These Irishmen have called us 'cowards and sons of cowards'!
Shall we submit to have our citizens shot down by a set of vagabond Irishmen?

The Columbian Artillery was one of a number of ad-hoc Irish militia companies formed mainly for pomp, parade and after-dinner speeches.

'The Irish were called in to protect a slave from being freed, who was being sent back to Virginia!' Patrick told her.

'Shame on them!' she remonstrated. 'Sending a man back to his slavery, and they not long, themselves, out of theirs.'

'He was a runaway!' he argued with her.

'And so were we, Patrick, so were we!' she said angrily.

But the Irish got ahead. As Lavelle put it, 'All against a background of Know-Nothings and credit agents like R.G. Dun, who describe us as nothing else but "tricky" or "too fond of horse-flesh".'

She was glad she had never to seek the approval of the all-powerful R.G. Dun and the inevitable commentary on her sex and race; to be told you were 'good for nought credit' – to be marked that way.

The 'Bridgets' were another phenomenon of Boston life.

'The Boston Bank of Ireland', Lavelle called them.

'Without the "Bridgets", Ireland would be sunk.' Mary, ever interested in Erin's daughters, supplied the facts. 'Last year more than one million pounds was sent back by the "Bridgets". Without them, many would never have escaped Ireland. The "Bridgets" made the "Daisy Chain".'

Ellen understood what Mary meant. The 'Daisy Chain' of female emigration, 'Bridgets' bringing out more 'Bridgets', all bound for either the 'loom or the broom', in the mills and mansions of Massachusetts.

'If it wasn't for the "back-door Bridgets",' Patrick piped up, 'and the priests creeping round taking their hard-scrubbed pennies, half the churches in Boston would never have been

269

raised,' much at odds, Ellen thought, with his stance a few years ago at Eliot School.

They were all taking shape. Mary, the thinker, studious, given to the facts and figures of life, passionately interested in the role of her own gender. Building up in her mind some catalogue of the 'silent and steadying contribution' the 'Bridgets', mill girls and needlewomen made to life on both sides of the Atlantic. A store of knowledge, Ellen had no doubt, Mary would one day put to use.

Then, Patrick. Politically aware, always rebellious, resistant to 'the weight of Church and State bearing down on the small man'. And then the 'Bostooning of the Irish', as Patrick called it, worse in his eyes than 'all the English betrayals'. 'The Irish now betraying themselves, colonizing their own countrymen, in the name of being American.'

In each of them she could see the disparate parts of herself. At night she prayed that neither would fall prey to the vagaries of mind and emotion to which she was once given.

And Louisa. Louisa was her silent angel, a kind of touchstone for all of them, and most of all for Mary. She and the girl were inseparable. Not only that, but Ellen had long ago noticed how ably they seemed to communicate. By touch and look, and something extra. Their favourite recreation was to play pieces of music for each other in a tit-for-tat musical game, much loved by Ellen.

'Music,' Ellen had said to Mary. 'That's how you two *talk* to each other, like the way...' She paused, at the remembrance. 'Like what you and Katie had.'

'It's something like that, Mother,' Mary had replied, 'but nobody will ever be Katie. It's though she's never gone at all, that she's here still – inside.'

Ellen understood.

35

Like 1854, the next twelve months continued Boston's Golden Years, the city flourishing on every front. For Ellen, too, it was a better year. Memories of Montréal, once such a deep wound within her heart, had with time begun to close. Until now, almost healed, the wound itself would never be re-opened. She worked at sealing away the past as she had sealed away Ireland, to be both forgotten countries in the wasteland of memory. Soon it would be frozen there, have no pulse at all, be unable to speak, to trouble the present, or the future.

But she could not yet sever the past completely. In moments of melancholy she would take out his book from among the skirt-folds in her bottom drawer, escaping with it to the Great Elm. There, she would read – and remember 'To His Mistress Going to Bed' or 'Farewell to Love', brushing her thumb over the unresponsive words. Sometimes, when strollers-by, hopeful lovers taking the Long Path, were at a safe

271

distance, she would hold the page to her face, imagining it still held some scent of him, as if the words might preserve some faded sensual remnant. Then she would put the book away again for months, bottom-drawered, out of harm's way.

Once, she had lain the book on the piano when Mrs Brophy called, summoning her, as of a sudden her husband had been taken ill. Ellen was gone longer than anticipated. When she returned, she found Louisa seated at the piano reading the *Love Elegies*. The girl closed the book and without handing it to her put it back where Ellen had left it. Louisa then commenced playing from 'Cantata 208, Sheep May Safely Graze' – a favourite Bach piece of them both.

She didn't know what to think, wondering which of the poems Louisa had read. Maybe the girl wouldn't make that much of them. The words had no living meaning for Louisa. She waited by the piano, the music lulling her worst imaginings. When the playing stopped, she took the book calmly.

'Thank you, Louisa. That was truly beautiful!'

The girl smiled in appreciation, moving into Cantata 147. As Ellen mounted the stairs, *Love Elegies* in hand, the circular rhythm of 'Jesu, Joy of Man's Desiring' rose with her. As she put the book away into its safe and rightful place, she wondered what message it was Louisa sent to her through the music.

Two days later, Lavelle appeared through the door with Stephen Joyce in tow. She welcomed him, as steadily as she could, the heart pounding the life out of her.

How could he have come here? With no warning ... breaking his word to her? He apologized almost immediately.

'I am sorry, Mrs Lavelle, to arrive in on you like this, unannounced.' He smiled. 'But your husband insisted and he is a convincing man.'

'Yes, Ellen,' Lavelle added, 'and I have insisted he stay for the evening. We have much to talk about of events, and have seen too little of him of late.'

'Yes, of course you must stay!' She heard herself echoing Lavelle's words, little of herself in the sentiment. 'And take some supper with us later.'

He demurred, but Lavelle would have none of it, so she excused herself to go to the grocery store. 'Now I have caused a commotion in the household,' she heard him say as she buttoned the coat about her.

She had to get out, away from the confines of the house, from him. Once gone she felt better. Somehow, the clack of her shoes on the pavement, leaving them both behind, was a reassurance, albeit a temporary one. How was she to get through the rest of the evening?

Her mind went in circles, searching out possibilities for absence. Too late to call on Peabody, or any of their other customers. None of her meetings to go to, and she had only recently called on Mary and Louisa's piano tutor. Then it came to her – a visit to Mrs Brophy and her sick husband. Dear Harriet, always to be relied upon. That was it. Immediately they had

273

finished supper, she would announce it, make her apologies and leave. It would be too late to cancel the arrangement then. By the time she returned he would be gone. Well pleased with herself, she travelled homewards, laden with provisions; but the more weighty burden of his visit now lightened.

'The biggest problem hindering our advancement in America is not Nativist, the Orangemen of Ulster, nor the "blue-bloods" of Beacon Hill – it is black,' she heard her husband argue on her return.

Stephen did not agree. 'Only two thousand are here in Boston, mostly in run-downs on Nigger Hill. They are not a threat, Lavelle.' She smiled to herself at the familiar Trinity twist of his accent.

'I think it is the Irish themselves,' Patrick piped up. 'Too many running after the same jobs, driving down the wages. Even the blacks are against us, signing petitions to keep us out of their neighbourhoods.'

'Exactly,' Lavelle interjected. 'And if Boston Yankees free more Southern slaves, then where will they flee to?'

'To the North, where the Irish are,' Patrick answered.

She thought they were all arguing the wrong point. 'Whether they come here or not doesn't make it right to keep them in chains – deny them freedom,' she stated.

'What freedom, Ellen?' Lavelle turned to her. 'Will it be freedom for the Irish with four million *free* Negroes swarming the docks, the tunnels and the railroads? Look at the South,' he continued. 'His master will not risk the Negro's life in a tunnel or a canal bed while there are Irish with shovels to be found.'

She was about to interrupt him, stop the words he spoke.

'But it is the South which supports repeal of the Union of Ireland with Britain,' Stephen said, ahead of her. 'Is that why you, Lavelle, go with Southern slavery?'

She was becoming exasperated with both of them. 'Are we to be used as pawns from across the Atlantic, when the real question is what shall our future as Americans be?' she demanded.

'Whatever happens between the North and the South will determine that future, Mrs Lavelle.' It seemed so cold to her the way he kept referring to her as Mrs Lavelle, so cold ... and correct. 'But if the South is defeated,' Lavelle cut in, 'black slaves will trample over the "free" Irish and the Know-Nothings of Boston will help them. Because in their minds, Paddy is only a "turned-inside-out nigger".'

She wondered as they spoke, if somewhere in Stephen's life now there was someone else for whom he saved his words of love, words far removed from these words of war. He had not exorcized the old devils in the blood, handed down from generation to generation. Devils of children on bridges, forced to jump into Porta-down waters, devils of birthing mothers sliced like Peabody's Virginia hams. Virginia – in the South.

Stephen was speaking. 'But if the South is

275

defeated and the North aided in that defeat by Irish militiamen, then at last we will gain our recognition as Americans. Both we and the blacks will be liberated – become white.'

She listened as the three men she most dearly loved, each followed a different path to his own truth. 'Whether it benefits this "Irish-America" or not, no man, or woman, should be in another's bondage,' she said in defiance of all of them.

Her pronouncement, and the hiatus it produced, provided as good a time as any to make her departure. Although Stephen's presence had not been as fraught for her in the manner she had feared, it had unsettled her in other, less predictable ways. Her plans, however, were thwarted in the worst way imaginable, when Stephen suggesting that he had overstayed his welcome stated he 'would escort Mrs Lavelle along the street'.

Lavelle thought it a good idea, adding, 'I notice my wife shares a common interest with you, Stephen.' She looked up, alert, earlier fears resurrected. 'In a book I have previously seen in your possession, a copy more recently in this house. It will give you both some light relief from talk of Abolition and war.'

Ellen felt a pang of alarm, yet Lavelle had made the remark with no guile. 'What book is that?' she asked, surprising herself by her lightness of tone.

'A book of poems, on the piano some days past; *Love Elegies* and other metaphysical questions – I hadn't noted it before. Is it only recently arrived at the Old Corner Bookstore?' he asked, without anything more than common interest, she thought.

'No,' she answered truthfully, yet lying, 'my copy is from Montréal.'

'Well,' Lavelle smiled, 'I thought you must have had it a while – it seemed well-thumbed, some pages more so than others.' Then to Stephen, he said, 'Strange matter for a clergyman to be writing upon, don't you think?'

Ellen was conscious of Louisa watching her, then the girl's gaze switched to Stephen, as he answered.

'I think not, Lavelle. The clergy must understand all human life if they are to be its shepherds. Donne has as much to say about love of God as he has to say of human love. I read him regularly – I did not know Mrs Lavelle had a similar taste,' he said boldly, fixing his full gaze on her.

'It appears she has,' Lavelle answered, bidding him farewell.

In the street she held on to his arm for dear life. 'Do you think he suspects?' she asked him.

'There is nothing to suspect, Mrs Lavelle, is there?'

She grew angry at him – she was deeply concerned. 'You know what I mean!'

'I genuinely think not, Ellen,' he replied, more solicitously than before. 'Your husband would not play so cruel a game on you. It is not in his nature. He is a good man.'

'Yes, he is,' she answered, 'and we have sinned terribly against his goodness. You, as his friend, I, as his wife.'

'There is not a single day on which I do not reflect on it,' he replied.

'Do you read the *Elegies?*' she asked.

'Yes, frequently – they are the pale glass through which I see you,' he answered, asking in turn, 'and you?'

'Yes, but as *infrequently* as I can,' she answered.

He fell into silence until she spoke again. 'But you are locked for ever deep, here,' and she put her hand above her breast.

He placed his hand over hers. 'In your frozen heart?' he asked.

'Yes, Stephen. It must remain so – of necessity, not of choice,' she said gently.

'Then mine, too, will be for ever frozen.'

'You will be too busy fighting wars to remember,' she laughed. 'You men always need ideals for which to do battle, to die for,' she added, remembering how he had spoken.

'I would die for you, dearest Ellen.'

She knew he meant it, and slowly removed her hand, dislodging his.

'Ellen, is that you?' The voice of Harriet Brophy calling from an open door startled Ellen. But it saved her from the indiscretion of speech or act she felt compelled to commit by his last statement.

'I thought I recognized you from my window – and bring over the handsome gentleman escorting you! Do I recognize him?'

Ellen started to say something, stopped, then waved a hand at her neighbour. The last thing she wanted was for tongues to start wagging now, long after everything.

He bade her 'good-bye' quickly and made his way along the street. She hadn't had time to part properly from him. Maybe it was as well. She

278

gazed after him a moment, before turning to cross the street. Something about his tall, angular figure, his steadfastness of gait, made her wonder if she would ever see him again.

36

Her first inkling of something amiss was when Peabody sent a boy to summon her to Quincy Market 'with all haste'.

She, or Lavelle if she couldn't, called on Jacob regularly. Any matters regarding orders, delivery, price or payment were dealt with on these occasions. Now she wondered what commanded the 'haste'. Perhaps he'd had some breakages and needed replacements urgently? Perhaps a complaint? A rare enough occurrence, since Frontignac Père et Fils selected their growers with great care. Serious enough, however, if it came from an important customer on Mount Vernon Street, or the literati of Louisburgh Square amongst whom word of a poorly-nosed Burgundy would spread with great alacrity.

As soon as she had fixed her out-of-doors self, she hurried to South Market Street.

'What is it, Jacob? It sounded urgent and you look grave,' she said, noting that his customary sparkle was absent.

'It is, and I am,' he said brusquely. 'Look at this!' He came from behind the counter and took her by the arm, but not in the usual flirtatious

279

way. 'You had better sit while you read it!' he said, wiping the top of a tea chest for her with the underside of his apron.

She took the letter, her heart already in a sunken state, and started to read. 'Dear Mr Peabody, We beg to advise, that as from the twenty-first proximo, our newly acquired bonded warehouse in the city of Boston will be available for your inspection...'

She read, eyes widening in disbelief, right down to the end to the flourished signature of Jean Baptiste Frontignac. Below it, the red waxen seal of the French cockerel, the one she had seen so many times on deliveries, that which guaranteed their intactness.

She read the letter again, slowly; '...the full range of our extensive selections of *grand cru* from the Châteaux of Bordeaux, Burgundy, Cognac and the Champagne district as well as exciting *vins nouveaux* from the emerging regions ... all deliveries without of warehouse, two days only within the Greater Boston area. Pricing list attached...'

'When...? What...?' she began, not knowing what she wanted to say, all questions redundant, all answers devoid of hope.

'Today, Ellen!' Peabody supplied. 'I sent for you immediately. I am sorry – had you no intimation from them?' he asked, hand resting on her shoulder.

'No, nothing,' she whispered. 'Yes ... yes!' She changed her mind. 'In Montréal. A feeling ... nothing said.'

'They never do, the French,' he said quietly, as

much surprised at this turn of events as she was.

'Let me see the pricing list, Jacob,' she said, wanting to confront the worst.

'No, Ellen,' he answered, 'it would serve no purpose now. I am sorry to be the bearer of such bad news. It was a bolt from the blue to me, but I'd rather you heard it from me first ... from your Jacob.'

'Jacob, I want to see it. Now!' she demanded, angry, not so much with him – it wasn't Jacob's fault – but with them.

Reluctantly, he shuffled back inside the counter and, reaching underneath, produced a small sheaf of papers, which he brought to her.

'Here you are, Ellen, but I think you should wait, not cause further upset to your person today.'

She took the sheets from him, thumbing through the listings of wines and spirituous drinks. It was vast, beyond any stock she and Lavelle could hope to carry. Her eyes scanned the prices, those of vineyards whose names she recognized. To a bottle they were ten cents in the dollar cheaper than the prices she was currently paying to Frontignac!

'They are out to ruin me, Jacob!' she said. Peabody remained silent as she went through each page, at the bottom of which was printed in bold lettering, to further affront her, 'Deliveries over One Hundred Dollars, F.O.C. Greater Boston Area'.

'Free of charge!' she exclaimed, her mind in turmoil. 'Jacob, it's not all black is it? I can overcome this?' she asked, desperate for any glimmer of hope he might offer.

He put his arm around her. 'Ellen ... my dear,' he began carefully, as if not wanting to extinguish all hope. 'Before this week is out, I imagine, every fine liquor store in Boston will have received one of these missives. You can survive for a while. Frontignac is big – you are small.' He paused, before delivering what he knew would be the *coup de grâce*. 'Firstly, they will likely stop supplying you.' He let this sink in for a moment with her. 'But if you had another supplier, and the prices compared, you could possibly survive. But you will need capital too to finance the additional range of stock, in order to compete with the Frontignacs.'

She took in every word he spoke, the grim picture of the future he had painted, but was grateful to him for painting it with the truth.

'Thank you, Jacob, my good friend,' she said, resolutely adding, 'I am going to fight it. Damn them, Jacob, I'm going to fight it!' she swore. 'I will go to Montréal, to France itself, wherever necessary, to find new suppliers.' She turned to face him. 'Jacob, will you stand by me?'

She saw him hesitate a moment, open out the palms of his hands.

'Ellen,' he began tentatively as if not wanting to say to her what he was about to say. 'My accountant has long since told me how bad a bargain I made with you at the start.' He smiled a little ruefully. 'Especially now my custom in fine wine is well established. This agreement we have, wherein you sell to me at your cost from Frontignac and I pay you when I sell, splitting

282

the profit, is not now as advantageous as it once was.'

Her heart dropped; what was he saying?

'But it works—' he carried on, 'I have the benefit of extended credit and you take the risks – as I have explained to my accountant … and,' he added, 'as I have also explained to him the very excellent attention to business which you offer Peabody's.'

'Jacob,' she started, disbelief in her voice, but he went on more quickly now, his tone changing as if he had given her too much the wrong impression.

'Besides all, Ellen, we are friends. We argue, you hide your secrets from me – but we are friends, dear friends.' He reached to encircle her shoulder again, still soothing. 'Friendship is more important than profit. Accountants do not understand these things, they have no souls … as we have.'

She did not like this round-the-counter talk and shook off his arm. 'Jacob, out with it! Don't hide behind your accountant!'

'Ellen…' he began in the same silvery tones as before, but she pulled away from him, saw the ingratiating smile wane from his face. 'All right then, have it your own way. I am trying to accommodate your new circumstances with Frontignac. It is an unfortunate coincidence that events should collide together like this.'

Maybe she was too abrupt with him. It wasn't Jacob's fault, how the Frontignacs had moved against her at this time. Peabody continued, helpful, understanding her plight.

'I will extend to you a further six months on the

present arrangement. After that, of course I will continue with you, Ellen,' he affirmed. 'But it must be exclusively a business arrangement not based on friendship.' He hastened to add, 'Not meaning we shall not be friends; we will be that, always.'

That, always, but she would not give it to him to see her any more defeated than she was. 'You are right, Jacob – Boston is built on business first, friendship second. We should be no different.' She stood up and stuck out her hand to him. 'Six months, then, Jacob – that's fair notice!'

He took her hand, clasped it warmly, seemed relieved it was this easy. 'Six months, Ellen,' he repeated.

'Oh,' she held on to his hand, keeping him close to her. 'What did you mean, Jacob, "hide my secrets from you"? You are my trusted confidant – I have no secrets from you.' She could play the old fox at his own game; *buried standing up* is right – as Lavelle said of the Jews.

Now Peabody seemed uncomfortable, but she refused to let go of his hand. She saw the little red spark rise in his glinty eyes, then be masked. This man, this Job's comforter, who under the guise of comforting her distress, merely aggravated it – he would not give her six months. Despite their clasped hands, their 'dear friendship'. This was his Judas kiss.

'Oh, nothing, Ellen,' he answered, the white eyebrows inscrutable underneath her gaze, 'one of my teasing phrases, as you call them. Just that you have changed – as any woman would in rising circumstances. Not as reliant on old Jacob

284

as you once were – a good thing,' he added quickly. 'That's all, nothing more!' And he shook her hand to release his own. She held it a moment longer.

'Jacob, you know I couldn't have survived without you. How could I have? For that I will be for ever grateful to you,' she said, before disengaging her hand.

She knew he would be watching her from the door, so she pulled back her shoulders, looked up at the New World skyline, and headed homewards. She felt betrayed. Betrayed by those smooth-talking Frontignacs in Montréal. She had given them their entrée into Boston and now this. They had led her up the garden path, timed their moment well and then set about the ruination of the business she and Lavelle had built up over years. She should have listened to her instinct in Montréal, then set about seeing other suppliers as Stephen had advised. Any person exercising prudence would have done so but she had talked herself out of her fears, allowing herself to be distracted by his presence. She had sacrificed the future of their business for fleeting hours with him.

Another instinct had told her that Peabody would at some stage betray her. Out of some petty vindictiveness, some imagined slight, or the jaded jealousy of an old man. She had ignored that too, despite Lavelle's frequent warnings, thinking Jacob would never do such a thing to her, castigating Lavelle for being so mean-spirited. Even so, for Jacob to seize his opportunity now in which to do it...

And what secrets did Peabody imagine she was hiding from him? He never said anything without cause to gain an effect, or promote a response. It didn't matter anyway, the die was cast. Her mind tried to focus on solutions, if indeed there were any, she could not go home, burden Lavelle and the children with the news, unless she had some plan, some way out.

Her feet led her to Holy Cross. An hour she sat there, huddled into the corner of a pew. Churches were so different without the pomp and ceremony, and the crowds of worshippers. Now, apart from the odd set of footsteps slipping out of the city's hub-a-bub, the big cathedral was silent. But not empty; there was a sense of Presence there. She prayed to that Presence, offering contrition, seeking deliverance from what lay ahead, aware that what she was now facing was the real penance for her sin. Lavelle, Patrick, Mary, Louisa, they too would suffer. Would pay the price of her fall from grace.

Eventually the place imposed some calm upon her. As if its great arches, high altar, tall perpendicular stained-glass windows and the sheer stolidness of its slabbed granite, over-powered the smaller human components of flesh and fibre huddled within its interior. Maybe it all just came down to sin and retribution – that most fundamental of relationships, between creature and Creator. She the creature had sinned, He the Creator had punished.

Had her God deserted her? She had deserted Him and come back – but perhaps not fully. She remembered her last encounter with Stephen, when they had walked from her house: his touch, his voice, his nearness. Had they been alone somewhere else – in Montréal – she knew she would have relapsed. Even five minutes from her own doorway, except for Mrs Brophy, she would have done or said something, let her resolve slip. She had been prepared, to have chosen him again over her God.

She left the Cathedral of the Holy Cross, more confused than ever, heading homewards to face them without any way out of their calamity.

37

'It's not your fault, Mother!' Mary said, full of concern. 'You couldn't have foreseen this. You mustn't take it all on your own shoulders.'

Lavelle's anger was reserved for Peabody. 'His true colours are at last showing – I never liked the man.'

'It's not the first time the French have betrayed the Irish,' Patrick stated, 'and as for the Jew, he is never to be trusted. This is what we are up against here.'

Louisa, not understanding what all the commotion was about, but knowing from Ellen's manner that it was something serious, was visibly distressed, and came and stood by her mother, embracing her.

When the initial burst of feelings had subsided, Patrick and Mary each offered to give up their schooling and engage in whatever profession – high or low – the situation demanded.

'We'll get through this, one way or another.' Lavelle added supportively. 'There are still plenty of tunnels needing digging in this country and I'm still an able-bodied man!' Lavelle added supportively.

Ellen's spirits were greatly uplifted by this demonstration of combined love and goodness. She could get something herself, mill work, anything, but first she was not prepared to let go of what she and Lavelle had built up without a fight.

Then Louisa was tugging at Ellen's arm, bringing her to the piano. It was not really the time she wanted to listen to anything, but it seemed Louisa wanted to play, to express something to her. She waited as Louisa moved behind the keyboard. But the girl did not sit down. Instead, she crouched, turning the palms of her hands outwards towards the instrument, miming a pushing movement. Ellen wondered what it was the girl was doing? Then Louisa straightened up again and with the finger of one hand pointing towards the doorway, with the other hand caught her mother's arm, putting her face up close to Ellen's in an attempt to make her understand. Ellen watched carefully as Louisa tried to shape the words with her lips.

'The piano to go? The piano to go, Louisa? Is that what you're trying to tell me?' Ellen asked.

The girl wanted her to get rid of the piano – sell this great joy of her life. Helpless at being unable to offer any other suggestion, this was her way of sharing the burden.

'Oh no! No! Louisa ... my dear child. No! They'll carry me out of here first before that piano goes,' Ellen said, more defiantly than she felt.

The girl looked at her, shaking her head from side to side, disagreeing, tears rising behind her silence. Ellen embraced her.

'Don't worry, Louisa dear, it will be all right, I promise. We've come through a lot together – just pray for me,' she asked, knowing prayer itself was not enough to save them.

Louisa seemed to understand. She withdrew her head from Ellen's shoulder, then, taking her mother's face in her hands tenderly, exquisitely, she kissed Ellen on the lips.

After further discussion between Ellen and Lavelle, it was decided she would return to Montréal, to first see the Frontignacs and then seek out other suppliers. Lavelle had wanted to accompany her, but she was uneasy about him coming to Montréal, as if somehow his presence there might uncover her. She talked him out of it. In any case he was needed in Boston, lest there was any further deterioration in the local situation.

He came to the train to see her off, kissed her and wished her well, saying, as she boarded, 'I will be waiting all the hours till you return.' Then he shouted something after her about 'not spending too long in those Montréal bookshops!' in an effort to lift her humour. He was a fine man, such a fine, fine man.

Three train journeys, same destination, but this

one so different, no gloss of excitement rising from the grinding wheels now, the rhythmic *clacketyclack*, once sensual, nothing but an ungainly thud of wheel on track. She, having no sense of travelling hopefully, only wanting the journey behind her, and life, as they had known it, preserved.

Rather than stay again at the Hôtel Fond du Lac and dredging up past memories, she considered Dillon's Hotel on the Place d'Armes, close to Notre Dame. Eventually she decided against Dillon's, fearing the popular hotel would be filled with 'big bourgeois' members of the Beaver Club, which met there. These once *voyageurs* and fur trappers, now barons of Montréal, still played at being Nor'westers. She didn't think she could stomach their songs, their noisy exuberance, their campfire boisterousness.

At the Fond du Lac, they gave her the same room she had shared with Stephen. She peered into it before entering, as if their story was still unfolding there, waiting for her to re-inhabit it. Then she sat on the bed seeing the room: the floorboards with the unplanned gaps, something she hadn't previously noticed; the door betraying an ingrained griminess above its handle – *seigneurial* grist from the mill owners of the Saguenay Valley who stayed here. Perhaps even from hands resined by lumber or furred by the soft under-coat of beaver pelts.

She thought she could detect tobacco – the telltale slightly soiled lace on the curtains – and wondered if, after all, this could be the same room? She rose, and from where she had sung to him, stood by the window, searching the sky for a sign. Looking over her shoulder back towards the bed, to where he had lain, she was sure then that it was.

38

The Frontignacs refused to see her, at first pleading prior engagements until she threatened 'to remain darkening the doorstep from now to Kingdom Come if I have to!'

At the possibility of an unseemly scene at Manoir Frontignac, prior engagements seemed to become mysteriously disengaged and it was now Frontignac Père who glided out to meet her, all charms and smiles, behind his luxuriant but well-sculpted beard.

'Ah, Madame Lavelle, *bonjour*, pardon the delay, unavoidable, but inexcusable – what brings you back to our lovely city?'

'This does,' she snapped, pushing the letter to Peabody at him.

He raised his eyebrows. 'Ah, the letter!'

'Yes, the letter, letters – why didn't you tell me?'

'But Madame Lavelle ... come, come, if we told you, then you would know,' Frontignac Père said plausibly, as if it were all self-apparent.

'And...?' She wanted to hear it from himself.

'Then you could make, shall we say, alternative plans – which is, I suspect, why you are in Montreal now?' he said, the essence of politeness, the hint of a smile tracing his lips, unperturbed by whatever she might attempt to do.

'So you, Monsieur Frontignac, did it, shall *I* say ... underhandedly?'

'Dear Madame Lavelle – "Lavelle",' he paused as if her name had now taken his interest, 'it is a French name, *n'est-ce pas*, *"Le val"*, of the valley, perhaps?'

'Yes, it is,' she said, not batting an eyelid, 'and so is *"bhastaird"*!'

He looked at her, head raised quizzically, the tailored beard at a tilt towards her. She didn't explain to him that 'bastard' was the same in any language, thinking he had caught her drift. Frontignac Père chose to carry on as if he hadn't.

'In business it is a rough-and-tumble world even for our gender,' he replied, picking a speck of dust from his sleeve.

'It is a great mystery to me, Monsieur,' she fumed, 'if I should call you *Monsieur* Frontignac, that you should know what gender you belong to. Being on the one hand not man enough to be open and proper with me, and on the other lacking any virtue and honesty common to my sex.'

For the first time she saw his face darken, the bemusement on his lips disappear, but she had more yet to say to *Monsieur* Frontignac Père.

'We have a word in our language for your likes – *stagún!*' She spat out the insult to his masculinity, spun on her heel and left, fluttering pieces of the letter in a trail behind her. Outside, she was glad at what she'd done. He was too polished by far, standing there like some little oily Napoleon, manoeuvring her, talking down to her about her 'gender'. Now that she had burned her bridges with the Frontignacs, she had to build new ones elsewhere – and quickly.

'Cartier et Charbonneau (*maison fondée en 1763*)' looked promising. Large and well-stocked, it was obviously a *maison* of some substance. However, the most fundamental of problems beset her – language. Cartier et Charbonneau, it seemed, catered to an exclusively Francophone clientele. The only person there with a smattering of English was a packing clerk, who was summoned to make sense of what she was saying. She tried to explain as best she could the object of her visit. He translated to either Cartier or Charbonneau, she wasn't sure which, dress and bearing decreeing him one or t'other. She picked up the words 'Boston' and 'Frontignac', and saw the frown cross Monsieur's face.

'Non! Non madame!' and then Monsieur disappeared, leaving the clerk to show her out.

At Maison Barthélemy Richelieu, she had better luck as regards the language, but the response was still the same. 'No, *madame*, I am sorry, I could not go against Frontignac – here in Montréal we have an arrangement – Boston is too difficult for me.'

Later that day she found Jacquemart et Fils. As elsewhere the Frontignacs had prepared the ground well and another polite *'Non!'* greeted her ears.

As far as the wine merchants of Montréal were concerned, Boston was a closed shop. No one would supply her.

Originally Lavelle had suggested they write to Father McGauran in Québec who had, in the first instance, arranged the introduction with the Frontignacs. She had been against drawing the priest back into their problems. In any case, with what she had learned from Stephen during her last visit, she was suspicious of the Catholic Church here, which derived from the old French aristocracy. Acting like Irish landlords, he had told her, these *Seigneur*-priests had extracted tithes from their tenants, in turn building up trading monopolies and ensuring the Church controlled Canadian commerce in every respect.

The *Seigneurs* didn't like the Paddy-Irish. The Shiners and other Irish rioters had seen to that. The Shiners, who sailed from Cork in their 'shiny' silk hats, had for two decades fought openly with French-speaking workers along the lumber camps of the Ottawa Valley. The continuing contretemps had become known as the 'Shiners War'. Too, Montréal's Irish also liked to 'celebrate' Queen Victoria's birthday. A little arson, some stone-throwing, cudgel-fighting and other such party games in the city's streets, ensured the monarch was 'given a good day'! Like the Shiners War, this over-exuberance by her race was not overlooked, nor forgotten.

Now the *Seigneurs* of Montréal had flexed a muscle or two against her – Irish, and a woman. A troublesome speck of dust on a frock-coat, she had been firmly and effectively shut off from the Francophone merchant princes of the city. Her choices now were limited. She could go to France itself, but she would need an interpreter.

Stephen – he could speak French, the thought flashed in her mind – but she extinguished it as quickly. It was out of the question. France in any case would be a costly journey, perhaps necessitating up to a month there.

Australia? The wines could not compare with the French, no *raffinement*, and it would be difficult to convince the refined taste buds of Boston to change. In time, perhaps, but it would be a long haul, full of risk. As always Frontignac Père et Fils, Québec, Montréal and now Boston, would be there like a giant shadow, smothering her every move.

Dispirited, she trudged back to the hotel, took dinner in the shabby gaudiness of the dining-room, noting that the silver-gold chintz curtains were not at all suitable for a room impaired by age, needing an infusion of life. The *joueur de violon* recognized her and approached in his drooping way.

'Madame is alone?' The moustache lifted a semi-quaver, then full-quavered into an octave of teeth. 'No with Monsieur this time?' She gave him a watery smile, hoping it would dampen his enthusiasm, make him go away. It didn't. 'Ah ... is no good.' The moustache drooped again in empathy with her solitude. 'I make *musique* – you no be alone?' The moustache rose, revealing a greater pearliness than earlier.

She shook her head. 'No, no music,' she answered.

It was all so faded, she thought as she mounted the stairs, so very, very faded. She undressed and

295

lay on the bed, on what had been his side. When he had asked her to sing it had been a strange moment, he lying there making no sound, watching her silhouetted against the window, drinking her in note by note. She had physically felt it, felt the flow out of her body towards his. That's what it was – the love act. A distant inter-coursing. Some songs should always be sung in full nakedness.

She stood up and went to the window. It was bright. She folded her arms around herself, the light yellowing her goose-flesh. In an outside corner of the window, golden-threaded, pure gossamer carat, a cobweb. Its inhabitant, fever-ishly working against the moon, spun out the sticky fluid from its spinnerets, the light itself seeming to transform the liquid extrusion into an ever-widening entrapment.

She wondered how one small body could create such an endless labyrinth. Where was it all stored? Or was what it spun merely streams of spider-thought, solidified by contact with the outside world – moon-yellowed into life?

She put her palm against the windowpane, watching mesmerized as the web grew like magic mist around the tips of her fingers, turning them to long hairy stamens of spiderwort plant. A busy little fellow. She put her lips close to the glass, making her own hoar-frost, remembering when she had sung to Stephen and the moist white rose her breath had formed on the window.

Deciding that it spun in 'jig-time', she started to lilt the lively 'Round the World for Sport' to the spider's workings. Nobody ever sang to a spider – she would be the first. And this one's industry deserved a song.

She liked the notion, the naked madwoman who sang to spiders.

39

Lavelle came to meet her, knowing by the tentative way she alighted from the train that it had been a wasted journey. He held off asking any questions until she herself was ready to tell him.

'They have it all sewn up. No one will go against the Frontignacs. But the Frontignacs will certainly go against us after...' She told him the story.

'You were right!' he affirmed. 'I'd have given him worse!'

'I never intended saying what I did, but Frontignac got me so angry.' She paused, admitting, 'We badly needed some stay of time from them.'

'It's not the end of the world, Ellen, and I'm glad you didn't let off that jumped-up little *Francac* without a tongue-lashing – such as only you can give,' he added to cheer her up. 'People deserve what they get.'

She thought for a moment on his last statement.

'Sometimes,' she said, looking at him.

With the situation now blackening, there was nothing for it but to reduce their outlays. They had previously dispensed with Sullivan, and if any little crumb of consolation was to be gleaned from the sorry state of things, it was from ridding themselves of the 'surly hill-topper', as Lavelle referred to the Kerry lad. Now they would have to sell off existing stock and then rid themselves of the warehouse. In this latter respect, at least, things fell their way. Their lease was up for renewal within four months. As they were required to give three months' notice of quitting, they would in effect only be at the loss of one additional month's rent.

'It could have been nine or ten months,' Lavelle said, trying to take a bright view of the situation.

The stock, however, would first have to be cleared. Their few other customers who had been contacted by the Frontignacs took what they could at its full price. Indeed, paying more quickly than usual, protesting that if she and Lavelle could find suppliers elsewhere, they would 'stick with you rather than the Frenchman'.

Cornelius Ryan was a disappointment. Ensconced behind the counter of his Emporium, he folded his arms, asking her, 'How is the childer and the boy what stood up to the Orangemen?' Then telling her, 'The Bordelaux isn't selling too good around here, missus! True as my word, other than that I'd take some off your hands.'

She said nothing. *No flies on the Tipp'rary man*, she thought, and thanked him.

'Not at all, missus! Not at all – anything to

support our own! A pity about the Bordelaux.'

Still with quite an assortment of wines left over, she had no option but to go back to Peabody. Of them all he had the largest capacity, with his three outlets, to clear the remainder of her stock.

'Of course, Jacob,' she said, business-like, when reservedly he expressed an interest – if the price was 'fair' to both of them. 'Of course I will sell it to you at a special price to clear!'

He would have to come to the warehouse to 'see with my eyes what I would be taking on'.

He duly did, walked around with her noting everything, then making what she considered to be a derisory offer.

'Jacob, I said a special price, not a give-away one!'

'Ellen, you know that I am already well stocked and this,' he swung out his hand, 'this is a lot of additional stock to carry for an indeterminate period.'

'Jacob, you know the prices,' she said, tempering her speech. 'I am prepared to offer you this lot to clear for one-third below cost. You, on the other hand, are offering me a price which is *two*-thirds below cost! That is not business, Jacob ... it's robbery!'

'Take it or leave it, Ellen.' He shrugged. 'I'm trying to help and it's the best I can do.' He was treating her like some sort of *shiksa*, trying to get her to beg.

'Jacob, do you want me to go on my knees to you, is that it?'

He smiled. 'You have a genteel way of putting things, Ellen. That is well past ... for me at any rate,' he added after a pause. He had purposely mistaken her meaning, as he always did, but this time it had a different kind of barb to it. She ignored it and certainly was not going to haggle with him now. She wanted done with him.

'It's a deal!' she said, and extended her hand to him.

His face registered a fleeting surprise, but he said nothing. He took her hand and squeezed it a moment, looking at her with some expression in his eyes.

Then he let go. 'I knew it would be.'

Lavelle was again furious when she told him. 'It was a bad thing, Ellen, to be dependent on the likes of Peabody and those French. One worse than the other, but both true to form.'

'You were right – right all along – I didn't see it,' she answered.

'A leopard doesn't change his spots, nor a Jew his money pouch. You're far too trusting,' he stated.

And she was, she knew, too reliant on how she could win people over. Maybe it would have been better if all along Lavelle had done more of the dealings with Peabody and the Frontignacs. He would have kept things clearer, been less distracted by Peabody's clever conversation. Now it was too late for that.

She did not tell him about Peabody's innuendo and the fact that she believed something else, other than mere profit, lay shrouded within his behaviour. Some sexual jealousy against Lavelle ... or another! Some imagined betrayal in which she had engaged. She'd never know now. Peabody's behaviour puzzled her but there was a much bigger question – their very survival.

Every outgoing was looked at, every non-necessity pared back. Milliner and dressmaker alike were stricken from her list. Charitable offerings were suspended. The purchasing of newspapers and magazines, even the *Pilot*, was discontinued. There were no more visits to the Old Corner Bookstore – anyway, she'd had little stomach for books of late.

Of these early deprivations, the one which most grieved her was the cancellation of Mary's and Louisa's pianoforte tuition. Both had continued to develop in aptitude and love for their music. Lessons were eagerly looked forward to each week, with joy on their faces when they burst home with a 'new piece', taught to them by their tutor. Their practice sessions resembled musical duels, each seeking to outplay the other. The good Miss Wigglesworth had offered to 'keep them in tuition with a moratorium for the time being on fees'. Kind as it was, Ellen could not accept such an offer and politely refused. Louisa, at least, had her regular Sunday-afternoon practice in the cathedral, with the organist, who professed her to be 'showing much promise for sacred music', though Louisa, of yet, had not been allowed to play on any formal occasion.

The girls had taken the loss of Miss Wigglesworth with great grace, but Ellen knew how much both of them missed the lessons. She tried to comfort them, saying it would be 'a temporary arrangement until such time as things improve'.

In the intervening time their lives had taken on

the semblance of slow death. In her mind, Ellen paralleled it with that time in Ireland, when she was forced to ration their daily portions of potatoes in ever-diminishing numbers, knowing there would come a day when none would be left to divide. It was not that same life-or-death situation now, but to her it had the same inexorable impetus.

Bit by bit life, as they had known it, was being deconstructed. The conspiracy of boundaries was at work again, boundaries which were no longer static, which no longer merely defined their lives. Now, the boundaries had become an ever-reducing and compressing force. Ever-reducing the options available to them, ever-compressing their lives – closing in on them.

The first deconstruction was watching Lavelle remove the racking and shelving in the warehouse, the same fittings he had so enthusiastically constructed when they had come here. When it was all dismantled, they tried to sell it, but finding no takers were forced to burn it. All that they had built up, now going up again, this time in smoke.

Then the sign – the New England Wine Company. The sign that proclaimed they were ready for business, and was a statement of their survival from the Old World, of arrival in the New. Now with Patrick, she held it steady, both of them perched on borrowed ladders, while Lavelle, on another, clawed out the supporting nails. She and Patrick were finally forced to let it crash to the ground when they could no longer take its weight.

She cried for the death of the sign.

They considered what other enterprise they might undertake, while they still had some remaining funds, before Lavelle would 'take up pick or shovel', herself 'the loom or the broom'. He never criticized her, was a tower of strength, solid as she knew he would be, wanting 'to go West for the better wages'. But she wouldn't let him. Now that her 'restlessness' was over she feared that if he went he might never come back, that she would lose him like Michael ... like Stephen. There was still hope for them in Boston. The city was always her dream, her saviour. She wouldn't give up on it yet, wouldn't give up on herself and Lavelle.

Despite a strong Temperance movement and the visit of its 'chief apostle' from Ireland, Father Theobald Mathew, Boston had more than fifteen hundred establishments selling liquor to its thirsty citizens. Of these, two-thirds were Irish-owned. Despite the best efforts of the Nativist legislature to eliminate 'Rome, rum and robbery', replacing it with 'Temperance, liberty and Protestantism', the sale of 'intoxicating beverages' was still big business in Boston. Many of these establishments, however, were no more than rough groggeries, where whiskey, ale and porter flowed freely, inflaming men's passions into loud and often riotous behaviour.

A grocery store, they decided, would perhaps be a safer bet. Many such stores run by the Irish opened up and shut down again with alarming regularity. Often first started in the corner of a room in one of the tenement buildings, where the Irish swarmed, they required no great initial investment or continuing overhead cost.

'That is their problem,' Lavelle said, 'they are too easily set up, too many dogs at the same bone.'

She and Lavelle had walked the city looking at the better-placed stores, their vegetables freshly laid out in boxes, their barrels brimful-bright with apples and fresh fruit. Beef and lamb were kept inside, away from the spoiling sun. Outside, under the stretched canopies, starch-coated grocers carefully scrolled 'Today's prices' on the stand-up pavement signs. Some, more vocal, proclaimed their wares to passers-by, singing the praises of 'green cabbages, rose-red apples and ripe juicy pears', all in the same luscious mouthful.

In the right neighbourhood, away from the fly-by-night vicissitudes of the 'tenement Irish', they could, over a period of time develop a decent grocery business. Patience, hard work, sufficient capital to start with and a tight rein on credit would be the four cornerstones to success. Having some, but not sufficient capital, Ellen, it was decided rather than Lavelle, would approach the credit agency, R.G. Dun, they both fearing Lavelle's brush with the law might disadvantage their request.

Everybody knew of R.G. Dun, what hopeful or perspiring businessman didn't? It would be a process of questioning not dissimilar to the one she had undergone with Mr Jellico, a situation she had disliked intensely.

She felt as if on trial for her life. The agent of

304

R.G. Dun, a bulbous little man with a notebook, probed into every corner of her existence, then pompously informed her, 'Intellect, industry and integrity of character are the three *sine qua nons* for credit with this company. Qualities not widely found in your countrymen, I regret to say, Mrs Lavelle.'

And him not regretting a word of it, she knew.

He quizzed her about the children, their ages, their schooling and 'the suitability of her gender being absent from the marriage hearth'. He queried Mr Lavelle's absence, wondering if 'that name hath hitherto crossed before me?'

Then, in his primped-up little way, he asked her, 'And your ... eh ... previous business experience, Mrs Lavelle?'

So she told him the story.

'And what provision did you make against such an occurrence?'

'Well...' She fumbled for the words. '...I had no cause ... I never expected ... we had such a history of business...'

'In business, as in life, Mrs Lavelle,' the R.G. Dun man admonished, 'we must expect the unexpected and provide against it.'

She felt the whole discussion was going nowhere.

'Mr Peabody? Mr Jacob Peabody?' he enquired at the name. 'Now there is a provident man, close and shrewd, with a keen and grasping intellect. Three stores he now has, I believe, all primely located.'

'You know him?' Ellen asked.

'Peabody is known to me, as are many of

305

Boston's business fraternity,' he replied, writing something in his well-guarded notebook. The dust would hardly be settled after her, before he would be scurrying down all importance and red-faced to Peabody. This convinced her all the more that she would get a 'good for o' recommendation from R.G. Dun and this *toadeen* before her. She hated being made to squirm before the likes of him. However, she sat it out until he had finished.

'Well, Mrs Lavelle.' He closed his book and twined a rubber-band around it. 'We'll wait and see what we can do.'

She didn't need to wait and see. She knew they would not be entering Boston's grocery trade or any other trade which required borrowed capital. The word from R.G. Dun would go out.

'Troublesome of her race and gender. Good for o.'

And so the boundaries tightened further about them, constricting their present choices, limiting future ones. While, all the time, their assets dwindled.

This process of the disestablishment of their lives was at its most heartbreaking when she was finally forced to sell back the pianoforte. Getting it in the first place was a luxury, a powerful affirmation of how far life had advanced for them from the penny whistles and gut-fiddles of Ireland. Now she ran her hand along its grained brown top – it was a substantial instrument and would leave the room bare in its absence; but more than that.

She lifted the lid, looked at its hammers and dampers and metal strings silenced there, waiting to give voice. It was like opening a door into some wonderful world, framed by cantatas, and concertos, instead of the barefooted one of jigs and reels. She loved the Italian words of this new musical language she had discovered here in America. *Oratorio, andante, allegro, largo* – they had such a swing to them, and a reverence for that which they spoke of – like at Mass. She tinkled a few of the notes – yet it hadn't been something for her. She felt she could have mastered it, lost herself through it, in those long nights of the soul, when nothing could comfort her. Still, that didn't matter. The doorway into the refining world was for them, Mary and Louisa. She had opened it for them. Now she was closing it again.

The evening before the removers came, they gathered around it for the final time. 'For the parting tune!' Lavelle said it was. One of the leg coverlets had slipped its tie, sagged on the floor like a discarded dress. She reminded herself to remove all of them before it was taken. It was such a silly prudery, anyway; so like Mrs Brophy.

When she had faced them with the news, both Mary and Louisa had been stoically brave, understanding how her having to tell them was as grievous for her as the loss of the piano itself was for them; that it was her defeat too.

She had later found them comforting each other, Mary telling Louisa, 'We will always have the memory of it – the memory of tunes. We can still play them ... in our heads, can't we Louisa?'

Louisa had simply nodded.

This evening now would be their last memory of it.

Mary played first, her favourite piece, and Ellen's, 'Jesu Joy of Man's Desiring'.

Louisa stood next to the piano, hand resting on it as Mary played. Ellen closed her eyes, as she did when she herself would sing, but even with her eyes closed she would have known which of them it was. Mary played the piece full of the hope that the 'joy of desiring' brings, accentuating the absolute magnitude of its brightness. When Louisa played it, she on the other hand drew from all the longing of desire unfulfilled – the recognition of loss sustained, rather than the hope of Heaven gained. She watched as they exchanged places, smiling, touching each other. What would be Louisa's choice? What message within the music, for them, for her?

The girl composed herself, looked first at Mary, then at Patrick and Lavelle, finally at Ellen, her face softening into a distant smile. Then she commenced playing.

Ellen had never heard the melody before. She looked to Mary, but Mary was too engrossed in her sister's playing to notice. Louisa must have practised it at the cathedral in anticipation of this evening – to surprise them – giving the piece its once-only recital.

It was slow. What was the word ... *largo?* Incredibly beautiful – the notes so delicately falling like angels' dewdrops in the light of Heaven, clear and bright in the sad dawn of the minor key; shining, until Louisa's fingers melted them away into little trills and fragile, faltering triplets.

She played, eyes closed, the utmost serenity on her face. Unhearing now, unseeing, except in the sound and light of the soul. It was Bach, Ellen knew, Louisa's left hand rising and falling like the footfalls of God, shepherding the melody into the souls of all who listened; and He, the Good Shepherd, watching over His child as she played the broken melody.

When she had finished, all were still, brought into her silent world. As the last chord hung there, like a life unresolved, the girl closed the lid over the keys for the last time and came to Ellen. Her tears, when they came, Ellen knew, were as much for her – for the closing of life as they had known it – as for anything.

40

Lavelle's reputation as a 'fightin' man' led to encountering difficulties in his search for employment. He picked up some casual work as a forgehand and stableman, enough to stem the more rapid erosion of what they had put by, but nothing more consequential than that. The money from the sale of the piano had helped. But in the end, she wondered if the pitiful few dollars they gained was worth the grief of losing it.

Ellen's own choices were also narrowing. Married women were not common in working life, the myriad single women, many her own countrywomen, swamping what available work there was, driving down the wages. 'There has to be something better than being a needle-woman or a "Bridget",' she joked to Mary. 'I'll end up either blind or befuddled.'

She had that day seen three of the countless needle-women in the city, wearing dark blue glasses, creeping 'like mice at dusk' through the Common. Three blind mice, as she had unkindly thought of them. Their blindness caused by Boston blue-bloods, who, respectable behind their purple-tinted windows on Beacon Hill, kept these unfortunate women chained to their machines in dimly-lit sewing shops.

On the other hand, to be one of Boston's two-thousand-strong army of 'Bridgets' normally required one to live in, behind those same tinted windows to lessen the chance of bringing 'moral contamination' into the home. As well, a 'Bridget' had to be on call twenty-four hours a day. Pay was docked for such crimes as 'breaking tea-cups', 'pilfering apples' or even 'spoiling a dish of prunes', as reported in the *Pilot*. In some newspaper editorials such misdeeds were seen as part of a 'conspiracy' by the Papist Church against Yankee Protestant homes where the unfortunate 'Bridgets' were alleged to have been 'put up to it by their priests'! Whatever solution Ellen would find, neither taking up her needle nor a broom would be it.

It was a Tuesday in early October of the year 1855. Mary was sixteen, going on seventeen, Louisa perhaps a year or two older. Clear as crystal it was, but a hardy day, crisp as a crab apple, the browns and yellows and reds of fall bringing an illusion of warmth to the Common. She still brought Mary and Louisa there, not that Patrick came with them any more. And they would stroll arm in arm, talking of the day, or the doings in Boston, even just watching the leaves do their slow dance to earth. She never burdened them with her own worries when they had these 'precious times' together, as she thought of them. Another year would see their schooling complete, all of them, even Patrick. She would get them through that next year, no matter what. At least she would see to that properly. Beyond that ... who knew what way the world would scatter them.

Patrick wanted to 'enlist in an army', a thought that always sent a shudder over her, but he seemed set on the idea and she wasn't the only mother to have to live with such a cross. It would, she hoped, at last make a real American of him – in the uniform of his adopted country. She worried that he still harboured deep-rooted grievances against England and talked about 'rising an army of the Irish in America to fight the Crown!'. She prayed that when the time came for him to enlist, these sentiments would be drilled out of him. Louisa would need thinking about; she was bright, winsome too, but she would still need shepherding. She couldn't just be let out in the world like another could.

Mary was a different story. Mary would make her way anywhere, but it was always Ellen's hope that Mary would go on to higher learning – she thought it was Mary's hope too. Now, because of their situation, it began to look more and more as if that wish would never be fulfilled. Anyway, all that was a year off yet and God was good.

Whatever thoughts lay on her own mind this Tuesday, there was something too on Mary's and Louisa's. The two seemed to be on the edge of getting out something ever since she had met them after school, looking from one to the other, an excitement on them mixed with nervousness.

'Will we sit a few moments under the Great Elm?' she asked. It was as good a place as any for secrets to be shared. But they wouldn't wait there long, the pre-winter nip already in the air.

They sat, the girls not flanking her, as was usual, but both to the one side of her, Mary nearer.

'Mother...' Mary began, an unusual tremor in her voice, 'Louisa and I ... we've got something to tell you.'

Ellen waited, wondering what all this schoolgirl drama was about. Mary delayed the telling, looking back at Louisa, half-hidden from Ellen behind Mary's shoulder. It was obviously some prank or scrape involving the both of them.

'Louisa is going to be leaving ... and...' Mary managed to get out as Ellen looked at Louisa, alarmed. Had someone come for her after all this time? '...And ... me too!' she thought she heard Mary say, through her bewilderment. 'We are going to be nuns!' her child said, reaching for her hands.

'Nuns!' Ellen repeated, as if the giant tree had pronounced its worst sentence on her. 'Going to be nuns...' she said unbelieving, needing to hear the words again. She looked from one to the other of them. 'But...?' she started to ask.

'Because it's the right time, for both of us,' Mary answered, as if that were all there was to it. She was losing them to God. Her mind flashed back over all the little things, the signs...

Louisa's devotion to prayer; the image of Veronica wiping the face of Jesus; the music; the organ-playing. It was all there. Only she was too blinded by her own inward gaze to have noticed it.

'Are you sure, Mary? Louisa?' she heard herself asking. It was a fruitless question.

Louisa made a soundless little laugh of happiness, nodding her head up and down, throwing her arms around her mother's neck.

Within Ellen a huge gap of loss was opening. It seemed no length of time since the famished waif she had grown to love so much had first appeared. Now, as silently, mysteriously, as she had come into their lives, she was leaving again. With them for only a short time, a borrowed angel called back to her God.

And Mary – she reached to embrace her other child, confused, caught between their obvious joy, her own sorrow. Mary had flourished so well here in Boston, developing a social consciousness and a compassion for others. She had of late begun to let her hair grow longer, as Ellen's once had been.

'All those one hundred strokes I gave it, Mary, every time before Mass,' Ellen would say to her, 'do you remember, when you were small?'

Now here Mary was, long beyond those years, a full woman almost. The world at her feet, throwing it all away.

'Oh, Mary!' was all Ellen could say.

'*A Mhamaí* ... aren't you happy for us?' Mary answered, falling back into the old language.

'Of course I am, oh yes ... but to lose the two of you...' She couldn't see it any other way. 'Why now?' she asked, as if reason or its timing would lessen the blow.

Mary paused a moment. 'I have thought it to be the life for me for some time, and I knew, too, that Louisa did – she's much holier than me,' she added, like a little girl. 'God called us now and the way things are, *a Mhamaí*, it seemed a good time to answer Him.'

That was it. They both had decided to go, deeming themselves to be burdens – burdens because of her; giving up their lives for her sins.

'I've let you all down so badly,' she confessed, 'I've caused all of this.'

'No you haven't, *a Mhamaí*. You could never do that. You've done so much for us all against everything.' Mary hugged her so tightly.

'Jesus wept,' was all she could say in reply, and cried bitterly.

As she held the two of them to her, she thought of the futility of loving any other human being. It was such a secondary, dispensable thing, quickly dashed in the chaos of life. Like everything else, Mary and Louisa were now being stripped from her, stripped away from her by God. Heartbroken, she felt Louisa press against her.

'When you played that piece, you were telling me, child, weren't you? You were telling me, Louisa,' she whispered to herself.

It was Louisa's going-away gift to her, the only way the girl knew how to tell her – through music. She rocked them then, like the children she still wanted them to be. In her turmoil she imagined Louisa would enter an enclosed order, where her silence would be revered, a normal world at last for her. Mary would go with her. As they had been in the outside world, so too would they go to God, silenced away together contemplating the face of the Saviour.

Once they entered such a convent all contact with the human world would be broken. Their only release would be in leaving this life, bound for the higher glory.

'We are entering the novitiate of the Sisters of Saint Mary Magdalen,' Mary whispered as if reading her mother's thoughts. The import of what Mary was saying almost passed Ellen by, so locked was she within her own imaginings.

'Saint Mary... The Magdalens... It's, it's not enclosed!' she said, a rush of joy taking over her. She held them both back from her. 'I never thought ... oh thank God! I thought we'd ... I'd ... never see you both again!'

41

Later that evening, when Lavelle returned, she told him.

'They're doing it for us, Ellen.' He was adamant. He summoned the two of them.

'Now, Mary, Louisa,' he began, 'I am not your father and it is not my practice to interfere in matters of the household, so I will say only this. Whatever vocation you may choose, it is yours alone to decide, but I do not want you to go because of recent events,' he said, concluding with, 'I will leave it to be discussed between your mother and yourselves. Listen to her – she won't put you wrong.'

It was the longest 'speech' on domestic matters he had ever made. Now it was over to Ellen. She was, he had reminded them, their moral guardian, who would not advise them wrongly. The words rang inside her head. How could she rightfully shape their thinking, when her own was so tainted? She found she had no need to, Mary taking the lead.

'If the coming of the call coincides with the needs of the family then it is the will of God that Louisa and I should answer it now.'

That was it. The will of God. The call and the answer. Mary had put it beyond discussion.

Albeit their dwindling resources had been augmented by the sale of the pianoforte a finely crafted walnut dressing-table, Lavelle had once bought for her, the will of God would now much more significantly ease the burden on the household.

They had recently decided to vacate their present accommodation, it being at a high rent, and move to a lesser neighbourhood. She was aware of how much of a reversal of fortune this was, in the sense that the Irish who were rising into consequence, not falling from it, were leav-

316

ing the area into which they were now about to move.

When Mary and Louisa would depart the household for the convent, something even smaller again would be sufficient for just the three of them: Lavelle, Patrick and herself.

The following month the girls were both gone. She missed them around the house. First she went readying their room as if they were still there, making the bed, pounding the pillows with her hand, putting a shape on them. Then fingering the dresses once designed for the lovely bodies of young women, hanging there lifeless now, replaced by the sombre habit of the Brides of Christ, shapeless, sinless. She was glad the piano was gone; she couldn't have borne looking at it, standing there waiting to be played, the dust of years gathering on it, a constant reminder.

When they moved to the smaller dwelling on the fringes of the West End, its compactness, the nearness of everything – walls, doors and windows – only served to emphasize the girls' absence, contrasting with the bustle that had once accompanied their comings and goings, the music of lives once mixed with hers. While she tried to be happy for them, she mostly failed to be other than profoundly sad at their not being there.

Their absence was more than non-presence, seemed much greater than a mere physical withdrawing; it had to do with almost not existing without them. Lavelle and, to his credit, Patrick, did their best to be around her, consoling, putting to her the bright side of 'them being called to God'. Mary and Louisa, she imagined, would at least be able to sublimate their own feelings of absence, tie it to the higher good, offer it up like a chalice. She couldn't.

Christmas was their bleakest yet in Boston, guests were not even a consideration. Strange how they too had evaporated. Stephen, Peabody – not even the good-hearted but meddlesome Mrs Brophy dropping by for a sweet sherry or with some 'newses' that couldn't wait the telling. It was just herself and Patrick and Lavelle, the meal itself penitentially frugal for a Christmas 'feast' – no trimmings only bittersweet memories of Mary and Louisa, full of the joy of the season, flapping about under her skirts like chickens round a mother hen. She felt older this Christmas, older than her thirty-six years. A lot older.

She was reminded again of Jacob Peabody, shortly into the New Year, in a manner unexpected, one which filled her with some indefinable apprehension.

'I knew it! I knew it! Didn't I tell you, Ellen, that Peabody was at the back of it? Read this.' Lavelle slapped the letter into her hand.

It was from Father McGauran, in Québec. Lavelle, despite her protestations, had written to the priest enquiring as to why, after all these years, the Frontignacs had moved to ruin them.

Now, in his reply, the priest was most upset at the turn of events and had gone directly to Montréal to see Frontignac Père. 'Monsieur

318

Frontignac admitted under my severe questioning,' Father McGauran wrote, 'that they had only
acted as they did, having first received intelligence from Boston of a nature warranting their
actions.' Frontignac Père had not revealed to the
priest the 'nature' of the 'intelligence' from
Boston, or if he had then the priest had
considered it to be *sub-confessionem*, and had in
turn not revealed it to Lavelle.

She read on, her heart pounding. 'They,
although at this stage unable to reverse their
decision regarding commencement of business in
Boston, would nevertheless *be prepared to enter
into some form of partnership with Mrs Lavelle and
her husband, despite "voiced differences".*'

She couldn't believe it! It was an eleventh-hour
miracle, brought about by the priest who had
first introduced them to the Frontignacs. She
had misjudged completely how Canada's
Catholic *Seigneurie* would react. She looked at
Lavelle, who, filled with delight, grabbed her,
swinging her off the floor.

'Now R.G. Dun will be fawning all over us to
advance credit,' she said loudly, banging her fists
on his back.

Lavelle had been right all along, right to involve
the priest. She was wrong on that, and wrong
about the Frontignacs too. They had been
gracious well beyond what she could have
expected after what, with gross understatement,
they had called her 'voiced differences'. She
hoped Frontignac Père hadn't informed the
priest how shameless she had really been.

'It's the girls, Lavelle, it must be Mary and

Louisa – their prayers,' she gasped, still fully unable to accept this turn of fortune. 'How else could this have come about now?' She thanked them silently in her heart, thinking that at last things would now be reversed, the effects of her sin lifted from their lives.

'Well, somebody is watching over us,' he said, more grimly adding, 'but it's no thanks to Mr Jacob Peabody.'

'Lavelle, you've no proof it was Jacob. Just let it be,' she said, though the certainty that Jacob was somewhere at the back of things was like a jagged edge, razoring her spine.

'It had to be him, Ellen!' Lavelle shook her by the arms. *'Intelligence from Boston!* What intelligence? Supplied by whom? Peabody is stamped all over it, Ellen, and I am going to have it out with him at last.'

Her mind raced furiously. The last thing she wanted now was Lavelle confronting Peabody. Something was wrong, but what, she didn't yet know. Monsieur Frontignac could merely have been covering up for his own profiteering, pretending something had happened in Boston without specifying anything in particular. Peabody's name was not mentioned anywhere in the letter.

She wouldn't have been surprised if somebody like that *slieveen* of an agent from R.G. Dun had taken it into his head to contact Frontignac directly, in the hope of attracting the business to Boston. This in turn would position R.G. Dun to 'validate for credit' all potential customers of Frontignac.

'You can't go to Peabody!' she remonstrated with Lavelle, 'accusing him of something of which you have no proof. Besides, we're going to have to deal with him again,' she continued, 'and he's too important a customer. We have much other work to do to establish the nature of this "partnership"; to reclaim the warehouse, if it is not already let. Peabody is only a small part of it all.'

But he would not be shaken this time. 'I listened to you last time, Ellen...' He didn't complete the sentence, put her at fault. Instead he said, 'What if Peabody repeats his actions? We must know if it is him, or if it is not him.'

The jagged edge at her spine scraped more furiously, filling her with deep dread. She mustn't let him talk to Peabody. Some awful, terrible result would come of it.

'Jacob will deny it in any case,' she said, fighting to find a solution. 'The answer is not with Peabody, it is with Frontignac – only he knows what this "intelligence" is – if it exists at all!'

'Then I will go to Montréal, I will have it out of them,' he asserted.

'No, Lavelle!' she countered. 'I must go. I have done damage there and I must repair the situation with Monsieur Frontignac ... and apologize.'

'They're the ones who should apologize,' he argued. 'They moved behind our backs on the pretext of some flimsy information. If it wasn't for Father McGauran, I'd shortly be bending my back to some railroad track and you'd be praying for the sound of the whistle to vacate your loom!'

321

She was at her wit's end. She just had to override him. Lavelle in Montréal filled her with as much dread as the thought of his having it out with Peabody.

'Lavelle!' she said, raising her voice in one last desperate attempt. 'If you are to replace me in dealings with either Peabody or Frontignac, then you will undermine my standing with them. They will never revert to dealing with me, a woman, again. I will be perceived to have been the cause of the difficulties.'

She had never spoken to him like this before, never unfairly brought her sex into it, never brazened the lie to his face. She saw the start in his countenance. He took a moment, then a breath, before replying.

'Have you ever considered that you might have been, Ellen?' he asked. She knew the way he meant it, yet was surprised, even so, that he had said it at all. But she knew also that he wouldn't now interfere, would leave it to her. He came to her, held her, saying softly, 'It's a day for celebration – what are we at each other for, Ellen?'

And she could never tell him.

42

She had not been expecting to ever travel again to Montréal. This time was eating into their meagre reserves, and though she should have travelled with a lightness of heart at their unexpected reprieve, she did not.

Once arrived and when she tramped through the March snows to Manoir Frontignac, she had no difficulty with admission. Nor were there any other engagements requiring cancellation before she could be seen.

Frontignac Père received her again and was all of a fuss, making fulsome references to 'our friends in Mother Church'. It was, as she had suspected, old liaisons, the workings of a long-standing, but still functioning tradition, one stretching back to an old country – France. The fracture between herself and the Frontignacs was now healed and sealed with the blessing of 'Mother Church'.

But the fracture itself?

Frontignac was vague. She let him talk without interruption, waiting for the 'water-under-the-ground-words' to surface. And surface they did. Not as a stream but as tiny tricklings, here and there, to the main flow of his careful *non-dénouement*. Words like 'merchants ... 'trusting heart'... 'better an open enemy'.

'You have heard of *Les Maximes du Duc de la Rochefoucauld?*' Frontignac Père asked her, stroking his beard.

She had not, she said.

'*Le Duc* was a man who understood men ... and women too of course, Madame Lavelle!' Monsieur Frontignac explained, as if there had never been a bad word between them. '"The height of cleverness, is to conceal one's cleverness,"' he quoted. 'Rochefoucauld had a reflection on all things, Madame Lavelle. It would be well to read him if, in the United States of America, you can ever find a good English translation!' he said, in a manner making her doubt that she ever would.

She said she would try.

'And what does she read, *la belle madame?*' Frontignac Père continued, calling for 'English tea' for her.

'The American novelists and the English poets,' she answered, 'but sadly nothing in French.'

'Oh, but you should make the endeavour. I could teach you.' He smiled benignly, like some longtime friend. 'Rochefoucauld has as much to say on love, for example, as Byron or Donne. Consider the aptness of this: "Jealousy is always born with love, but does not always die with it."' He looked at her. 'Would you agree, Madame Lavelle, an aphorism well worth remembering?' He never once mentioned Peabody's name directly, spoke only of 'growing opportunities in Boston for us all'.

But all the while she felt that in everything he said, despite its charm and carelessness, it was as if he were drawing her a map. But a map of a country foreign to her, unsignposted, needing something more so that she could understand its terrain.

'The letter, Monsieur Frontignac – can I see it?' She spoke out boldly, seeing the surprise register for a moment on his face.

'Ah ... dear madame, *je regrette!*' he said apologetically. 'There is nothing written in it that is not already written in your heart. I would be breaking a confidence to a friend – or an enemy!'

So there was a letter, 'intelligence from

Boston', but she still didn't know from whom, or what 'intelligence' it contained.

'Don't you think, Monsieur Frontignac, that I have the right to know? I'm sure *le Duc* has something to say about matters such as justice?'

He laughed at how she attempted to turn the tables on him. 'I am tempted to, for you, madame. But again I remember *le Duc* – "The intellect is always fooled by the heart".' He laughed again. 'But for once, I must try and prove *le Duc* incorrect and not let my heart be swayed, even by you, Madame Lavelle.'

Then he kissed her hand most punctiliously, politely bidding her *'adieu'* and again calling her *'la belle Madame Lavelle'*.

She left, finding it hard to feel any antipathy towards Frontignac Père. He had a vigour and charm scarcely impaired by age and when she had tried to apologize for her insulting outburst on the previous occasion, he had brushed it away with a wave of his hand. She had learned enough from him. So, it was Peabody who had written to him. But what had Jacob put in the letter still held by Frontignac? And more to the point – why?

'The height of cleverness is to conceal one's cleverness.' That maxim certainly fitted Peabody. 'Better an open enemy than a close – supposed – friend?' Peabody again. 'Jealousy is always born with love, but does not always die with it.' Who? Love of her? Jealousy of whom? Try as she might, she couldn't fit Peabody with this particular *dictum* of *le Duc*. Maybe it was something Frontignac had just thrown to divert her attention. It wouldn't be beyond him, she knew.

Travelling homewards on the train, she considered it all again.

Peabody didn't, couldn't, love her. She had never given him any encouragement apart from the odd flirtatious banter, maybe let him paw her hand too long at times. But she was sure Jacob behaved in like manner with other females of his acquaintance, that all his amorousness was not totally reserved for her. And the thing about jealousy not always dying with love – where did that come into it? It was all a *pishogue*, a nonsense, the bearded old charmer playing games with her. It seemed to be a way with old men. What dictum did *le Duc* have about old men and younger women, she wondered?

Whatever, she was somewhat relieved. Montréal had gone well – if Frontignac Père hadn't lulled her into a false sense of security. They were prepared to enter into an arrangement with herself and Lavelle to manage the business in Boston, expand it across Massachusetts. She didn't reveal to him how desperate they were, but she supposed he knew; his 'intelligence from Boston' would have informed him. But he wasn't going to hear it from her. *Is binn béal in a thost* – it's a sweet mouth that is silent. And a safe mouth too! The Irish had their own maxims.

She had noticed that of late she had started to fall back into some of the old Gaelic expressions. Remembered, too, how Mary had begun again addressing her as *a Mhamaí*, before she and Louisa had entered the convent. She hadn't minded it then, not like on the boat leaving Ireland. How Mary had reacted – as if cut off from all she had previously known – being forbidden those two words: *a Mhamaí*. But it had been a necessity, a symbol of leaving the old life behind, of cutting ties. Strange how they both had fallen back into it.

She wondered what life would now be if they had stayed in Ireland. Ground-down peasants, she supposed, trying to get out, scrabbling together the money for America. Maybe Mary would have escaped and become a 'Bridget'. Droned away, day in, day out, under the backbreaking workload, taking all the abuse, the insults, the 'thick-as-ditch-water' remarks. Mary, she knew, would have suffered all that to get the money to send back – to start the 'Daisy Chain', bring the rest of them out.

Peasant life, *pshaw*. She had heard them talking in Boston about the 'old Ireland', dewy-eyed and all dreamy, as if it were some *Tír-na-nÓg*, filled with green fields and red-haired maidens dancing at the crossroads. It sickened her craw, all that stuff, and then the 'gi' us wan o' th' ould songs' kind of talk. That's why she never sang them any more – *keening* and *ochoning* for the old life and them with plenty in Boston, hanging their lace curtains and buying pianos, to show how they had 'upped' themselves.

She remembered what it was really like, grubbing around in the filth and the muck for the odd lumper that might have been missed; the cabin so small they could all hardly stand up in it together. Then, at night, huddled together for warmth – on straw, like animals. That was the real Ireland.

Stephen and his lot were just as bad. Except, in their Ireland, the fair maidens came in visions, instead of dancing at the crossroads. And all the fair maidens were virginal 'Mother Irelands' – if you could have such a thing! She wondered if Stephen was still awaiting his 'vision virgin' who would lead the Irish out from bondage to the rapacious John Bull. God help the lot of them, but those Trinity bucks at least should know better – they were educated, the Connacht hill-farmers weren't.

Instead of getting on with life in America, their lives had become one big *mixum gatherum* of past and present, impeding progress, the swamp of history clogging up the future. All of them infected with a kind of miasma of memory.

And the longer they were in America the worse the miasma would get. Be handed down from generation to generation like an enshrouding vapour, polluting their children's minds, holding 'Irishness' at a standstill within its cloud. She looked out as the train *clacketyclacked* through the vast white terrain of Québec – an Ireland, she thought, for ever suspended in time like a great frozen heart.

She rarely let her mind wander like this any more. She put it down to the Frenchman's meanderings and *Les Maximes du Duc*. Maybe trains had something to do with it – your feet being off the ground. Rhythms, sounds, *clacketyclack, clacketyclack, clacketyclackety, clacketyclack.*

She fell into drowsiness with the soporific song

of the train, dreaming of angels and dewdrops falling in a minor key and the frozen hearts of the red-haired maidens dancing ... *clacketyclack, clacketyclack, clacketyclacketyclacketyclack. A Mhamai, a Mhamai, clacketyclack, JesuJoyof-clacketyclack, Jesu Joy, Jesujoy, JesuJesuclackety-clack...*

43

She marched right in on Peabody.

She had turned it over and back in her mind a hundred times on the homeward journey to Boston.

'Jacob!' He was surprised to see her. Surprised that she was not slinking in the door to him like the *shiksa* he thought she was.

'Intelligence from Montréal to Boston?' She went straight into it.

His face turned ashen, his hair a shade bare whiter. But the hardness was in his eyes, something she had only noticed the last few times she had dealt with him.

'So, Mrs Lavelle has been travelling again,' was all he answered. He stayed behind the counter, no rushing round the end of it to greet her, falling all over her. Barriers had grown. He would give her nothing.

'Well, Jacob, it was you, wasn't it?' she accused, making for him around the counter.

He made no reply, faced her, stood his ground.

'Set out to ruin me – why? For money, for greasy dollars, was that it, Jacob?' she demanded.

His reply, icy, unflinching, made her recoil. 'No, Ellen, I had no need to ruin you – you ruined yourself!'

She knew then all that would follow. First, here in his pork-loined little store, before it would spread to her world outside of it.

'Walking in here like the Queen of Sheba! Thought you had all of us fooled, thinking you were someone – a jumped-up Biddy with your fine wines, instead of slopping out lane-ways on Nigger Hill with the rest of your kind.' Peabody scarcely drew breath. 'Aahh ... but Jacob Peabody helped you, held out a friendly hand when none else would,' he said in a voice steeped with bitterness. 'Oh, yes! Don't think I didn't know the amounts of shoe-leather you left after you on the streets of this town, the places you were run out of, before old Jacob gave you a break. You and that fool of yours, Lavelle.' He poked his finger into her chest, prodding home each word, forcing her to retreat. 'Then, it was all sweetness and smiles and *shiksa*-smarminess. But all that soon changed when you found your footing, got above your station.'

She could hardly believe what she was hearing – the venom thickening his slightly accented way of speaking, the accumulated litany of accusations against her, long-harboured.

'Next, you wanted "ediccatin" as you called it then, and "litterture, Jacob", and again it was more sashaying and flashing green eyes and "come to Christmas dinner, Jacob",' he mimicked, 'to cover for your fancy man – your Irish patriot.'

She knew it. Somehow, she had given it away to Peabody. It wouldn't have taken much. She started to protest, but it was useless against all that he had stored up.

'Am I blind, Ellen? I saw it the minute I set eyes on him and you, doe-eyeing him like you used to do in here, when you wanted poetry and philosophy, wasting my day. A Trinity Protestant and you a good Catholic girl from the Virgin Isle – the man you had not good enough for you – no "poetry" in him. Setting *us* both up to be fools with your journeys to Montréal.'

How could he have known? Had they been seen – Frontignac? She started again to say something.

'Don't!' he silenced her. 'I saw it all – first when you availed yourself of my listening ear to sound out your own feelings. Then, when you were seeing your *paramour*, you were like one of those books you took to reading – all on the page.'

She remembered Jacob watching her at that time, feeding her lines from poems, gauging her reaction. Was it all so obvious? And if to Jacob, then to others too? Lavelle?

He continued to upbraid her as if it were *him* she had deceived and not her husband. 'How you kept an honest face on you, when brazen as a hussy, you allowed a discussion at your table on the virtues of your gender, I do not know. Seated there in the company of your lover with your cuckolded husband and your despised Peabody. I

331

resolved then to do what I must, before we all were tarnished.'

'He wasn't... Then...' She started to defend herself then stopped. Everything at Frontignac's now seemed clear. So, it wasn't just business, more profit for Jacob, as she had thought. It was some crazy notion he had that he and she inhabited some make-believe world, cocooned within his precious grains and spices. A world filled with poems and imaginings. He had mistaken her affection, her allowing him to be both protagonist and mentor, for something more. He, Peabody, the intellectual peacock, fanning his feathers of knowledge to impress her. Spurned once in some past life, twice when she had married Lavelle, thrice-spurned when she had fled to Montréal to be with Stephen. Damn him, she thought. She rounded on him fiercely.

'The letter, Jacob – what did you put in the letter – what did you say?' she demanded.

'I said nothing but the truth,' he answered, his head thrown back, righteous. 'That you had disgraced your sex, fallen into low virtue with a compatriot of your husband, thus tainting my own business and the House of Frontignac with the sordid affair,' he said defiantly.

'How could you, Jacob? How could you do such a thing?'

'Because it was true, Ellen. I hear no word of denial from you...?' he said, challenging her.

'I don't deny it, Jacob. God knows I don't deny it,' she admitted vehemently, '*and* regret it every living minute. But to shout it from the rooftops, like you did... What else did you say?' She fired the question at him.

He smiled, a strange waxen smile. 'Having presented Frontignac with the problem, I then offered him the solution. I would discontinue with you, but would instead give him my business directly – on terms of mutual benefit. Naturally he agreed.'

So that was it.

'Jacob,' she said, lowering her voice, 'you accuse me of having despised you. You are wrong, I never despised you, never, Jacob – but I despise you now!'

It was the end. The end for her, for the business. The Frontignacs would never again deal with her – how could they? It had all been a charade to mollify Father McGauran and his more powerful superiors. Frontignac Père had released enough information to her to deflect any blame from himself – to point her back towards Jacob, knowing that by doing so, the discovery of the contents of Peabody's letter would silence her. Then, there would be no more ruffling letters to the priests of the Catholic Church in Canada. Nothing to disturb the old *Seigneurie*. She had been forestalled at every turn, blackmailed by her sin.

Peabody seemed shaken by her words. She looked down at him. He was a pathetic figure. 'You are a Jezebel, Ellen, unfit for the role in which life has cast you. Once ... every time ... when you walked in, it was like the sun had lifted the gold from Faneuil Hall and placed it ... here.'

She remembered days like that when they would sit and talk together him and he would

333

quote Byron and Whittier and Donne. But that was it – pleasant times only – no more to her, not like when she was with Stephen. Was that what Jacob had desired?

Now, he looked around. Bewildered. Holding out his hands over the open grain bags, the cured sides of ham in dampened cloths, the tea chests from the Assam Valley, the wine-racks built by Lavelle. All the things that made up his merchant's world. As if they had once been something more, something golden, now transformed back again to something less: themselves. He looked at her, the cold draining out of his eyes.

'Why did you do it, Ellen? When everything was in its place – why?'

Everything had been in its place, she thought, looking at him, noticing how the apron, always before on its peg, now strangely encircled him, binding him like a white amice. He had been her priest; she had confided in him, given him more trust with her feelings than her own husband, let him take her hand, counsel her about the world, about herself. Was that love to him, she wondered? Before her eyes Jacob seemed to crumple, in disbelief at all he had said, crushed now by his cruelty to a loved one. His hands flapped in no-rhythm against the stained wiping-place of his apron, one hand trailing the other. He had said it all, she knew. Was deflated, the bile of years, fuelled by an old man's imaginings, spewed out of him now. His own miasma of memory, some old love in a far-off Hebrew village of the mind, that somehow she had replaced. Some Byronic

334

love object he had imagined her into.

His own Yiddisher vision-virgin.

'I don't know, Jacob,' she answered, her anger at him subsiding, 'why we act as we do. Once, do you remember, you taught me that we are neither masters nor mistresses of our own affections, only the ministers.' How true, she thought, not only in relation to herself, but also to the decaying Peabody. 'The Element of Fire, I think you called it another time, Jacob. Apart from that I just don't know, but I'm sorry, truly sorry,' she said, as gently as she could.

'"The sun is lost and th' earth,"' he said faintly, in reply.

She left him there repeating the line, hands trailing against his apron, trying to make some sense of it all.

44

She didn't go home.

She couldn't, else she would blurt everything out to Lavelle – the one blameless person in all of this. Instead she walked to the Common. Touched the bark of the Great Elm, then went on up to Louisburgh Square. Why she didn't know. Back again, down State Street across to the Long Wharf, down to its very end, ignoring the catcalls of its longshoremen, down to look at the sea.

It was a calm bright afternoon, the blue of the

water edging out to where it met the sky, beyond the islands. She still remembered their names: Deer Island over on the left, Noodles Island to the right of it, Apple Island, Pudding Point ... and the other one, what was it? Spectacles Island. It didn't seem to fit with the rest, the 'food' islands. She wondered if Spectacles island had been named for the needlewomen of Boston. She imagined not. And still the ships came to the many wharves, ploughed low in the water, heavy-laden.

What could she now say to Lavelle? It was broken with Peabody. There would be no more business with him than there would be with the Frontignacs. Lavelle himself would go to Jacob or Frontignac, to discover what had gone wrong, and this time there would be no resisting him. Frontignac would again play the innocent, send him back to Peabody. Jacob, once recovered, would be again filled with the venom with which he had inveighed against her, and reveal everything to Lavelle.

How would she face him then? Beg forgiveness, or lie to him that she was sorry, when she knew in her heart that her weakness still remained? Lavelle would desert her, and who would fault him? She and the children would be shamed; what she had done was unheard of. Mary and Louisa, their reputations tarnished, would be expelled from the convent, denied their calling because of her. Patrick would be held up to ridicule – his mother a harlot – the Pope's whore. He, or Lavelle, would seek out Stephen. The

336

Pope's own Church would shun her, her sin all the greater for it being with a black Protestant. Wasp-tongued Mrs Brophy would wring enough discussion out of her downfall to fill a month of Mondays for the Daughters of the Commonwealth. She would be reviled everywhere.

She closed her mind to it. There was only one course of action she could take; to spare them sharing her shame, being dragged down with her.

She knocked at the door of the convent. Sister Mary Lazarus answered. 'Mrs Lavelle – are you all right?' she enquired, seeing her distressed state. 'Won't you come in, sit down? I'll get some water,' the Sister offered.

'My children – I want to see my children.'

'Mrs Lavelle, they are at prayer, at Vespers!' Sister Mary Lazarus said. 'It is impossible for you to see them at all until they are professed. You must remember they are no longer your children. They are God's children now.'

Ellen said nothing, turned to go.

'If it is important, some calamity?' Sister Mary Lazarus offered, 'I am sure Mother Superior will allow a message to be passed tomorrow – if it is of importance,' she repeated.

'No, Sister, nothing of importance,' she said, turning again, leaving the House of Mary Magdalen.

45

Ellen reached for the wheel, turned it in reverse until the needle rose out of the feeder-plate.

'Damn it!' she said.

These new-fangled Singer machines couldn't keep the needle threaded, no matter what you did with them. She wished she had her older Howe machine. Maybe it was herself, she was tired, so tired. She lifted the guide foot and winkled out the bobbin with her finger. The thread had gone all tangled. Maybe her tension wasn't right; she thought Clegg had set it too loose anyway. That way it became slack and when she put her foot on the treadle for another burst of sewing, the slack snapped up too quickly. But that was the way the bosses wanted it – eight stitches an inch; more would cost time. She thought the seam needed ten stitches, maybe twelve per inch, but in the Massachusetts Cordwaining Company, with its working environment of 'stretchouts and speed-ups' – workers stretched to the pin of their collar to operate extra machines and then the speed being constantly cranked up – it was quantity that made the bosses smile, not quality.

'You, "lace widow", you lost your thread again?' she heard Clegg, the Closing Room fore-man's voice, above the hum of the machines. 'Anything to swing the lead – you Irish niggers!' he said, in an accent thick as Lancashire fog, and loudly so those around her would hear.

She ignored him.

'Here, get off! No wonder your husband up and died on you – for lack of proper threading,' and 'Peg-Leg', as the women workers called him, laughed suggestively.

Roughly, he bundled her off the wooden stool, tossing the narrow cushion she had made for herself to the ground. She picked it up, cradling it against her chest, and waited while he fiddled with the machine, all the while muttering epithets under his breath.

'There, it's set, and if I get one more shoe back from Finishing ruined by needle holes, you're fired, Irish! Do you understand? You're fired!'

She nodded and sat down again, carefully easing the two pieces of leather under the needle. She bent her head in close to see where she had already punctured the leather, back-tacked her stitch, securing it, then filled the empty needle holes with thread.

Libby Corrigan called over to her. 'Peg-Leg's got it in for you, Ellen, or at least he'd like to,' the woman laughed. 'Why don't you let him, the once even? It would make life easier for all of us!' she suggested.

Libby was from Wicklow, or 'Wickla' as she pronounced it. A 'widow', like Ellen, and deserted by 'himself' – 'a long dose of Wickla buttermilk that scalded himself off to California at the first smell of gold!' Not that Libby was sorry to see himself go, although he left her with 'a parcel of children – the most of them reared by now'.

'It wasn't going to work out from the start,' the

woman had confided in her, when first Ellen had come here, two years ago, in March, after Paddy's Day, as Libby Corrigan referred to it. 'Didn't I hear his father tell my father,' Libby had rejoiced in telling her, 'when they were fixing the dowry: "She might make a good wife all right, but she'll never make a pretty one!"'

'And what did your father say, Libby?' Ellen had asked.

'He was every bit as bad,' the pixie-faced woman crackled back. 'Says my own father back to him, "Faith, then I'll make her pretty – with cows," and he did. Three fine heifers it cost to make me pretty – and look at me still!' She had laughed, 'All the cows in the world wouldn't make a whit of difference on me!'

Ellen liked Libby Corrigan. Since she had started here in this ramshackle five-storey building, Libby had kept an eye out for her. What must she, herself, have looked like when she first came here, Ellen wondered? Her hands soft and white, genteeled by a different life to that of the cordwainers. Their lives were filled with the whiff of leather, their hands scarred with thread burns, a careless finger punished by puncturing needles or the razor-sharp clicking knives. Hands used to shaping the tough hides of leather-bearing animals to put shoes on Massachusetts.

Whatever about being made 'pretty with cows', Libby Corrigan was one of those gritty women who kept going at life, even when it wasn't that much of a life. And she kept those around her going too, with her sharp Wickla tongue – 'a tongue that could cut butter', as Libby herself said. It was that tongue, Ellen had learned, which had christened Clegg the foreman with the appellation Peg-Leg, from the habit he had of leaning over behind the young farm girls from New England when fixing their machines. 'Sticking it in between their shoulder-blades, and them not knowing whether it was an awl or a small-handled screwdriver or what,' according to Libby. But Libby knew, warning Clegg: 'Keep that thing away from me or I'll give you eight stitches per inch – and it wouldn't take the too many more than the eight either!'

But Libby was an industrious worker, never soiled her bib that way, and the foreman used her to train the 'green hands' of girls fresh from the wharves 'who otherwise wouldn't know a needle from a haystack'. In that way, Libby had become a kind of spokeswoman for the Closing Room girls, but kept them in order too, her sharp tongue being a kind of two-edged sword, as often useful to Clegg as it was used against him.

Apart from Clegg, Libby didn't seem to have much time for men in general, telling Ellen that having been 'downed for cows, I had a great mind to go to America ever after that. It wasn't "the hunger" that drove us out or anything, but me that kept nagging at himself – I knew once I got here I'd easily shift him and be me own woman,' she had said, not putting a tooth in it, cool as a breeze.

'And what about you?' she had then asked, cocking an eye at Ellen. '"Lace widow", arriving here all in your fine green dress. What's your story?'

Ellen had held out against telling her then. 'He passed on young, before we had any children,' was all she would commit to, some truth in both parts of her answer.

'I don't believe a word of your mouth,' Libby had said. 'But if you don't want to tell, then I'll not ask.' And neither had she.

Now, when Clegg was out of earshot Libby said over to her, 'Would you marry again, Ellen, or did you make a bad bargain too?' adding between the bursts of sewing, 'No girl back home now will settle for marriage until all hope of America has faded.'

'I know,' Ellen answered, keeping her head down.

When she had eased the leather around and was sure her corner-stitching was even, she did answer the second part of Libby's question. 'No, Libby, it was he who made the bad bargain,' she said, laughing it off.

Libby laughed with her, vowing, 'Well I wouldn't go near the altar again 'less he had a hundred acres of New England farmland – and a bad heart to go with it!' she added, wickedly.

Ellen heard the 'zuzzz' of Libby's machine; the woman could run up a seam like a hare up a mountain, while she herself would still be trying to gauge the three-eighths of an inch seam allowance. Libby turned, depositing another dozen pairs of stitched shoe uppers in the bin between herself and Ellen.

'I bet he did get a bad bargain,' she said, referring to her earlier question. 'You have a temper like a Lucifer match, when it's ris. You'd be great

342

in the Sisterhood,' she added.

Libby always wanted her to join in some cause or other, mainly the 'Sisterhood of Toil' – the women's trade union movement, for which Libby was a leading proponent.

'You're right about the first, Libby, wrong about the second,' Ellen answered, not entertaining the idea at all. 'It's people like you they need. Strong and clear-headed, and not afraid to speak out – I'd only be good for starting trouble, not finishing it.'

'The Lucifer match women are needed too, Ellen. Someone has to start the fire in people.'

'I don't want any more fires, Libby. I've started enough already,' she said, leaving the widow from Wickla all the more wondering at her.

Ellen hated it here, but it was all she could get, where she could 'disappear', far removed from Boston's West End and Quincy Market, and anywhere else she could be recognized. Once she had made the decision to 'disappear herself', two years ago, she knew she would have to stay 'disappeared'. She had taken little – the clothes she wore, the few dollars in her purse alongside her rosary beads, the crucifix from over her and Lavelle's bed – and Stephen's book.

Lavelle would have gotten on with his own life by now, initially, having gone looking for her, when she hadn't returned from Montréal. He would have found the note she had left for him and Patrick; a note explaining how she loved them, but had to leave their lives and praying for forgiveness for the ruin she had brought them.

Lavelle would have then gone to Peabody and

Jacob would have told him the whole story. He would have been shocked beyond belief, understood then why she had disappeared. For a while, he would have been angry, his pride wounded. Finally, she hoped, he would have put her behind him.

Patrick: she wondered about him. He was a man now, almost twenty-one years, out in the world making his own way, not needing a mother like her. Patrick had been slow to forgive her, if ever he did, for 'deserting' them when they were children; then, for having 'a fancy man in America' – Lavelle. Patrick would consider that she had run true to her character. He would never forgive her. Men deserted their families for fame or fortune, or neither, it was part of the Irish disease in America. That was the way. But it was not the way for women. Except, how could she have faced them, gone back? Patrick, too, would have found out in time that she had tried to contact Mary and Louisa, but not him – a further betrayal.

When she had first left, she had grieved that she hadn't seen the girls, then thanked God that they hadn't been available to her. Even if she had said little to them, just that she was going away, they would have guessed. Louisa would have known – looked at her with those large all-seeing eyes of hers. That would have been worse, not having to defend herself, not even to be able to ask forgiveness. And Mary, what would she have said to the mother who, she regarded, 'could never let us down – always put us first'?

But she had let them down. She had put

herself first.

Perhaps they had already suspected something; women sensed things from each other. The thought often struck her, whether that had been the real reason they had entered religious life – that they already knew, wished to spare that acknowledgement between them. At least in the convent they were cared for, safe. It would be another few years before they were professed, allowed out in the world. Maybe they didn't yet know about her. She prayed that this was the case.

And Stephen? She had many times wondered what had happened to him. Had Lavelle sought him out? Maybe he had returned to Ireland, or gone elsewhere within America, on whatever particular cause was in current vogue, feeding off the romanticism of the 'scattered' Irish. At one point she had thought to try and find him. She was exposed, her life and that of her family ruined because of him, at least she could then be with him. But in a moment of clarity it had come to her. If she went to him, then her self-imposed banishment would be set at nought. She would be embracing that for which she had exiled herself. Hers would be no true act of repentance. Still, it did not stop her from thinking of him.

Here at the Massachusetts Cordwaining Company she had spun them the story about being widowed. The other women thought she was deserted, a common enough occurrence masked by assumed widowhood, which drew a more sympathetic response than desertion. She had earned the name 'lace widow' because of the initial finery of her clothes, compared with the homespun smocks worn by most, and her air of general refinement. It was, too, a sly reference to the circumstances into which she had grown, but was now fallen from. To others she was the Widow Malley, a needlewoman, like themselves, having reverted to her former name for fear of being traced.

The cordwainers of Massachusetts had long campaigned for a ten-hour working day and better pay. No legislative improvement had been gained but the thirteen-hour day had, for a period, been reduced to eleven. However, the thousands of young, mainly single, Irish women and men who flooded into the Bay State needing work forced wages down. And by the sheer weight of their numbers in competing for the same jobs, they had also allowed the bosses to push up the hours again to twelve. It earned for the immigrant workers the name of 'Irish niggers' from the New England farm girls, who had left the land in favour of the loom and the last. So from sun-up to sun-down, six days a week, Ellen worked nose to needle in the unremitting drudgery of life as a shop machinist. Eye-straining, arm-aching, mind-numbing work of *set and stitch, turn and stitch, crank and stitch.* Stitch, stitch, stitch, the tiny fibres of hide, tanned for the feet of America, flying to escape the punch of her needle, filling the air, clogging her nostrils and mouth with an itching dryness. She would either suffocate or go blind if she remained here.

She threw aside a pair of un-skived uppers. It

346

would break her needle to attempt to sew the un-thinned leather. The last time she had been day-dreaming this had happened. Her rhythm had been broken and the forefinger of her left hand had slipped under the descending shaft. She well remembered the pain of the stunted needle-head piercing her skin, crushing tissue and bone beneath. She was so in shock she had been unable to crank back the machine with her free hand to reverse the steel out of her finger. By the time Libby had come to her rescue, she thought she would pass out with the agony of being nailed to the needle-plate. A rough, untrained, but matronly woman, 'Nurse', had dressed the throb-bing forefinger. Company rules allowed for the first three of such injuries to be dressed free of charge. After that, deductions for medical attention – five cents for each injury – would be made from the already slim wage packet she received. She couldn't afford to have that happen.

She continued to think of Stephen setting up a fresh pair of uppers, these with the edges skived to the right thickness. She fed the machine, watching the needle rise and fall, its eye dis-appearing each time the leather received it, lock-stitching the parts together in one unbroken seam. Then the next ... and the next ... and the next, her life lock-stitched before her into an unending eight stitches per inch.

At night, when she crawled home, weary-boned, to the tenements of Half-Moon Place, sandwiched between Broad Street and Fort Hill, she had no thought for lost love, and no malaise afflicted her except tiredness. Her only thoughts before she fell asleep were prayers for the needs of her children, prayers for her loves, Michael and Lavelle and Stephen, and a prayer to be at her machine next morning before the whistle blew.

On Sundays, her one rest day in the week, after Mass at St Vincent's on Purchase Street, to the south of Fort Hill, she sometimes took out Stephen's book of poems. Even then she could not be seen with it by any of the other needle-women, lest she suffer on Monday – 'the lace widow and her notions.'

The Massachusetts Cordwaining Company had hundreds in its employment. Men, women and children, some as young as nine or ten years old. Pattern-graders, clickers with their small curved-blade clicking knives, eyeletters, bottomers, lasters and stitchers like herself who seam-stitched, top-stitched, bottom-stitched and every-which-way-stitched.

She had never thought of boot-making as such a manifold job when, before this, she had laced on her own. How times had moved on from the solitary cobbler tacking at his last, to this. The bosses were always trying to find new methods to 'break down' the assembly operations. Now, instead of the machinists having to slowly learn every stitching operation and make-through a complete shoe, they had only to learn a few. Soon, she thought, the assembly of boots and shoes would be so broken-down that as Clegg put it 'even the non-Irish niggers from down

348

South' could be put on machines. It was her first taste of industrialization and she didn't like it. De-skilling meant de-humanizing. You became an extension of your machine, rather than the other way round. But to young Irish girls, it was simply a job in America, money to buy food other than potatoes. They had not, as yet, aspired to any higher rung of the ladder above the bottom one of survival.

Nor were any such higher notions close to Ellen's mind. A year ago, the Great Panic of '57 had struck and wages slashed to fifty cents a day. She had hardly been able to survive the Depression, skipping meals, taking up her needle when she went home at night – and, God forgive her, on Sundays – doing homework. The shop-floor girls hated the homeworkers, who undercut wages even further. Generally the Irish women would not take work into the home, trying, however ramshackle it was, to maintain some dignity there. Homework was left to the Jews, 'making sweatshops of their bedrooms', or the Italians, in whose houses, according to Libby, 'You'd like as not get bolognesed shoe-laces served up to you quick as spaghetti!'

After the Great Panic and with the advent of further speedups and stretchouts from the bosses, a new militancy had crept in amongst the workers with Libby urging Ellen all the more to join the Sisterhood of Toil.

'American ladies will not be slaves – why should the Irish be?' she had challenged Ellen, who still resisted all such rallying cries. She understood the underlying philosophies, had discussed them many times in her previous life with Mary: 'work to live – not live to work.' But while at heart she supported these ideas, she had avoided attending the workers' meetings. Anonymity was what she craved, not reform.

The Abolition of Slavery cause was also strong among the cordwainers of Massachusetts, who adopted as their own the Abolitionist slogan: 'Power concedes nothing – no struggle, no progress.'

Whatever her thirst for anonymity, Ellen couldn't help but be excited by this new enthusiasm for the abolition of all slavery; human bondage for black slaves, industrial bondage for white workers. Amongst the cordwainers, there was now the whiff of leather in one nostril and the whiff of a new dawn in the other, a potent mixture if ever there was one.

'Women will be in the front line, Ellen – wait and see,' Libby proclaimed. 'Arm in arm, black women and white women, the Irish, the Jews and Italians too, joined with the American ladies. There will be no division of colour, creed, or sex. It will be a New World, made by women.'

Ellen thought it would be – maybe not as easily, and as harmoniously, as Libby saw it – but things were coming to a head on many fronts; of that she was sure. How it would affect her own life didn't much matter to her, but she wondered, and worried, about how it would affect the lives of those she loved and had left behind her.

46

If Libby Corrigan's vision of a new world, linked arm in arm across the colour and gender divide, had some hope of being realized among the needlewomen of Massachusetts, it had no possibility of ever happening in the place where Ellen now lived.

Since she had come to Boston in 1848, over ten years ago, Ellen had experienced little of the other side – in fact the main side, as she had since discovered – of Irish life there. She had deliberately eschewed all Irishness, wanting to be American. So she had given a wide berth to *céilis* – gatherings – and the groggeries and dramshops where her people congregated. The few Irish she knew were like Mrs Brophy; the 'coming Irish', those who had 'upped' themselves to be 'of wealth and standing', Boston's commercial Irish. Not the potato peasants, like herself.

Now, as she picked her way under the arch and into the long passageway of sub-divided warehouses, having to step around the privies and water hydrants, it was as if life had grabbed her by the throat, turned her around, and hauled her back to where she should have been. Back among her own, back to being a 'tenement Biddy'. 'Sheds, shanties, and tottering rookeries'; Half-Moon Place had been well described. Only that the rooks themselves wouldn't even rest here.

She held her nose against the sink of pollution on every side, the backwater of drains flushed out by high tides.

Children, ragged, unshod, played in the filth shouting, 'We don't want to be the Protestants this time!' Flinging any garbage to hand, in a 'Battle of the Boyne', Boston-tenement style. She dodged some rotting evil hurled her way. It mashed against a rickety staircase behind her, dripping its sludge from step to step, to be later squashed by the bare feet of those same children. Not that anyone would take much notice.

'Is that you, Ellie?' a voice called out to her. Blind Mary. The woman always sat on her stoop at that doorway looking out. At what, Ellen didn't know, for Blind Mary was a casualty of the sewing trade and had the 'needle blindness'. 'Them childer have me tormented, Ellie,' the woman complained to her, 'with their shoutin' and throwin' things, knocking skelps off one another – me poor heart's not able for it.'

'Don't mind them, Mary, they're only playing, having fun,' Ellen said to her.

'Well they should be learnin', that's what, ediccating themselves. If I had me sight that's what I'd be doin', readin' books and learnin'. Here, take a drop,' and she pushed the gin bottle out from behind her skirts at Ellen. 'It keeps body and soul together … keeps me alive, until hisself comes back.'

The gin, indeed, did keep Blind Mary alive. Half of the basements in Half-Moon Place had been turned into illicit dramshops, and in half of the other half, the women ran little sidelines in gin to supplement the borderline or no wages their husbands earned. With Mary blind, permanently on the brink of starvation, her 'gin trade' was a necessity. How she managed, being unable to see, Ellen couldn't imagine, with a clientele which ranged from that of the sailor dance halls, set up in other basements, to common night-walkers and tricksters of every kind.

'Ah, he wasn't a bad man when he left, not a bad man!' Blind Mary said, referring to her Dan, who had upped and left her. ''Twas the forges, Ellie, the furnaces in them forges, Ellie. Sure the heat o' them melted the poor man's brain.'

'I know, Mary, I know.' And she did, after more than two years, she knew Blind Mary's story by heart.

'Then comin' home here to this hell-hole, not a streak of light nor a puff of air,' the woman continued regardless, 'sure, bad and all as the forges was, it was the only sunlight the poor man saw, those roaring furnaces,' she explained, nodding her head up and down towards Ellen, 'and it melted his brain – dried up all the juices in it. But I know he'll come for me, Ellie. Down that passageway, under the arch, I can see it in me mind's eye, and him running down, scatterin' them little bastards that's been dannoyin' the head o' me, and him calling out me name – "Mary! Mary!"'

'I'm sure he will, Mary, I'm sure he will,' Ellen said to her, her own head 'dannoyed' from listening to the woman.

Blind Mary fumbled out her hand, caught

Ellen's arm and pulled her in close to the doorway. 'Ellie,' she whispered, 'it's the niggers. I heard tell one of them's gone into my Dan's job at the furnaces,' the head was nodding furiously, dannoyed at the niggers now, 'and the black man won't melt, Ellie – black as the Divil at the gates of Hell – he won't melt. What will we do at all when the war comes and they let them all out of the cages down South, and good young Irish boys killed freeing them. Well, Ellie, what will we do at all then?'

'I don't know, Mary, I don't know what we'll do.'

She didn't know what to say to her. The woman's mind was half-gone with gin; it was no use arguing with her. Yet Ellen knew she was only saying what a lot of them down here thought. Here there was no table-talk like that she remembered with Patrick and her own Mary and Lavelle, discussing the merits and demerits of Abolition – the moral issues. Here it was survival. As Blind Mary had put it, 'the black man won't melt'. Whatever work the Paddies, 'the turned-inside-out-niggers', could do, then the 'smoked Irish', the blacks, could also do – and cheaper.

She went on up the passageway – the state of this place they all now lived in. These people, her people, peasants from the hills and valleys back home; bad and all as it was there, they never lived like this, never behaved like this. In the mountain villages, no matter what, in the worst of the Famine, in the blackest of the black potato years, some semblance of dignity and humanity remained with the people.

Here, three thousand miles away from the correcting eyes and tongues of the village, all restraint had been loosed. The same upstanding, God-fearing villagers were now the froth and scum, the backwash of Boston. The old 'conspiracy of boundaries' of village and church, even of landlord, was smashed and smithereened. Now there were no boundaries, nothing sacred or decent. Even the air itself was foul and feculent, redolent of the life the Irish here led. Here no cooling breeze whipped up the Maamtrasna valley. Here in the basements there was no light, no windows to look out. Even if you did have a window above the ground or in the cramped attics – a mere two to three feet high – you had neither field nor valley to look out on to gauge the mood of a day. No certain mountain, only the flap of half-scrubbed washing, which hung from pillar to post at every corner. No sound of a bird, only the 'thwack' of Jacob's Ladders against the outside walls. These, a rumpled knot of life-threatening rope and wood, she wouldn't put a step on for love nor money. No scent of the wild honeysuckle in Half-Moon Place, only the wretched smell of diarrhoea and cholera and dysentery hanging on the air, waiting to drop on them.

She rounded the corner. Biddy Earley, streelish as ever, door-stepped her. Biddy didn't like Ellen, and she, in return, didn't like Biddy Earley. It was not so much the unkempt look of her circumstances; most here couldn't help that. But Biddy was an agitator, about anything and everything, and moreover, wasn't happy unless

355

everyone else shared her agitation. 'The rack-renting landlords and middlemen, our own the worst!' – 'the mill-owners taking the flower of Irish youth, imprisoning it from dawn to dusk' – 'the state of this place, the Land of Liberty me arse!' And, in particular, 'them niggers'.

Biddy had recently told her, boastfully: 'I had a house mobbed, down there,' she had pointed through the archway, ''cos there was a blast o' blacks living in it. Living there just like white folk – just like us!' she had added, indignantly sweeping back a greasy lock under the neckerchief she wore on her head.

'And why shouldn't they?' Ellen had said.

''Cos they're not fit to live with us, spreading in here from Nigger Hill, bringing down the neighbourhood,' Biddy had said contemptuously.

'How far down is down?' Ellen had replied acerbically.

'I could tell you were a nigger-lover, you're not like the rest of us down here, widow-woman. You don't fit!' She had prodded Ellen with her finger. 'Like a bit of liquorice in your bed now and then? Believe all this stuff about them being just "smoked Paddies", do you? Well they'll be "smoked Paddies" before the night is over!'

'What do you mean, Biddy?'

'What I mean, Widow Malley, is this – fire and brimstone, the wrath of God on the heathens! It's all they understand. Now, shut up and listen,' she ordered, 'you're lucky I'm telling you after how you cut me last time!'

And Biddy Earley proceeded to tell Ellen that there was going to be 'a smoke-out for the smoked Irish' that night, down at the end where Ellen lived – in the single shanties. Ellen, like the other Irish, was to light a candle in her window. That way the so-called 'Irish Fire Brigade' mobbed-in for the job from 'further up Fort Hill' would know which shacks not to torch.

Ellen was aghast. 'This is madness! People will die – it's murder, Biddy!' she accused the woman.

'Murder? Sure they have no souls – isn't that why they're the way they are?' Biddy answered her, as if it was as plain as the nose on Ellen's face. 'How could it be murder? Anyways, sure they'll scamper away like monkeys out of any harm, get a bit more smoked maybe, that's all,' she laughed.

'If the fire spreads...?' Ellen started.

'The lads in the "Fire Brigade" know what they're at, they've done it before, sure; anyway, it's a still night. So just go home, widow-woman, light your candle and keep your trap shut!'

She left Biddy and went home. What was she to do?

Two doors up from Ellen lived Maybelle Tucker, a black woman with two children, 'runaways' from Alabama. Her husband was still in hiding after a few years of having escaped. Perhaps, Maybelle had told her previously, he had even been spirited out of Massachusetts to Canada on the 'underground railway', as the escape route was known. Ellen often spoke with her across the washing lines at weekends. She was a fearful woman, wondering when they'd be discovered and forced back South under armed guard or when she'd be 'mobbed by dem white niggers – dem Irish'. She was also afraid to move; how would her husband find her if he returned? And movement could provoke discovery. Life in the 'free' North didn't provide much freedom for her, Ellen thought. 'Only dat dey is no chains here, Miss Ellie.' Unlike the chains, Maybelle seemed unable to leave this deference behind her, even though Ellen had often spoken to her about it.

So far Maybelle and her two children had been left alone. Indeed, some of the Irish in Half-Moon Place mixed freely with the blacks, and some of the Irish women but not the men, had taken to marrying them. Given time, it would all work out, but before that it would split the country in half, and the Irish too.

If the Irish and the blacks fought each other for low-paid jobs, then they'd both always be ground down, exploited by the bosses who didn't care whether you were a white nigger, Irish – or smoked-Irish, which they called the blacks. But work was what both races needed, dangerous, backbreaking, brain-melting labour of any sort. There was no way out of that, just as there was no way out for her with regard to Maybelle Tucker and her two children. If she didn't put a candle in her own window she would be burned out, like Maybelle; mistakenly, maybe, but burned out nevertheless. If she warned Maybelle, then Biddy Earley would know it, and then what would the consequence be for herself? Maybelle would still be burned out and, as likely, herself too. That would be the end of her – out on to the passageway.

She had sunk low, very low, because of her own failings, but she was surviving. Hadn't she one room, one window, a small hard bed and her own door, enough money for a bit of food and wood in the winter? At last, by her prayers and the penance of the life she lived, she had begun to fall back into God's grace, feel some peace of mind. If she became homeless, with the few possessions she now owned gone up in smoke, she would have nowhere to turn to. Not even the charities – for fear of being discovered. Maybelle Tucker, at least, would get by. The anti-slavery charities would help her and the children, and as long as no one got hurt... She agonized and agonized over it, turning it this way and that in her mind, went out into the passageway on her way to Maybelle, then turned back. Why did it have to be just her – couldn't it be someone else? Others had been told as well. Was she the only one who felt differently from Biddy Earley? The only 'nigger-lover' in this whole higgledy-piggledy hive of human misery? The impatient rattle of knuckles on the door startled her.

'Come on out here, widow-woman, into the light, and read this for me!' she heard a voice demand.

It was Biddy. God blast the woman, she thought, what did she want now? Hadn't she caused enough trouble already? She went out.

Biddy hardly gave her time to pull back the flimsy wooden door. 'It's about the niggers – in the *Pilot*. I cannot make out what it's saying. Read it out loud to me!'

Ellen took the crumpled page of the *Pilot* from

359

her and started to read the lines from Boston's weekly. 'When the Niggers shall be free, To cut the throats of all they see...'

She stopped, scarcely believing what she was reading, what was printed in front of her.

'Go on! Go on, read it, widow-woman! That's not me saying them words, that's the Church, our Holy Roman Catholic Church. I'm tired of tellin' you – one of these mornings you'll wake up with your own throat slit!' and she snatched the paper out of Ellen's hands. 'Blind Mary'd read better than you!'

When she had gone Ellen sat down on the bed, head in her hands. What was it all turning to?

The *Pilot* was their paper, and ran news from the 'Old Country', railed against the Know-Nothings and the sectarian bias in Boston's schools, and defended the 'Bridgets'. The defender of the poor and oppressed Catholic Irish had now become the oppressor of the poor and enslaved Negro, with the blessings of Holy Mother Church.

It was wrong – all wrong. Maybe they were right about the four million freed slaves that would swamp all over the Irish like a black plague – just as the Irish had swamped Boston. She had often heard Lavelle say so, and Patrick too. If there had been one *scatterin* of the Irish fleeing from the blackened praties of Famine, then there would be another *scatterin* of the Irish, this time from the black Southern plague. But it was still wrong. Worse still, was the Church kindling the flame of hatred, succouring the likes of Biddy Earley and her Irish Fire Brigade mobs.

360

She took her candlestick, crooked her finger through the loop of metal, lifted it to the window. The Lucifer match flamed into the gloomy interior and she held it to the wick.

Lucifer, the fallen angel.

47

Later, she waited, listening for the commotion outside, wringing and unwringing her hands like Pontius Pilate.

She would go out when the Fire Brigade had done their foul deed. Extinguish her candle, make sure that Maybelle and her two children got out safely, give them shelter for the night. Put the children in the small bed, herself and Maybelle up on the edge of it, keeping watch. That much at least she could do.

She sat, and sat, and waited, watching the candle in case the night wind down the alley should snuff it out – and they would mistake her shack for Maybelle Tucker's. She prayed, asking forgiveness for her cowardice, the cold eating in at her bones, shivering the fear further into her.

Then she heard them. First, just a distant tremble in the ground, causing her to bolt upright. Then closer footfalls, whispered voices from Kerry and Mayo, echoing down the passageway – the Irish Fire Brigade at their work. Next, the flicker of a torch across her window. A face for a moment, looking in, checking, then gone. She padded across the floor, barefoot, half-crouched like some hunted animal, and waited behind the door, petrified; relieved that they had passed her by, terrified they would return. She was tortured by the thought of what she was part of. But they'd be all right, Maybelle and her two children – what had she called them – Magnolia, and the little one with the big eyes, like Louisa; Blossom? Called them not after saints like the Irish did, but after flowers; Blossom and Magnolia.

How would she ever face their mother again and ask about them, listening to Maybelle Tucker talk about 'dey is trouble a-brewin' in dem cawnfields' or 'de black blood is gonna be runnin' outen dat white cotton', nodding and agreeing with her that it was a terrible thing, just because a person was born in Carolina instead of Cork and was black instead of white.

Then the shouts and the whoops told her the deed was done. Then she heard the crackling noise of fire, the passageway outside flickering into life, purged of its darkness. The faint pleasant smell of smoke seeping in through the gaps and cracks assailed her every sense, suffocating her with the enormity of what she had allowed to happen.

Outside, the sound of running feet. A yell: 'Smoked Irish!' Laughter. She yanked open the door, ran outside, almost immediately the thump of a body send her reeling backward. A mobber fleeing, shouting at her: 'Stay indoors, missus!'

It took her a few moments to recover, to scramble to her feet. Across the passageway from her she saw the candles, one here, one there, now guiltily snuffed. No one else came out. Desperate, she stumbled to Maybelle's door. Already the flames were licking the sky above the woman's shanty. There was no sign of Maybelle and her children. Panic-stricken, Ellen saw that someone – one of the Fire Brigade – had rammed a stout stick against the outside of the door, held into the ground with a rock.

They were still inside. Frantically, she knocked away the stick shouting, 'Maybelle! Maybelle! The door!'

God, they'd be burned alive – the children! With her hands, she tried to grasp the smoking doorframe. But the wood was hot and burned her fingers. The stick ... somehow she forced the knob of the stick into the gap and wedged it open with all her might, but the whoosh of heat that met her drove her backwards. No matter how she tried she couldn't get in.

She shouted again. 'Maybelle! Maybelle! Oh my God, what have I done?'

Then she fell in a heap on to the lane-way, beating down its filth and its evil with her fists, cursing the evil in men's hearts. Sobbing at the harsh realities of life and death in this Half-Moon Place. She didn't know how long she was there, half-lying, half-sitting, head sunk on her breast, blackened with grime and smoke.

'You can go home now, Miss Ellie; we's safe,' she thought she heard a voice say – her conscience, salving her guilt. 'Miss Ellie!'

Startled, she looked up. Before her stood Maybelle, holding the hands of Magnolia and

Blossom. She shook herself in disbelief and looked at them again. Maybelle standing, looking down at her, the children's big sad eyes on a level with her own. They were alive. Somehow, miraculously alive. Someone had warned them, helped them get out. It didn't matter. Only that they were safe.

Ellen staggered to her feet. 'Oh thank God! Thank God, you're safe, Maybelle, all of you! Oh thank God – you can stay with me – it's not much...' she gabbled on deliriously, her burden lifted. 'Until you get–'

The woman moved back as she made to embrace her. 'No, Miss Ellie. De children an' me – we's gonna make ou's own way.'

She was questioned, by the Night Watch, like all others in Half-Moon Place, but no arrests were made. When it had quietened down Biddy Earley came to her all brazen and smug-in-the-knowing.

'You told her, didn't you, widow-woman?' she accused. Ellen never answered, let her think what she liked.

'You'll see!' Biddy pointed her finger up over the sprawling rooftops. 'When up there, when Beacon Hill is swarming with black "Bridgets" and there isn't a place to be had for a decent Irish girl, you'll see then, widow-woman, you'll see then I'm right.'

For months afterwards Ellen was on her guard, for fear of reprisal, but it never came. It would have been better if it had. She deserved it, not for the telling, as Biddy imagined, but for the not telling. She wondered who it had been, who had warned the black woman? Which of the women – she was sure it was a woman – had given the word to Maybelle? However, in the close-by-the-wall stoop life of the passageway, no clue was forthcoming and she knew the whole rotten gallery of them thought it was her.

She told Libby Corrigan what had happened, saying how ashamed she was at her cowardice. If she was expecting pity, she got none from Libby.

'You've a right to be ashamed, Ellen! At the same time, I don't know what I would have done!' she said forthrightly.

'You would have done the right thing, Libby,' Ellen said, convinced. 'You would have stopped them! Like I would have once.'

'Who knows what the right thing is when your own roof's in danger? There's one law in thinkin' things, another in livin' them,' Libby said, having previously in her head worked out all such rules for 'livin''.

After this Ellen decided to throw in her lot with Libby and commenced attending her Sisterhood of Toil meetings.

48

Early in 1859 her eyes began to give her trouble at last. First it was tiredness, a winter tiredness brought on by harsh, bleak light, everywhere caked white with the cold. Next it was the odd headache; then a more constant one. Even into the light-giving summer, she had some difficulty. So that more and more at her machine she pierced her finger until the crown of it bore the raised shape of a continuous welt, dark and bluish and purple. Eventually she got the blue glasses. They helped the headaches and her purple finger. Now she could laugh about being one of the three blind mice, remembering the needlewomen she had once seen, creeping homewards along the waterfront.

Less and less could she read her book of poems. All of that, Stephen, Montréal, seemed so irrelevant now. Still she held on to his book – a small, dimming comfort. Whenever she did read a few lines it was rarely from the *Love Elegies* any more. Now edging past thirty-nine, it was as if growing older, like the poet himself she was inclined more towards Heaven than towards Earth. She found solace in Donne's *Divine Poems*, like 'A Hymn to God the Father':

Wilt Thou forgive that sin which I have won
Others to sin, and made my sin their door?
Wilt Thou forgive that sin which I did shun
A year, or two, but wallowed in a score?
When Thou hast done, Thou hast not done,
For I have more...

And she dwelt on the words, as if they were her own. Putting flesh on her sins, sins of the flesh itself, sins of omission – Maybelle Tucker. There, in the spartan solitude of her tenement sanctuary.

Sometimes Blind Mary came up to her 'for the company', tired of sitting on her stoop 'looking out for hisself tripping home to me at last'. She had a fund of the old stories and songs, mainly from the south-east coast of Ireland and East Munster. Songs to Ellen's ears like 'The Connerys', about three brothers transported to New South Wales for the attempted murder of a landlord's man. The song threw a curse on those who informed on the brothers ending with a hope they would soon be returned home again.

Is a'guí chun Dé,
Ar na Connerys a thabhairt saor abhaile chugainn,
ó New South Wales.

And praying to God,
The Connerys to bring home safely to us,
From New South Wales.

At first, Ellen had trouble with some of the words; so long it was since she had spoken or heard the language. It made her ashamed, what with Blind Mary telling her, 'Sure, you have the best of Irish, coming from the West. It's a grand thing to have one's own language, what with all them foreigners that's here!' Ellen agreed with her. 'Read another piece o' the English rhymes to me – the one about the eyes,' Mary now asked. Ellen read from 'The Message': 'Send home my long strayed eyes to me...'

Blind Mary waited a moment, nodding to herself. 'He was a priest, Ellen?'

'He was,' she answered, wondering what the

woman was thinking of.

'He had such soft words for a priest,' Blind Mary said.

In this way they shortened the nights for each other, trading songs and rhymes. The blind woman with the old sure Gaelic, the red-haired woman with the soft words of an English priest.

Then, one evening, Ellen went for the book, to find it gone. She kept it always beside her bed, and knew it had been stolen; there was nowhere within the narrow confines of her room for it to be misplaced. Nothing else of the small parcel of her belongings was missing. She grieved over the book. It was as if the final vestige of her old world had been stripped from her, the last link with Stephen.

'Maybe it'll come back, *a stór*,' Blind Mary said, as if the book had its own life, its own motion. 'God is good,' she comforted, 'maybe it'll come back, Ellie.'

Ellen knew differently. The book going from her was part of a pattern. Like the candles in the passageway, going out one by one on the night Maybelle Tucker's house was mobbed, so too, had the candles in her own life gone out – Stephen, Lavelle, her children, the business, her sight, the book. All candles, light-offering, snuffed out by sin.

'It's gone, Mary,' she said, 'gone for good.' The book would no more 'come back' than the poor woman's Dan would.

'I'll look out for it for you,' Blind Mary replied, and Ellen knew she would, would keep looking out for it, as she did for Dan. Blind Mary had hope. It was all she had, hope and gin and a handful of old songs.

She, herself, had no hope. It was better that way. With no hope there was no extinguishment of hope.

Each day was then the same as the next, the same as the last, no better, no worse – to be survived. Her life had become a round of survival: rising, going, stitching, coming, sleeping, rising again, like the round of a jig or a reel. You always knew the tune would turn, come back to where it had begun with wonderful certain monotony. Not like Bach, who took you off to the sky, weaving you in among the clouds' lining, until you never knew when again he would land you safely back to earth. Bach's music was air-music, floating on hope and desire. Irish music was earth-music, grounded, safe. Her life now demanded earth-music, that repetitive round of certainty. She mustn't lose the earth – Heaven could wait.

Not that she ever thought of Bach much nowadays. The missing book was her only connection to all those notions she had, all that rising above herself. The book was her forbidden treasure, her pearl of light, among the stitches-per-inch of life, and the drudgery, sewage and garbage of Half-Moon Place.

What was it Mary had once said to Louisa before they had come to take away the piano? 'We will always have the memory of it – the memory of tunes.' At the time she thought it such a wise thing to say. Now, with her book gone, she too would only have a memory – the memory of words.

369

There was so much of life that was just a memory. How much could one memory preserve, she wondered? Not that she was creating any new ones. And if she ended up darkened like Blind Mary, then her memory would need to hold pictures, as well as poems and tunes.

That thought preyed on her, so that more and more as the decade turned, she found herself looking at her face in the fragment of mirror glass she kept, touching each part, committing it to the memory of skin, for the time when she could no longer see it. The memory of skin ... like when she and Stephen...

Even when he wasn't there her skin had still remembered. So that when undressed, when she put her hand to her body, where he had gone – 'Before, behind, between, above, below' – it was not her hand, but his.

Then she would put the mirror down, close her eyes, remembering, and touch her hair at the line where it met her forehead. Still like the sun, but now streaked here and there with seams of whiter sun-fire.

'Ellen Rua, how do? Soon it will be Ellen Bán.' She smiled to herself, thinking how once she had wanted to lose the 'Rua' from her name; Rua – red. 'Rua for fire,' Peabody had once said. She wondered about Jacob – if he had found love, or just more money. That white-cocked plume of his hair, unless he had lost it to age. He must be the sixty, she thought. Strange the way he had worn the white apron, the last time. A boundary line, white and shop-soiled, something to rub his hands into, degrease them. She remembered his hands against it. Like crippled wings they were, flapping and beating, wanting to lift him up again, give him flight out of this bitter-beaked world. Yes, she thought, Jacob was more to be pitied than anything.

Still, with eyes closed, her fingers followed the line of her nose to her lips, spread out across the extent of them, each side from the dividing central furrow. She then picked up the glass, repeating this exercise of exploration, mirroring the visual reality against the touch-memory. 'I don't know which one of you I best like!' she remarked to the mirror.

On one occasion she had undressed and stood with her body buttocked against the rough grain of the wooden wall. Raised her arms out either side of her like a crucified Christ. 'Full nakedness! All joys are due to thee, As souls unbodied, bodies unclothed must be...' She stopped herself before the words '...To taste whole joys'.

That now was a not-to-be-remembered reason for bodies to be unclothed. She continued the remembering exercise, first turning her upper body and stretching her right hand over to her extended left arm. With her eyes marking each movement, each memory place, she traced her fingers back along her forearm, elbow and upper arm to the sinews of her shoulder.

There they felt the raised, but long-healed ridges of *munggaiynwun* – the cutting of the body – the 'sorry cuts' she had inflicted on herself at Annie's death all those long years ago. Three

371

times she had dragged the jagged quartzite knife across her skin, so great her grief was in the Coorong on Australia's southernmost coast. That memory her skin, her whole body could never forget. Annie would have been fourteen by now. Maybe if she still had Annie to rear, maybe it would have saved her from all that preoccupation with wanting to 'up' themselves, all her chasing after poems and preludes ... all that thinking about herself. Stephen had asked her once about the scars. When she had told him the story, that it was the custom of the Ngarrindjeri women after great loss, he had gentled his lips along the course of each scar. Sealed the memory. His long Trinity tongue tracing down her shoulder, underneath to its moist pit. Quickly she banished the thought of him, moved away her hand. Some wounds would never be sealed.

Next, she extended her right arm in the Calvary position and repeated the discovery with her left one. Still flexed against the supporting wall, head now on her chest, she followed the descending path of her hand over breast and rib, releasing each part from the tension in which it was held, as it was committed to the sum of memory. Pelvis, vulva, each crease and fold, each purple-grained ridge of skin stretched by birth-giving. She had no regrets about the disfigurements of birth.

Here was where the *mewe* was – the life-source, the energy centre. Again, she remembered, the medicine-man of the Ngarrindjeri, placing his hand there, telling her: 'You have good *mewe*,' when she had asked him to do 'bad *mewe*' –

anything to save Annie. She wondered now, where all her good *mewe* had gone? How had she lost it?

She stood for a moment distracted by her thoughts of Annie, suspended, motionless, then let herself sink to the floor. This was not good *mewe*, trying to store up memories against a sightless future. This memorizing of her body was treating it like a hollow temple, seeking to freeze its decay into middle age, making it the for-ever-to-be-desired body of a one-time lover. *The miasma of memory.*

It was all to do with pride. Her deadly sin was never lust, or 'great love', as she thought it then to be, but pride, putting herself at the centre of everything. Being the redeemer of her children; building up the business, *her* way. Shaking off her Irishness, wanting to be 'upped' – the new-American lady, German music filling her house, and the pernicious poetry of a lascivious English cleric, her head. Now here she was again, displaying such vanity, trying to preserve some immaculate image of *herself*.

Disgusted, she threw on her clothes, then her spectacles. Not that she really needed them for outdoor use ... yet. But they had another purpose – anonymity.

She stepped out into the passageway. Strange, how in blue, the effluent, the fly-infested faeces, the garbage all took on a different dimension, a mysteriousness of hue. Whatever hue of the tenements, their unremitting stench was invested with no such redeeming feature.

Since the onset of her creeping blindness, it had

long been in her mind to do what she was now about to do, but fear of being discovered had held her back. She had long been gone from her old haunts, Long Wharf, Quincy Market, the Cathedral in Franklin Street, the Common – all no longer within the geography of her world. She had never gone back, not once crossed the boundary she had imposed on herself.

But while she had fallen into a new routine of life, she still constantly wondered about her children, and Lavelle – and Stephen. Oftentimes she had wanted to go back, hide somewhere, watch them. It had been a temptation hard to resist, but she had resisted it.

Now she wanted to have one last picture of them in her mind before the blindness set in. Not approach them – just know they were all right.

It was safer now, with less chance of her being recognized, the bent gait of a needlewoman, and her hair no longer the crowning glory it once was. Her eyes, dulled by leather, no longer sparkled with the water-dark green of the Mask. Bespectacled in blue they would help pass her off as one of Boston's myriad blind mice. As she went down the passageway, Blind Mary was in the doorway, perched on her stoop.

'Ellie, is that you? Where are you off to? I think today might be the day!' she said, her voice full of excitement. 'Hisself always liked the fine crisp day to be out in,' Blind Mary went on. 'He didn't like it too hot, the way the sun would be melting his brain.'

Ellen didn't want to be delayed, but stopped anyway. It was a hard station for the old woman, this blind waiting, sitting on her stoop, nodding away, the children 'dannoying the head of her' – a kind of nodding-speak-stoop life, looking out for her Dan with little hope of her ever seeing him, even if she had the sight.

'Here, Ellie! Have a drop for the journey.'

Blind Mary proffered the bottle. She took it, swallowed a mouthful, felt the perfumed rawness tear at her throat. It would give her courage.

49

She went first to Holy Cross. Sunday afternoon was practice time for choristers and organist. Taking her place quietly to the rear of the cathedral, head bowed, she held a faint hope that somehow the organist might be Louisa. A sound like geese flapping made her look up. A brace of nuns flitted by intent on being somewhere else and quickly. She lifted her head to see their faces, but instead saw only the distinctive white-winged head-covering of the Daughters of Charity, flying blue-tinted, beyond her vision. Disappointed, she waited.

This cathedral had been many things to her. Her consolation and refuge, a place of devotion and the place of her condemnation. She looked around at the Stations of the Cross – still hanging there, as they had been, as they would be, long after her. Her eyes rested on the blurred Sixth Station... Louisa's Station. Veronica, all in blue, wiping the face of the blue Jesus. She sat there, silently wrapped within her blue world. Eventually, she heard the shuffling sound of feet in the organ loft behind her. When the music started she did not recognize it.

It wasn't Louisa, or even Mary, playing. She was sure of that. But it was years since she'd heard them – they would have advanced, or maybe had to relinquish their playing altogether. She didn't dare turn around to look up – in case anyone above should look down. It was a bad idea coming here and as unrealistic as Blind Mary waiting to 'see' her Dan. However, Ellen continued to wait until the rehearsal was complete, to her chagrin none of the pieces familiar – no Bach.

She shouldn't have built up her hopes like that, but yet still she remained until the sound of feet leaving the gallery had faded. She darted a look behind her then crept out into the cathedral porch, using one of the great stone pillars for cover. From there she watched them disperse. There was no Mary, and no Louisa.

It had been too much to hope for. A forlorn hope, born of desperation. She returned inside the cathedral and with all humility offered up her deep disappointment to her blue-crossed Redeemer.

On leaving the cathedral, she started out for the Long Wharf, going via Washington Street, still with its patchwork of buildings. She stopped for a moment under the sheltering Old South Meeting House, across from it the doorway leading up the four flights to their first home in America. In it, she pictured Lavelle and herself that Christmas night, she holding the door for him as he left and Lavelle cheeking her with, 'You know, Ellen, we should get married after Lent.'

She saw herself, giddy as a girl, call after him, that she had the same notion herself, then he crunching homewards haloed by falling snow, whistling the white length of Washington Street, because she had said 'yes'. Ah, poor lovely Lavelle, he got such a bad bargain in her. Such a bad bargain.

At the Long Wharf she knew the New England Wine Company would be no more, and only hoped the sign they had taken down would have been replaced by *Frontignac et Lavelle* – like one of those French companies in Montréal. The names ran well together – *Frontignac et Lavelle*. She found their old warehouse, refurbished, resigned, now home to an ice-exporting company.

She left the Long Wharf, nervous lest she be recognized by one of the many longshoremen, who would have known the tall and red-haired 'Irish' of old. The only comment she attracted, however, was a respectful, 'Ma'am, mind you be careful down here of those slings and pulleys!' After the thousands of times she had been up and down this pier! It must be the glasses, she thought. She decided to give the Quincy Market area a wide berth. There were always comings and goings to Faneuil Hall and she never knew who she might bump into. Peabody, if he was about, was always eagle-eyed.

Twice she scuttled past Stephen's house. He

had probably gone years since. What did she hope to find – him standing on the doorstep waiting for her? She lingered a little longer near their own old house, No. 29, but down a bit from it, pretending she was looking for a house across the street. The work they had put into it: No. 29 was their real home, the place where they were all together, she and Lavelle and Patrick and Mary and Louisa. Those were happy days – hunting down the second-hand bargains, Patrick wanting to 'get at' the gone-to-seed cabbage patch, the family all gathered round the piano – days full of beginnings and hope.

A woman perched on a doorstep, on the opposite side, was paying her too much attention. Could it be her old neighbour, Mrs Brophy? She couldn't be sure, could only make out the shape of the woman, so she kept her head down. An Irish accent came across to her.

'Off with you! Get on – you don't belong around here!'

She realized then how different she must look to the ladies 'around here', with her smock and her simple crimped bonnet, and her blue glasses identifying her as a needlewoman.

She trudged on, having resolved not to visit the house in which they had lived after No. 29, in the West End. She had few happy memories of there. With Mary and Louisa already gone and the business sliding away from them, the West End was the beginning of the end of the happy days. Besides, Lavelle or Patrick might still be there. She hoped not, hoped life had given them a lift again. One more call to make; this one saved until last, hoping fervently it would prove fruitful.

The Convent of St Mary Magdalen was well named. A refuge from temptation, it sought to 'reclaim the thoughtless and melt the hardened'. It provided a basic grammar school and domestic skills education for young girls who had been exposed to moral danger. These were the Preservatives, not requiring major reclamation, just mild correcting and the preservation of their 'character'. The Penitents required more rigorous redemption. These, women with a sinful past, were, by a continuum of prayer and penance, 'regenerated'. As a symbol of their regeneration they threw off their worldly names, taking instead the names of saints and martyrs. The Penitents then at various stages returned safe and virtuous to the society they had left. Some Penitents remained on, becoming Magdalens. These, for ever enclosed against the outside world, adopted a special brown habit, took vows of poverty, chastity and obedience, and became contemplatives consecrating their lives to meditation and prayer.

As she drew ever nearer the convent, she considered that she herself was a Magdalen. She had committed the sin of Mary Magdalen – adultery. Now, like that woman, she had turned from her sin and repented, denied herself the world she once knew – apart from this temporary relapse. Her life had become one of poverty, chastity and, mostly, obedience to the rigours of the needlewoman's lot. Her factory smock, plain, unflattering, was her habit. More and more as her sight failed her, she would be shut away from the outside world. She would be forced by blindness to live within her own interior world, become a contemplative.

The thought struck her that perhaps she would be better to throw herself on the mercy of some house such as this one, to become a contemplative within a community of nuns, instead of in a tenement hovel, with only Blind Mary for company. She would not fear utter silence, the incessant meditation on the mysteries of life and death, nor indeed the company of other Penitents like herself. To live with them and die with them, be laid to rest in a little cloistered plot of consecrated ground – it was a comforting thought, although she had of late noticed the first signs of longing in herself for *'bás in Éirinn'* – 'death in Ireland'. It was every emigrant's wish to die in the birthland. And she could imagine no place surpassing the elevated *Crucán* above the two lakes at the mouth of the Maamtrasna valley. To be laid down there, with Michael, her first love, and her darling Katie. There, close to the mountains and the sky, she knew she could finally be at peace.

Her mind returned to where she was – the Magdalens. Something was bothering her about the Magdalens ... and Mary and Louisa. The Magdalens, she remembered, however much they rejected the world, the flesh and the devil, could not become fully-fledged Sisters of the order. For that, a young woman must be of 'spotless character', like Mary and Louisa, and of a family with a 'blameless reputation'. She stopped. If it were known how far *she* had fallen, how much 'blamed' her reputation was, then Mary and Louisa would never become Sisters; at best, they would be condemned to the cloisters as mute Magdalens. Maybe they already had been? If, by the grace of God, they had not, her presence here was putting them in jeopardy.

She took a faltering step, confused by her need, frightened of its possible consequences. *Her* need – what *she* wanted. Not trusting in the Jesus who had once forgiven Mary Magdalen, unable to leave a thing, even in the hands of God. Always had to do and see for herself – be a 'doubting Thomas'.

She would never be whole again until she drove that mote from her eye. She should leave them as they were. They were safer in His arms than they could ever be in hers. Reconciled then, she turned away, each footstep leading her further along the pathway of purification.

Foot-weary and heart-weary, she reached the arch of Half-Moon Place. She relaxed. It was what she knew. Out there, beyond the arch, she felt exposed, uncertain. Here, she could fade back into the din and the smells, the rookeries and the rickety stairways – the secure underbelly of shanty-Irish Boston.

She was hardly in the door when Blind Mary scratched at the outside of it.

'You've had a long day, *craythur!* A long day – here, swallow a dram, it'll ease whatever longing aches you.' Ellen threw back her head, tilted the bottle, felt the welcoming kick of the malted grain in her mouth, the dark purple bite of the juniper berries.

'It's the prickly leaves,' Blind Mary said as she caught her breath.

'What's that, Mary?'

'The prickly leaves ... the juniper, what gives it the sting.'

She wondered how the blind woman knew. She hadn't heard talk like that since back in the valleys, in the time of Sheela-na-Sheeoga, and her herbaceous mixtures. They sat there in the dark, Ellen not bothering to light the candle, passing the bottle between them. When it was finished, they sat in silence with nothing now to connect them. After a spell, Blind Mary spoke, in her kind of nodding-talk.

'Did it help you forget what it was you couldn't find, Ellie?' she asked.

Ellen never queried the woman as to what she meant or how she knew. 'It would take the full of Boston Common of juniper berries to do that, Mary,' she whispered back, her voice unsteady.

'Well, if the gin can't do it, the next best thing is prayin'. God forgive me for puttin' it that way!' Mary crackled with laughter. 'We'll make a novena to St Jude, the patron of hopeless cases – 'cos that's what we are, Ellie – hopeless cases the two of us,' and she started up the novena with the opening petition: 'For the safe return of my Dan, and your own special intentions, Ellie–'

'Will you stop it, Mary! For God's sake stop it! All the praying in the world won't make a blind bit of difference to either of us – St Jude, St Anthony, nor the whole litany of them.'

She was sorry as soon as she said it, but Blind Mary bit back at her. 'Well, maybe it won't, Ellie, but what else have we got, except melting our minds with the gin?' She added, 'And I'll have no more o' that till tomorrow, when the gin-man comes.'

'It's all *trína chéile*, Mary, everything is...' she fumbled for the explanation, '*trína chéile*,' she repeated, failing to find one. 'There's no blasted English word for it!'

'"Mixed-up-together", Ellie – it's all the one whether it's in English or Irish – it's all the one to Blind Mary,' she muttercd.

'Is the dark different, Mary?' Ellen asked, her mind gin-jumping on to something else.

'It is – it's not as hard on the eyes!'

Ellen was about to ask what she meant when the woman burst out laughing. Laughing at her own blindness, mocking Ellen for asking about it.

'No, Mary ... I don't mean ... I was wondering what it'll be like ... for me?'

'Have you the spectacles, Ellie? Well put them on and I'll tell you,' the blind woman instructed.

Ellen did so. She never wore them at night; there was no need to filter out the dark. Now the woman before her took on a different bluish hue, paler than the darker shape of her nodding head, making waves of light and dark – an *Aurora Borealis* between them – as she talked.

'Now, Ellie, move the spectacles out from your nose a bit.' Ellen did so and the black-dark moved in on her again, filling up the blue-dark.

'Now take them away from you altogether,' Blind Mary ordered. 'That's how it will be, Ellie;

383

the blue will all go and there will only be dark. Blue-dark by day, black-dark by night – but all dark.'

Ellen wasn't frightened by it, as she thought she would be, visualizing her blue-darkening blindness the way the blind woman described it.

'The black-dark tastes different in your mouth, Ellie, like dark berries 'stead of brighter ones – you'll know it all right,' Blind Mary said consolingly. 'You'll surely know it!'

Ellen was glad when Blind Mary scratched out through the door again. She was tired. Tired even before the gin, tired and foolish. What a *seafóid* – a nonsense – everything was, her journey a wasted one – a *turas in aisce*.

She hadn't seen sight of one of them.

She cursed herself for getting up her expectations. What did she think? That on this particular day, at that certain time, in the exact place she was, they'd be there, where she wanted them to be, waiting for her? She was growing into a foolish old woman. As foolish as Blind Mary, holding up her doorway, day in and day out, waiting for her Dan to come *snawvauning* down the alleyway, back to her. Or instead offering up her cracked novenas to St Jude.

She put on her blue glasses, looking at the ceiling, laughing and cursing in her first tongue. Into the blue-dark, while she still had it.

Her sleep, when it came, was fitful, filled with visions of a black St Jude, astride *Crucán na bPáiste*, calling on the smoked-Irish peasants in blue-valley fields to give him back his sight. And she, among the souls of the damned, dark-

384

purpled juniper on the waves of Lough Mask, dancing, ignoring the brown-penitented pleas from the Magdalen-priested shore.

50

In the morning, not even the stench of the new day could rouse her for work. It was the first day she had ever missed.

She lay there, temples throbbing, the roof of her mouth dry as tindersticks like it was twined with thatch. Disoriented, waiting for the work-whistle, knowing that if it didn't sound it meant some impending doom for her.

But she just couldn't face the noise, the needle-weary repetitiveness. She would probably damage more uppers than she stitched. Run that God-blasted needle into her finger a dozen times before the day was over. She was better off here, ginned to the gills as she was.

Outside the rain pelted down.

She dreaded the rain. Somehow she pulled herself out of her skimpy cot, placed the knotted lump of cotton Maybelle Tucker had once given her against the gap under the door. The passage-way would soon be a river of sludge, if it kept up like this, slushing anything and everything in its path under the doorways, down into the base-ments. She pitied those in the basements, even Biddy. How did they survive at all? No wonder cholera had ripped through the place a few years ago. She got back into bed. The sound of the rain drummed into her skull like a marching band, its lambeg drums unrelentingly clatter-thumping her soaked brain.

She remembered rain – Good Friday rain.

It had all been so different then, so sensual, beating down on her skin, throbbing into her, drenching her, and him. Her hair raining down as he unbuttoned her, coming between them in her mouth that very first kiss; and the heat rising off her body like steam from a pavement, needing the cooling Good Friday rain.

She shouldn't even be thinking like this. The gin had her tormented. The rain had just kept on falling, pouring down agony and passion in equal torrents. He damp and wet when she tore off his shirt, fingers slipping on his back, needing to dig into him. Eventually, her hands clinging to the long wet tail of his hair, twisting it around her fingers, wrenching his head back, long-necked, like a great white swan, as he beat down on her.

Oh God, how she wished those lambegs would stop pounding! She closed her eyes against them. But they were already in there filling her up with sound, thumping the inside of her skin. Frantically, putting her hands to her head, she tried to dampen the sound. But it kept on burrowing deeper, louder, moved down and away from her, escaping.

When she thought she had finally found it again, trapped it within her hands, the sound had gone strangely quiet, pulsing silently. It was the same quickening pulse from the same deep core when she had arched him back, his face gaunt and pale, his white-ribbed bone searing her red feather-down, impaling her while the crucifixion bell tolled. The lambegs swelled into sound again. She couldn't control them any more, didn't want to now. Just wanted their killing loudness, when the white rush came and he shouted her name. The fierce drums, resisting confinement, pushed against her hands, it all exploding inside her at once – the bells of Calvary, the clattering lambegs and the rushing, releasing torrent of the Good Friday rain.

Blind Mary called on her again, that same night – the night of the rain.

'It was the Famine, Ellie,' she started, after producing the bottle, saying the gin was 'only for the cure, mind!'

'The Famine? What, Mary?' she asked, bewildered, still not the whole of herself.

'The Famine changed everything – for the women!' Blind Mary began. Ellen, wondering where all this had come from. 'It drove us out because we were only a burden and with no chance of a dowry, on account of the potatoes being sickened. Then, over here, if we did get into marriage life itself the priest got into the marriage bed with us, interferin'. They were never like that before the Famine, Ellie?' she asked, but having it already worked out in her own head.

'No,' Ellen replied, 'they weren't. I suppose afterwards there were less of us and more of them. It gave them more of a grasp on the people.'

'But the priest is much worse here than back home,' Blind Mary interrupted, winking her useless eye, as if she knew it for certain. 'Only here the women isn't rushing like sheep to get into marriage life!'

Ellen agreed. The woman paused for a moment, giving weight to what she was about to say.

'If hisself was dead – and even if I knew for sure he was – I wouldn't do it again, Ellie.' Another pause, no nodding now. 'Would you?'

Ellen was almost on the point of telling the woman the truth, that she wasn't a widow-woman or a deserted wife, none of that. What harm could a doddery old blind woman do, who never went further than the lane-way? But she didn't tell her, answering her instead with another question.

'Why should we women give up what we have here in America? The men don't.'

This seemed to please Blind Mary. 'But it's the men what rules the Church and the Church what rules the marriage bed!' she stated matter-of-factly. 'That's the start and finish of everything.'

Blind Mary was right. Once the marriage bed was ruled, then 'God's plan' worked. God's plan for a woman, being 'to perpetuate the human race and minister to the happiness of her husband. Never to undermine his position by going out to work and to bring up *her* children in line with the Commandments of God and the edicts of the Church.' Blind Mary, who didn't see, saw enough.

'You're right, Mary, the Church has colonized

us, just as sure as the Crown did,' she said. 'Put sin and children around our necks in equal doses,' she added, 'and what do we do? Produce a whole new generation of *gasúrs*, who are tied to its teaching, keeping it powerful.' Ellen found herself nodding now, emphasizing each point. That was how the nodding-talk started, she supposed. Talking to yourself in the dark, no one there listening, but nodding to them, pretending they were. 'We've made slaves of ourselves, Mary!' she concluded.

'Faith, that and we have – slaves and breeders!' Blind Mary laughed. 'And if they could hear us talking now, Ellie, we'd be hanged on Boston Common like the witches of old. Why is it always the women, Ellie?'

'Because they're afraid of us. Deep down, the men are afraid of us, of our bodies!'

'Our bodies?' the blind woman asked.

'Yes, Mary, the power of blood frightens them. We are unclean, the temples of sin, but the temples of pleasure – men's pleasure!'

'That's quare talk, Ellie!' Blind Mary nodded, gone into herself again, working it out.

'Is it, Mary? Think about it! And we can withhold that pleasure, be apart from it. That frightens them too. A man cannot be apart from his pleasure. His pleasure must end – ours need not.'

'Holy God, Ellie!' Blind Mary said, blessing herself hurriedly, twice. 'I think you have it right – but no one ever says it.'

'No, they don't, Mary. But they think it when they hang witches – and they'll think it when they hang you and me, Blind Mary!' she added, bursting into laughter with the other woman.

'They won't need to hang us, will they, Ellie, the way we're going?' Blind Mary replied more soberly, shaking her bottle at the dark. 'Even the dancing...' she started off again, back on the Famine, '...it was different, you know, Ellie, before the Famine, wilder. You could hit against the young men, feel the "scythe-stones".' Mary laughed at the remembering. 'After the Famine, it was just the feet ... not the dancers themselves, just the feet that danced. No swinging of the scythe-stones.'

'Scythe-stones – I haven't heard that a while, Mary,' Ellen answered, thinking of the valley girls and Peabody. And Stephen. Scythe-stones, she thought now, was more earthy, more substantial, more full of the frolic of happenstance. Not so sure as the arrow of love, the *flèche d'amour* as Stephen and the French had it. 'But you can't lessen a sin by setting it to music, Mary,' she mused out loud, recalling a sermon once, railing against the 'carnal pleasures of the waltz'. The waltz ... the waltz had been her downfall.

'But you can heighten it for sure!' Blind Mary chirruped.

'That you can, Mary, that you can,' she answered, 'especially the waltz.'

They were both silent then, thinking of different dancing days, and how it was, as Blind Mary had said at the start of the conversation, that the Famine had changed everything for women. Ellen wondered if it was all just 'gin-talk'. Or did other women talk like they did? The

Daughters of the Commonwealth discussed wider issues – 'woman's place in society'; 'the economic role of women'; 'the refining role'; 'the reforming role...' All very interesting, in a dried-up kind of way, but the discussions always skirted around the basic issues of female functions and feelings. Were women afraid of blood as well, she wondered?

With Blind Mary she could discuss everything. Dancers in the dark, the both of them.

51

Libby met her next morning.

'Are you all right, Ellen? The cramps, was it?' she asked, concerned.

'I'm fine, Libby – something like that,' she answered, wondering if the woman could smell the gin.

'It's a curse, every month!' Libby said, not seeming suspicious.

'It is.'

'Peg-Leg was like a bull yesterday,' Libby warned her, 'so watch yourself; there's a bit of a backlog at your machine.'

And indeed there was. Stacks of uppers in bins piled sky-high waiting for her. She threw on her overall, keen to get at them. She would already be docked a day's pay, almost a dollar. It would leave her tight for the week, less than five dollars in all. With two for rent and thirty-six cents for fares, what was left wouldn't go far. But that was the way it was, and it was her own fault lying on in bed full to the gills with gin and 'lambeggin' herself.

Clegg bided his time. He caught her by the arm in the washroom. She had held off going for as long as she could, trying to catch up on the work. Tried to gauge when too many of the men wouldn't be in there – the clickers were the worst! Each day she and the other women ran the gauntlet of their lewd remarks, and being felt for quality and width, like sides of leather. Despite complaints from Libby and the Women Workers' Union, the factory bosses refused to segregate the toilets.

'Wouldn't even buy separate drinking mugs for us,' Libby referred to the beer-stained and tobacco-spittled mugs they were forced to drink from in the summer months, the place like a dry oven.

'Back to work you – Irish,' Clegg said to her, 'no fanny-breaks until you clear that work!' He jerked her arm until it hurt. 'Where were *you* yesterday?' he asked, his face close to hers. 'Don't tell me, I can smell it. Just like the rest of them.' He jerked her arm again. 'Lace widow, my sainted arse. Come down a bit in the world since we first came here, haven't we? You're no different, a jumped-up shanty-Biddy. Back on your machine!' he ordered.

He pushed her out to the shop floor, wiping his hands as if they had held something odious between them. Until the midday break came she thought her kidneys would kill her. Clegg watched and watched her but she wouldn't give in, held on somehow, banging out the God-forsaken uppers until the mountains of cowhide on every side of her had diminished.

Libby approached her in the washroom. 'I saw that bastard, Ellen. We have to do something, take a stand – what do you think?'

In the heat of the moment, she agreed, later regretting it.

'What do I want, getting into all that?' she said to Blind Mary. 'I've been fighting half my life just to stay alive. Now I'm tired of it – just want to be left alone, no notice taken of me,' she added.

'Who'll do it, Ellie, if the likes of you what's ediccated won't?' the blind woman asked, adding, 'The likes of me wouldn't know nothin' about them rights and things – just do the little I can while I'm waiting for hisself to come.' She paused. 'That ediccation is a great thing and shouldn't be let go to waste, Ellie.'

There was something about the way Blind Mary spoke that caught Ellen's ear. She looked at the blind woman, her head nodding up and down, the thin scrawn of a neck on her, loose bits of hair, like spiderwort, hanging about her face.

'It was you, wasn't it, Mary?' she said quietly. Ellen felt the woman go still, the nodding stop.

After a while, the question. 'Me? What, Ellie?'

'It was you who warned Maybelle Tucker, the night she was mobbed out, wasn't it? You saved their lives,' she insisted, now more sure than ever.

'What are you talking about, girl?' The nodding started up again.

'I didn't have the courage to do it,' Ellen told her. 'I was fearful of what Biddy and her Fire Brigade might do to me,' she continued, 'but thank God, somebody had more courage than I did and warned the poor woman in time.'

'Ellie, you know I don't have no time for them niggers. They moved in and took my Dan's job at the forge, soon they'll be crawlin' all over the place with their quare talk of "dem, dat, dese and dose". The troops is readyin' to try and keep 'em held back and good luck to them is what I say.'

'But you still did it, Mary?' she asked again.

'Will you stop at me, bad cess to you, and take a drop o' the gin,' the blind woman said, angrily. 'Sure, no one knows who it was – else that Biddy be after 'em!' was all she would say on the matter.

Ellen decided not to pursue it. But she was sure she was right about Blind Mary and was filled with admiration for her – 'unediccated an' all', as she referred to herself. Blind, hating the black people, afraid of what might happen to the jobs in the forges and everywhere else if the coming war was lost. 'Free the blacks and blacken the Irish – that's what'll happen,' as Mary saw it. Yet the human spark lived in her, the spark that would have lived in the valleys back home, that had been all but extinguished here, in the mad scramble for survival amongst the rookeries and basements of Boston. Mary would have picked up wind of the 'mobbing-out' along the passageway. Must have crept then, by dark, feeling her way along the walls to Maybelle's house, and warned the black woman. No one would have suspected her, Blind Mary stuck on her stoop, waiting for her Dan.

'Biddy has been awful quiet lately, Mary,' Ellen said, thinking back on that awful night.

'She has. Biddy has her own troubles ... like the rest of us. God help her!' the woman answered mysteriously. The head began again, the hair-spiders jiggling with it, in their own kind of nodding dance.

'Well, she makes enough of them for everybody else,' Ellen replied.

'She has her reasons,' Blind Mary said, without revealing any of them. 'Some people just bring trouble on themselves and when they have it brung down, want to set it on everyone else around them, too!'

The woman could have been talking about Ellen's own life, instead of Biddy Earley's. She felt the woman was somehow chiding her for her remarks about Biddy, though Mary was also saying something else about the woman, but in a strange, 'sure, God help her', protective way.

Ellen wondered if she herself had judged Biddy too harshly. She had gravely misjudged Mary, who, while apparently supporting one course of action against the blacks, had, when needed, taken another and saved Maybelle Tucker's life and those of her children. Had she also mis-judged Biddy? What were the troubles Biddy had brought on herself? And what had caused her to be the way she was, do the things she had done?

52

For the next three days the rains hammered down on Half-Moon Place. At least, she thought, as she wrung out her sodden doorstop, it would clear the air of the reek of urine and excrement. Even if in doing so, it washed some of it down on top of the unfortunate wretches who were the basement dwellers. With only one privy for every hundred occupants and the constant backwater from overflowing drains, those who lived in the tenements were in constant companionship with a host of diseases.

That year alone, Blind Mary had told her, seventy children under the age of five had died. Some from 'arsenical wall-paper', some from disease brought on by the mix of fresh and stale milk sold from the unwashed barrels of McGinty, the milk-dealer. Some had died, unable even to swallow McGinty's milk, their throats closed by life-squeezing mucous membrane – the scourge of summer, diphtheria.

Many of the mothers along the passageway who nursed new-born were in such straits of ignorance and poverty that they fed the infants anything they could lay their hands on. Beans, cucumbers, and other half-cooked, sun-spoiled vegetables, washed down with mother's milk if it was to be had, McGinty's if not. Even Blind Mary's gin, watered down, became the liquid sustenance of many a child.

'It was a miracle,' Ellen said to Mary, 'not that so many died, but that any survived.'

The cut-shortedness of tenement life did not apply solely to the very young. 'It's the older young, in their twenties, who are perishing too!' Blind Mary told her, nodding seriously. 'We're nothing but a perishing class, Ellie, that's what the Irish are, a perishing class.'

Yet the ships still came, ferrying in more of the perishing class to replace those already perished. Ellen herself had now been in Boston almost twelve years. On average, Irish life in the city did not exceed fourteen years. She, only in her fortieth year, was already in decline. Everything about her life pointed to it.

She knew by Biddy Earley's face there was trouble. Normally dour, that cross *crawmogue* of a nose on her, the woman's eyes now held something else – panic.

'Can you come, widow-woman, come quick and help me?' Biddy asked, a previously unheard pleading in her voice.

Ellen's first response was to have nothing to do with her. She was only trouble, and had done terrible things. Now, what difficulty she had got herself into God only knew. Blind Mary's words about the woman came back to her – 'she has her reasons, her own troubles'. But why come to her? Hadn't she all her cronies, her 'mobbing-out' gangs and her Irish Fire Brigade? Why her? Unless Biddy had fallen out with the rest of them?

'Please help me, widow-woman?' she said, grabbing Ellen's hands, beseeching her to come.

Ellen followed her out into the passageway, Biddy hastening ahead of her. Down they went into the gloom of the basement in which she lived. Ellen had to steady herself more than once on the slime washed down on to Biddy's stairs from the sink of the lane above.

'Take your shoes off!' Biddy called back to her.

Ellen ignored her. She wasn't about to filthy her feet on the contagion that was underfoot. Her eyes not yet accustomed to the cavernous darkness, she took the last downward step, her foot landing in water. The whole of Biddy Earley's basement was a pool of dark mucus-like water.

'Oh!' she exclaimed, feeling it swill around her legs.

Biddy didn't answer, but made some sound and then called into the gloom. 'C'mere to me, where are you, you little black bastard?'

Her eyes at last becoming accustomed to the dim light, Ellen could make out the shape of Biddy's bed in the corner, cobbled out of flimsy wood, tea-chest material maybe, the water lapping its edges. Like a giant fetid stew, articles floated on the membrane of the water: a pot, bits of firewood, a few sodden vegetables, and a shoe. Something smooth touched her leg. She dreaded to look down, fearing the worst, and hurriedly withdrew her leg, stepping back up the slimy staircase.

Biddy's basement was a veritable cesspool, filled with the flotsam and jetsam of tenement life. She saw Biddy grab for something – a box, floating around the room like a small boat.

'C'mere to me, will you?' the woman repeated.

Then Ellen saw what the object was. It was a makeshift coffin, the lid not yet on it. One more piece of flotsam in this flooded crypt. She then saw something within the coffin-boat. It was the body of a small child, maybe two years old ... motionless ... black.

'Oh my God, Biddy!' she started to say.

'It's my Patrick,' Biddy said. 'Patrick Joseph Earley, my little black bastard, and he's almost gone, widow-woman.'

Dumbstruck, Ellen waded over to where Biddy stood, relieved that at least the child wasn't dead. But he wasn't far from it – hardly a *giog* out of him.

'I put him in the box to try and keep him dry,' Biddy explained.

The child's dark forehead glistened with fever. When Ellen put her hand to it he made a small whimper of a noise.

'He's fevered, Biddy, I don't know what – we'll have to get help, get him out of here. Bring him to my place, it's fairly dry,' she said, all of a panic, not knowing if anything she did would save the child.

'No! No! We can't bring him out. No one knows ... that's why I came to you,' Biddy said, trying not to raise her voice.

'But he'll die, Biddy, unless we get a doctor!' Ellen entreated.

'He stays here!' Biddy said, defiantly. 'I had him here in the dark and he's never been a day outside it since. Nor will he,' she added, 'until the lid goes on him!'

'I won't breathe a word to a soul, Biddy. I'll wait with you, if that's your wish,' she said.

So they sat, the two of them, keeping vigil, Ellen on a step of the stairs above the water, Biddy on the partly submerged bed, rocking the coffin-boat. Ellen wondered how much longer the wood could hold out the fetid water.

'One little nigger less in the world,' Biddy said, to no one in particular. 'I hated him when he was born,' she continued, 'all black and blue and bloody, like a forest animal. But he grew on me, the little savage. And a quare thing, widow-woman, when he started his gruntin' little sounds, he made them just like us – like he was Irish!'

Ellen didn't know what to say to her. Biddy hated the black people with a vengeance, yet here she was, forced to love one of them. One of them out of her own body, who fashioned sounds like her. It must have altered her mind, that, her own flesh and blood – hating and loving it at the same time.

'It must have been hard on you, Biddy?' she said, after a while.

'*Hard* on me, widow-woman? You don't know the meaning of hard. I cooped up here with him, trying to keep him hid, with his big hungry eyes ... wantin' feedin'. Me thumb stuck in his mouth to stop him crying. But I couldn't put him to me breast. I just couldn't do it!'

Ellen said nothing.

'I prayed the Lord to take him, but He wouldn't. He was hardy, God love the little bastard,' she said, Ellen knowing it was probably the nearest Biddy would ever get to a prayer for her 'little bastard'.

Outside the rain had stopped. If it held off a while, the water would gradually subside, leaving behind whatever debris and detritus it had brought. Leaving behind Ellen, and Biddy, and the dying child. They were the real debris, all of them down here in Half-Moon Place and in Fort Hill and the North End too, raised and lowered on the tidal backwater of tenement life. Eventually discarded, in basement hovels and makeshift coffin-boats. Her and Biddy, each with their secrets, all of a muchness. And Blind Mary, with the dream of her Dan, her crazy novena'd dream. Three blind mice they were, poking about in the under-dark. Creeping through the alleyways of life, keeping each other company with nodding talk and stoop-life gin, until one by one, each of their tails would be cut off.

'I had to stop them!' Biddy broke into her thoughts. 'I had to stop them in the end, widow-woman. But they were too worked up by then, so I let them – but it wasn't her fault,' she said.

'Who, Biddy?' Ellen asked.

'The nigger-woman. It wasn't her fault, it was her runaway husband ... I had the drink on me,' she added. 'And...' she looked down at the child, 'so I upped and I warned her!'

'*You* warned her?' Ellen couldn't keep the amazement out of her voice. 'But you ... I thought it ... you blamed *me!*' she said, more angrily now.

'I know. I had to, otherwise ... I did you a

401

wrong...' Ellen had never seen Biddy Earley so lost for words. 'I'm sorry about the trouble I brung on you!' she eventually got out.

Ellen didn't know what to think. She had assumed it was Blind Mary who had warned Maybelle Tucker, and that the woman had only been parrying with her by not admitting to anything. Never in a hundred years would she have thought of Biddy herself. What turmoils the woman must have gone through, the dark secret she had to keep hidden – her 'smoked-Irish' child.

'It's all right, Biddy,' she said, her annoyance subsiding, 'you had your own troubles,' she reassured the woman. 'But I have one question.'

'Ask away!' Biddy responded.

'Was it you who took the book – the book of English poems?'

'I'm no common thief,' Biddy said angrily. 'What would I be doing with them pernicious English poems, any more than them poisonous dime novels? You know I'm not well-got with the readin'.'

Ellen had thought that Biddy had taken the book out of revenge, believing that it was she who had warned Maybelle Tucker. But, with what the woman had just revealed to her, that could not have been her motivation. If Biddy was telling the truth, then who was the 'common thief', who had taken Ellen's book of 'pernicious English poems', as Biddy called them?

The two women sat and waited, didn't say very much after that, both engrossed in their own thoughts. The water dropped an inch or two, not much more. Biddy still held the side of the coffin, from which now no sound emanated, peering into it every so often, as if expecting some sign.

'Do you think he's gone?' she asked after a while.

'I don't know, Biddy,' Ellen answered, and made to get up to have a look.

'Stay there where you are!' Biddy ordered, and pushed out the coffin-boat towards her. It was like something out of a dream, reminding her of a story her father used to tell about Hades and Charon, the boatman of the Underworld.

The Styx, he had told her, was one of the five rivers of Hades, over whose infernal waters Charon ferried the souls of the dead for an *obolos* – a farthing – placed in the corpse's mouth. If the boatman was not paid then the dead became lost souls, never reaching Elysium, the abode of the blessed. Left to wander eternally on the Stygian shores.

She went down a step to where the water level had dropped and caught the coffin-boat. Patrick Joseph Earley, his dark curly hair dampened with fever, lay there, his eyes open, some last whimper framed in his mouth. She laid her hand on his forehead. While beads of perspiration still remained, there was no heat in them now. He was gone all right. Gently, she closed the child's eyes and mouth.

'He's gone, Biddy,' she said, blessing herself.

'Push him back here till I get the lid,' she ordered Ellen, asserting that 'there's no point in prayin' for them, they don't have no souls.'

'What about the half-soul he got from you,

Biddy?' Ellen asked.

'Well, if he did, itself it's as black as me own for what I done. As black as his own little savage's heart!' Biddy said, still defiant.

Ellen looked at the 'little savage's' face. It was just the fresh-formed face of a child in sleep. Whatever fine looks it held had come from his father, not from Biddy Earley, she couldn't help but notice. She said her own prayer for the safe journey of the boy's soul to the Elysian fields, then pushed him back over the divide between herself and his mother.

53

Later, under cover of darkness, she helped Biddy carry the coffin-boat down the passageway; they placed it in the burned-out ruins of Maybelle Tucker's house. Visible, so it would be found before the tenement dogs would shred the frail timbers. She offered to let Biddy stay at her place until the waters went down, but Biddy refused.

'This don't change nothin' between us, widow-woman!' was how she put it.

For the few remaining hours that night, Ellen lay awake. Was nothing as it seemed with people? And Biddy – was she a good or a bad person? She was sure the woman herself didn't know. And, if Biddy didn't know, did it really matter if anyone else did?

She was getting like Peabody now, addling her

brain with questions that had no answers. Still, she supposed, it was important to raise them, now that she had the time. Life, if it was just a journey from here to somewhere else, was not about working, or doing, or sleeping, or eating. It was about questions – peeling them off like the skin of an onion till you got to the next one to be asked, then peeled that question back, and so on.

Eventually, before you left it, you perhaps got somewhere close to the core of life, and were ready for the next step. Then, there would be no more questions, only the face of God. That sight she was beginning to more and more hunger for, but she was not ready yet. She had to peel away her own skins first, root out the imperfections, her attachment to things of this life, like the book; she still wondered what had happened to it – but did it matter? And the much worse attachment – remembering, holding on to forbidden memories, however infrequently she entertained them. Slinking round Boston like a wraith, looking at the past, that was a grievous relapse. That was not the path to spirituality, the road to the real life, to redemption.

Then again, maybe the real life was no more than puncturing a series of holes in endless shoe-leather without managing to puncture her finger; accepting her lot. Did it really matter which life was which?

She couldn't fathom one, couldn't escape the other.

54

'There's going to be a war, Ellen!' Libby Corrigan stated categorically a few days later, during the time of Advent. Ellen thought minds should be more turned to the coming of the Saviour's birth than to war.

'A time of great change is coming in America and it's going to be our great chance too,' Libby enthused, no thought of Christmas on her horizon.

'I don't see anything exciting about war, Libby,' Ellen replied. 'Fat difference it'll make to you and me, except longer shifts, making marching boots.'

'It's time now, before that, for the Sisterhood to start the struggle,' Libby said, her voice laced with something Ellen remembered. A zealot's voice – Stephen. 'No struggle, no progress, you know that, Ellen. Boss-power gives nothing without labour-power taking it.' Libby beckoned her closer. 'The men are ready – Washington's birthday, in the New Year!'

Ellen looked at her. It *was* like going to war for Libby. All worked up she was, like Stephen used to get. Did everyone always need a cause, to be going against something? Fighting for some freedom or other: Ireland, the blacks, the workers, women? Once she had thought 'causes' only afflicted men. She looked at Libby, the small pixie-like face shining, the sing-song of her Wickla accent, flattened and hardened now, three thousand miles away stirring up the women of America.

'On February twenty-second next, the biggest march in the history of the United States will happen – here in Lynn, Massachusetts,' Libby laid it out like a military plan, 'otherwise we'll end up back at fifty cents a day like three years ago!'

Ellen well remembered the '57 depression. She, Libby, and thousands of other workers had barely survived it. Since then, the Massachusetts cordwainers had become more and more militant, pushing for increased wages, reduced hours and a minimum set of working conditions. If they didn't hold together now, up the pace of the struggle, the pressures of the almost-inevitable civil war would be used to squeeze them down again. 'Patriotism' would demand that they do more for less.

Her heart wasn't really in it. It was a distraction from her own path, a further lack of acceptance. But Libby had stood by her from the start when things were tough.

'All right, Libby, I'm with you!' she said, not sure what she could contribute to Washington's birthday.

Libby Corrigan's face lit up, so that Ellen was glad she had thrown in her lot with her. 'Good, we need women like you. What's going to happen,' Libby explained, 'is that thousands of the men will march on the factories and hand in their tools. Then, before Paddy's Day, we'll take to the streets. We'll show them what fanny-power is all

407

about!' Libby said, full of it.

Ellen agreed to help with the making of banners, each night, by hand, laboriously stitching in the words of Libby's banner-cry.

American Ladies will not be slaves

Give us a fair compensation

And we will labour cheerfully

It was slow tedious work, further aggravating the welts on the fingers of her left hand. The poor light and her own failing sight causing her to misjudge time and again the exit point of her stout needle. But she persisted, offering it up against time in Purgatory.

'Bottleneck!' The word went around the Closing Room at the Massachusetts Cordwaining Company.

'Bottleneck' was the signal for the women to bring the factory to a standstill. But in a manner in which nobody could be blamed, because unlike a strike, there would be no downing of tools. The opposite, in fact, as Libby had put it.

'We work out of our skins until we've emptied our own section and clogged up the next,' she explained. 'Then we'll have nothing to do and the finishers too much. Peg-Leg will go mad with us sitting here, and Bull Jenkins in the Finishing Room – wait till he charges in here blaming Clegg.'

Ellen couldn't help a tremble of excitement at the notion of causing trouble for the foreman.

'Next,' Libby went on like some pint-sized general, 'Peg-Leg will slump off to the Cutting Room looking for more work. But the clickers will be slowed down, examining every hide twice for "bad-grained leather", delaying us even further. With *no* work coming from us, Jenkins will be back again, bullin', that now his section is idle. It won't be long then, before the bosses are down and they'll all, Clegg, Jenkins, the whole lot of them, get it in the neck. Except us – only tryin' to work as hard as they'll let us!'

It was a master plan, Ellen thought.

'It'll dawn on them eventually,' Libby concluded, 'that there's more to needle-life than boss-power! This is just to give them a taste before the Christmas of what's waiting for them after it,' she said, relishing the thought.

If leather ever flew, it flew that week. Ellen had never worked as hard. Clegg couldn't believe his luck at how the output from his section set new levels of production, and how few 'fanny-breaks' there seemed to be. It was the best Christmas present he could get, and given all the unrest that was abroad, he could pride himself that his section, at least, was trouble-free. However, his natural Lancastrian cautiousness kept him alert. There was a lot of talk going around and the place was infested with Biddies and Bloomerists, neither to be trusted. The Irish the worst, well-schooled in skulduggery of every sort by their Popish Mass-men.

When Jenkins came he came at him true to his name, snorting and stomping like a bull through the line of machines, just as Libby had forecast. 'Clegg, what in God's name are you at?' the bull demanded. Ellen, Libby and the rest of them straining to catch it all. 'Trying to show me up, is it? Piling it on to my lasses?'

Peg-Leg defended *his* 'lasses': 'Well, get back bloody up there and get them to work as hard as mine!'

Jenkins thundered off, to the continuing clamour from his own 'lasses' about thread problems, feeder problems, loose bobbins and uppers not properly bound, until like little hillocks of leather, the work piled higher and higher at every workstation under his supervision.

Next, as Libby had forecast, the supply from the Cutting Room to the binders slowed down. Bundles of work, when they did arrive, came unskived and mismatched. Now Clegg was forced to go to the Cutting Room complaining that 'my lasses' after breaking their backs' now had 'no work due to slackers' in the Cutting Room.

And so the bottleneck spread from one production area to the next. The Bottoming Room, Lasting, Eyeletting, Topstitching. Finally the checkers started to send work back wholesale, that 'the speedups' ordered by Clegg and Jenkins had caused quality to plummet!

By the end of the week each floor of the five-storey building was in chaos. Partly-finished shoes and boots lay everywhere. Half-filled boxes jammed the stairways, everybody blaming everybody else, while empty dispatch carts were stacked up one behind the other waiting at the loading bays for goods to fill them.

Libby was ecstatic. Ellen, too, exhilarated that after years of drudgery, they had somehow 'gotten back' at the bosses, proclaiming to Libby that it was 'the best day's sport since I stepped foot in this place'.

Bloomerism worked.

However, she was having second thoughts about taking to the streets in March. Appearing in public was different, inviting discovery and the risk of raking up all that she had managed to keep buried for the past four years. Still, it was good to be part of something she had always believed in – before it had any names like 'Sisterhood' or 'Bloomerism', or even Libby Corrigan's 'fanny-power'!

Blind Mary took great interest in the banner-making, getting Ellen to describe it to her – what the words said, even the colours of the threads. Then she would feel the raised rump of the stitching, running her finger around it, nodding her head as though the banner itself were talking to her.

'Oh, it'll be a fine banner, I can tell. If I only had the sight, I'd march ahind it meself,' she said. 'Will you be the one to carry it, Ellie?'

She had no intention of carrying it, and was hesitant enough about being just one of the crowd.

Up to this Ellen had never mentioned anything to Blind Mary about Biddy or the child, but now Mary herself drew it down.

'There was a great commotion the other day while you were at work, Ellie. They found a casket with a little blackfella in it up at the burnt house. It near went out o' my head to tell you.'

Ellen said nothing.

'Mind, it wasn't one of hers...' Blind Mary explained, '...the nigger woman what got mobbed-out!'

'I suppose it could have been any poor waif,' Ellen replied, trying to get rid of the subject.

''Tis well known to some whose waif it was!' Blind Mary said, starting the nodding again.

Ellen didn't know if the woman was referring to her, or was instead letting her know that she, Blind Mary, knew. She let the remark go, and waited a moment before changing the conversation.

'They say, Mary, there'll be war before long, on account of John Brown last year – attacking the Government gun station at Harper's Ferry.'

'I think you are right, Ellie,' Blind Mary said, the head going strongly. 'But no Irish supported him, nor even the niggers he was trying to raise up!' she added, as if John Brown had received his proper come-uppance.

'They were foolish to hang him,' Ellen believed, 'making a martyr out of him. The British always made that mistake with us!'

'Sure, he wasn't a right American at all,' Blind Mary started to disagree, 'a black Protestant he was, the spawn of Cromwell hisself! They didn't hang him half high enough. It's our poor innocent Irish boys who'll be sent out in the end because of the like o' John Brown – our lads don't want Lincoln neither!'

For a blind woman who hardly moved off her stoop, Mary had her ear well glued to the ground, Ellen thought. She probably got it at night from the sailors and militiamen, when they were well juiced up on her juniper berries.

'Lincoln will be President, with or without the Irish vote, Mary – he's a good man,' she argued.

'He's nothing o' the kind, he's a nigger-lover and the Southern States won't have him.' Blind Mary argued vehemently against Abraham Lincoln. 'He'll show the cloven hoof yet, Ellie, and burst the country apart!' she predicted, adding dolefully, 'Oh, it's terrible times we're living in; I hope we'll all be spared – and poor Dan. I'm thinkin' o' startin' a new novena that he won't come back at all now, afore the trouble starts and he be drafted to fight for the niggers. The heart is scalded in me, Ellie, tryin' to work out what's right and what's wrong.'

The woman was right about the troubled times ahead, and there was nothing Ellen could say about Dan that wouldn't sound false. Not that Blind Mary, once she got started on her favourite topic, gave her much chance.

'It's a shame, the trouble them savages is bringin' on people, after the Court giving it down that they was inferior and unfit to mix with us white folk.'

Mary, was referring to a case two years previously, whose judgment that a Negro had no rights equivalent to a white man was widely supported amongst Boston's Irish. Ellen didn't like to hear talk of imminent war and Lincoln going to 'burst the country' as Mary put it. If there was a civil war, then everything else would fall into second place – the Sisterhood, higher wages and better conditions. Factories might even be closed with the war soaking up men and money on every side.

That night she thought on the war.

What of her own? They all had strong views on the Southern question. Patrick was twenty-two now, almost twenty-three. If he went to war it would be with the South, of that she was sure. Lavelle also, she thought, would stand with the South. Stephen she couldn't tell. He would regard the South trying to free itself from the American Union as the mirror of an Ireland bent on breaking its union with Britain. On the other hand, he was always for 'freedoms', for the abolition of slavery. It might even depend on what stance his comrades took. Some had already indicated they would join with the South. Others had spoken out for the North. So it would be Young Irelander against Young Irelander, sons and lovers against fathers and husbands. She closed her mind from thoughts of it.

At least, she consoled herself, the girls would be safe from the war, in the sanctuary of the convent. It must be soon, that they would be professed, take their final vows. It was nearly five years now, she'd never forget the day; a Tuesday, October 1855, under the Great Elm. Maybe they had another year to go yet, she wasn't sure. Then they would come out from their solitude, and rescue poor sinners, the Preservatives and Penitents. Help them back towards a blameless

life. They were young women now, Mary twenty-
one, Louisa a year or older. Of marriageable age,
but Brides of Christ – Mary's red hair cropped
short, hidden modestly behind the brown
Magdalen head-dress, Louisa's dark and shiny
tresses, similarly gone. But their smiles ... she
could imagine that radiance, them having found
the real life. She wondered if Louisa had yet
spoken. These past five years she would have had
no need, Ellen supposed, in a life consecrated to
silence. Still, it had always mystified – if Louisa
had the power to speak. The old woman, Sheela-
na-Sheeoga's prophecy still stood. 'She will speak
at the moment of silence...' Sheela had said of
Louisa, '...in the far-off land.'

Ellen couldn't work it out. Maybe 'speaking'
wasn't 'speaking' at all, perhaps some act, some
sign, something the girl would do. Maybe it was
as simple as Louisa 'speaking' by taking vows –
'the moment of silence' her entering the silent
world of a convent, America – 'the far-off land'.

She left it there, turning instead to pray for
them all, that they would be delivered safely from
whatever lay in store for them.

55

In the cold New Year snows Blind Mary came not
as often to visit her as she previously had – 'until
the weather picks up again!'

The woman kept her going, could put talk in a

bottle, and frequently did, especially on the nights she swigged her juniper juice. Blind Mary never called it gin any more or 'Geneva' as Ellen told her she heard it named in Westport once. The 'juice of the juniper berry' seemed to put a different character on the grubby bottle, whose neck the blind woman would wipe with the heel of her hand before passing it to Ellen. 'And sure it *is* for the good of our health, Ellie!' Blind Mary would argue, 'while we're alive. We'll be in the grave long enough, then where'll we get a sup o' it?'

But Ellen was well relieved that Mary and her juice of the juniper berry had banished themselves, at least temporarily. More and more she valued solitude, regarding herself 'a Magdalen on the outside' having passed from being a Preservative to the higher, Penitent state. She was not yet ready to be a full Magdalen, a contemplative, her life devoted totally to sanctification, a life of complete self-denial, of absolute abnegation. She had a loose idea that by the close of the year, when perhaps Mary and Louisa were taking their final vows, she too might be ready to advance to the final Magdalen state. It was something to aim for.

Already she had taken the shard of vanity glass she kept as a mirror and cast it away. What use had she of it anyway, at her age? It was well named – 'vanity' glass – for primpin' and posin' in front of. Her, with the eyes hollowed back in her head from stitching and sewing, eyes needing 'her little blue windows', to see any bit of detail at all. And her forehead, furrowed with being scrunched up over that infernal Singer machine, worrying about her eight stitches per inch, and discoloured from years of tannic acid. Above it the fine *dos* of hair she once had – gone wild, its lustre lost, like gone-to-seed corn.

Mostly she kept it pinned back – bad enough catching fingers in the feeders, without her hair too. She ate sparingly, 'not enough as would put flesh on a sparrow's shin', Blind Mary used to castigate her. That showed in her face too, the skin either side of her nose now pinched a little, exaggerating her cheekbones. And the little furrow below her nose that ran down to her lips – the one Lavelle always watched when she became impassioned about something, or in passion itself – had flattened a bit, the tiniest of creases attaching themselves to its ridges. Creases she couldn't see but could feel all the same.

Since the day she had cut herself away from her previous life, the only condescension she had allowed to it was to 'beautify' herself with a solid bar of carbolic soap. Not a speck of powder, not a jot of rouge had she ever put on since. Now, in her simple smock with her wild hair and clean-scrubbed face, she could have been any of the young women teeming off emigrant ships straight from the valley-life in Ireland.

Apart from her sight – and her age, being the forty now.

56

The cordwainers' strike on George Washington's birthday, produced a triumphant turnout. Thousands upon thousands of shoemakers and bootmakers clogged the streets of Lynn and handed in their awls, lasting hammers and clicking knives. Thousands more citizens turned out to support the striking workers.

Ellen was in a dither about the women's protest, the following month. After all the preparation involved and Libby's unbridled enthusiasm, part of her looked forward to the march. The cause was just and right, one she had always espoused. She remembered Mary, at thirteen, being all fired up about notions of 'a society for the promotion of industry, virtue and knowledge'; how she herself had told them that 'mill life should be more than the tyranny of employment replacing the tyranny of unemployment'. In that sense she felt duty-bound to the children, as well as to Libby, to uphold those views, to march.

The other half of her ached for anonymity. She had a fear of being recognized, her shame revisited on Lavelle and the children. Increasingly, too, she saw all activities such as marching and agitating as distractions from the inner life, from contemplating the Divine and her soul's delivery.

She decided that on balance, she should go. In

any event, she would be downing tools like the rest of them after the march – 'walking off the machines', Libby called it. She wondered what she would do, how long she could hold out for, without even the miserly few dollars she now earned coming in. And while Libby was convinced that 'the bosses will break, when the machines don't sing', Ellen wasn't. God will provide, she thought, even if the bosses wouldn't.

On the day of the march itself snow was falling. This did little to dampen the spirits of the eight hundred or so women who turned out.

'Though we are smaller in number than the men, our protest will be as important – it will show other women what can be done!' Libby said, undeflated by the numbers or nature's climate.

So they marched in the falling snow, her banner boldly out front, she further back, under the umbrellas. It was exciting. Crowds lined each side of the street, some to gawk at the brazen shoewomen, others shouting support, bosses' men to heckle them.

From a makeshift platform Libby addressed them, Ellen marvelling at this gritty woman prettied with cows.

'Sisterhood of Toil,' she began to a huge cheer, 'sewing at once with a double thread a shroud as well as a shoe...'

The cheering swelled. It was a favourite theme of Libby's – that they were all 'sewing themselves into an early grave'.

'When Massachusetts supports the freedom of the black slave, what do we say?'

'Yes!' sprang up the roar.

'When we, white slaves of the North, seek our freedom, what do we want Massachusetts to say?'

'Yes!' came the clamour of hundreds.

'American ladies – we will not be slaves!' Libby Corrigan shouted at the top of her voice.

'No!' The roar of the needlewomen and mill girls thundered against the white, falling flakes.

That was as far as Libby got. She was immediately drowned out by the *derumptyturn* of a marching band. When she stopped speaking the band stopped playing. When she started up again, so too did the band. The bosses and Tory shoe barons had sought to ridicule the women workers, to reduce the protest to a carnival with music as the weapon. Women, the bosses held, violated their sphere by public speaking.

It was stalemate until Libby, incensed by this treatment, leaped from her makeshift platform and made for the hapless musicians, umbrella flailing.

'I'll give you music!' she shouted, much to the delight of Sisterhood and onlookers alike, a bevy of them joining her in similarly belabouring the band. The musicians took to their heels under the assault from the angry needlewomen with nary a toot nor a *derumptytum* between them, the only sound ringing in their ears, the flat battle-cry of Wickla.

'Musicians, is it?' Libby shouted derisorily, 'ye haven't a sping of spittle between the lot o' ye!'

Ellen hadn't enjoyed a day like it since the bottlenecks.

The strike spread right across Massachusetts – some twenty thousand cordwainers downing tools – the greatest walkout in American labour history. Lincoln, campaigning for the Republican Presidential nomination in New England, declared support for the workers.

'I like a system which lets a man strike when he wants to' Lincoln said, likening that freedom to the same freedom slavery sought to deny. Ellen liked Lincoln with his 'Capital is the fruit of labour', but labour 'greatly the superior of capital'.

But Abraham Lincoln or no, the Tory bosses ignored the workers' demands. The very reasons for which the strike was called, 'The High Wages List', bit by bit forced the striking workers back to work – when they had no wages.

Two weeks later, the machines still not singing and the Massachusetts Cordwaining Company still silent, so too were the Tory bosses to the workers' demands.

'Libby! I can't stay out any longer,' Ellen was driven to tell her friend after a meeting to decide the future. 'I have nothing to pay the rent with.'

By early April Libby had returned to work, one of the last few remaining strikers to do so. It was all over. The cordwainers' strike had failed and the factories sang once more to the sound of the Singer sewing machine – eight beats to the bar, eight stitches per inch. Though she did not say as much to Libby, Ellen was glad. She didn't have the heart for such things any more. Just to put in her day was all she wanted, and to talk to Blind

Mary at night, hear the old songs and the old stories. Even Blind Mary's praying and then her not praying for Dan's return was a sort of blessed normality. The woman didn't require her to do anything – just be willing to talk or more often to listen.

When the brighter spring days and longer nights had edged in over Half-Moon Place, Blind Mary had once again begun to visit her with more frequency, cabin-hunting along the passageway for talk. Ellen herself did not engage in the cabin-hunting talk, lapsing more and more into silence, listening, letting Mary ramble on about everything under the sun. How 'wicked proud' she was, of her Dan, and America being 'a land without stars' and 'the sun not dancing on Easter morning on account of the place being full of "niggerology" – with Lincoln and his likes!'

They would recite the Litany to the Blessed Virgin or whatever saint it was that week, who was in vogue with Mary, and who would bring Dan dancin' back under the archway to her or else keep him away – 'safe till the nigger-war is over'. Then Blind Mary would spin out songs of tryst and treason, and tales of young girls forced to marry old 'dead' husbands and 'Rise up Your Blanket', and the like. Rattling them off like a litany. Songs she had 'picked up' or 'got' back home in Ireland or had been kept alive here in the late-night dram shops. One she had learned from Biddy Earley, 'Lord Gregory'. 'The babe is cold in my arms, Lord Gregory let me in,' she pleaded in her gin-cracked voice.

In return, Ellen recited what she could remember of the *Holy Sonnets*. Without her missing book, it was difficult.

'Then, as my soul, to heaven her first seat, takes
  flight...
So, fall my sins...
For thus I leave the world, the flesh, the devil.'

And the blind woman would cross herself three times. 'Jesus, Mary and Holy Saint Joseph, Ellie – you have the heart put crossways on me...' And she would hurl back the gin. 'I'll ha' to give up the drink, I will ... do d' other one instead, Ellie – the one about wakin' up again when you die!' And Ellen would recite:

'Death be not proud...
One short sleep past, we wake eternally,
And death shall be no more; death, thou shalt
  die.'

'Death, thou shalt die,' Blind Mary would repeat, 'that's a better class o' a poem altogether,' and she would pull at the bottle again, all thought of giving it up gone now, that death was dead. 'You never say d' other ones no more, Ellie – you know, the ones you used to ... about love and his mistress and the like?' Blind Mary would ask, nodding in agreement with herself.

'No, not any more, Mary, they're ... I got tired of them.' Instead, she would sing one of the old songs – in Irish, the words now sitting better with her, the rust of years fallen away, their beauty

423

shining in the blue dark between them.

'All the same, Ellie, you can't whack the old songs,' the woman would say when Ellen had completed singing.

'I suppose you can't, Mary,' she would answer. 'They're not just songs, they're what we are.'

And so it went into the early summer, everything in its place, everything settled. She diligently went to work, partaking in none of the Bloomerism – or the cat-calling at Clegg. Once, even, when he leaned over, rubbing himself into her back, asking him without malice, 'Mr Clegg, to which God do you kneel at night?'

And like the singing rhythm of her needle puncturing leather, the talk and nodding songs of Blind Mary became part of the safe fabric of her material world.

57

In the late summer, when the heat rose, Dan returned.

'Jesus, Mary and Joseph and Holy St Jude – hisself came back!' Blind Mary croaked at Ellen, all excited. 'But we always knew he would, didn't we, Ellie?' she insisted.

Ellen agreed. The woman had shown unshakeable faith. 'How is he, Mary?' she asked.

'Oh, he's great in hisself, great entirely, though...' She hesitated, came closer to Ellen. '...I think the old complaint still ails him – from the furnaces,' she explained.

'Oh!' said Ellen, understanding. Dan's brain, she felt, must still be 'melted'.

'Yes,' the blind woman said, a hint of melancholy in her voice. 'He's talking about going again, when the war comes. I suppose that's the way with the men, coming and going? Sure, he has to, I suppose?' she added.

Her heart went out to the woman. Ellen herself had never believed that 'hisself' would return, yet Blind Mary had prayed her novenas, sat on her stoop every day at the doorpost, 'looking out for him'. And sure enough the scoundrel had come 'buck-leppin' down the passageway whistling as if he hadn't been gone a day, scattering the unclad urchins just as Blind Mary always said he would. She had no recriminations for his long absence. Blind faith was followed by blind love; no questions asked, no answers expected.

It wouldn't be that way for her if she returned, not that she deserved it. She hadn't been 'just gone', like Dan. She had transgressed, crossed the forbidden line, and while a man might cross over it, he could cross back again. A woman, she knew, couldn't.

About a week later, Blind Mary visited Ellen again. She came in sheepishly, hands behind her back, the sun lighting her spidery frame in the doorway.

'What's the matter, Mary?' Ellen asked, concerned. 'Is it Dan?'

The woman shook her head.

'What is it then?' She went to take her by the

arm, but, before she could do so, Blind Mary brought the hands from behind her back and pushed something towards her.

'What...? Oh, Mary – it's my book! Where...?' She was beside herself. After all this time her book that was lost was found. Her joy had been returned; it was a small, tender miracle. 'Thanks be to God,' she said.

'I'm sorry, Ellie,' Blind Mary was saying, her voice barely audible. 'I should never have took it. I wanted to have it for when hisself came back ... to read them out loud to me, the way you did,' she explained.

Ellen took the book, hardly heeding the words, running her hands over the cover, thumbing open the leaves, hearing them fall together again, whispering like paper-bound lovers free at last.

'Hisself made me take it back to you,' Blind Mary continued, Ellen at last starting to take notice of what she was saying. 'He wouldn't have that English filth under the same roof as hisself, he said.'

'Filth?' Ellen repeated, the word leaping out at her, the full bent of what the woman was saying beginning to dawn on her at last. It was she who had taken her book!

'That's what hisself called it,' Blind Mary went on, making nothing of the fact that she had stolen the book, only of what 'hisself' thought of its contents. '"Fancy filth" – that you were trying to turn me into a common night-walker from reading it!' she said more defiantly, the nodding head now backed up by a higher authority, her Dan.

'But do you think it's "filth", Mary?' Ellen asked, dazed by the events unfolding before her, remembering all the nights the woman had sat there, listening to her read or recite from it.

Blind Mary shook her head, this time deliberately. 'It's no use going against what is, Ellie,' she explained. 'It's not what we were reared to, like the old songs and stories. I'll be off with meself, anyway,' she concluded, adding, 'Hisself said not to be delayin'.'

With those words Blind Mary left and Ellen doubted that, unlike Dan, she would ever return again. She sat on the bed holding the book. Glad to have it back, like a lost friend. But where did it leave her? The friend she had shared it with, the one person she had never suspected, had been the one to steal it. And even after she had taken it, squirrelled it away, had carried on as if nothing had happened. Kept cabin-hunting down to her, sat there listening as she, Ellen, struggled to remember the stolen lines. All the time the book stashed away in her own cabin, like a fatted calf against the return of her 'Wanderin' Dan'.

More and more, everything was getting *trína chéile* – turned inside out, upside down. She had trusted Blind Mary, sucked gin from that soiled bottle of hers, talked up and down with her about the Old Country, the new country, the 'Bridgets', the blacks and the Bloomers. She had traded songs with her. They had, even, prayed on their knees together, for the safe return of her absentee husband.

How wrong could she have been about Blind Mary? Thinking first that it was she who had

427

warned Maybelle Tucker, then blaming Biddy for stealing her book. She had been doubly wrong. Then again, why was she surprised? People always concealed their true selves. She herself had been one thing to Lavelle and her children, a dutiful wife, their moral guardian. But another thing with Stephen – a different kind of being entirely – a trollop. Did the one deny the other? Or were they just two conflicting parts of the same whole, temple and tempted locked in a life-long struggle?

Once it had all been easier, more clear-cut. The Crown, the landlords, the proselytizing clergy-men selling 'soup for souls' to the famished, were clearly the bad. Likewise, the famished, the downtrodden peasants, were the good. 'Blessed are the poor in spirit; they shall see heaven.'

Here, nothing fitted the old moulds. Peabody had been her saviour once until imaginings and jealousy had turned him. The Frontignacs had helped her, but only because of an old and Church-led landlording system. Stephen Joyce, Lavelle's fellow revolutionary, had dishonoured that comradeship. Patriot and Protestant, he was one of the hated Scots-Irish, but a Young Irelander too. And the Irish themselves? What of them? Here in Boston, they preyed on each other in a dog-eat-dog existence – the Irish landlords the worst. And the rabbit warren-Irish, living in corners and dugouts, hated the other suppressed race, the Negroes. This hatred in turn spurred on by the *Pilot*, the voice of Holy Mother Church, whose greatest commandment was 'Love thy neighbour as thy self' – but not thy black ones!

Everything in contradiction with itself. And what of the contradictions within her own character? *Kathleen Ní Houlihan* – Mother Ireland – on her back in a dowdy Montréal hotel, wet with sin. Or kissing the feet of the crucified Christ, staining him with her lust. A 'Jezebel', Peabody had called her. A thousand times worse than Blind Mary ever was, carrying on to the outside world as if nothing was amiss. Yet, all the time with the worm in her heart, eating away at it, gorging itself on her deceit.

She leafed through the book lovingly, squinting at the words, most of them denied to her now, even with the aid of her little blue windows. Some she could retrieve, tilting the book towards the light. 'Full nakedness! All joys are due to thee...'; 'Love built on beauty, soon as beauty, dies...'

As the words floated to her, so too did the memories they brought, her hand reaching to her cheeks, her hair... She flicked on from the *Love Elegies*, disturbed by their immediacy, searching out other lines. With difficulty, she found them.

'The element of fire is quite put out;
The sun is lost, and th' earth...'

Peabody, he had seen it all along in her; the Element of Fire, her fatal element. The fire of passion – now long since extinguished. Now only the fires of Purgatory ahead of her, stoked for the purification of her soul.

'Fancy filth!' she muttered. 'Fancy filth!' She had heard it all before, from the pulpit and the

Pilot; 'literary poisons ... pernicious English writers, soiling the flower of our womanhood'. Driving Boston's maiden aunts and its moral guardians like Mrs Brophy, to patrolling the libraries, blacking out the lines of Byron and Shelley and Donne. Or into the Old Corner Bookstore, surreptitiously ripping offending pages from books. Soon, words wouldn't matter to her. Soon, the world would be as dark to her as it was to Blind Mary. She longed for that darkness. If she was dark, then she would have no need of books, no need to be worried if they were stolen or not. It was unnecessary to life, her book, proof that she was not truly contrite. Despite all that she had imagined she had stripped herself of, the book was a remembrance of sin – a silken, sensuous thread of attachment, one she at last should break. She closed Stephen's book for the final time.

The following day at her machine, she was again reminded of the book and of her intention to break her attachment to it.

She lifted the connecting thread between the batch of uppers she had just stitched, so as not to mix them with the next batch of a different size, and brought the thread to her mouth to break it, as was her practice. At once she felt the crack, the tooth give way against the thick gauge of the thread, the broken crown fall on to her tongue. She spat it into her hand – it was the second one she had partly lost. Soon she'd be as gap-toothed as some of the older needlewomen. It was a sign.

That evening she took the book, denying herself a last opening of it, but holding it tenderly, like a child. She had thought of leaving it at the Magdalen convent for Louisa. Mary knew little about the book, apart from the evening Lavelle had mentioned it. But Sister Veronica, or whatever Louisa was now called, would understand the significance of her leaving it there, this final divesting of self. Eventually, she decided against the idea. By letting Louisa know in this manner, she would be calling attention to herself, negating the act. Her self-serving revelation would only cause distress, distract them in this most sacred of times, before the final profession of their vows.

Instead, she went back to the long stretch of pier that necked out into the Atlantic. The Long Wharf was where, all those years ago, her journey into a new life had begun. It was fitting that here she should cast off the last remnants of that life. All about the wharves Boston had the smell, the noise and nervousness of a coming war. People talked more loudly than she had remembered. A small group of militiamen passed her by, the stale smell of gunpowder on them, their uniforms sweat-soaked from quick-marching. Everywhere was a rattle and hum as groups spontaneously gathered on street corners to discuss the latest events.

She went to the very end of the pier, passing the crimpers and hussies; and the Festys and Lostys in their green ties still waiting to bilk the new arrivals. As she hoped, no one took notice – unremarked, unremarkable, of declining middle years, a needlewoman of no account in the Athens of America. Through the roll of the summer sea-mist, blue-shadowed, almost indistinguishable shapes to her, scudded silently across the bay.

She stood and waited a moment, feeling the sea-turn in the wind. When at last she let it slip from her hands, the book, her cradled child, made no protest. She heard the entering splash, imagined it dance a moment, pirouetting, swirling downwards, its cries trapped in prisms of air, silenced before they reached the surface.

When the disturbance within the water had ceased, she observed a momentary respect, before turning and retracing her steps along the wharf. The consignation to the deep had been reverential – all that it should have been. She allowed herself a smile, the newly-broken diagonal of tooth catching the side of her tongue.

She was still smiling when, at last, she returned home, the slight rawness now at the side of her tongue seeming to cause her no hindrance.

58

The next day Libby Corrigan noticed the difference in her.

'Why, Ellen, you look more like your old self today!' Libby greeted her with.

'Every day is a new start, a blessing, even in here!' she replied.

Libby peered at her. 'There isn't love in the air, is there, Ellen? You'd tell me, wouldn't you?'

'No, Libby, there is certainly no love in the air,' she said, thinking of her book swirling, dancing, committed to the deep. 'I've had my share of love,' she added.

'You're right too,' the woman answered. 'It's only a bother, stops us from getting on with life. If God was a woman, She'd never have invented it!'

And they both laughed.

Ellen needled her way through the day with gusto, avoiding her newly-chipped tooth whenever she had to break thread. It was a nuisance. If she lost any more of her teeth her mouth would soon resemble the peaks and valleys of Maamtrasna.

Somehow the day didn't seem as long as usual, the whirr of the machines singing her through it with mesmeric insistency. *The Irish make the machines sing – and the bosses too!* But now the battle-hymn of war was everywhere in the factories.

'South Carolina will be the first to go!' Libby confidently stated.

Ellen had told her she had gone to Boston, seen all the excitement, the militiamen.

'Were they Irish?' Libby asked, her face alight with mischief.

'How should I know?' Ellen answered, expecting some sting-in-the-tail reply.

'Well, if they had *sugawns* of hay-rope tied to their ankles they were Irish,' said Libby, 'to teach them their right from their left!' she added, bursting out laughing.

Ellen started to laugh with her. 'That's not true, Libby!' she said.

'It is! It is! On my mother's grave, it is. Wouldn't the men make a show of you?'

Everywhere there were whispers of war and boots. Boots in which to march brothers and sons, husbands and lovers to the battlefronts. Boots made by sisters and mothers, wives and sweethearts. Boots that someday, perhaps, would rattle down the welcoming streets and alleyways when they came back home again. Whenever. If.

Every time that the talk was of war, she thought of her own. What far-flung battlefields would this great American war take them to? It wasn't even their own war – a war to free them from the Crown, to sever the Union with the 'Old Enemy'. This was an American war.

She remembered Patrick talking about the years of being ground down by Famine and poverty resulting in the great *scatterin* of the Irish. This American war, she knew, would produce a further *scatterin*. This time, to the four corners of America. In which blue-grass plains of Kentucky, under what Tennessee moon, would the Irish battling for America now be scattered? No matter where, they would be frightened, unable to sleep for what the morning might bring. Many wouldn't see the next night, would be ripped to death, God help them. Patrick's words came back to her: 'If we can't live as Americans then we will die as Americans.' That was the way it would be. The Irish would die their way into American hearts. Irish blood on the prairies and cottonfields of America, would, she knew, let the 'niggers turned inside out' at last be white! Martyrdom was a long and sacred tradition in Ireland.

As she came home, under the arched entrance of Half-Moon Place, even in the passageway the garbage-throwing games had changed. No longer were heard the cries of the Battle of the Boyne – Orange against Green. No more were campaigns mounted with rotting vegetables against Cromwell. Now it was 'North against South', 'Paddies against nigger-lovers'.

Paddies against Paddies, more like, she thought, as she left the battle-scene and went in.

Despite everything she missed the visits from Blind Mary. Between them, they had created their own little world, where Mary's blindness and her own exile never mattered. The songs and stories and poems carried them beyond the conspiracy of boundaries, beyond sight and severance into the place of memory, suspended the ordinary. In her heart, she had forgiven Blind Mary. Forgiveness was like food; everybody needed it all the time. She wondered how it was between the woman and her Dan, whose long absence and further threatened desertion Mary had already forgiven. Dan would soon be off again, no doubt, mustering in on the Common. Ellen imagined Dan to be one of those men filled with wanderlust; any cause, any place, as long as it was 'away'. His like loved the excitement of going and the self-importance of coming back, the notion of being accorded a hero's welcome, even if they'd only been clearing swampland in Louisiana, or digging coal in Pennsylvania. Adventurers, heroes and patriots exacted a high price, for ever expecting the home front to be locked in time, frozen to a 'before-the-going'. Unassailed, and unassailable. A high price indeed.

She ate a little. A brew out of some bones, laced with a smathering of mashed potato. She didn't want much for food, didn't see the point, as long as she had enough strength to do her work. Food was a luxury, too. Didn't Christ fast for forty days and forty nights in the desert, with the Devil coming to tempt Him with food? And Saint Patrick, too, all those nights alone, at the top of the Reek, only the *Cloghdubh*, his black hand-bell, to pelt at the devils. Anyway, after the rent, her money went nowhere.

Afterwards she knelt and prayed. One of the few possessions she still retained was the crucifix she had taken when she had left the note for Patrick and Lavelle. Up over her bed it was – 'the alphabet of spiritual knowledge' – looking down over her always. With it there and her dead Saviour, she was never less alone than when alone.

She prayed for the dead, her children and Michael first. Then for her father, the *Máistir*, and *Cáit*, her mother. She prayed for the about-to-be-dead in the great American war, that death wouldn't be lingering and painful when it came; that they'd be taken quickly and cleanly. Then she prayed for the living, all those she had forgiven; Clegg, Blind Mary, Biddy, Peabody,

436

even Pakenham, the landlord from the old, bad times. Then those whose forgiveness she could never earn, Lavelle, her living children, that they all would be removed from the cloud of shame under which her sin had placed them. She prayed for Maybelle Tucker and her children. Finally, she prayed for her own salvation and that of Stephen Joyce, then crawled into bed.

59

When Clegg asked if she'd take in some homework, she agreed. It would be the worst of needlework – by hand, in the gloom, with only the strength of her finger to force the needle through the resistant hide. But they needed the extra work, more boots were being called for, for the militiamen. It was her country asking her, Clegg said, not the bosses. Libby refused, as did the other Irish women and the young farm girls, but the Italians and Germans said 'yes'. She didn't care. She had nothing against Clegg or the bosses and besides, what better had she to do? The few cents she would get she could put by for the rainy day around the corner, when she could no longer see.

So, in the evening times, she lived now in her own company and the company of leather. The 'war boots' they had kept to manufacture within the confines of the factory, the ladies' boots and shoes they had given out. It was laborious work.

The first week, the thumb and forefinger of her right hand became so welted that she had to stop working. Gradually, the welts became calloused, as hard as the hide itself. Still, every time she forced through the needle, the pain seemed to come out the other side of her thumb, as if she herself had been threaded.

She talked to the unformed shoes as if they were the people who would inhabit them. Oftentimes she would sing to them, the old songs, breathing the words over them, investing them with life. So, one pair would be *'Úna Bhán'*, destined for some fair-haired beauty from the upper-side of Boston, forbidden her true love by a Brahmin father not wanting her to marry beneath herself. Or *'Bean an Fhir Rua'* – 'The Red-Haired Man's Wife' – a creature of unblemished nature, anonymously but passionately loved by the writer of the song, who wishes her husband dead. Another pair might draw from her a song in praise of *'Bean A' Leanna'* – 'Woman of the Alehouse' – a woman who could plentifully dispense the consoling powers of drink.

Her imagining of the lives of those who would inhabit her handiwork were drawn from insights into those past lives preserved within the memory of the tunes. She hoped she was not putting any *mi-ádh*, or curse, on future lives by her stitching songs. It was only her sung celebration of life, its dreams and hopes, its tenderness and passion, her wanting to create a space for them all in the tenement of her heart.

At times she sang for herself alone.

'*A Stór mo Chroí* in the stranger's land
There is plenty of wealth and wailing,
Where gems adorn the great and the grand,
There are faces with hunger paling.
When the road is toilsome and hard to tread
And the lights of their cities will blind you,
O, turn *a stór*, to that Eastern shore
And the ones that you leave behind you.'

She should never have thrown the old songs from her. They held the truth; the feelings, the hope and despair of earthly life, expressing it in the ordinary language of real people. Songs born out of the rocks and the bare acre, not couched in anything that you had to understand about the clever words of poets. Cleverness, 'living too much in the head', as Blind Mary used to say, was a bad thing. The scalded heart was the place to live. But look where it had gotten her. She thought about this for a moment. It had started in the head, her malaise – wanting everything to be new and better, dissatisfied with her lot. 'Shedding Ireland like last year's skin', Lavelle had said. You could never be right with living too much in the head. Jacob had taught her that. 'We cannot know our own minds,' he would say, 'because we have only our minds with which to do the knowing.'

They all had their own wisdoms; Lavelle, Stephen, Jacob, Blind Mary, Biddy. Like herself, all were fumbling towards the light. Confused, most of the time. She should have listened more, the way she had always done to the *Máistir*'s voice – until she had blocked him out too.

Listened to the wind and the rain and the rocks and high places, only you didn't get them in cities. Even the wind and rain didn't speak in the same way when it pelted down on you from city skies, or blasted against your face on a busy street. There was less of God in cities, of that she was sure. Cities with all of their bustling commerce forced Him out, kept Him in the oceans and valleys and mountains. He was out there all right at the end of the Long Wharf, beyond Spectacles Island and Noodles Island, or in the whispering fields outside Montréal, in the Château des Messieurs. And was in the frozen anvil of the far north, silent, waiting.

But maybe he was somewhere in the tenements too: Biddy warning Maybelle Tucker; Blind Mary clinging with blind faith to the faint hope for 'her Dan'; Mrs Brophy – tea and sympathy, the times she needed it. She had been too quick to rush to judgement, too slow to have faith in God's mercy, had doubted even that He would forgive her. She thought of the Stations of the Cross – Veronica wiping the face of Jesus. It was the small tender mercies of life – the forgivenesses – that mattered, not the great passions or the gestures of *grande hauteur*.

She kept stitching, singing to her shoe people. She should never have thrown over the songs. One came into her head; she started it, stopped, started again, deciding she had nothing to fear from it any more. 'O My Fair-Haired Boy...' She had sung it to Stephen in the room at Montréal, naked and brazen at the window, every fibre of her being waiting to be on the bed with him; and she had sung it before that, in the fever sheds of Grosse Île, singing it out over the great St Lawrence, and it was the song Michael – her dark-haired boy – always called her to sing in the gathering places of Maamtrasna all those years ago.

'If not in life we'll be as one
Then in death we'll be,
And there will grow two hawthorn trees
Above my love and me.
And they will reach up to the sky,
Intertwined be,
And the hawthorn flower will bloom where lie
My fair-haired boy and me.'

She finished the last pair of shoes for the night, wondering what young Boston girl would walk in them? Maybe down the Long Path, hand in hand with her 'fair-haired boy', flush with the excitement of love, praying he would not stop under the gingko tree or the Great Elm, go the full stretch of the Long Path with her.

Maybe they would grace the feet of some young soldier's sweetheart, waving him 'good-bye' on the same Common, as he mustered into an infantry regiment bound for God-knows-where. She put her thumb to her lips, moistened it then crossed the instep of each shoe, that the girl's soldier boy would be brought home safely. It was a thing she used to do at night on the children's foreheads, when they were small, to protect them from unprepared death. She put away her work for the night, thinking still how she missed Blind

Mary. Her shoe people never sang back to her.

Then she lost them altogether. Clegg took the homework back, saying her hand-stitching was like 'piss-holes in the snow – all over the place'. She didn't think it was that bad; her sight not that far gone. But she said nothing. He was probably right. And why would he do it, without good reason?

That night she prayed for him.

A month later, in the early fall of September 1860, she still prayed for him. Even when he had fired her.

She had known the day must come when her sight would fail enough. She didn't blame Clegg for finding fault with her work. Even, when in the days leading up to that, he had referred to 'bottlenecks and banner-makers', and how lace widows had 'come down a peg or two'. They had all suffered one way or another for the strike, Clegg weeding out from the workforce those he held responsible. Now it was her turn. It was as simple as that.

Libby took her part, making representations through the union, but in the end there was nothing she could do.

'They're bastards, all of them, unrefined bastards – but our day will come, Ellen, our day will come!' her friend tried to console her with.

They had embraced each other and said goodbye.

She tried the other cordwaining shops, but it seemed word had gone out that she was trouble – a Bloomerist – and there were plenty of fresh green hands and clear green eyes still swarming the wharves in Boston, ready to make the machines sing.

In one smaller shop she managed a week, before they let her go, citing her failing eyesight and the cost of good leather. For a while she managed to gather in some homework, that somehow Libby had put her way – from the Italians, she thought. But while homework was a hard-won addition to her income while she had worked, now its paltry rewards alone could not provide for her. She took up her needle from dawn to dusk, endeavouring by sheer dint of labour to compensate for the lowly price of four dollars per one hundred dozen pairs of uppers bound. At the start each pair took her five minutes, so that in one hour and with no break, she would complete a dozen pairs. Working for twelve hours as at the factory, she completed only twelve dozen pairs, so that the hundred dozen took her not a week, but eight and a half days. She worked two extra hours each of the seven days, except Sundays, which she took off for Mass, to win back the week. So that now, in seven and a half days, she completed her quota, thus saving a day. By candlelight, she would try to feel her way along the rows of stitching, gauging by touch what she could not gauge by sight.

Her fingers caused her more trouble. Each evening before kneeling to pray she soaked them in water to soothe the bruising. Then, in bed, she would lick the wounds with her tongue, like a sick animal, until she fell away from the world.

60

Then she fell behind again, because her hands could no longer take the daily punishment. First to eight days, then nine, finally to ten days for the hundred dozen. So that in a space of thirty days, she earned only twelve dollars. Fogarty, the landlord's middleman, took two a week in rent, leaving her four dollars for the month with which to get her 'sparrow's shin food'. She laughed at the idea of it. But it did her fine, she didn't want much and when the fruit over-ripened and the vegetables browned a bit, tanned like the leather, she got them cheaper. She remembered well how to spare out potatoes; a drop of water or buttermilk mashed into them. Sunday, she always had the scrap of meat for dinner, at the old-fashioned Boston time of two o'clock. It was perhaps the last remaining relic of previous life that she retained, apart from praying. And pray she did, never missing a morning or a night, no matter how tired or sore she was. Kneeling there in front of her Jesus, her little blue windows kept on to see Him, putting the pain of her hands in His hands.

Some nights she felt that at last she was reaching the state of sanctity she so much desired. Other nights she felt it was a presumption – a vanity, a lacking in humility. He would decide, not her, when the time was right to consecrate her a Magdalen, fit to dry His feet with her hair. The pain in her eyes had now grown so extreme it was a daily crown of thorns. She considered it a sign of her deliverance, her redemption secured, that He had allowed her to conjoin her suffering with His.

And when she sang to her shoe people, her voice had a new clarity, and she only sang now in the old tongue, God's own language as they used to call it back in the valleys. And she knew it was beautiful, more beautiful than she had ever sung before, her voice truly between the air and the angels – adoring her God; not man – not for her own glorification. In every song He was her joy of desiring. When she sang the words of *Úna Bhán*:

'*Ó a Úna Bhán nach tú a chuaigh idir mé is Dia?*
Oh fair Úna, wasn't it you that went between
    me and God?'

she knew that nothing now came between her and her God, and nothing ever would.

Her needle had by now slowed to such an extent that she knew it was only a matter of time before they took the homework back. Scores and scores of the younger, clear-eyed Irish girls were beating down the factory doors looking for work at any price, at any cost to themselves. Girls with strong backs, whose quick ungnarled hands and steady sight would be good for a handful of years. And sure 'they needed the start in America', she told Him the night the last batch of shoes went.

And the Italian women, the pasta army, who gobbled up the homework with increasing appetite – she couldn't fault them. They had been kind to her too – keeping her going the while longer. She had a few weeks' rent put aside, and she might get a few weeks' grace from Fogarty – he wasn't the worst. After that she didn't know. The fall wasn't too cold yet, she wouldn't mind sleeping outside except for the filth and the rats, and those unfortunates from the sailing ships who frequented the passageway at night, fired with Blind Mary's gin.

She could fall on charity, she supposed, throw herself at the mercy of God and the nuns, but not the Sisters of Saint Mary Magdalen. Whatever, she wouldn't want that – Mary and Louisa to see her in the state she was.

Her prayers took on a different tone. She still worried the Cross about everyone else, but now as well – selfishly, she knew – prayed more for herself, for release from her mortal coil. Blessed release, but only if it was His will and He required no more of her in this life. Nothing was left now in her own hands, everything in His.

She wanted nothing except reunification with her God. Neither was there anything of this world to which she clung. No possessions, none of the false promises, the deceits, the honey chilled in wine. Not even the hoped-for sight of her children and Lavelle. Like a Good Friday altar awaiting the Resurrection, she had stripped herself bare of all human longings. 'Jesu, Joy of Man's Desiring, look with pity, upon me.'

As she retreated from the light of this world the clarity within never shone more brightly. Like the Mask on one of those hot August mornings, its

446

transparent waters flashed with sunlight, its islands like dotted emeralds – it was all made clear to her. Everything that had happened had led her to this moment. Even her sin. A deep calm filled her. She had nothing to be doing, to be wanting. Only to be ... only to be.

61

Blind Mary, when she heard that Ellen was sleeping under the arch, brought her a bottle of gin; she didn't say anything, just pushed it at her, nodding. She refused, thanking the woman, blessing her for her thoughtfulness.

Biddy was a more regular benefactor. Scraps of food and a drop of milk, an off-handed offer of shelter in her basement 'for a few nights, widow-woman, till you get a place of your own!' Ellen was grateful to her, but it was no earthly haven her soul craved. Still, it must have been hard for the woman to make such an offer given what had passed between them.

At night, sometimes, she thought she heard Biddy's shrill voice driving a hard bargain with the men of the sea. Then again, she couldn't be sure – it was wrong to make a judgement. Even if it was her, Biddy, too, had to live with the cold hard lessons of love. She wasn't to be judged. Love, like life along the passageway, came and went, like the tides which regularly flooded the basement cellars. In the end no one took much notice. Nor did she, not even when the children stole her blue needlewoman's glasses, and the following night the sailors took her clothes.

Next day, when the two young nuns came, searching out Penitents, they found her sitting amongst the garbage, naked, singing, th' earth lost to her, and the sun.

The one the other young nun called 'Sister Veronica' ran to her, wiping the dirt from her face, cradling her nakedness.

Blinded by Heaven's light, lost in the rapture of her song, Ellen did not see her, nor did she hear the words the woman spoke.

'Mother?' she cried. 'Oh, Mother!'